WHO'S AFRAID OF MR WOLFE?

Hazel Osmond has been an advertising copywriter for many years, working on a variety of accounts, from house builders to building societies; furniture stores to museums. She won the 2008 *Woman & Home* short story competition sponsored by Costa. She lives in Northumberland with her husband, two children and two cats. She is currently working on her second novel.

WHO'S AFRAID OF MR WOLFE?

Hazel Osmond

Quercus

First published in Great Britain in 2011 by

Quercus
21 Bloomsbury Square
London
WC1A 2NS

A CIP catalogue record for this book is available
from the British Library

ISBN 978 1 84916 418 4

10 9 8 7 6 5 4 3 2

Typeset by Ellipsis Books Limited, Glasgow
Printed and bound in Great Britain by Clays Ltd, St Ives plc

To everyone who likes to have the last word . . .

ACKNOWLEDGEMENTS

Thanks to my sisters, my mum and my beautiful daughters for their enthusiasm and support, to those friends and family in the UK and US who read, gave feedback and did not snigger (unless it was one of 'those' bits) and to all those on the C19 website for the hilarity and generous advice.

I'm also indebted to *Woman & Home* magazine for kick-starting things and to Broo my agent and Charlotte at Quercus for 'getting' Wolfie right from the start.

What, no men? Yup, three lovely ones. Thanks to Dad for the humour (I know somewhere you're still causing laughter), the actor Richard Armitage, because without his cravat and scowls there would be no Jack Wolfe and most of all to Matt my husband, ever patient and ever romantic in the face of dreadful housekeeping and writer's flutters.

CHAPTER 1

'. . . and then the knickers are going to sing,' Ellie said.

'Sing,' Hugo repeated slowly, running a finger between his thick neck and his stripy shirt collar.

'Yes, and if possible do a little dance. It's meant to be funny.' She grinned. 'Very tongue in cheek.'

Across the room she heard Lesley, her creative partner, snigger, a surprisingly large noise from such a petite person. That was one joke they had missed during the two days spent kicking around the singing-knickers idea.

Hugo made a huge 'Puhh' noise and loosened the knot in his tie, pulling it downwards aggressively.

'They'll be little models of knickers, of course,' Ellie added.

That fact didn't seem to make Hugo any happier. He frowned and his piggy eyes, already alarmingly small, disappeared altogether.

'And Gavin's cool with this?' he snapped.

'Loves it,' Ellie said, and then instantly hoped that Hugo

hadn't picked up on her little mistake. Gavin, her boss, was too icily sophisticated to *love* anything. He was a creative director who prided himself on stamping on everything that wasn't arty or filmed in black and white. Luckily, at this moment he was shooting an ad for suntan lotion on an island somewhere in the South Pacific.

Ellie's mind flitted back to the telephone conversation during which she'd tried to tell Gavin about the knickers idea. Hugo need never know that it had consisted of huge bouts of static and Gavin shouting, 'Pardon?'

Her advertising guts told her this was a good idea; her writing guts told her this was a good idea; she wasn't backing down.

'Gavin thought it was really . . . cutting edge.' She crossed her fingers under the desk.

Hugo continued to eye her suspiciously and a little red spot appeared on both of his cheeks. He threw his pen down on the desk.

'I can't believe this,' he said, shaking his head in disgust. 'You really think that the San Pro market is ready for your idea? While our competitors talk about "peace of mind" and "wings that won't let you down", this agency is going to throw a load of singing knickers at the client?'

'Not literally,' Ellie said.

'And besides,' added Lesley, her short, spiky crop bobbing as she got into her stride, 'you've let the client motor along nicely for too long. It's time for a radical departure.

All this stuff about wings, it's like they're selling model aeroplanes, not panty-liners.'

Ellie yet again thanked whoever the god of advertising was for pairing her up with Lesley. Designers came in all shapes and sizes. Ellie could have got a monosyllabic one who only knew how to draw and work an Apple Mac. Or one who viewed themself as a personal reincarnation of Michelangelo and thought that Ellie, a mere writer, was pond life. Instead she'd got lucky with Lesley, and three years down the line their creative brains were spookily in tune. Now they couldn't always remember whether a good idea had started with Lesley's images or Ellie's words.

Hugo rubbed a hand over his eyes in a weary fashion and Ellie saw that the wet patches under his arms were spreading rapidly. He was in danger of disintegrating into a puddle of sweat and hair gel.

She looked away and kept her lips firmly sealed; a little trick she had picked up from Hugo and knew unnerved him. Anything that unnerved Hugo was fine by her. He had always been her least favourite account executive, or 'pig in a suit', to give him his proper title. Apart from actually looking like an overfed pig stuffed into a pinstriped suit, he had a public-school bray that made her fillings vibrate. The important thing with Hugo was not to be browbeaten by his assumption that, being a man and owning half of Shropshire, he was predestined to get his own way.

To him, females came with an Alice band and a trust fund and they stayed at home and pushed out heirs to the family seat. He was unable to cope with any deviation from that norm, and as far as he was concerned, Ellie and Lesley were way off the scale. Particularly Lesley, who, as a 'gal who liked other gals', was practically a witch in his eyes. Like Queen Victoria, Hugo obviously doubted whether lesbians actually existed at all.

When he couldn't argue his way to a victory, he would use silence, on the assumption that nobody had as stiff an upper lip as he did. The opposition usually caved in, if only to avoid any more embarrassment.

Ellie found this all the more irritating because of the fawning and toadying he lavished on those higher up the food chain in the agency, such as Gavin. As she remembered one particularly vomit-inducing display, she glanced across at Hugo, still rubbing his eyes, and gave a little cough. Hugo lowered his hand and stared at her. She opened her mouth as if to say something and saw a look of triumph start to spread over his face. A silent count to three and she closed her mouth again. She was pleased to see from the expression now on his face that Hugo realised she was baiting him.

Then they were all back playing the silence game.

Ellie distracted herself by looking around at the way Hugo had decorated his office. A large framed photograph of a gun dog dominated one wall. It was the famous

Stumpy, who, Hugo had once proudly informed her, had survived having his tail accidentally 'shot orf' by his father. On the other wall was an aerial view of Hugo's family home, strategically placed, no doubt, to cow any visitor with its size. It looked ancient and crumbly and cold, very much like his parents, whose photograph was displayed on the third wall. On Hugo's desk was a snapshot of Cicely, his girlfriend, who had a lot of forehead and even more jaw. Ellie noticed that her picture was much smaller than Stumpy's and drew her own conclusions from this.

Other than that, there was nothing in Hugo's office to hint that he had any kind of inner life at all. Except Ellie knew that he had a drawer stuffed with soft porn. Rachel on reception had told her, although how she knew was anybody's business.

Ellie preferred not to think about Hugo sweating over those magazines and hoped to God none of them featured a 'bitch of the month'.

Hugo jutted his chin out, what little there was of it. 'Now listen, you two. I have looked after the Sure & Soft panty-liner account for three years. Three good years.' His tone of voice reminded Ellie of the one teachers employ to talk to not very bright children. 'It is a product that needs our finest work and delicate, delicate handling, so when the account came up for review, I knew I should let all three of the creative teams have a sniff of the brief.'

Ellie wondered if that had been an intentional pun on

Hugo's behalf, and then remembered that this was 'Hugo the humourless' and went back to listening to his little speech of reasonableness.

'I decided I would give you all a chance, as it were,' he was saying, 'and then I could take the best concept forward to the client. It isn't rocket science.' Hugo turned an accusatory look on Ellie. 'Two of the teams have given me some lovely stuff.'

Ellie knew that across the room Lesley would be thinking the same as she was: the other teams had probably gone down the tired old route of subtle treatments featuring pert women wearing white trousers. Thanks to the product, their lives were carefree, their world transformed.

Ellie sensed that it was time to break her silence. 'Sorry to correct you, Hugo, but it's not you who's deciding on the best concept. It's not even going to be Gavin – he won't be back.' She ignored Hugo's poisonous look and carried on. 'I'd heard we were all going to pitch our ideas to Jack Wolfe. He's the one making the final decision about what goes forward to the client.'

Hugo gave a nasty, dry little laugh. 'And you think Jack Wolfe is going to like your idea any more than I do? You must be mad.'

Ellie decided not to respond to that.

'I should have known you two would come up with something difficult.'

Lesley gave a groan. 'It's not difficult, Hugo, it's different.'

'I'm their account executive,' Hugo shot back. 'I handle their account week in, week out. I listen to what they want from their advertising. I sort out their problems. This isn't what they expect.'

'Hugo, that's the whole point. We don't want to give them something they expect.' Ellie could not help letting her exasperation show. 'We've come up with something new and memorable that will make the client stand out from their competitors.'

While she had been speaking, the small red spots on Hugo's cheeks seemed to have taken over his whole face. He was a very peculiar colour. Ellie was absolutely certain that she wasn't going to give him mouth-to-mouth if he keeled over. For a second or two Hugo locked eyes with her and it was like 'Lord of the Manor meets peasant wench'. Ellie held her ground and saw Hugo's shoulders start to sag. The next time that he spoke, his voice had a pleading tone.

'You don't honestly want us to go in and see Jack Wolfe and pitch him this idea, do you?'

It was no surprise to hear that Hugo was scared of Jack Wolfe. If Hugo was Lord of the Manor, Jack was the game-keeper who could break your leg with a look and then shag your wife in the shrubbery.

Ellie folded her arms and saw out of the corner of her eye that Lesley had done the same. Hugo treated them to his full repertoire of angry and disappointed expressions, so Ellie simply turned and stared innocently out of the window. Hugo's office had one of the better views and if she leaned slightly to one side, she could see the spire of a Hawksmoor church, the tops of some trees and the edge of a wall of glass that formed part of a trendy art gallery, but today it was all uniformly dull, with the rain slashing down and the sky a low, unremitting blanket of grey. A single, bedraggled pigeon was sitting on the windowsill blinking in at them. It reminded Ellie very much of Hugo. She turned back to look at him and saw he had progressed to drumming his fingers on the desk.

If Ellie had to abseil down the side of the building and break into Jack Wolfe's office to make sure he saw their idea, she was going to do it. Even in the rain, even with her fear of heights.

With Gavin out of the picture for a few weeks, the singing-knickers idea just might make it through to the client. It had a fighting chance of escaping Gavin's 'Net of Immaculate Taste'. While the thought of pitching the idea to Jack Wolfe was already setting up all kinds of palpitations in Ellie's chest, it had to be better than seeing their idea suffer death by sarcasm courtesy of Gavin.

Ellie chanced another look at Hugo. He couldn't physically stop them from pitching their idea to Jack, but he could drop a few poisonous words in his ear beforehand. Never mind that the little runt would have to stand on a box to do it.

She had to be realistic, though. Locking horns with Hugo didn't seem to be getting them anywhere. Ellie plastered her best smile on her face – this was going to hurt.

'Hugo, I appreciate that you understand your client better than we ever could, but really you have nothing to worry about . . . if you play this right. Why not put the other two teams on before us with their nice ideas and Jack will see that you know your stuff? He'll be very impressed.' Ellie widened her smile. 'Then you slip us on last with our wacky idea and Jack will give you points for having the guts to suggest something different.'

She tried to ignore the impressive eye-rolling and fingers-down-the-throat actions that were coming from Lesley. She couldn't blame her: flattering Hugo was making her feel a bit queasy herself.

Hugo stopped drumming his fingers on the desk, but he still appeared to be weighing up the risks. 'What about when Gavin comes back?'

Ellie fired up her encouraging smile again. 'When Gavin comes back, it will all be sorted. Either Jack Wolfe will have strangled us with his bare hands or he'll have chosen our idea. And Gavin's not going to reverse any decision that Jack's made, is he?' She didn't add that nobody in their right mind would change a decision that Jack had made. 'It's a win-win situation for you, Hugo.'

There was a beat of hesitation and then Hugo tightened

the knot in his tie and sat up straighter. 'OK,' he said slowly. 'OK, we'll give it a go.'

She had judged his level of cowardice correctly; he would stick a neck out as long as it wasn't his own.

'Great,' Ellie said, jumping to her feet and gathering her papers. 'All we're asking is that you give us a good build-up in your little introductory patter to Jack and don't make any "I don't like this idea" faces behind our backs.'

Hugo opened and closed his mouth, a picture of hurt innocence.

'Come on, Hugo,' Lesley said, standing up too. 'If you get behind us, we'll get behind you.'

There was a loud barking noise that confused Ellie until she realised that it came from Hugo. 'You'll get behind me?' he said. 'I don't think so. Personally I think it would be better if we all got behind something solid, like a table on its side.' He put the top back on his pen with an unnecessary flourish. 'You know what Jack's like if he takes against something.'

'Oh well,' Ellie said lightly, trying to mask the very real panic that was rising in her at the thought of being on the receiving end of Jack's temper. He had a reputation for not suffering fools or foolish ideas gladly. The swirl of panic in her stomach did another couple of revolutions before she got control of it.

'See you, then, Hugo,' she said quickly, and headed for the door. Prolonging the meeting might give Hugo the opportunity to change his mind. Or even worse, he'd try to make small talk, which in Hugo's case was absolutely miniscule and made him sound like one of the Royal Family desperately trying to bond.

As she reached the door, Lesley was right behind her. 'Run,' she heard her whisper, and they both shot out of the room and raced past the moody black-and-white photographs of London to get to the stairs.

Back in their office, Lesley shut the door firmly behind them. 'Bit sticky back there in places, but I don't think it went too badly – tit-head was almost happy at the end.' She plonked her papers on her desk and caught the side of her pencil pot, sending the contents cascading over the desk and on to the floor. 'Oh bugger,' she said, getting down on her hands and knees to pick them up. Behind her, a small blow-up Elvis drifted off the bookshelf and bounced across the floor.

Ellie bent down to scoop up Elvis and tried to balance him back on the shelf. When that didn't work, she pulled open a filing-cabinet drawer and shoved him in there. As she closed the drawer, she automatically reached out to steady the mini-fridge, which was wobbling on top of the cabinet. For a little space under the eaves their office certainly held a lot of stuff. If they didn't have another good tidy-up soon, they were going to disappear under piles of paper, pens and Post-it notes. It was now touch and go whether Lesley's Elvis collection or the tower of paperbacks Ellie had never got round to taking home would win the battle for domination of the office.

Ellie looked over at Lesley as she put her pencils back in the pot and couldn't help smiling – unsharpened ones in the middle, sharpened ones round the outside; always the same. Hard to believe that this woman, now humming away contentedly as she made order out of pencil chaos, had once seemed seriously intimidating. Or that, in the days before they were partners, Ellie used to give her a wide berth if she saw her in the pubs and bars frequented by the advertising mob.

Everything about Lesley had made Ellie feel like some gangly, over-ripe frump just up from the country. She had a trim little figure poured into something edgy, her hair colour changed almost every week, and always, always there was a slightly spaced-out girl hanging around her. Ellie had invariably reacted by saying very little and trying to poke her own hair back into whatever half-arsed version of a French plait she had cobbled together that morning.

Ellie had been forced to remove Lesley from the 'trendy and heartless' pigeonhole into which she'd shoved her when they'd both ended up judging a student advertising competition. They had agreed right down the line on the marking, chucking out anything that was so far up its own backside you couldn't tell what product it was selling. They ended up giving the prize to the dorkiest guy in the room, reasoning that he needed more encouragement than the rest.

When Lesley had revealed later that she felt music had died along with Elvis, Ellie realised that all the cool and scary stuff about Lesley was simply a layer of armour that allowed her to appear tougher than she was. This was something Ellie could relate to, having used her sense of humour in a similar way for years.

A few weeks after that, when Lesley suggested they get together and persuade Wiseman & Craster that the company needed another creative team, Ellie didn't hesitate. Now, between them they managed to present a united front against the waves of testosterone that powered the rest of the agency.

Lesley finished arranging the pencils and Ellie knew that the next thing she would do would be to polish her glasses. Sure enough, Lesley reached for the faux leopard-skin case and was soon rubbing the lenses vigorously with a cloth.

Ellie switched on her computer and dragged her mind back to the tricky subject of Hugo. They'd have to keep an eye on him. He couldn't be trusted further than you could throw him, which, with so many expense-account lunches under his belt, wasn't very far at all. She knew he was going to drop them in the poo somehow.

She was aware that Lesley had stopped polishing and was now looking at her. 'Quit worrying, Ell,' she said. 'It's going to be fine. No one's going to stamp on our idea this time.' She got up, went over to the mini-fridge and pulled out two bottles of Italian lager. 'And may I say congratulations on that excellent bit of massage you did on tithead's ego? Have yourself an Oscar.' She placed one of the ice-cold bottles in Ellie's hand and then scrabbled around in her desk for a bottle-opener. 'Little swine, making us jump through all those hoops when he's not even the one we've got to impress. He'll agree with whatever Jack thinks.' Having found the opener, she leaned over and took the top off Ellie's bottle and then her own. 'Cheers.'

Ellie raised her bottle, tapped it against Lesley's and there was silence as they drank.

'Well, that should get the creative juices flowing,' Lesley said, sitting back down. She glanced at her watch. 'There's a fair bit to do to get these knicks knocked into shape. You need to ring Sam, tell him you'll be late?'

'No, he's out again entertaining the Germans. Doing his bit for whatever "*entente cordiale*" is in German. However late I'm going to be, he's bound to be later.' Ellie took a long drink and then opened an art pad. The paper glistened up at her, white and inviting.

'So . . . no good trying to busk it with Jack. We'll need to set it all out clearly – why we think it will appeal, how much it's going to cost. One slip-up and Jack will tear us apart.' Ellie took the top off a fine liner and started to write a list of things that they had to cover in the pitch.

Then she stopped: Lesley was staring into space, her glasses hanging from one of her fingers.

'Jack tearing us apart,' Lesley repeated softly, and then gave a low whistle. 'What wouldn't most of the women in this agency give to be in our shoes?'

Ellie rolled her eyes. 'Oh, no, don't start. Not all that again.'

'Just think, Ellie, Jack sinking his—'

'Nooooooo.' Ellie ripped the page off the art pad, screwed it into a ball and threw it at Lesley's head.

'Sorry, Ellie, but come on,' Lesley said, ducking, 'you must be a bit excited. You're a woman, heterosexual, and our first chance to pitch our work to Jack and you get to flash your knickers at him.'

Ellie made a vague noise in reply. Jack Wolfe had been at the agency for just under two weeks and it was as if he were pumping pheromones into the air-conditioning system. Colleagues who appeared perfectly sane in every other way had suddenly taken to flirting and giggling when Jack was about. Even some of the men.

Lesley retrieved the ball of paper and lobbed it into the bin. 'It's all right for you – you're such an old married woman you're immune to Jack. Either that or you need your eyes testing.' She took a swig of her lager. 'Hell, I'm a lesbian and even I can see why women fancy Jack.'

'My eyes are fine,' Ellie said, putting the top back on her pen in a manner she hoped said, 'Can we talk about something else?' but when Lesley continued to look at her, she held up her hands in mock submission. 'OK, OK, I admit Jack's a good thing for the agency, especially if he manages to give Gavin a kick up the backside.' Ellie took a second or two to savour that image. 'And I think it's great, if a little scary, that we get to pitch to him, but I'm not stupid. He's here to streamline the place and everybody seems to have overlooked what he's done at all the other agencies he's ever worked at. Poor Hardy & Wades. By the time he moved on they could have had their Christmas party in a phone box there were so few of them left standing.'

'Yeah, but they didn't need to have it in a phone box, did they?' Lesley was triumphant. 'They took over the whole of Gordon Ramsay at Claridge's because they'd won nearly everything there was to win that year. He might have cut them to pieces, but the ones that were left were laughing. Simon Winchester's driving around in a Porsche now, you know?' Lesley clutched her lager bottle to her chest. 'Just think, that could be us come Christmas, sitting on Gordon Ramsay's lap and counting how many times he says f—'

'Fairly sure you're going to still be here then, are you?' Ellie flicked the top off her pen again. 'Sure you're not going to be one of the ones standing outside Claridge's with your nose pressed to the glass? Simon Winchester might be happy, but Gabi and Paul are still schlepping around trying to pick up work.'

'Yeah, well, they were pretty rubbish. It's not surprising he turfed them out.'

'OK, bad example, but you know what I mean.'

Lesley grinned, put on her glasses and started sharpening a pencil, her ritual preparation to actually getting down to work.

Ellie watched her for a while and then shook her head sadly. 'Well, don't say I didn't warn you. Don't cry on my shoulder when we're out on the streets selling the *Big Issue* or we're one of the few teams left and he's piling on the work. Jack's got a seat on the board and his name on the door here. That's a first. He's obviously got big plans for the place.' She took another long drink of her lager. 'I think we're going to find that there's only one way of doing anything around here and that's Jack's. You wait until you disagree with him. Then you'll see him completely lose his temper. I bet he throws back his head and howls.'

Lesley stopped sharpening her pencil. 'Oh my God, we could definitely sell tickets for that. Do you really think he does?' Her eyes went misty behind her glasses.

'No, and I don't think he gets hairy palms when there's a full moon either.' Ellie frowned. 'The culling is going to start soon. Bet that stops all this swooning and that other stuff . . . all that going on about him being Heathcliff.'

'Yeah, that's getting a bit tedious . . . Although . . . although as an impartial observer of male–female flirting, it's been pretty entertaining. Some women are as subtle as a brick.'

Ellie made a 'You're mistaking me for somebody who gives a toss' face and tried to concentrate on what she was supposed to be writing.

'Rachel's the best,' Lesley ploughed on. 'Taken it as some kind of challenge, evidently. Skirts getting shorter, tops getting lower every day. Doesn't seem to be getting anywhere, though. None of them does. He has a thoroughly good flirt and then wanders off.'

Lesley put down the sharpener and gave the point on her pencil a critical look. 'These ones don't sharpen as well as the ones from Finland,' she said thoughtfully, and Ellie hoped that finally, finally they could get on with some work.

Lesley didn't appear to be in any hurry, though.

'Want to hear my theory about why he's not interested in anyone at work?' she said, raising and lowering her eyebrows suggestively.

'Not really, Sherlock.' Ellie made her voice sound as bored as possible. 'But is it anything to do with industrial tribunals, impotence, latent homosexuality?'

'Nope, Watson. Too knackered.'

'Right.'

'Rachel's kept a tally. Started it the first time she spotted him at that awards do in the Festival Hall.'

'Tally?'

'Girlfriends, odd dates, one-night stands, that kind of thing. He's a busy man.'

'Lovely. Great. Happy for him. Now, see this pad of paper?' Ellie held it up. 'See what I've written on it?'

Lesley peered. 'Nothing.'

'Yup, and if we don't get a move on, that's exactly what I'll be reading out in front of Jack, and I really don't think me saying, "Sorry, but Lesley insisted on telling me about your sex life," is going to cut it with him as an excuse.'

'OK, keep all that hair of yours on.'

Ellie stuck her tongue out goodnaturedly and then put her pad back on her desk. 'Jeez, all this fuss over a guy who looks like a six-foot-three, permanently scowling, sharp-nosed wolf.'

There was a spluttering noise as Lesley tried to laugh with a mouthful of lager. 'Blimey, you do need your eyes testing,' she finally managed to say, wiping froth off her black top.

Ellie could not help laughing too. 'Perhaps that was a bit cruel, but talk about looking at him through rose-coloured spectacles. You know why?' She didn't wait for Lesley to reply. 'They've all read too many of those romances with alpha males striding their way through them. They think that beneath all that granite they're going to find a tender, injured soul crying out for their healing touch. Whereas I see someone whose mother didn't tell him to "make nice" enough when he was little. If he ever was little.' Ellie finished off her lager and threw the bottle in the general direction of the bin. They both watched it miss and roll until it hit a pile of papers. 'Jack wouldn't get away with all that scowling if he wasn't a director and built like a tank. Imagine if we tried it – we'd have to put up with all those premenstrual jokes.'

She paused and gave Lesley a hurt look. 'And that thing you said earlier, about me being an old married woman. That's not fair. I'm not old and I'm not married.'

Lesley was looking at the point of her pencil again. 'I meant to say "settled". You know, "settled" as in "in a permanent relationship".'

'Somehow that sounds even more boring.'

'No, no,' Lesley said, waving her hand about but still not looking directly at Ellie. ''Course it isn't. I meant . . . you know, not bothered by all that . . .' she seemed to be casting around for the correct word or phrase '. . . hormonal stuff,' she said at last.

'Gee, thanks. Now you make me sound like I'm terminally set in my ways and dead from the waist down.'

Ellie noticed that Lesley didn't leap in to contradict her.

Well, she probably had a point, besides the one on her pencil. Ellie did feel settled. Good luck to the Lesleys and Jacks of the world, out there playing the field, but when you were happy, the secret was to stick with it.

Lesley saying, 'Oi,' very loudly made Ellie jump.

'Miss Eleanor Somerset,' she carried on sternly, sliding

her glasses down her nose, 'are you going to sit there all afternoon daydreaming, or are you going to pull your finger out and get this pitch into some kind of shape?'

Ellie made a very rude gesture with two of Lesley's pencils, but very soon they were discussing the finer points of knickers and how many words in the English language rhymed with 'gusset'.

CHAPTER 2

'Which one do you think, Sam?' Ellie said, holding up two shirts on their hangers. She placed one over her body for a couple of seconds before swapping it with the other.

Sam pulled on his earlobe and then went back to checking through his texts. His blond hair was falling into his eyes and Ellie had the urge to go over and brush it out of the way. She gave a smile and then threw both shirts on to the bed and did a little naked jiggle.

'Or perhaps, big boy, you prefer the one I'm not wearing?'

'Yeah, very nice.' Sam didn't even look up.

Ellie slowly bent down to pick up the discarded shirts. Time was when she only had to open a top button and Sam would have been all over her. Now she had to practically install landing lights and put a big sign over her head saying, 'Sex, this way,' to give him the hint. It wasn't his fault; it was that ruddy job. He was working too hard, that was the trouble. He had black shadows under his eyes and he was never off his mobile.

It was a rule of life: whenever you were snowed under at work, your libido took a nose-dive. It was like your body closed down the extraneous stuff so you could send all your blood to your brain.

Ellie wondered whether she had enough time to lure Sam over to her side of the room and then try some gentle seduction before they both had to leave for work.

She looked at the bedside clock. No, not really. Shame.

Bit different from the early days at university, when they had stayed in bed all day, only surfacing for food. Sam had got seriously chewed out by his engineering tutor for missing lectures. Especially when he said he'd been doing his own in-depth research on stress points and angles of thrust with Ellie.

Not that university was the last time there'd been any romance in their lives. Whenever they had the luxury of limitless time and no deadlines, things got nicely over-heated. Like last year in Siena. There'd been something about that hotel room with the windows flung open and the noises coming up from the street below. Their siestas had seemed to stretch into the evening, with the sheets twisted in a heap on the floor. Lying there in each other's arms, they'd watched the sky growing darker and darker.

Just like a honeymoon but without the wedding, they'd joked. Ellie grinned. And this year, who knew . . .

Thinking about those days made Ellie have another look at the clock and then another look at Sam. Even dressed in his suit, it didn't take too much imagination to see him as the eighteen-year-old she'd fallen for. He still had that easy-going charm about him, even if the boyish enthusiasm that used to reach out and grab you was slowly being strangled by work. Right there she wished she could take them both back to that first meeting on the lawn outside the pub, him in his tatty jeans and T-shirt, his feet bare, dancing with such earnestness to the music that she hadn't been able to take her eyes off him. She remembered the thrill of realising that he was dancing closer and closer, and that moment when he'd reached out his hand and tilted his head and looked at her. He hadn't even said the words 'Do you want to dance?' Hadn't needed to.

His T-shirt had a couple of studs in it. She remembered they'd dug into her when she held him tight, but it hadn't seemed to matter. All she'd been conscious of was how his heart thumped along with hers. And how it couldn't have been from the exertion of dancing. They'd stopped moving long before that.

The urge to get back to that intimacy was tempting. Perhaps if they were really quick. 'Sam—' she started. The sound of his mobile ringing cut her off.

'Sorry, Ellie, important call.' He darted out of the room.

Charming. This time she couldn't hide her disappointment. Maybe if she wanted some uninterrupted time with him, she ought to phone him herself. No, that wasn't fair. At least both of them were free this evening. There was quite a bit more work to do on the pitch for Jack, but if she got a move on, she should be home by eight at the latest. They could have a nice meal, a good bottle of wine and then reacquaint themselves with each other's bodies.

Ellie struggled into her bra and knickers, making a mental note to try and get some more alluring stuff on this evening, ready for Sam to peel it all off again. She looked down at the two muddy-coloured shirts on the bed, picked up the first one and then opened her wardrobe. Jeans, jeans or jeans today?

Five minutes later there was only her hair to do. The hardest part. 'Lively' was how her mum had described it when she was little, and it hadn't got any tamer now that she was grown-up. She bent forward from the waist and dragged the brush through the curls and waves, then stood up and finished it off. Even in the gloom of the bedroom, with the blinds only half up, she could see the red and gold in it glinting in the mirror.

'Sam, you're going to be late,' she shouted, picking up some earrings from the bedside table.

Sam's face appeared round the bedroom door. 'Didn't you have all that on yesterday?'

'No, it's all different, even the shoes.' She lifted up a foot to show him her baseball boots and he came right into the room.

'Yeah, stunning difference. Your hair looks gorgeous, though. Lovely when you've just brushed it.'

Ellie looked at his sleepy brown eyes and the way his hair was flopping forward again. 'You don't look so shabby yourself,' she said with a grin. Then she noticed the phone still clutched in his hand. She nodded at it. 'Trouble?'

'No. Only the arrangements for tonight.'

Ellie blinked. 'Tonight? But I thought we were both in tonight? I was going to cook, get a good bottle of wine. You know, have an early night.'

'Sorry, love, it's the Germans. They want to go out on the town tonight. I can't really leave them to do it on their own.'

'But isn't there someone else who can give you a night off, take your place? Your hours are becoming as crazy as mine. You're meant to be the nine-to-five one.'

Sam came over and put his arm round her and she felt the muscles under his shirt. She breathed in his familiar smell.

'I'm sorry, but I told you it would be like this once we'd bought the German company.' He gave her a squeeze. 'Senior management is keen on us all getting along, breaking down the barriers. I can't wriggle out of it.' He kissed her on the lips and then pulled back and made a funny face, aping her pouting mouth.

'I suppose if you've no choice, then I haven't got any either,' she said, trying not to sound sulky. 'But this isn't only about me having to put up with another evening without you. I'm worried about how hard you're pushing yourself. There's no way you can keep up these late nights and long days for ever, and they shouldn't expect it of you. Then you've got that Barcelona conference. I don't want you keeling over.'

Sam pulled her in for another hug. 'Don't worry,' he said into her hair. 'Tough as an ox, me. And tell you what . . . I'll wangle it so someone takes my place on Thursday night. We'll get together then, eh? That's not long to wait. I'll even cook.' He gave her another quick kiss on the top of her head and then moved away, picking up his keys from the bookcase. 'I'll do my curry. Or maybe my chilli?'

He looked so enthusiastic that Ellie didn't like to tell him that she honestly couldn't tell the difference between the two dishes.

'OK.' She was still pouting a little. 'Your curry it is, then.'

'That's my girl,' he said, before checking his phone. Then, a final kiss on her cheek and he was out of the bedroom and then out of the flat.

Ellie peered through the window as she fastened her earrings and watched Sam run down the road, his mobile jammed to his ear once again. She'd conveniently misplace that thing on Thursday. Let them ring; nothing was going to come between them and their evening in together.

She kept watching him until he had gone round the

corner and, once more checking on the time, quickly went into the kitchen to throw some things in the dish-washer.

Forty minutes later Ellie pushed open the door of Cavello's and inhaled deeply. Coffee, tomatoes, basil, bread and people, lots of people. She joined the back of the queue and put her book in her bag. Pointless reading in here when there was so much other entertainment.

As usual the noise in such a small space was deafening. Tony Cavello was holding court as he served, dispensing jokes and wisdom along with the cappuccinos, sandwiches and pasta salads. The coffee machine was spitting and hissing, people were shouting orders, and Tony's two sons, Tony Junior and Marco, hurtled about scooping food into plastic pots, cutting meats and salamis and splitting open bread. Every now and again Marco would burst into a snatch of song before reverting to 'Hey, you want that in focaccia or ciabatta?'

The huge mirror running along the length of the wall behind the counter was meant to make the place look bigger. In reality it made it look twice as manic and even more crowded. The queue shuffled forward and Ellie exchanged a smile with a woman she saw most mornings. She heard her order her usual black coffee, plain bagel, salad with no dressing. No wonder she could fit into that dress. Ellie toyed with the idea of following her example and then caught sight of the lasagne, which was particularly plump and creamy-looking. So that was lunch sorted; now she just had to decide what to have for breakfast. Ellie's gaze travelled over the various pastries and cheesecakes, and then suddenly she was at the front of the queue.

'Ah, Miss Eleanor,' said Tony, managing to wring four whole syllables out of her name. 'And what is it today, my beautiful darling?'

'Watch it,' said Tony Junior. 'He's feeling frisky this morning. Fulham won last night.'

'I'll have a latte with a bacon bagel and then a lasagne and green salad, please, Tony.'

'Excellent, excellent.' Tony beamed at her. 'I make the lasagne myself this morning. Very good, very creamy' – he bent forward – 'like your skin, Miss Eleanor.'

There was a little murmur of laughter from the people behind her in the queue and Tony Junior broke off from slicing some prosciutto to shout, 'Told you so. Careful, Ellie.'

Tony gave a belly laugh and set about pulling her order together, barking into the kitchen and chivvying Marco on the coffee machine: 'Hey, singer boy, a latte for the lady.'

'Yo, Ellie,' Marco called across, ignoring his father. 'We're doing you on my art course. You know those women with all that hair? The ones that guy painted?'

Tony was packing her food into a large paper bag and reaching out for napkins and a knife and fork. 'Who? You mean Rubens?' he said, winking at Ellie.

She didn't need to look in the mirror to know that she was blushing. She covered it up with a joke. 'Thanks, Tony. Perhaps I better not have the lasagne after all. Got any crispbreads?'

Tony's eyebrows shot up. 'Hey, nothing wrong with your curves.' He picked up two melons from the cold counter and started to juggle with them. There was more laughter from behind her.

'Nah, not Rubens,' Marco shouted. 'That Millais bloke. You're just like a Pre-Raphaelite chick with all that hair.'

'Thanks, I think,' Ellie said, and self-consciously flicked her hair back over her shoulders. She reached out for her bag of food and coffee. Tony held on to the bag and lowered his voice a little.

'How you getting on with that Jack Wolfe, eh? Not giving you a hard time, is he? Hear women are fainting all over him at your place.' Tony did an extremely bad impression of a wolf flexing his claws and Ellie was going to make a face but thought better of it. You never knew who was behind you in the queue.

'Oh, he's not so bad,' she said lightly. 'He knows his stuff. He hasn't scared the pants off me yet.'

Tony let go of the bag. 'Well, you watch yourself, Ellie.'

'I will,' she said, and handed him her money. Then, in

a much louder voice than she intended, she added, 'Although maybe I should faint too – I do hear Mr Wolfe has an incredibly big tail.'

There was complete silence as Ellie finished talking and she watched Tony's smile disappear. Before she even looked in the mirror she knew what she would see. Jack Wolfe's grey eyes stared back at her. He didn't appear to be blinking; his reflection regarded hers with a steady gaze.

How had he managed to get right behind her like that? For a big guy he was light on his feet. He'd obviously heard the 'tail' comment, as now she looked closer, she could see there was a kind of smile on his face and a distinct slant to one of his eyebrows. It was a look that managed to appear both amused and threatening and Ellie felt as though something cold had been tipped down her spine. She thought back over all those stories that had followed Jack to the agency, the ones involving how tough and unpredictable he could be if people started hacking him off.

'Hello, Mr Wolfe,' Tony said. 'Your order is all ready. I get it for you.' He skittered off to the kitchen and Ellie felt Jack move from behind her to stand by her side.

Please God don't let him have been there for the melon juggling. She gave him a quick sideways glance and couldn't work out how she'd failed to notice him. She'd been called 'lofty' since she was about fifteen, but even she had to lift her chin to look Jack in the eye. Worrying profile too. You wouldn't want to mess with that chin or nose. There was something about him that made Ellie want to step away. She executed a subtle side shuffle to put a bit more distance between them and hoped that he hadn't noticed. The way that he turned his head and studied her suggested he had.

Well, however he'd managed to sneak up on her, she'd have to talk to him at some point. Politely.

'Hello, Mr Wolfe. I didn't know you came in here.'

'Evidently,' he said, managing to put layers of meaning into the word, most of them disturbing.

Wonderful, he was going to enjoy making her feel uncomfortable. She decided that it was time to go and started to move, but Jack made no attempt to stand aside and let her pass. In fact, she wasn't sure that he hadn't closed the gap she had created between them. It looked smaller, although she hadn't seen him move. What was he on, castors or something?

Ellie was now crammed against the cake display and Jack continued to watch her with that supercilious smile on his face, as though he were weighing her up. Ellie felt the first stirrings of anger beneath her irritation. Jack was obviously in the habit of using his size to intimidate people, and she guessed if that didn't work, he simply scowled them into submission.

She regarded him bleakly. Mr Heathcliff Lite. As far as she could see, all the fuss was about a Yorkshire accent and dark hair and eyebrows. Hardly enough to send you hurtling over the moors after him.

Not everyone thought like her, though, and as if to illustrate that, a woman on Jack's left leaned across him.

'Excuse me,' she said breathily, 'could I get one of those biscotti?' Her hand, which was waving in the direction of the counter, managed to meet Jack's. Ellie heard a little squeak and 'Ooh, sorry' and the woman was looking up at Jack, wide-eyed, her lips parted.

'Here, let me.' Jack's face was infused with life and he reached out, took the biscotti from the pot and handed it to the woman.

'Oh, that's so kind of you,' she gushed. 'I know I shouldn't, but they are so lovely.'

Ellie cast a jaundiced look in the woman's direction. She was so thin she could have eaten Tony's entire stock of biscotti and still slipped through a crack in the pavement.

Jack smiled and continued to look down at the woman. 'I really don't think you should ever deprive yourself of something that gives you pleasure,' he said, and his tone was so deep and the look in his eyes so intense that it made what he said seem like a direct invitation to a lot more than an Italian biscuit.

The woman obviously thought so too, as she coloured and laughed and said, 'I agree. Depriving myself would be a sin.'

It was then that Ellie must have made some kind of noise – she hoped it wasn't the retching one she had in her mind – because something about the set of Jack's shoulders changed.

'Perhaps I'll see you in here again?' he said to the woman, before turning towards Ellie. Up went the eyebrow. 'Have you got something stuck in your throat?' he asked her. Slowly.

'Possibly,' Ellie said. 'I've always had a weak stomach.'

Jack did not reply, but he continued to glare at her until the woman who had been flirting with him touched him on the arm. She was holding a card and handed it to him with a little self-satisfied smirk before making her way through the crowd to the door.

I bet she does that thing where she looks back over her shoulder, Ellie thought, and couldn't help smiling when the woman did just that. She stopped smiling when she realised Jack was looking at her again, and it wasn't a particularly friendly look either.

Well, he could keep on glaring. He might be made of sardonic Yorkshire granite, the hardest substance known to man, but being held hostage in a café wasn't part of her job description. She raised her chin.

'Excuse me, Jack, can I get past?'

'In a minute,' he said, but didn't move.

Ellie felt her anger ratchet up another notch and was contemplating trying to dodge round him when Tony returned. He was a little out of breath. 'Exactly as you like it, Mr Wolfe. Very good pastrami this week, very good.' Ellie noticed Jack's order was in a neat box.

'Thanks, Tony. Am I still in credit? Do you need another cheque?'

Tony made an 'Oh, let's not talk about money' gesture that made Ellie suspect that even if Jack had owed anything, Tony would have been honoured to keep right on providing his lunch.

Jack turned back to Ellie. 'Come on, then, let's get you to work,' he said. 'Or would you rather lounge around here chatting and juggling melons?'

Tony gave a sycophantic giggle and Ellie was severely tempted to reach out and grab a handful of Jack's choppy black hair and pull it hard to wipe the mocking smile off his face. When Jack moved, she stomped past him, noticing with bad grace how she didn't have to elbow her way back through the crowd today. Even the thickset guy from the building site who normally barged past Ellie took a covert look at Jack and stepped aside.

Out in the street, they walked along in silence, with Ellie first keeping pace with Jack's strides and then making a definite decision not to. There was no way she was going to look like one of his little skipping groupies. She started to walk as slowly as her long legs would allow, which meant that every now and again he had to stop and wait for her to catch up with him. The last time he did it, she said quickly, 'You don't have to wait for me, Mr Wolfe. I know my way.'

'I've told you before, Ellie,' Jack said, starting to walk again, 'you don't have to keep calling me "Mr Wolfe". If you do, I'm going to have to call you "Miss Somerset".'

'I'm sorry. It's just that "Mr Wolfe" has so much more comedy potential. You know, "What's the time, Mr Wolfe?", "What are you having for lunch, Mr Wolfe?"'

'"Eaten any of the pigs in suits yet, Mr Wolfe?"'

Now that was a surprise. She grudgingly gave him points for his sense of humour. Or perhaps he wasn't joking. She could well imagine that Jack was a man perfectly capable of biting an account executive.

'OK,' Jack said with a wry smile, '"Miss Somerset" it is, then.'

A few more yards and they were at the agency. Ellie's gaze was drawn to the new nameplate that had been fixed to the wall when Jack had bought into the company. 'Wiseman & Craster' was now 'Wiseman, Craster & Wolfe'.

Payback time, Mr High and Mighty.

'Sorry it couldn't have been "Wolfe, Wiseman & Craster",' she said, not sounding at all sorry. 'It would have read so much better.'

Jack reached for the door handle and gave her a sidelong glance that quite suddenly made the image of a wolf licking its lips slither into her mind.

'Oh, I don't think it matters really,' he said, pulling

open the door. 'I don't mind if I'm in front or behind. Any position's fine by me.'

Ellie wasn't quite sure she had heard him correctly, and if she had, whether he was still simply talking about the nameplate. His face betrayed nothing, whereas she knew hers had probably gone bright red. She walked past him into reception trying not to touch him, but acutely aware of his height and breadth. He filled quite a bit of the doorframe, and as she squeezed past him, a smell of warm sandalwood reached her nose.

Reception was the usual madhouse. Clients were arriving and leaving; leather-clad motorcycle couriers dropped off packages; pretty girls posed; and testosterone-pumped guys were leaning over the reception desk to talk to Rachel.

Well, to talk to Rachel's breasts to be exact.

Gavin had spent thousands and given the contractors a nervous breakdown to create the setting for all this activity. Slate had been brought from Wales for the floor, and the walls lined with metal that had been selectively weathered and dented. The reception desk was a single solid piece of wood, distressed to look as though it were driftwood. All the seats, even the sofas, were upholstered in creased leather. It was a little like sitting in a disused industrial complex in the company of some very old cows. Jack was known to detest it.

As Jack followed behind her, Ellie watched with amusement as people who were previously absorbed in their own storylines nonchalantly fell over themselves to say hello to him. Rachel was out of her chair in a flash, teetering and wobbling round the desk and holding out letters for him.

How was it possible, Ellie wondered, for Rachel to push her breasts out that far and not fall over? She couldn't help looking down at her own breasts, which were safely stowed away out of view in her shapeless shirt. She had more going on down there than Rachel, so how come Rachel looked about three times larger? Glancing up, she met Jack's gaze and looked away abruptly.

'Thanks, Rachel,' Jack said, taking the letters and flashing her a smile that made Rachel find an extra couple of centimetres of thrust. 'Ooh, nice shoes today,' he added, raising his eyebrows.

Rachel obviously spoke fluent flirt and translated that as 'God, those heels make you look hot' because she contentedly purred her way back round to her side of the desk and leaned forward, treating Jack to a full view of her cleavage. When Jack gave her the ghost of a smile and simply put his head down and started sifting through his post, Rachel looked as deflated as anyone so pneumatic as she was, could look.

Ellie sensed that now might be a good time to break away, and she was wondering if she could get away with saying, 'Bye, Heathcliff,' very quietly when Jack looked up at her.

She knew what was coming next.

'How are you getting on with your ideas for the Sure & Soft pitch?'

Yup, that was typical. He'd had plenty of time to ask her that while they had been walking. Now everybody was listening and she felt cornered. Which was presumably what he wanted.

'All right,' she said, trying to look unconcerned.

Jack turned his head slightly – a small movement but a powerful one. '"All right" doesn't exactly fill me with confidence. Do you want to try that again?'

Ellie didn't really. What she wanted was to be in her safe little office among the books and papers and Elvises. Trouble was, there was no doubt that Jack was issuing an order rather than an invitation.

'It's going incredibly well. I think you're going to like it.'

Jack narrowed his eyes a fraction. 'You "think" I'm going to like it?'

Ellie wondered what effect screaming would have.

'Know . . . I meant I *know* you're going to like it. It's great. Wonderful. Something fresh and exciting.' Her teeth were almost clenched.

'Excellent,' Jack said, and turned away, trying to hide his smile.

One nil to him, Ellie supposed, and now she was even more annoyed. She could feel a headache starting to form, spreading up from her tense shoulders to her tense neck to a place right between her eyes.

Jack started to walk towards the lift and Ellie decided there and then to take the stairs. She had nearly reached them when his voice sounded out again across reception. 'Oh, Miss Somerset?'

There was something about the way he was moving back towards her that she didn't like. He got really close, lowered his head slightly and fixed her with an un-wavering stare. It was a look that had already become known in the agency as a 'bodice-ripper'. That was the polite version.

'You were right,' he said softly, 'I do actually have a very, very big tail.' For the third time that morning Ellie blushed right to the top of her head. Then mercifully Jack was gone, padding off towards the lifts.

Rachel shot her a 'You lucky sod' look and Ellie felt the dull pain between her eyes turn into a stabbing one. She looked like a cross between a cooked lobster and a tomato and he was going to think she was another one of his fans. Or did she mean fannies?

With a disgruntled look in the direction of Jack's back, she walked towards the stairs.

At first she climbed them slowly, and then the thought that Jack might also decide to take the stairs occurred to her. Very soon she was running up them two at a time, not stopping until she had reached her own floor.

CHAPTER 3

It had been a long day. Ellie had gone back over all the creative arguments in favour of the singing-knickers campaign, setting them out clearly and memorising them. After a quick break for lunch, during which she and Lesley had demolished the lasagne, the pair of them had worked up the storyboards showing, frame by frame, how the TV ad would actually look on the screen. The smell of Magic Marker filled the room as Lesley drew everything out and Ellie sat and marvelled at how just a few squiggly lines could make something come to life. Then Ellie tightened up the copy and the song lyrics. Singing the song in front of Jack and Hugo and the other creative teams was going to be nerve-shredding, but she had written the words, she was the one who had to breathe life into them.

By seven o'clock they were in need of further inspiration, and as the mini-fridge had been ransacked long ago, they set out for the Side of Beef, next door. A twenty-first-century reconstruction of what a traditional London pub should look like, it had become a kind of informal annexe to the agency. From time to time, particularly when the Creative Department was celebrating the winning of a big account, the more 'collectable' items in the pub would find their way into the agency and then have to be tactfully returned. Ellie herself had not been above liberating a toasting fork and a stone hot-water bottle one particularly boozy night. She noticed that the brewery wasn't taking any chances with the old metal advertising hoardings for long-vanished products: they were all bolted to the walls.

The pub was packed at this time of night, and looking around, Ellie knew that this particular watering hole would make a great setting for a nature programme. Here were all the different social and feeding groups of the agency at play. The media buyers exchanged the odd word with the creatives; the creatives sneered at the suits; the suits patronised the administrative staff. It was nearly impossible for anybody to transcend these barriers, except for Rachel. She moved between the groups like some exotic gazelle, gloriously uncool and unfailingly sexy. To Ellie's knowledge, Rachel had slept with roughly one-third of the male members of the agency, regardless of whether they collected the post or schmoozed clients. Ellie caught her eye, waved and then steered a path towards the little group of writers, designers and studio jocks that was her natural habitat.

'Peronis all round?' Lesley asked, and clicked off in her high heels to buy the drinks.

A large girl with dreadlocks touched Ellie's arm. 'How's it going?' she said.

'All right, I think, Juliette. How about you? You ready for tomorrow?'

Juliette wrinkled her nose. 'Well, if I can keep Mike under control, we'll be fine. You're a little bit hyper about it all, aren't you, Mike?' She jabbed a blond-haired guy next to her in the ribs.

'Well, our idea's brilliant,' he said, and then leaned across Juliette until his face was close to Ellie's. 'Tell you what . . . we'll show you ours if you show us yours.' Ellie guessed Mike had been in the pub a while.

'Ignore him, Ellie,' Juliette said, and pulled Mike back into his seat. 'You know the rules, Mike – nobody tells anyone anything about their concepts before the pitch. Hugo's the only one who knows what we're all doing.'

Mike mouthed a 'sorry' at Ellie, but Juliette wasn't finished with him.

'Honestly, when am I ever going to get you house-trained? If you're not trying to hump every woman in the agency, you're bouncing all over people in an effort to get information out of them.' She lowered her voice and nodded towards a table over on the other side of the bar, where two sour-faced men dressed in black were nursing their beers. 'I caught him earlier trying to cosy up to Jon and Zak. They sent him back with his tail between his legs.'

Ellie made a face: she'd had enough of thinking about tails for one day.

Lesley returned from the bar and handed round the drinks. 'What are you talking about?'

'The pitch tomorrow and Mike's unfortunate habit of trying to hump every woman in the agency,' Ellie explained.

'He hasn't tried to hump me yet,' Lesley said.

Mike shot her a cheeky grin. 'Well, I might be dumb, but I'm not bleedin' suicidal.'

There was laughter and then they moved on to other topics: how much they all distrusted Hugo; why the cappuccino machine never worked; what that woman in Media Planning was doing wearing her hair like that; and, of course, Jack Wolfe. As if on cue, he walked into the pub. There was a discernible ripple of excitement and Ellie saw Rachel stop purring at an account executive and manoeuvre herself into Jack's sightline.

'Ahhh, look at Rachel,' Mike said. 'It's like poetry in motion.' Rachel wove her way towards Jack and moved in close to smoulder up at him. 'You've got to give her marks for trying,' Mike went on. 'It doesn't seem to be getting her anywhere, but she keeps on giving it a go.'

They continued to observe Rachel's efforts until Jack gracefully extricated himself and moved off to talk to Alec, the financial director.

'Well, I don't blame her,' Juliette said. 'I mean, who wouldn't want to try and bag Jack?'

'If she mentions Heathcliff, please kill me,' Ellie said to Lesley out of the corner of her mouth.

Juliette stumbled on, 'You know, with Jack . . . well, don't you think there's something a bit . . . unevolved about him? Like he might be quite capable of stalking you and bringing you down . . .' Juliette's voice trailed off.

Ellie shook her head sadly. It was spreading, and to Juliette too. Engaged, singer in a choir, dutiful daughter.

'Well, he did punch someone once,' said a voice behind Ellie, and they turned to see Rachel. She had a smug smile on her face, as she always did when she had a nugget of information that she knew would be fallen on with glee. 'Someone made an improper suggestion to Mrs MacEndry, so he punched them.'

'Mrs MacEndry?' Ellie said in disbelief. 'Jack's secretary Mrs MacEndry?'

'It's true,' protested Rachel. 'Jack is very protective of Mrs MacEndry and this client said something insulting and so Jack took him to one side and punched him. Broke his nose. It was all hushed up.'

They sat there processing that news. Mrs MacEndry had worked for Jack for years, and when he moved agency, she always moved with him. When Ellie had first met her, with her grey hair and sensible clothes, it had been hard to believe that she really was Jack's secretary. Once or twice rumours had circulated that she was actually Jack's mother.

'I wish I was Mrs MacEndry,' Rachel said with a wistful look towards Jack, and then drifted off to lean provocatively against a wall.

Jack's defence of Mrs MacEndry forced Ellie to concede that maybe there were some good things about him. Moments later she had changed her mind again, as Mike steered the conversation round to Jack's love life.

'He's seeing that skinny bird from the Frogmortons agency.'

Juliette made a little 'tsk' noise. 'Woman, not bird . . . and you might need to narrow that down a bit, Mike. You need to have an eating disorder on your CV just to get an interview there.'

'Nah, that can't be right,' Lesley said, taking a swig from her drink. 'The one at Frogmortons is a redhead, but that bloke in Media Planning said he'd seen Jack entangled with a very blonde blonde. The one whose father owns those Sushi Max bars.'

Rachel's voice dipped back into the conversation. 'It's both. I know someone who's related to his cleaning lady and it's definitely both. Big secret.'

'Lucky bugger,' Mike said.

Ellie was appalled. 'He's carrying on like an old-fashioned potentate with his harem.'

'Oh God, that's some image,' Juliette said with a little hiccup.

Ellie looked around the table incredulously. 'Oh, come on. You've got to be kidding. You know women got the vote, don't you?'

'I'd give it up for one good seeing-to from Jack.' Juliette clapped her hand to her mouth. 'God, you don't think he heard me, do you?'

Jack was listening intently to Alec, his face impassive and his body completely still.

'Well, I hope you have more luck than I'm having,' Rachel said, tossing her hair peevishly.

Mike moved a little closer to her. 'Don't worry, baby,' he said, snaking an arm round her waist. 'He probably doesn't like mixing work and pleasure. I, however, do not have the same problem.'

He was puckering up to land a kiss on Rachel's cheek when she wriggled free of his arm. 'Nice try, puppy boy, but even I don't go for creatives.' She gave him a hefty push and everyone except Mike burst out laughing. It wasn't just the crushed look of disappointment on Mike's face, it was the look on Rachel's, as though having any kind of sexual congress with a creative was akin to going to bed with a warthog.

Rachel stalked away to join a group of account executives and the rest of them made fun of Mike until they sensed he'd had enough and bought him a compensatory drink. Ellie put her arm round him and told him not to take Rachel's rejection personally; she had her eye on bigger game.

After that they had another round of drinks, gossiped some more, groaned at how much more arrogant Gavin would be when he came back, and then decided to call it a night. They all had a big day tomorrow.

Outside, London was cold and glittering and noisy, the traffic still grinding its tortuous way home. Ellie sniffed the air and felt the restless excitement in it. She never got tired of coming out into the lights and thinking that anything, anything would be possible. It was what had drawn her to London and what, despite all the other irritations of living there, made her miss it whenever she was away.

They said their goodbyes, and when Ellie gave Lesley a big hug, Mike said in a rush, 'You two, you don't ever . . . do you?'

'No,' they said in unison, and smacked him round the head.

By 11 a.m. the next day Jack was slowly simmering. Was this the best this bloody agency could do? They were halfway through the first pitch and he felt as if he'd seen it a hundred times before. Smiling women discussing how their lives had been transformed by their panty liners. Then, surprise, surprise, one of the women caught the eye

48

of a passing bloke and ended up trotting off down the street with him, her white-trouser-clad backside swaying appealingly, no doubt. It was bland; it was unimaginative; it was indistinguishable from anything else that was out there. In short, what the client probably wanted, but not what they needed.

Jack made a point of looking at his watch and then stared hard at the guy dressed in the red T-shirt who was still talking. What was his name? Jon? Jon without a frigging 'h'?

Well, Jon was about to discover that missing consonants out of your name didn't make you a good creative. Jack tuned in to a few more seconds of the tripe about the happy women and swivelled slightly in his chair to look at Jon's partner. Ah, the famous Zak. Earning twice as much as the others and producing half the stuff. Living off past glories. Cocky-looking too. Just sitting back and letting his partner do all the hard work.

Jack caught Zak's eye. Well, that had solved that – the guy didn't look so cocksure now.

Jon blathered on for a bit longer and then there was silence in the room. Jack let it stretch out for a while as he searched for something to say that would sum up what he thought of Jon and Zak's creative treatment.

Yeah, he had it: 'Give me bloody strength.' He watched them crumple in their seats. Now they didn't look so super-cool; more like schoolboys waiting to be caned.

A sweating Hugo lumbered to his feet to introduce Juliette and Mike. Jack put his elbows on the desk and rested his chin in his hands. They made an interesting combination, these next two, but was it a combination that worked? Jack had sensed a bit of tension between them already. Perhaps Mike, fresh out of college, was a bit too impetuous for his partner. Good designer, though, and she was a good enough writer.

Mike stood up and launched straight into the pitch. He was rattling along so quickly that Jack had to concentrate hard to make out what he was saying, and his arms were all over the place. Jack saw Juliette reach out and tug at the back of Mike's jeans. When he turned round, she gave him a searing look. 'Slow down,' she mouthed. Yeah, that was it – he was too bouncy, like a big Labrador, and she hadn't got him trained yet. Still, with a little time they might come good.

Jack focused on what Mike was saying and then caught sight of the first storyboard that he was holding. Utterly unbelievable. They were about to be treated to a heart-warming conversation between a mother and daughter about panty liners. Like that wasn't going to make every young girl watching the ad curl her toes in embarrassment. Jack knew what his sisters would think of the approach. By now they'd be making retching noises and chucking things at the telly.

A few minutes later and Jack could feel himself coming

to the boil. What the hell was wrong with this agency that it could take so many bright, creative people and turn them into drones? That slacker Gavin was probably at the bottom of it. He never came up with a fresh idea, so why should they? Well, Mr Cool had a nice surprise waiting for him when he got home unless he pulled his finger out sharpish.

Jack cast a sour look at Juliette and Mike again. At least they were having a go at selling the idea, rubbish though it was. Juliette's dreadlocks were bouncing around as she got into her stride. Trouble was, you could see from their faces that they didn't really believe what they were saying. They should be standing up fighting for it, getting him emotionally involved. At this point he couldn't care less if they were winding up or winding down.

Finally, Jack presumed they'd finished. He watched as Juliette sat down abruptly and then, when Mike continued to stand, she reached across and pulled him down into his seat.

It was no good Juliette turning her big, brown eyes on him like that. There were people earning a pittance back in his old agency in Manchester who could run rings round her and her partner. They had more energy, more hunger, more everything. He turned a stone-making gaze on them and uttered one word: 'Unbelievable.'

Swivelling his chair, he turned to face the third team. Great, the wise-cracking, scruffy Pre-Raphaelite who might have a bit of an issue with authority, and the scary, trendy lesbian. Like a couple of mismatched bookends. Tall and curvy meets short and stick-thin. Mind you, the lesbian was doing that nervous jittery thing with her leg, so perhaps she wasn't that sure of herself. Not a good start. Not guaranteed to inspire confidence. Jack gave a yawn, but for courtesy's sake did it with his mouth closed.

Hugo got sluggishly to his feet and pulled a face. 'And now Ellie and Lesley,' he said, as if announcing the arrival of Black Death to the village.

When Hugo sat back down, Ellie swore that once the pitch was finished, she would see whether pigs really could fly. What a tepid little vote of confidence that introduction had been. Right now, though, she had to focus on selling their idea. She rubbed her sweaty palms down her jeans and tried to find any drop of saliva that might still be in her mouth.

Going on last hadn't been such a great idea after all. The atmosphere in the room had become increasingly toxic with each pitch and now, by the look of him, Jack was at his most annoyed. His lips formed a completely straight line. It was going to be like coming on stage after the previous act had died.

She could feel the potential to do something dangerous rolling off Jack like a scent, and now all his attention was on her. Slowly she reached out and put a hand on Lesley's knee to stop it moving, then stood up. She decided not to return Jack's look; he'd probably turn her into a pillar of salt. Instead she fixed her eyes on Mike and reached into her pocket and fished out a pair of knickers.

Well, that had got *his* attention at least.

'It's only a pair of knickers,' she said, ignoring the way her hand was shaking, 'but Lesley and I will show you that they play a vital role in what women feel about sanitary protection.

'At the end of the day, there's no real unique selling point for the product. All these products offer more or less the same benefits, and we've never met a woman yet who wanted to know the science or believed her panty liners were going to make her a more fascinating person.' She fired a scathing look at Jon and Zak. 'That's really patronising. All you want to know is that your protection isn't going to let you down, embarrass you in public and ruin your knickers.

'Most advertising skirts around this or makes vague reference to "peace of mind", but we want to make this lack of worry into a positive image. And to do that it's back to the knickers. We make them happy. We give them personalities.'

Lesley stood up and set off at a cracking pace, explaining exactly how the ad would look. 'We're going to use models of knickers that convey different kinds of women, from career girl' – Lesley started to shuffle through the pack of storyboards – 'to young mum to sex kitten. And they're going to be so happy they're going to sing.'

'This won't be preachy,' Ellie said, stepping forward again, 'it will be fun. We believe that while life has moved on, this kind of advertising hasn't, and it's time it did. We think modern women are ready for humour where this product is concerned. We think the youth market particularly would really relate to how ballsy this is.'

She chanced a glance at Jack. His face was unreadable, his eyes watching her intently. Ellie swallowed with some difficulty, knowing that this was make-or-break time. It was the moment when she had to sing the song.

'Right.' She heard her voice falter a little. 'Obviously we'd have professional singers for this, but for now you'll have to put up with me. So here it is ... "The Thong Song".'

She knew she was going to die right there in the room, but she wasn't going to go down without a fight. Sod Jack Wolfe and his granite face. She allowed herself a few moments to remember that time at school when she'd hit Derek Cooper around the head with *Jane Eyre* because he'd kept calling her a swot. She was brave; she could do this.

Then she was off, warbling a bit, but in tune: 'You might like cotton. You might like lace. A satin thong might put a smile on your face. But whatever your choice, whatever the day, Sure & Soft will make your knickers say,

"You can wear us. You can flaunt us. You can cut your skirts real high. You can chance the highest winds. You can flash a bit of thigh. Any day, every day, you know we'll be just fine. So listen up there, girl, here's the bottom line ... No need to get sad, no need to get bothered – with Sure & Soft you've got everything covered."'

Ellie stopped and felt light-headed, realising she hadn't been breathing properly. Her pulse was all over the place. She looked around the room at the faces, although it was hard to see Hugo's, as he had his head in his hands. Mike had his mouth open. Someone coughed.

So this was what it felt like, that mortification before the security guard escorted you from the agency.

Hugo suddenly blurted out, 'It's a crazy idea, Jack. I wasn't sure about it.'

Lesley and Ellie looked at each other and simultaneously thought what a slimy, two-faced toad he was.

And then Jack started to laugh.

Hugo tried to ascertain if it was a happy laugh or a 'you mad witches' laugh and, until he could decide with certainty, played it safe with a half-smile, half-frown combination of his own devising. It soon became apparent, though, that it was laughter. Jack Wolfe was actually shaking his head and really laughing. Ellie winked conspiratorially at Lesley.

'Brilliant,' Jack said, ruffling his hair with his hand and then smoothing it all down flat again. 'Absolutely bloody brilliant. In fact, I would say it's so bad that it's good. Cheesy, ironic, even post-ironic, damn it. Singing knickers! People will love them.' He turned the full force of his smile on Ellie and Lesley and his grey eyes didn't seem quite so glacial as usual. 'Well done. That took guts. At last, something different, something original.'

He stood up and automatically everyone in the room stood up too. 'Get it worked up . . . a model of one pair of the knickers to give the client an idea of how the animation will look. And get somebody to record the song, just with any kind of music that's got the right rhythm for now. If the client goes for it, we'll have some music specially written. Think you can get it all done by the end of next week?'

They nodded. They'd have agreed to have it done by that night if necessary.

'Good. OK, then. That'll give us time to do a rehearsal properly. Hugo, you can be in charge of that. Oh, and pull together a focus group too, will you? Run the rough idea past some suitable women and see how they like it.' He paused. 'Pauline Kennedy will have taken over as marketing director of the Sure & Soft team by then, will she?'

Hugo gave an enthusiastic nod. 'Oh yes. Old Hetherington's filling in time now really, counting off the days until he can spend all his time on the golf course. He'll be leaving the big decisions to her.'

'Good. Pauline's much more open to new ideas than

Hetherington's ever been. From what I know of Pauline, I think this will definitely appeal to her.' Jack started to gather up his papers. 'I also know she can't stand the MD of at least one of the other agencies invited to pitch for the account.'

'Oh, I d-don't think there's any suggestion that Sure & Soft want to m-move agencies,' Hugo stammered. 'I mean, they're simply being seen to do the correct thing with this review. They're terribly pleased with the service I've . . . we've provided over the years.'

Jack gave Hugo an amused look. 'There is nothing guaranteed with clients, Hugo. But if we're fighting fit, with a cracking idea and Pauline Kennedy's the one making the decisions, that's half the battle. I'll be here to hold your hands on the day. Let me know if you hit any problems between now and then.' He chuckled and Ellie saw a nasty glint come into his eyes. 'Shame Gavin's going to miss out on the whole thing.'

Hugo waited a nanosecond after Jack had left the room and then turned his beaming face to Ellie and Lesley. 'Fantastic work, girls. I knew it was a winner the minute I saw it.'

One of the words Lesley said to him was 'off', and even Zak and Jon cheered.

CHAPTER 4

'All I'm saying is I don't think we've got the sex-kitten pair right yet,' Lesley announced, as she laid the knickers out on the coffee-shop table. 'We've gone down the black and red "electrocute yourself on the static" nylon route and I think they should be more upmarket sexy.'

The man on the next table inhaled the froth on his cappuccino and coughed noisily. Ellie rubbed one of her feet and looked at her discarded shoe with hatred. A whole afternoon hunting down potential knickers that could be made into a model for the client presentation had mauled her toes and created a blister on her heel. She should have put on her well-worn baseball boots this morning. Right now she didn't care if she never saw another pair of knickers in her entire life.

'We need something really erotic,' continued Lesley, 'like you get in Agent Provocateur or somewhere like that ... You know the kind of place I'm talking about, don't you? If you want, I could draw you up a list of—'

'Excuse me, but I have bought underwear before, you know. I'm not wearing something under my clothes that I've constructed from two coconuts and a surgical mask.'

The man on the next table looked at Ellie and did some more froth-inhaling.

'Well, it wouldn't surprise me if you had,' Lesley said, trying not to laugh. 'I know how much you luuuuuurve fashion.'

'Ooh, that was below the belt. Literally.'

Lesley gave her a round of applause. 'Very good. You should be a copywriter.'

'Thank you.' Ellie did a little half-bow. 'Just because you have totally failed to convert me to the vanity and self-absorption that is fashion does not mean I cannot appreciate nice things.'

'Just not wear them.' Lesley was again attempting not to laugh.

'You are pushing your luck,' Ellie said goodnaturedly. 'I thought we'd declared a truce on trying to smarten me up. I thought we'd agreed that I'd start spending less on books and more on fashion when you started sleeping with men rather than women.'

There was a crash as the man on the next table dropped his cup. Ellie watched him dabbing coffee off his cardigan and then turned back to Lesley, who was checking her phone.

'OK, I'll do a detour on my way in tomorrow, have a look at a couple of shops.'

'Not ones where they sell knickers in packs of three.'

'I am ignoring that remark,' Ellie said, slipping her shoe back on. 'Tomorrow I will be reinvigorated, but not tonight. Tonight I have a date with a large bowl of warm water and some foot balm.' She stood up very slowly. 'So what about you? What are you up to while I'm having my wildly exciting night-in soaking my feet?'

'Meeting someone here, actually. She's a pharmacist . . . finishes at five.' Lesley broke off from checking her text messages and suddenly looked young and vulnerable. 'Third date, Ellie. She's called Megan. Gorgeous, soft Welsh accent. I like this one a lot.'

'As in want to keep seeing?' Ellie asked, and made a poor job of trying to keep the amazement off her face when Lesley gave a little nod in reply. Ellie had become used to Lesley's strictly-for-fun, quantity-not-quality approach to her love life. To see her awaiting the arrival of a girlfriend with something that smacked of nervousness was a bit like finding Casanova reading a wedding magazine.

'Well, best of luck, then,' was all Ellie could think to say, but Lesley wasn't listening anyway. All her attention was focused on a spot somewhere behind Ellie's left shoulder. Ellie turned to see a slim girl with her blonde hair pulled back in a ponytail coming towards them. She had a scrubbed, shiny look and a light, bouncy walk. She trotted past Ellie and landed a big kiss on Lesley's cheek.

Ellie could only describe the expression on Lesley's face as 'goofy'.

It had been a long time since Ellie had felt like a goose-berry, surplus to romantic requirements, but she felt like one now. In fact she wasn't sure Megan and Lesley even knew she was there any more.

Ellie gave a little cough. 'Right, I'll be going. OK? I'll be in late in the morning . . .'

'Yeah,' said Lesley, staring at Megan.

'Nice to meet you,' said Megan, tearing her eyes away from Lesley for a second to smile at Ellie.

'Likewise,' said Ellie, and left them to it.

Later, on the bus, Ellie rubbed a clear patch in the steamed-up window and looked out at the traffic. Nose to bumper again. The rain was tanking down and only the cyclists were going anywhere, slaloming through the cars and buses. A driver up ahead stuck his hand out of the window and made a rude gesture as a bike clipped his wing mirror.

She wondered where Lesley and Megan were now. Not sitting on a bus, that was for sure. Probably still drowning in each other's eyes. Ellie wiped at the window again. It had been positively unnerving to see Lesley acting like a jittery teenager when Megan had walked towards her. Lesley had always been in charge in relationships, picking up and dropping women as regularly as she dyed her hair a new colour.

Such a tiny little blonde thing too, Megan, and she looked as though she might even be sporty. Lesley hated any kind of sport. What a turn-up if this was 'the one'.

The bus lurched forward a few yards and then stopped again. If Megan was a sticker, Ellie could stop fretting about Lesley's chaotic love life. No more having to field phone calls from sobbing women whom Lesley had dumped. Megan was kind of wholesome-looking too. And she had a profession. A real one. Not like that snake dancer. Or the healer. Or that woman who did performance art.

Ellie prayed that Megan liked Elvis and pencils.

As the bus edged nearer to her stop, thoughts of Lesley and Megan were replaced by visions of a steaming bowl of hot water. Her feet twinged in anticipation as she got off the bus and rounded the corner at speed, pulling her coat around herself more tightly to keep the rain and cold at bay.

She stopped. Her feet would have to wait.

Sitting on the doorstep was Great-Aunt Edith, slightly worse for wear by the look of her, and sporting a pink Lurex top and a tweed skirt under what looked like a grey velour poncho. Her umbrella appeared to be all spokes and not much material. Ellie hurried towards her.

'Locked yourself out of your house again?'

Edith grinned sheepishly. 'I had the key when I went into the Queen's Head. Then . . .' She made a vague motion with her hand.

Ellie suspected that Edith's regular appearances were more to do with loneliness than lost keys. That house of hers round the corner was probably feeling a bit too big for Edith tonight. Gently she helped her to her feet and into the flat.

Once Edith was settled on the sofa, Ellie put the dying umbrella in the sink, abandoned her torturing shoes in the middle of the kitchen floor and made some sandwiches and tea. She doubted whether Edith had actually had anything to eat today, although judging by the way she was now singing 'Smoke Gets in Your Eyes' from her perch on the sofa, she had kept her fluid levels up.

How come other people's great-aunts smelled of lavender water and face powder, while hers smelled of gin? Ellie peeped round the kitchen door to check on her again. Yup, still upright, still singing. The loud noise she was producing definitely matched her personality rather than her stature. As Ellie's father used to say, 'Edith is tiny enough to put in your pocket, but there's no way to keep her there.'

Ellie loaded everything on to a tray and carried it through to the living room.

'What was it this evening, then? Book club, darts club or whist?'

'Ah now, something different.' Edith picked up a sandwich. 'We went for an interesting talk on the role of the servant in Shakespearian literature, and that led to a discussion on dining customs in Elizabethan times, and then, well, it naturally seemed to lead to the pub. Did you know that small ale was a watered-down version of the proper-strength stuff?'

'Yes, I did know that, Edith.' Ellie passed her a cup of tea. 'They don't do small gin, obviously.'

Edith took a bite out of her sandwich and her eyes twinkled. When she had finished chewing, she said, 'That would be sacrilege, my dear. Your great-uncle George always used to say to the servants in India, "Small glass, large gin."' Edith had impersonated Great-Uncle George's voice perfectly and Ellie had a sudden recollection of his bristly chin and watery blue eyes.

Edith reached for another sandwich and hummed merrily away while eating it. So much energy. For as long as Ellie could remember, Edith had lied about her age and had recently taken to telling people she was in her mid seventies, whereas Ellie was sure she was nearly eighty. Edith worked diligently to put people off the scent by dressing in what her affronted daughters called an 'age-inappropriate manner'. Where hair and make-up were concerned Edith believed you could never have too much of a good thing. Tonight, in addition to the pink Lurex and tweed ensemble, she was modelling red wedge sandals, gold hoop earrings and her trademark peroxide 'helmet hair'.

Edith stopped mid-bite. 'Oh, the knickers, I forgot to ask . . . Yes or no?'

'Oh, a big yes. A big thumbs-up from the Wolfman.'

Edith clapped her hands, scattering bits of sandwich all over herself. 'I am so pleased, darling. Clever you and clever Lesley. You were always a bright little thing and you've grown up to be a bright big thing too.'

'You make me sound like a fluorescent elephant.'

'Now stop it, Ellie. You can't fool me with that jokey thing. You're embarrassed at being paid a compliment. You never could take them. You know exactly what I meant – lovely on the outside, clever on the inside.' Edith raised her teacup in a toast. 'Here's to you.'

They chinked teacups, Edith sloshing a lot of tea over her hand.

'It was a bit hairy, though, Edith, presenting the idea. Jack wasn't very nice to the other two teams.'

'Well, I don't suppose they pay him to be nice. I expect he can be quite a scary prospect with all that height and those dark, brooding looks.' Edith gave a little shiver.

'Tall with dark looks? I don't think so, Edith. He's tiny with a bald head and wears thick, thick glasses.' Ellie laughed a little at her own joke.

'Oh, I'd presumed with a name like that he'd be a bit more imposing. A bit of a knickers-flutterer.' Edith looked disappointed. 'I'd imagined he was the kind of man who could walk past you and make you want to rip his clothes off, closely followed by your own.' She grabbed another sandwich. 'Well, that's a blow. I was picturing some Heathcliff-type figure and you've given me Mr Magoo. Most, most ... underwhelming.'

Ellie was tempted to put Edith right, but she resisted. It was comforting that in one person's mind at least, Jack was not Heathcliff.

'No Sam tonight, then?' Edith said when she had finally finished the sandwiches.

'Out entertaining Germans again, I'm afraid.'

Ellie braced herself for what she knew was coming next – those eight little words that she didn't want to hear, particularly tonight when her bed was calling out to her to come and sleep in it.

'Well, how about a game of Scrabble, then?' Edith said with a manic look in her eye.

Ellie groaned but got the board out anyway. Every game with Edith followed the same pattern. A few minutes of normality and then she would start to put down filthy, blush-making, paint-stripping words and pretend that she didn't know what they meant.

Most opponents faced with the prospect of having to explain them to her simply gave in. Not long after that Edith usually won. When Ellie's parents had been alive, her obscene Scrabble had become so bad that they had banned her from playing it with the children.

Half an hour into the game and Ellie knew that if the vice squad raided her flat tonight, both she and Edith would be hauled off to prison, no questions asked. Ellie wasn't even sure what one of the words meant.

After having pulverised Ellie in three successive games, Edith started to yawn alarmingly.

'Come on, you,' Ellie said. 'Let's call it a day.'

Edith did not object and sat quietly while Ellie slid the letters back into the box, folded up the Scrabble board and went to put it away. When Ellie returned, Edith was getting carefully to her feet. Ellie put her arm out for her to lean on and they walked slowly to the door of the spare bedroom.

'Have a lie-in tomorrow, Edith. You can stay here all day if you like. Take it easy.' She was careful not to sound as if she was fussing.

'Oh, there's no need for that, Ellie dear. A few hours' sleep and I'll be ready for anything.'

Ellie was not fooled. As Edith leaned on her arm, she could feel how light she was, how frail she had become beneath all that bluster and bizarre clothing.

'A little lie-in, eh?' Ellie cajoled. 'Just for me. You know I think you do too much.'

Edith patted her hand. 'I know you do, dear, and it's very sweet of you, but I like to keep busy.'

That was something of an understatement; Edith was rarely still, and Ellie had noticed that every time one of her great-aunt's ageing circle of friends dropped off their perch, she redoubled her efforts to make the most of every hour of every day.

'I understand all that, Edith,' Ellie said gently, 'but sitting here with your feet up would recharge your batteries. Put the telly on, get the heating toasty. I could make you something to have for your lunch before I went to work.' Ellie saw Edith do a little gesture as if she were about to remonstrate. 'Now, don't make me get all sentimental,' she said quickly, 'or I'll start telling you how much you mean to me now Mum and Dad are . . . well, you know.'

She felt Edith squeeze her arm. 'You're a sweetheart Ellie dear, but don't worry about me, please. I'll rest when I need to. You concentrate on those knickers of yours.'

Edith offered her cheek for kissing before toddling off into the spare room.

Ellie wandered back into the kitchen and found a spare key to the flat and put it in an envelope. She'd leave it on Edith's breakfast tray in the morning. If she was going to keep turning up on the doorstep, she might as well be able to let herself in.

Sam got back in the early hours of the morning, smelling of beer and giggling inanely. He snuggled up to her back, winding himself round her, and Ellie told him that her knickers had gone down well. She wriggled against him, being deliberately provocative and hoping he'd take the hint. He didn't, simply patted her on the bottom, said, 'Well done,' and then fell asleep.

*

Next morning Ellie stood in the lingerie shop and gulped. It was a real eye-opener. She held up a hanger and looked at the price tag on the attached knickers. Never had so much been charged for so little. Two teeny wisps of material held together by rhinestone-covered laces cost as much as a three-course meal for two. With wine. It was unbelievable what some people would pay for underwear.

Then Ellie's eyes strayed to the other things in the shop. Nipple tassles, blindfolds, handcuffs. All in the best possible taste, of course. She felt a bit uneasy. It was as if she were peeping through a keyhole at slightly forbidden stuff, stuff that people with more glamorous lives than hers would wear.

Silk, satin, marabou feathers: it was difficult to know what to choose. In the end she picked out a pair of the hottest, pinkest knickers with tiny black ribbon bows up each side. Perfect for the sex-kitten character. On the way to pay for them, she was distracted by a set of bra and knickers in pale gold with delicate cream lace trimmings. She expected that they only did the bra in svelte model-girl cups, but the assistant gave her an assessing once-over and produced Ellie's exact size.

In the changing room, designed to look like someone's idea of a brothel, Ellie looked at her reflection and actually blushed. The bra pushed her up in all the right places, and the knickers barely covered any of her important bits. She had never seen herself like that before. The colour complemented the gold and red in her hair and her skin tone, and the feel of the material was lovely.

She automatically crossed her arms over her breasts. She wasn't used to 'getting them out'. Her preferred way of dressing was to cover them up. Her breasts had arrived a good year earlier than any of her schoolmates' and the boys had all made icky comments. Hiding them had been her only defence.

Apart from developing a penis-shrivelling sense of humour.

Nonetheless, she still had that hiding thing going on. Her mother had been constantly pulling her shoulders back, telling her she'd get a stoop.

Ellie thought of Rachel and uncrossed her arms and stuck her chest out. Well, perhaps she'd save that for Sam's personal viewing. She did look hot, though. She gave her everyday underwear, lying on the floor, a pitying look as if it were some ugly relation who insisted on following her. Another twirl round in front of the mirror and she wondered whether she had the nerve to buy a blindfold too. No, definitely not. The only way she'd ever be able to tackle that was through mail order; she couldn't face an assistant. Although, by the look of the assistant on the till, she probably wouldn't have batted an eyelid if Ellie had wanted to buy a full-length, crotchless rubber suit with thigh-high tartan waders.

It was almost lunchtime when she got into the agency

and ended up sharing a lift with Jack and Mike, fresh from a client meeting in the City. Mike was talking nineteen to the dozen and doing his usual impersonation of an overenthusiastic puppy, which made Jack seem even more like a large block of granite.

It didn't take Mike's eyes long to lock on to the distinctive carrier bag from the lingerie shop. Ellie could almost see the drool on his shirt. Funny how most men were so predictable when faced with anything involving skimpy underwear. It pressed all the right buttons.

Except for Sam, apparently. He'd hardly been able to find the bed last night, let alone locate any of her erogenous zones. Another night without anything more than a beer-induced cuddle.

Ellie felt the bag being lifted out of her fingers by an almost panting Mike. Before she could stop him, he said, 'Let's see what you've got in there, then,' and pulled out her matching bra and knickers. He whooped with delight and held them up.

'Very nice, Ellie. Very classy, but sexy too. What's the bra for, though? Thought you were only doing knickers?'

'Those are mine.' Ellie said, grabbing the carrier bag from Mike and shoving the knickers back into it, cross that she had become so flustered. 'These are the ones for the campaign.' She pulled out the hot pink satin knickers and put them on the palm of her hand. They didn't take up much room.

Mike made a lunge for them and then whistled in awe at the price tag. 'Don't get much for your money, do you? I've never seen knickers that expensive.'

Ellie wished Mike would shut up. If he went on like that, Jack was going to think she'd been wasting agency money. Even now he was giving her that intense stare of his, the one that made you feel that he could actually see what you were thinking. Suddenly the lift seemed too small and Jack seemed too close and Ellie wished that she had taken the stairs.

Slowly Jack reached over and lifted the knickers from Mike's hand. He casually flipped over the price tag. 'Looks OK to me,' he said. 'Ellie's obviously an expert.' He dropped the knickers back in the carrier bag.

Ellie studied the lift floor in minute detail and tried not to think about how the knickers had looked in Jack's hand.

As the lift reached the next floor, she chanced one more look at Jack, only to be met by his cool, grey gaze. She felt the colour rise and spread across her cheeks. What was this? She was turning into some kind of chameleon that only appeared to do red.

When the lift doors opened, she darted out, glad to escape even though it was not her floor. She thought she'd got away with it too, until she heard the ever-helpful Mike say, 'You know you got out at the wrong floor, Ellie?'

'I do, Mike,' she said, thinking frantically. 'It's just the sign in the lift says it can only carry seven hundred kilograms and I'm a bit worried about how much all of that testosterone and drool of yours weighs.'

Hurrah, she had timed it perfectly: the lift doors closed before either of its occupants could say anything in response.

CHAPTER 5

Ellie knew from the moment she saw Mr Hetherington and the Sure & Soft team that things weren't going to go well. Hugo had obviously got his facts wrong because Hetherington was telling them that he was still very much in charge, although this was his last big outing. Pauline Kennedy stood next to him, her smile looking a little forced, and they all knew she wouldn't be making the decisions today.

It was no consolation to Ellie that Jack was glowering at Hugo, or that Hugo's eyes were bulging in a distressing way. She and Lesley were the ones who actually had to stand up there and sell the idea.

Ellie took another look at Mr Hetherington as he was introducing his team members to Jack. She imagined he was the kind of man who referred to 'monthlies' and 'having the painters in'. He was going to hate the singing knickers.

Jack gave an inspirational welcome speech in what Ellie

noticed was a more pronounced Yorkshire accent than normal. Hetherington, a Yorkshireman himself, smiled and nodded, his chins wobbling. Then a very nervous Hugo took to the floor. He had sensed that Mr Hetherington was one of the old school and that failure was in the air. Mercifully, he didn't pull any faces, but he undersold them and the reason behind the new approach so badly in his introduction that Ellie wasn't really sure he had finished until he sat down. She felt panic jitter through her and looked across at Jack, but he was helping Hetherington to some water.

She and Lesley did their best. They were bright and enthusiastic; they talked about how the TV ad would pan out, going through each storyboard and highlighting little details and finishing touches. They passed around a model of the hot pink knickers and showed how they would look when they sang.

The expression on Mr Hetherington's face grew grimmer and grimmer. The rest of his team was picking up cues from him and one by one their smiles died. In the end it was only Pauline Kennedy and Jack who were maintaining eye contact. At one point Jack smiled encouragingly, a genuine smile that went all the way up to his eyes, but his body language was telling a different story. He was ready for a fight.

Ellie concentrated on Pauline as she pressed the button on the CD player to let them listen to the song, complete with music. The atmosphere worsened as the song played, and as the track finished, there was a tremendous bang as Mr Hetherington slammed his hand down on the table, making all the bottles of expensive water jump and jiggle.

'I have never, ever seen such a load of amateurish nonsense in my life. I could go to any other agency in town and get something a million times better than this. A professional job. In fact . . .' he paused for effect '. . . we saw some impressive stuff from Padstow Scott earlier this week.' He let that little thought lie there for a while and then he turned to Ellie and fixed her with a baleful stare. 'Whose idea was this? Was it yours?'

Ellie opened her mouth and nodded. Her brain was crying at her to speak out and say that it was about making a creative difference, about setting his product apart. She tried to remember all the disparate bits of information she knew about demographic trends and audience outlook and the San Pro market, but all that came out of her mouth was, 'Urrrrrr.'

'You'll make us a laughing stock,' Hetherington bellowed directly at her. 'What are you, some kind of student here for the holidays? You want to get yourself out in the real world and see how it operates.'

He started counting out the ways he didn't like the concept. 'It's offensive. It's childish. It's in poor taste. When I think of my mother having to sit through this . . . this . . . filth . . .'

Ellie glanced around. To her left, Lesley was trying to say it was her idea too. To her right, Hugo was doing a passably good imitation of a side table.

Then Jack was on his feet, smoothing down Hetherington's anger and reminding him of all the good work the agency had done for his products over the years. He pointed out that there was nobody better at giving his company tried-and-trusted work, but that Hetherington shouldn't blame them for attempting something different.

Hetherington was still grumbling away, but less forcefully, when Jack suggested they all adjourn to the restaurant up the road, the one with the Michelin stars and the good wine cellar. Just to have a little chat. If they went now, they'd serve them a late lunch.

'All right,' said Hetherington, 'but don't bother to invite these two. Keep them and their stupid knickers out of my sight.'

Moments later the room had emptied of Jack, Hugo, Mr Hetherington and the rest of the client team, and Lesley and Ellie were left sitting among the debris of what had once seemed like a brilliant idea.

It had taken Ellie and Lesley quite some time to pull themselves together enough to make it back to their office. Ellie was still shaking when she got there, and Lesley wasn't saying a word.

Ellie put her head down on her desk and wallowed in

the shame and embarrassment of failure. She couldn't believe she hadn't been able to think of anything to say when Hetherington had shouted at her. The way Jack had looked at her like she was a complete idiot hadn't helped. He was probably planning to fire her now.

Ellie heard Lesley pick up the phone and then she was talking to Megan. Her conversation was peppered with swear words and negative comments about men who should have retired long ago. When she finished the call, Lesley stared down at her desk. She'd toned her hair colour down for the presentation, a dark black-blue, and sitting there like that, she bore a strong resemblance to a depressed crow.

If the knickers idea hadn't been so brilliant, perhaps it wouldn't have hurt so much.

As the afternoon ground on, a steady stream of visitors dropped in. Some, like Juliette and Mike, had come to offer genuine support. Others, like Jon and Zak, had come to gloat. Jon had at least kept a straight face, but Zak had barely been able to stop himself from laughing out loud. When he'd stuffed his hand in his mouth theatrically, Ellie had hoped that his black nail varnish would chip off and choke him.

Zak had also managed to drop two little bombs into the conversation that even now were blowing holes in Ellie's brain. The first was, 'Don't worry. I'm sure you won't have single-handedly lost the agency the account.'

The thought of what that might mean for people's jobs was horrendous. The second comment, 'Hmm. Wonder what Gavin will have to say about all this when he gets back?' was making her feel sick. Who was going to remember that Jack had thought their idea was good?

Gavin was going to really go to town on them. They'd never been his favourite team anyway. They probably came a very poor third after Juliette and Mike. Whichever way you looked at it, today had been a bad day at the office.

Eventually there was a noise in the corridor and Jack was standing in the doorway.

'Panic over,' he said. 'I couldn't talk him round on the knickers idea – he still hates it – but he's going to give us another chance. I tweaked Zak and Jon's idea a bit and ran it past him and Hetherington wants us to work that up and re-present it to him before he retires.'

Ellie didn't know whether to cry with relief or take bites out of the carpet at the thought of Zak and Jon's idea making it on to the TV. The way Lesley was digging the point of her pencil into the desk suggested that she felt the same.

Jack came right into the office, bending his head to avoid hitting it on the slope of the ceiling, and Ellie could see that he was carrying a bottle of champagne.

'Are you going to club us to death with that?' she said.

He gave her a lukewarm smile. 'Don't think I'm not

tempted. But really, it's not your fault. It was a good idea, a brilliant idea. Sometimes you just don't get the clients you deserve. He's a dyed-in-the-wool, don't-stick-your-head-above-the-parapet guy. You could have taken your own knickers off and waved them at him and he still wouldn't have liked it.'

As he finished talking, Mrs MacEndry arrived with two champagne flutes. She gave them a sympathetic smile and patted Ellie on the hand before going out again. Jack took the wire cage off the top of the bottle and opened the champagne, spilling some down his suit but not appearing to care.

'Tomorrow we'll have a bit of a post-mortem,' he said, putting the bottle down on Ellie's desk. 'There were places we all loused up, Hugo included, and I was at fault for assuming you'd had more experience of presenting to clients than today's performance indicated.'

That red-hot shame was back and Ellie wanted to say something about the fact that Gavin had never let them get much experience of presenting, preferring to keep them up in their attic, but she was put out to see Lesley nodding in agreement with Jack. She kept quiet and concentrated on watching the froth slipping down the champagne bottle.

'Look on it as an opportunity to see where we can improve next time,' Jack said, giving them both a meaningful look. 'But for now, congratulate yourselves on not being mediocre, then go home and forget about it until tomorrow.'

'Do you know, I really, really like Jack,' Lesley said when he had gone and she had consumed two glasses of champagne. She was all moist-eyed and smiley.

Ellie sighed. 'If you go on like this, I'm going to ring up the Lesbian Party and get you expelled. You need to get a grip.'

'No, I do not want a grip,' Lesley said very precisely, showing how drunk she was. 'I only have eyes and all other bits for Megan. But he is a sheep in wolf's clothing that man ... a gent and not a werewolf.'

'Crappity, crap, crap, crap,' Ellie heard herself say, forming the words even more precisely than Lesley had. 'You are so wrong you couldn't be wronger. You know nothing ... He is a wolf in wolf's clothing with wolf underpants and matching accessories. However, I will concede that giving us the champagne was extremely decent. Now stop talking gibberish and get Elvis out.'

Lesley stood up and, after much effort, did as she was asked, and they played a few games of Volley Elvis.

Another glass of champagne each and they were feeling greatly cheered up. They started to put the various pairs of knickers on their heads and take photos of each other. Then they finished the bottle of champagne, and once Lesley got her jacket sleeves sorted out, she went off to meet Megan.

Ellie packed up too and in the lift bumped into Jack. Perhaps she should give him credit for not tearing their heads off.

'I'm glad you came back when you did,' she slurred at him. 'We were about to make a noose by tying all the knickers together.'

'A little drastic,' he said dryly. 'Besides, much as I enjoy administering a good kicking where it's deserved, I do know you creatives need TLC in these situations. Otherwise next time you'll play it safe.'

Well, that was another surprise. He was right: sometimes you needed someone to let you be brave. Ellie gave him a big smile and concentrated on staying upright.

They had reached the ground floor and Ellie was halfway across reception when she heard Jack call out, 'Oh, Miss Somerset.'

This was getting to be a habit. She turned, unsteadily, to face him.

'Don't think I'm interfering,' he said, 'but you might want to take those knickers off your head before you go out on the street.'

CHAPTER 6

It was almost dusk and Ellie was standing really close to Jack in his office.

'This is very good copy, Ellie,' he said, smiling. 'In fact, it's the best I've ever seen. You're a very good writer. You know that, don't you?'

'Yes, Jack.'

'And you know how I reward good writers, don't you, Ellie?' His voice was so low that it was almost a growl. He took a step nearer.

Ellie lifted her head and saw the gleam in his eyes. He was so close that she could see the threads in his shirt, the stubble on his chin. He wasn't moving, just giving her that intense stare.

She wished he'd stop. Or start. Anything but this mind-blowing anticipation.

'This is how I reward good writers,' Jack whispered into her ear, and then, bending his head, he kissed her on the lips, pushing his tongue roughly into her mouth. That's all it took, one kiss and she felt a spasm of passion run through her. She kissed him back just as roughly and felt his hands come round to cup her bottom as he pushed himself against her to show her how turned on he was.

A few stuttering steps back and she was leaning against his desk; a deft movement from him and she was sitting on it. And then, glorious torture, he got hold of her knickers and dragged them down her legs and threw them across the room.

Now he had his hand on her and then his fingers inside her and she was burning down there for him. She didn't know what she was doing. She arched her back, pulling him deeper and deeper inside . . .

Ellie sat up quickly, breathing hard. She looked to her left. Yup, Sam was there next to her in bed, snoring into the pillow. There was no desk in sight. She lay back down. It was all Hetherington's fault that she had knickers on the brain.

After a few minutes she rolled over and waited for her heart rate to calm down before curling into Sam's back. Holding him close, she enjoyed his familiar warmth, the deep sound of his breathing.

But it was a long time before she was able to go back to sleep.

CHAPTER 7

Jack sat and gazed at the London skyline and waited for Ellie and Lesley to knock on his office door. Normally he enjoyed the view, the jumble of domes and spires, glass and steel that stretched away from his window. He liked the way you could look out at something that was 300 years old and then turn your head and see a building that had only been finished last year. All vying for attention, jostling for space. All that energy. If he opened the window, he could hear the traffic and the sound of new foundations being hammered into the ground somewhere close by. It usually made him feel alive and right at the heart of things. The city changing and evolving but never dying. A continuous, comforting thread of life.

Today all that noise and activity only seemed to be giving him a headache.

He became aware that he was frowning deeply and made a conscious effort to stop. Soon he was doing it again.

The trouble was, he wasn't exactly sure what to say to

Lesley and Ellie. The other little post-presentation post-mortem meeting with Hugo had been fairly straight-forward and mainly focused on Hugo's need to double-check his information, get better at thinking on his feet and never, ever undermine the creatives' efforts in an attempt to curry favour with the client.

With Lesley and Ellie, the logical route would be to stick to the facts. They needed to get a much better under-standing of the business case behind any creative approach so that they could have all the information they needed at their fingertips. That way, they could have hurled hard facts and figures at Hetherington when he had turned on them. They could have spoken the kind of language he understood, rather than sitting there like a pair of cata-tonic rabbits.

But there were a couple of other tricky things to be tackled, particularly with Ellie. He was mulling over the best way of handling those when there was a discreet little cough and he turned round to see Lydia MacEndry in the doorway, her notepad in her hand.

'Sorry to disturb you, but Ellie's been on the phone. She said she's sorry it's such short notice, but something's cropped up that means Lesley can't make the meeting this morning. Ellie wonders if you could rearrange it?'

Lydia's face told Jack that there was more, probably not good.

'And did she give any idea of what this "something"

was?' he said, knowing it would involve yet another of Gavin's cock-ups.

'Well,' Lydia said hesitantly, 'it seems to involve Gavin having given a verbal brief to a freelance illustrator for that Stagshaw Engineering job before he went away that turns out to have been . . . well . . . not particularly clear. The poor illustrator has arrived with his work and it's not going to do at all. He and Lesley have gone back to his studio to try and salvage something from the mess before the client meeting, which is' – Lydia checked her notepad and concluded, regretfully – 'in two days' time.'

Jack lowered his head and tried to remember that it was not fair to shoot the messenger, particularly when that messenger was Lydia, but it took most of his self-control to stop himself from bellowing that he was fed up with Gavin already and even more fed up of having to chase around after him with a mop and bucket clearing up his mess.

Lydia had moved closer to his desk and so he raised his head again.

'Can I get you anything, Jack?' she said in what he knew was her kindest, most mothering voice.

'No,' he said, mustering a smile. 'Not unless you can bring me Gavin's head on a plate.'

'I can do coffee and some paracetamol instead?'

He let her bring him both, not even bothering to wonder how she knew he had a headache. Lydia always seemed to know what was going on in his brain. He'd have found that intensely worrying with any other woman, but it was one of the things he liked about her.

'And the meeting?' she said as she handed over the tablets. 'Shall I have a look in your diary for a new date?'

Jack suddenly realised that this particular Gavin cloud could have a silver lining. Talking to Ellie on her own might be easier than doing it in front of Lesley.

'No,' he said. 'Tell Ellie to come down anyway.'

After Lydia had gone, he applied himself once more to thinking about the things he needed to cover with Ellie. For a start, he rarely saw her outside the Creative Department; her profile was so low she was practically flat-lining. She made no attempt to get to know the clients socially and didn't try to hide that she regarded most of the account executives as barely above slugs in the food chain. He could give her examples of that behaviour so that she wouldn't be able to wriggle out of seeing that he had a point. Which just left the much more thorny issue of the way she dressed. No wonder Hetherington had thought she was a student.

How to broach that subject?

Jack stared at his desk as if he could get some inspiration from the blotter and pens. He looked at the pictures on the walls, uniformly splashy and bright. He even glanced at his jacket, hanging on the back of the door, and at the large blood-red sofa with its curved back and stupid little chrome legs that annoyed him every time he saw them because he wished he'd picked the blond-wood ones. No, none of these things were giving him the slightest clue about what to say to Ellie.

Perhaps he'd leave the clothes thing for another day. Have a casual word when he knew her better, not bring it up now when they were still all pissed off about yesterday.

But those rumpled shirts she seemed to live in were hideous. Didn't do anything for her at all. He didn't expect her to walk around like Rachel, but with those things on, she might as well be wearing an invisibility cloak.

He wondered why that irritated him so much.

When Ellie arrived, he saw her look down at the desk and then blush. He wasn't quite sure what that was all about. And when he tried to establish any kind of eye contact, she avoided it. He felt vaguely put out that she wouldn't look at him.

'Sorry about the thing with Lesley,' she mumbled.

He tried not to stare at the way she had screwed her hair up on top of her head and secured it with a pencil, or how one of her baseball boots was fraying at the toe.

He opened his mouth to start his little speech about her getting to grips with demographics and markets, and found it came out as, 'Ellie, are you happy just being a copywriter?' He saw her eyes widen.

'Just?' she said, and sounded confused.

Jack wondered why the hell he had leaped in so abruptly,

but decided that he might as well carry on. 'You've never had ambitions to be a senior copywriter or a creative director?'

'Well . . .'

'Or are you content treading water like you are now?'

She stared at him. 'That's very direct. Am I treading water?'

'I'd say you are. Doesn't it annoy you when you see other, less talented people running ahead of you?'

'Well . . . yes . . . but—'

'People like Gavin, for example.'

Damn, he hadn't meant to say that. It was an open secret that he didn't think much of Gavin's abilities, but blurting that out in front of one of Gavin's staff wasn't on. He watched Ellie attempt to put a non-committal look on her face.

Jack tried another angle. 'You're a good writer, Ellie. You have great ideas. So what's holding you back? Lack of ambition? Fear?' A little line creased Ellie's forehead and he saw her shift in her seat.

After a pause she said, 'That's not how I see it, Jack. I'm quite satisfied with how things are going.'

'Really? You're happy with how far you've got in the years you've been working?' Jack's brain was now telling him to back right off, and Ellie was looking at him with an expression that suggested she was unsettled by the way the meeting was unfolding.

Tough. He stared back at her. Big eyes, generous mouth, generous . . . Jack whipped his eyes back up to Ellie's face and hoped she hadn't noticed the lapse.

'Well, the question is, Ellie,' he said quickly, 'are you really happy, or are you complacent? Could it be that you're so deep inside your comfort zone that you don't realise you're falling behind the pack?'

Ellie laughed out loud. 'That's a tortuous set of mixed metaphors.'

Any intention he might have had to go gently with her died at that point. He didn't pay her to pick holes in the way he spoke. That look on her face reminded him of Mrs Amehurst when she used to tear his essays apart in front of the rest of Year 10. There was no way he was bloody well having that. He'd noticed that tendency to backchat before, like the other morning in Cavello's.

He swivelled his chair and concentrated on the London skyline again until his anger died down. He didn't care that it made him look like a cut-price Bond villain. When he turned back to face Ellie, he expected her to look embarrassed or even sorry.

The cheeky mare was smiling.

'I am actually trying to help you here,' he snapped, and wondered how in a few minutes he had managed to veer so badly off script and she had managed to wind him up so effectively.

Time to stop fannying about and tell her straight.

'Look,' he said, 'the point I am making is that if you upped your game, there is no limit to what you could achieve. I'm trying to point this out to you in case one day you decide that you want more than a crappy little office with some blow-up toys.'

He heard Ellie take a breath as if she was going to interrupt. She could forget that.

'For a start, you need to be a bit more visible. Mix outside your feeding group. Try not to make it quite so obvious that you hold the suits in such contempt. If you bothered to find out what they do, as opposed to what your prejudices have made you decide they do, you might have a bit more respect for them. In case you hadn't noticed, we're all on the same side.'

Jack realised that as he had been talking, he had been jabbing the air with his finger. Damn it, in the space of one meeting he'd become the kind of guy who jabbed his finger at people who worked for him.

Ellie appeared to be gnawing her bottom lip from the inside.

He pulled his gaze away from her mouth.

'And perhaps . . .' Jack tailed off, everything telling him that he should not say what he was going to say next '. . . perhaps you ought to think about why Hetherington mistook you for a student.' Jack relaxed. That had come out OK. Not too direct, not too personal. Definitely no hint of sexual harassment. If the woman had any sense, she'd take the hint about smartening up a bit and they could move on.

'What exactly do you mean by that?' Ellie said, looking affronted.

Great. No hint-taking there, then.

'Are you trying to make some kind of personal comment about the way I dress?' There was a definite edge to Ellie's voice.

Jack couldn't stop himself. Despite visions of industrial tribunals swimming before him, he made a show of studying what she was wearing and then raised his hand in a kind of 'What can I say?' gesture. He saw her eyes flash at him before she gave her clothes a surreptitious check.

Well, that proved his point. She couldn't even remember what she had on. Probably dressed in the dark and hoped for the best.

He let her stew a bit and then decided now might be the time to get back to his planned speech, take some heat out of the confrontation. He slowed himself down, started on about the need for her to familiarise herself with the business side of things.

'We'll get Hugo to give you a couple of sessions on—'

'Why bother?' Ellie said. 'Why bother? Tell you what, I'll become a clone and wear the usual black creative uniform.'

'No, that's not what—'

'Or how about a tight skirt and some cleavage?'

Jack stood up. That was it. She could wear sackcloth and ashes for all he bloody cared and spend her entire life writing the small print on mortgage adverts. He wasn't being made out to be some kind of sexist pig.

'I think we've got as far as we're going to, Eleanor,' he said in a level tone, and then noticed with horror that she seemed to be crying. Not the really sobby kind of crying, but the gulping and wet eyes kind. Jack sat back down and pretended to look at some papers on his desk.

This was a nightmare. What century was she living in? Did she expect him to pass her a handkerchief and rub her back? Perhaps it was all put on. He took a look. No, she was really fighting to stay under control; he could see her swallowing over and over again. He fiddled with a paperclip. Didn't she know you had to be tough to be in advertising?

He gave her a few minutes and then glanced at her again. Now her hair was coming down, escaping in mad curls.

Perhaps he had been a bit harsh with the clothes thing. Zak wandered about looking like he hadn't washed in weeks, and there were plenty of other scruffy, successful creatives out there. If she wanted to keep going around like a bag lady, then it was up to her.

He couldn't help being hacked off about it, though. Why bury all that brightness so deep that nobody could see it?

As the sniffing and swallowing dried up, he searched for something to say to get her out of his office.

'Ellie,' he said in a gentler tone than he'd used so far, 'you're good. You understand that our job is all about getting our clients noticed and selling more of their products. You're not in it to massage your own ego. These are all excellent things. But in an image-driven business it's important to convey a positive message about yourself and about the agency.'

He saw her look up. There were tears on her face and he couldn't quite put his finger on how that made him feel.

'Look,' he went on, 'I appreciate it's difficult being a woman in this business ... well, any business. You get judged on all sorts of things men don't get judged on. It's tough, but that's how it is.' He lowered his voice even further, like he was dealing with a skittish foal. 'In an ideal world, people should be able to see through your clothes to the real Eleanor beneath.'

It was only when he saw Ellie's eyes widen in shock that he realised what he'd said. A blush reddened her skin.

Now he'd managed to humiliate her on top of everything else.

She stood up abruptly. 'Can I go now, Mr Wolfe?' she said. 'Or did you want to humiliate me some more?' She wouldn't even look at him.

Jack sat there after she'd gone, not sure what had happened or why he hadn't slapped her down for that last bit of cheek. Probably because he felt that she'd had a point.

He had to be thankful there had been nobody in the office with a hidden camera. They'd be showing that particular film to illustrate exactly how not to handle your staff.

She'd started it, though. How was it possible for one woman to be so touchy about everything? She'd gone out of her way to take offence. A less spiky woman would have sat there and nodded. And that crying was completely out of order. Did he have room in the agency for a cry-baby? Even a bright one?

He fumed for a bit longer and then remembered what he had said about seeing through Ellie's clothes to the real her beneath. An image of Ellie wearing a pair of high heels and only that beautiful golden underwear shimmered into his mind and refused to budge. Yeah, well, she might have her good points, two in particular, but he wasn't in the habit of touching up his employees. Even if he had been, there were plenty of non-scruffy, non-weepy women above her on the list.

Jack tried to concentrate on the papers in front of him, but he was still half furious and half aroused when it was time to go and meet Sophie or Leonora or whichever one of them he was ruddy well meant to be seeing tonight.

*

Ellie had stayed right out of Jack's way after that.

And now here she was in another office with another man in a strop. She was having distinct feelings of déjà-vu, but at least Lesley was bearing some of the brunt of it this time.

Gavin flicked an imaginary hair off his immaculate trousers and looked down his nose at the two of them. Underneath his perfect tan he was going red and blotchy. He lifted up one of the storyboards from the singing-knickers idea as if it were contaminated waste and turned it round in his hands.

'Schoolgirl standard,' he said softly.

Gavin didn't do shouting, much too impetuous. He preferred contempt, superiority and disappointment. He wiped his hand down his grey cashmere sweater as if trying to dislodge any residue of nastiness that had lodged there after handling their work.

'I'm away from this agency for a short while and what do I find when I come back? That one of my teams has, evidently, lost its mind.' He reached out and straightened a pen lying on his desk.

'Now, Gavin—' Lesley started, but Gavin held up a hand.

'Lost its mind and gone back to pre-school to play with plasticine knickers.'

Lesley crossed her legs and started bouncing one spiky-booted foot up and down. She couldn't have shown she was irritated any more plainly if she had written it on a sign.

97

Gavin smirked and patted his hair. 'Correction. Not only playing with plasticine but having a go at poetry too.'

Gavin plucked a copy of 'The Thong Song' off the desk and made a big show of reading it. He held the paper low enough so that they wouldn't miss any of his pained facial expressions.

'Oh dear,' he said when he had finished, 'I don't think the Poet Laureate has any competition there, does she?'

Ellie managed to get out, 'It's not meant to be poetry, it's selling—'

'Enough,' Gavin said, raising his hand again. He brushed some more fluff from his trousers and looked at his nails. 'Do you want to tell me what those are?' He pointed to his shelves.

Neither of them looked; they didn't need to. 'Your awards, Gavin,' they chorused.

'Yes, they're my awards. Won over many years for the standard of my work. For the creativity of my work. How many do you see?'

'Seven,' they said together.

'Not a bad haul.'

Ellie was tempted to say that he hadn't added to it recently.

'And I haven't simply won them for work I've done. I've made sure that the work coming out of this agency is of the same high standard. Every piece of work that comes out of this agency has my mark on it.'

'But—' Lesley said.

Gavin leaned forward. 'But nothing. I do not take kindly to you trying to get some substandard piece of work past me when I am away by going directly to Jack. He might be a good businessman, but he is not, by training, a creative.'

Ellie definitely wasn't in the mood to defend Jack after all those nasty, personal comments he'd made, but she didn't like the way Gavin said 'businessman' as though it were akin to being a male hooker. And Gavin was pushing it with that comment about Jack not being a creative. Jack's reputation was built on the fact that the creative ideas that came from his people sold products and won awards. Recent awards.

Gavin stood up and straightened a file on his cabinet that was slightly out of line with the rest.

'Gavin, we did not go behind your back,' Lesley said. 'Ellie rang you and told you what we were doing.'

'So she says,' Gavin retorted.

Ellie decided it might be a good time to look at her baseball boots.

Lesley battled on, but Ellie felt like telling her not to bother. They were in the doghouse and no amount of talking was going to get them out.

'Look, Gavin,' Lesley was saying, 'it was agreed before you went away that we would all come up with our best ideas, present them to Jack and he would decide which one went forward to the client.'

Gavin sat back down and folded his hands in his lap. His face assumed a hurt but brave expression. 'It seems that when it comes to loyalty, Hugo could teach you a thing or two.'

'What?'

'Hugo tells me that he tried to talk Jack out of the knickers idea, to get him to go with one of the other treatments.'

'Now hang on. Hugo was all over the idea once Jack had approved it. He's just trying to come out of this smelling of—'

Gavin's hand was up again. Even Lesley gave up then and they both sat there and let the rest of what he said wash over them. They'd heard it all before in some form. While he was talking, Ellie thought about the many ways in which she was going to torture Hugo over the coming weeks. Starting with telling Rachel that he fancied her. She hoped she was there to see the terror in his face when Rachel launched herself at him.

'You need to realise that you don't know it all. You need to listen . . .' Gavin droned on.

Ellie wondered why when Jack spoke sternly to her she had started to cry, but when Gavin did it she wanted to take the top off a pen and write rude words on his perfectly moisturised face.

At last Gavin stood up. 'Right, I have to go. Editing the suntan lotion ad. And when I've finished, I want you to have a good look at it.' He gave them a patronising smile. 'Watch and learn, girls, watch and learn.'

They shuffled out of the room and into the corridor, subdued and weary. Lesley didn't even slam the door.

'Having a good day?' a voice said, and they turned round to see Jack leaning against the wall. Ellie suspected that he'd only just moved away from Gavin's door.

She tried not to look at Jack. The memory of crying in front of him the other day was still making her feel sick with humiliation. That was when she wasn't smarting at the unfairness of what he'd said. She'd been right: if you crossed him, he was horrible. Wolfe by name, wolf by nature.

And who was he kidding when he said he was trying to help her? Using that gentle voice? He'd shown his true colours when he'd made that comment about seeing through her clothes. It was probably something he said to women all the time.

Worst of all, though, was remembering the other thing that was mortifying her: that dream. She tried to concentrate on breathing in and out and appearing normal.

'We've been chewed out by Gavin,' Lesley said. 'He's very disappointed in us and with us.'

Ellie heard Jack give a little snort and then he prised himself away from the wall and walked over to stand in front of one of the black-and-white photographs. It showed Tower Bridge, in the rain, shot from a low angle.

'Who chose these?' he asked.

Lesley nodded towards Gavin's door and they saw Jack smile. He had that same nasty glint in his eye he'd had when he had been relishing the thought that Gavin would miss the Sure & Soft presentation.

'You know,' he said, reaching up and grabbing hold of the framed photograph, 'things in a prominent position don't always deserve to be there. When you give them a long, hard look, they're pretentious, dull and incredibly uninspiring.' He lifted the frame from the wall, tucked it under his arm and turned to look at them. 'In fact, they really don't work any more.'

'You are still talking about those photographs, aren't you, Jack?' Lesley said.

In reply he gave them an evil grin and then wandered along to the next photograph. Very soon he was taking that one down too.

CHAPTER 8

Ellie smiled fondly at Sam. She was going to show him such a good time, love him so much that he'd have something really worth remembering when he was stuck in Barcelona and she was stuck in London. Seven days, one weekend – it was going to seem longer.

She casually undid her top button and then the one below that. Poor Sam, he couldn't bear being cooped up inside at the best of times, so how was he going to cope with being stuck in a stuffy conference hall listening to engineers wittering on?

Snuggling closer to him on the sofa, she gently lifted the TV remote out of his fingers and he got the hint. Wait until he saw her new underwear.

They had progressed to the heavy-kissing stage when Sam pulled away.

'Ooh, wait a minute. I've got a treat for you,' he said, looking mysterious. 'A kind of early birthday present. Stay there.'

He disappeared into the bedroom and for one heady moment Ellie thought it might be something she had seen in the underwear shop. Sam had recently hinted that he'd like to try something a bit more adventurous. Or perhaps she was way off the mark: it could be a ring. She thought about that and decided that didn't seem a realistic expectation. He wouldn't just bung it at her on the sofa, would he? Surely there would have been a bit more of a build-up.

Still, any present was good, and if it *was* something from the underwear shop, he'd definitely have some happy memories to take with him to Barcelona. Ellie felt deliciously wicked and draped herself over the sofa a little more artistically.

Sam returned from the bedroom and put an envelope into her hand. *Not handcuffs, then.* Ellie tore open the envelope with anticipation nonetheless. Maybe it was tickets for a weekend away together somewhere romantic.

She looked at the glossy leaflet for a makeover and photo session, and then stood up very quickly and went and locked herself in the bathroom.

When Sam eventually persuaded her to come out, and had removed the torn-up bits of leaflet from the toilet bowl, he took her to bed and apologised for getting it so wrong. It was only because a bloke at work's wife had been for a makeover and she'd looked amazing in the photos he'd brought in to show around, and when Sam had asked his sister if she thought Ellie would like it, she'd been especially enthusiastic.

Ellie wanted to say that this was because his sister was a scheming witch who had never liked her, but she let it pass. She also tried to ignore the fact that Sam obviously thought she could do with a bit of glamorising. And she was absolutely, positively, not going to let her mind wander back over the comments Jack had made about the way she dressed. Ignoring everything else, she threw herself wholeheartedly into getting back in touch with all the things she had missed about Sam recently. One in particular.

Later she helped Sam pack for his trip away, folding shirts and rolling up ties while he checked his travel arrangements on the phone. A couple of the shirts she hadn't seen before. She reached for a pair of his trousers. They still had a price tag attached.

She went to the full-length mirror and gave her clothes a critical look. Apart from the fact that she was somehow wearing earrings that didn't match and that the hole in her baseball boot was getting bigger, she didn't look bad. Bit shabby maybe, but she had that bohemian writer's thing going on, didn't she? People worried about their appearance much too much, especially women. It became like a stick to beat them with. All that 'Look at me, me, me' palaver was exhausting.

Perhaps she should splash out a bit, though, buy some

new stuff like Sam had done. She could certainly do with replacing some of her shirts. And the baseball boots.

She turned slightly, appraising herself, and then something in the mirror caught her eye.

'Ah, that's where you've got to,' she said with enthusiasm, getting down on her hands and knees. She reached under the bedroom chair and pulled out a book. 'I've been looking for you.'

She made herself comfortable next to Sam's suitcase on the bed and folded some more shirts for him. Then she eagerly opened the paperback and settled back to finish it.

Coping with the first few days of Sam being away hadn't been too difficult. It wasn't that different from how life had been recently anyway. Except there was less laundry.

Now she was hurtling towards the weekend.

Ellie stood waiting for the kettle to boil and thought about ringing up some friends to see if they fancied a night out. She'd ask Lesley along too when she got into work. And Megan, of course. Couldn't forget Megan.

She glanced across at Lesley's art pad, on which she had written 'Megan' in bold, swirly lettering and then surrounded the name with exotic flowers in bright colours. Lesley had fallen badly. Right now she was out arranging some photography for the engineering brochure, but Ellie had no doubt that later she would make a detour back past the chemist's shop where Megan worked. She spent so much time loitering around the pharmacy counter that people probably thought she was in the final stages of something.

Ellie grinned. Well, in a way Lesley was.

She settled down with her tea to finish some copy about a client's high-interest savings account. It wasn't exactly cutting-edge stuff, but as she worked through it, she felt her usual satisfaction at being able to transform complex information into something easy to understand. Now the people reading it in the bank queue wouldn't be scratching their heads.

The sound of the phone ringing cut across her thoughts and she picked it up. 'Why is Sam inviting me to go away to Barcelona with him and telling me not to wear underwear?' Chris, her eldest brother, sounded extremely confused. 'I mean, I know I've always got on well with him, but I never knew he felt like this about me.'

Ellie pulled the phone away from her ear and stared at it, then put it back and said very slowly, 'I have no idea what you are talking about. Have you been drinking, Chris? Do they let you have alcohol in the staffroom now?'

'Hey, less of your lip. I'm serious – go and look at your emails. It's obviously meant for you, but the idiot's sent it to everyone he knows. Including me.' Her brother laughed. 'Boy, has he got some explaining to do to his mum.'

Ellie put the phone down and clicked on her mailbox. *Meet you Hotel Cristo, Barcelona, 10 p.m. Don't bother with any knickers.*

Ellie felt a surge of excitement, and although she was embarrassed for Sam (how *was* he going to explain that to his mother?), part of her revelled in the fact that everybody would know she was being whisked off for a dirty weekend by her lovely boyfriend.

She needed to book a flight, get a toothbrush, rush home for her passport, buy something glam to wear. She wouldn't need much else; she didn't imagine they'd be going out a lot.

The phone rang again. It was Bob, the captain of Sam's rugby team. 'Why is Sam inviting me to Barcelona without my pants? I've tried to ask him, but his mobile is off. Thought you might know?'

By the sixth phone call Ellie had got her patter off to a tee: 'No, the email was meant for me. He sent it out to everyone by mistake. Yes, I am looking forward to it. No, it was a complete surprise. Yes, he does seem to have turned his mobile off.'

Four o'clock and Ellie was nearly ready. She wedged a chair under the handle of the office door and off came the work camouflage and on went the new underwear, a silky dress and high, strappy sandals. It felt weird to be wearing something so insubstantial and expensive. She did a quick calculation of how much it had all cost and then decided not to put a price on love.

Looking down, she found herself face to face with her cleavage. She tried to hitch the neckline of the dress up a bit and then thought about how she was meant to be exuding sexiness. She lowered her hands, but soon they were fussing with the neckline again. A nervous tic, she'd have to fight it. She should think about that makeover incident. Her hands lay still.

Ellie leaned over the desk and scrawled a hasty note to Lesley explaining why she was leaving early and then walked to the lift, sashaying in her high heels. She swung her hips and giggled.

It was Friday, she was dressed to seduce, and all was right with the world. In the lift she did a little dance before the doors whooshed back open.

Even the sight of Jack Wolfe striding into reception wasn't going to dampen her spirits. She lifted her chin and delayed putting on her coat. Stuff him and his views on her. She was off for a sexy weekend in a foreign city with a man who was worth three of big, bullying, woman-eating Jack.

'Ooh, nice dress,' Rachel said, as she passed. 'Special date?'

'Yeah, with Sam. Surprise weekend in Barcelona.' She hoped she'd said it loud enough for Jack to hear. She lavished a large smile on him and was pleased to see him raise his eyebrows in surprise. 'Bye, Jack,' she cooed. 'Have a lovely, lovely weekend.'

Jack began sifting through the pile of messages that Rachel had handed him, head down, engrossed.

Except he wasn't really concentrating on his messages; he was watching Ellie out of the corner of his eye, watching her in that dress, with those legs. He was especially interested in the way bits of her jiggled beautifully as she walked.

And then his mind went to another woman whose body used to do that when she moved and he looked away sharply and started to find his messages very, very interesting indeed.

The woman at the hotel desk seemed a bit spooked. Perhaps Ellie wasn't making herself clear; her Spanish was pretty good, but maybe they only spoke Catalan in this hotel.

Ellie tried again. 'Signor Bulstrode, here? This hotel?'

There was a breakthrough. 'Yes,' said the woman, but it was accompanied by a shifty look towards the porter.

Ellie felt weary and grubby and anxious to have her reunion with Sam. Her feet hurt in her strappy sandals, and the radio on the reception desk, pumping out a high-octane commentary on a football match, was hurting her ears.

'Could I please check in and go up to his room?'

'You want to go up too?' said the woman, the look of consternation in her eyes intensifying.

Ellie sighed. 'As well as Mr Bulstrode? Yes.'

The woman's brow furrowed, but she indicated to the porter to take Ellie's bag, telling him to go to Room 27. The porter gave Ellie a strange look as well, and she began to wonder whether they were very religious and upset by the fact that she obviously wasn't *Mrs* Bulstrode. That suspicion was confirmed as Ellie got into the lift and the woman called out after her, 'We're a family hotel, you know.'

Ellie tried not to look at the porter as the lift rose and instead studied the rather faded pictures of Barcelona. The photographer had managed to achieve the impossible and make the place look like Croyden.

Soon they were outside Sam's room and Ellie knocked on the door, pulled in her stomach and put on her best seductive look. There was a slight pause and the door opened a fraction. Sam peered out and she saw a look of panic cross his face.

'Ellie, what . . . ?' he said.

The porter looked at her and looked at Sam.

'Aren't you going to let me in, Sam?' Ellie purred. 'This was a lovely idea.'

Sam did not move and so Ellie gently pushed the door. Sam held on to it tightly and she noticed how his breathing seemed to have speeded up.

'Are you all right, Sam?' she asked, worried that he

might be feeling ill. She noticed that he only had a towel round his waist and was sweating a lot. His hair was plastered to his forehead. Perhaps he had a fever.

'Ellie,' Sam started to say, 'I'm ... I ...'

Ellie was definitely worried now. He couldn't even speak properly.

And then a voice sounded from inside the room. A female voice.

'Sam, *was ist los? Wer ist da?*'

Ellie felt as though somebody with an icy hand had reached into her chest and squeezed her heart.

She gave the door a hearty push. Sam backed out of the way and then she understood everything. All the late nights. Those new clothes. The torrent of mobile-phone calls he got at home but never answered in front of her.

Lying naked and dishevelled on the bed was a blonde woman, her long, tanned legs culminating in a pair of killer heels.

Ellie heard herself say, 'One of your German colleagues, Sam?' and Sam said something like, 'Yes. Lotte.'

And then she was back down in the reception area, but this time in the little office. The Spanish lady was pouring her a glass of wine and rubbing her hand and jabbering away in Catalan to the porter with such vehemence that Ellie knew it was something along the lines of 'All men are bastards and Englishmen are the worst.' The unsympathetic look on the porter's face told Ellie that however Catalans thought 'this is priceless', he was thinking it.

Ellie felt as if she were acting in a very bad farce and that soon somebody would leap through some French windows dressed as a vicar. Things like this did not happen to people like her. Except they did and they had, and now she was sitting in a Spanish hotel wondering how she could have been so deaf, dumb and pigging blind.

CHAPTER 9

Ellie could not remember much about the plane journey back from Barcelona. She knew the woman in the hotel had booked the flight for her and she had some recollection of the taxi drive to the airport, but after that it was as if somebody else was doing all the talking and sitting, while Ellie herself was limping along behind, unable to think about anything except how Sam had acted when he had opened the door to his room.

Somehow she found herself sitting on the sofa in their flat. It was dark outside, and she must have been sitting there for a while because she had pins and needles in her feet. Next to her, on the table, there appeared to be an empty bottle of wine and a pile of damp tissues. Everything else in the flat looked the same as it had when she had left on Friday, but she had no idea how that could be, as her whole life was different now.

None of this was possible. Sam and Ellie, Ellie and Sam,

they were a couple. They'd been through university together, the thrill and fear of getting their first jobs. She'd stood on the touchline at hundreds of rugby matches for him; he'd dragged himself round art galleries for her. He'd supported her through the death of her parents; she'd comforted him when his best mate had been killed. He understood she couldn't get started in the morning without a cup of tea; she understood how much he hated peanut butter. Big things, little things. It was Ellie and Sam against the world, for God's sake.

Except it wasn't any more. Some other woman had taken her place and all those little milestones of sharing, all those signs of infinite caring for each other, had been discarded. They'd been examined and found not to be enough. And she'd been lied to, for weeks, even months. Lied to and cheated on like some sad sap.

She should have known. She should have seen that the steam was going out of the relationship. Why hadn't she read the signs? Not just Sam's late nights and more frequent absences, but also the way she herself had reacted to them. What had been behind that failure of perception, her almost suicidal lack of effort?

Ellie hauled herself up from the sofa and collapsed on the bed with her clothes still on. She slept very little, relentlessly going over in her mind where she had gone wrong and how stupid she felt and how sad she was that someone who had loved her and whom she had loved back could have travelled so far away from her without her even noticing.

When Ellie got into work on Monday morning, she sat at her computer and scrolled through email after email asking her how her weekend had gone. She heard Lesley say, 'Ellie, are you feeling OK? I mean, I know you're not OK . . . but . . . is there anything I can do? Anything I can get you?'

She shook her head. Lesley had done enough yesterday when Ellie had finally got out of bed and telephoned her. She had listened to Ellie's barely coherent account of what had happened, made all the right, sympathetic noises and then come round and made her eat something and have a bath and wash her hair.

It was simple love, given without a fuss, and it had been in evidence again this morning when she had arranged to meet Ellie outside the agency and walk in with her. Fielding Rachel's questions, she had got Ellie upstairs without her having to talk to anyone else. She would have to face them soon, of course, but this little breather was what she needed before the real and the mock sympathy started.

Ellie stopped looking through her emails and felt as if she wasn't really sitting in the chair; it all seemed like a nightmare that was happening to someone else. Not to her and Sam.

With a sharp little pain in her chest, she realised there was no more her and Sam.

She leaned forward and started to type.

Thanks for asking about my weekend with Sam in Barcelona.

Well, in a word it was 'crap'.

Got there to find Sam in bed with Lotte from Dortmund. And I guess from the sweat they had worked up, they hadn't been doing much sleeping.

Seems he's been teaching her English, she's been teaching him German, and I've been learning how to be a stupid, blind idiot. It's been going on for months evidently, right under my nose. Now he's leaving me to live with her.

To those of you who didn't know, join the club . . . and please, please don't ring me. I know you will want to be nice and supportive, but I really don't feel that I want to talk about this at the moment.

And to those of you who did know, thanks, appreciate it. You've made me look a tit in two countries.

Well, three, if you count Germany.

Not to mention adding another layer of humiliation to the whole thing.

Ellie

Then she sent the email to everyone Sam knew, including his dentist, the Tesco grocery delivery service and his stuck-up ruddy sister.

CHAPTER 10

Ellie sat in the Creative Department meeting and marvelled that Gavin didn't bore himself to death. On and on he went about his wonderful suntan lotion ad and how it was nearly ready for its very first viewing by the agency.

Jack was saying nothing. Every now and again he took a deep breath in, held it for a while as he lifted his chin and glared at the ceiling, and then let his breath out slowly. It was perhaps some kind of testosterone yoga that was just about stopping him from grabbing Gavin by the throat and squeezing him until he stopped talking.

Ellie could see that everyone was losing interest, apart from Zak and Jon, who were like little nodding dogs, hanging on Gavin's every word.

She closed her eyes and went back to pick, pick, picking away at Sam's betrayal and all that had happened in the three weeks since she'd pushed open that bedroom door in Barcelona.

It had all been horrible, starting with the tearful phone

call from Sam's mother. She and Ellie had promised each other that they'd always make time to meet up and keep in touch, but they both knew that a leggy German blonde was now firmly wedged between them.

The absolute gut-wrenching low point, though, had been Sam's visit.

Ellie opened her eyes to check on how the meeting was going. Gavin was still talking; Jack was still doing his deep breathing. Next to her, Lesley was drawing a picture of Gavin with one large testicle and one very small one.

Ellie closed her eyes and steeled herself to go back over the way Sam had looked and sounded the last time she'd seen him. As he'd stood there on the doorstep, Ellie could see everything had shifted. He hadn't even smelled like Sam any more. She'd kept it together pretty well at the start, but then he had said that Lotte was in the car waiting for him and Ellie had felt like she'd been jabbed in the ribs.

Her intention to be calm had evaporated and she'd shouted, 'Why, Sam? Give me one good reason why.'

He'd proceeded to give her loads of reasons.

Ellie suddenly became aware that Gavin had shut up and Juliette was talking. Probably a good idea to open her eyes again. Juliette was giving a round-up of what she and Mike had been up to in the last week, starting with the e-book account.

Ellie should really listen to this – she was interested in

e-books – but very soon she had tuned out Juliette's voice
and was thinking about Sam's visit again.

'Look, Ellie, I didn't plan this,' Sam had said. 'It was . . .
Lotte just came along and we, you and me, we seemed . . .
stale.'

'Stale?'

He nodded and wouldn't look at her. 'We . . . well . . .
we were set in our ways. It began to feel like we were only
doing things out of habit.'

'It didn't to me.'

'Oh, come on, Ellie. You never suggested anything new.
When was the last time we did something totally off the
wall?' He fumbled with the zip on his jumper. 'Especially in
bed. Lotte and I, well, let's just say she's not as timid as you.'

Another jab in the ribs. She sat down on the sofa, the
tears running down her face.

'Timid? But we still had fun, didn't we?' she said between
sobs.

'We got into a rut, Ellie. I hadn't been having fun for
a long time. And, you, well, you'd given up making any
kind of effort as far as I could see.'

'What do you mean? What kind of effort?'

In reply Sam looked her up and down.

He started to move around the flat, putting things into
black bin liners. Ellie saw the little wooden box she had
bought him for Christmas go in, the book she'd got signed
by the author.

When he'd finished, he came and sat beside her. 'I'm sorry, Ellie, I'm going now. I'll give you a call about the flat, about the mortgage and everything . . . Don't suppose you feel like talking about it now.' He reached out to hold her hand and she let him. 'I'm genuinely sorry, Ellie. I should have had the guts to tell you earlier, not keep lying to you. It's a rubbish way to treat a friend. I wish you hadn't found out like that.'

'You mean you wish I hadn't found out at all,' she said, pulling her hand free.

Sam didn't answer and Ellie couldn't say anything for a while. She had a horrible, cramping pain in her chest, and when Sam got up to go, she just sat there. She was battling to retain some dignity, let him see what he'd chucked away, but then he'd said something about having to rush and before she could stop herself she had spat out, 'Yeah, better run. If you leave Lotte alone in the car too long, she might chew the upholstery.'

If only at that point Sam had got angry, instead of giving her a 'you sad little person' look, she might not have added, 'Still, at least you should be thankful that she's housetrained.'

It had given Sam the perfect excuse to slam out of the flat, probably feeling like the injured party.

Funny how having the last word had felt so unsatisfying and so final.

The sound of Mike's voice cut into her thoughts. He

was outlining some initiative that major book retailers were piloting involving child-friendly e-books.

She watched Mike's arms waving around like windmill sails for a while and then asked herself why she hadn't become angry with Sam after he had gone. There was still some of his stuff left in the flat. She'd read about women trashing their ex-boyfriend's suits, even their cars.

But perhaps there was a set sequence to betrayal and loss. Perhaps anger came after sorrow, and sorrow came after shock. She figured she was in the 'mooching around feeling numb' stage and—

'I said, Ellie, what do you think of that?'

It was Jack's voice.

Ellie was aware that nobody else was moving. The room had gone completely quiet. One look at Jack's eyes told her that he knew she hadn't been listening. The way they were boring into her, she wouldn't be surprised if he knew exactly what she had been thinking about.

'Well?' The little word snapped out into the silence.

Lesley was furiously scribbling some words on her pad, but Ellie couldn't make out what they said.

It didn't matter, though; she knew where the meeting had got up to, and she had done a bit of homework on the e-book market.

'Well, Jack,' she said, 'I think we could work with the libraries on this one. They needn't see this as a threat. They could in fact open up a whole new market for themselves by acting as the access point.' She stopped, aware that Jack's face was looking more and more granite-like and that Zak was making an unsuccessful attempt not to snigger.

'The libraries act as the access point?' Jack repeated slowly, dangerously.

'Uh-huh.' Ellie had a horrible feeling that she was about to walk over the edge of a cliff.

'Well, that's brilliant, quite brilliant, Ellie,' Jack said, leaning back in his chair and putting his hands behind his head. 'What a fantastic idea . . . if only we hadn't actually moved on from e-books to the new morning-after pill being trialled by Liphook Masters. Still, I'm sure that local government will leap at the idea of their libraries handing out contraceptives along with Harry Potter and Tracy Beaker.'

Ellie expected Jack to rip her head off there and then, but he didn't. He carried on with the meeting and then asked her to stay behind afterwards.

'It's not as though it's the first time, Ellie. You've been acting like you're on a different planet for weeks now,' he said, scowling at her. 'Look, we all have personal problems from time to time, but they should stay just that, personal. And private. And. At. Home.'

Ellie looked at the floor.

'I mean, how long is this sick bloody cat routine going to go on for?'

Ellie kept looking at the floor.

'Will you stop looking at the bloody floor?' Jack shouted, and brought his hand down on the desk.

Ellie looked up and purposely focused on the sky outside the window. She was fed up with this, with him picking on her. Fed up with his horrible hard eyes and that glower. What a bully. Next he'd be speaking ruddy German and pointing out how boring and stale she was.

'Look, this is a business, not a sodding bus,' Jack continued. 'We can't afford to carry passengers. God knows there are enough of them around here already.' He pushed a piece of paper over the desk towards her, his eyes almost colourless. 'Read that.'

Ellie read, recognising a piece of work she'd done last week. It was terrible: clunky, incomprehensible in places, clichéd. She'd rushed to get it done for Hugo. The swine could have told her it was rubbish, not handed it on to Jack.

'This belongs here.' Jack tore the paper from her hands and threw it into his wastepaper basket. 'I wouldn't accept that pile of rubbish from a student, let alone somebody who is meant to be one of the agency's best copywriters.'

'Right. I'll go away and write it again,' Ellie said, standing up. 'I'll go and polish it to Zak's high standards.' She was aware her voice was getting more and more strident with every word. 'And while I'm about it, I'll go and put on a goth T-shirt and black nail varnish so I can match his extremely high standards of sartorial elegance as well.'

'And what exactly is that supposed to mean?'

'Well, it seems there's one rule for some and one rule for me. I'm slightly off my game for a couple of weeks—'

'Slightly off your game? You're not even on the pitch. And this isn't about Zak, it's about you. Stop trying to take attention away from yourself by pointing out other people's shortcomings.'

Ellie felt hot and put upon. 'Oh, I'm sorry. I forgot nobody's allowed to have emotions. We're all supposed to be carved out of Yorkshire granite like you.'

Jack had suddenly gone incredibly still, but Ellie didn't really register it. She was on a roll. 'Why am I bothering? You have no idea how I feel. How could you, Mr Interchangeable Girlfriend for Every Day of the Week? It's like talking a foreign lang—' Ellie stopped. She hadn't actually passed that last bit through her brain before she said it. She felt her stomach go into freefall as Jack got to his feet.

His eyes locked on to hers. She had never been in a fight, but she guessed this was how it must feel.

Ellie found herself backing towards the door, trying to break eye contact with Jack as he started to move. She wanted to turn round but had a feeling that if she did, he would bring her down in an instant. She felt the wood of the door at her back and reached down for the door handle, clumsily managing to get the door open.

'I'm sorry,' she mumbled. 'That was too personal. I forgot where I was.'

'Too fucking right,' Jack said. He was close to her now. She could feel the heat coming off him and a flush of red was spreading across his cheeks. She took an awkward step backwards and felt the metal divider between Jack and Mrs MacEndry's office under her foot.

'Get out of my office,' he hissed at her, and she actually jumped backwards seconds before he slammed the door shut in her face.

Ellie stood staring at the door, unsure if her legs were going to support her. She knew Mrs MacEndry must be looking at her, so she tried to laugh, to pass it off as nothing. It sounded feeble, dead.

'I suppose you get used to him doing that?' she said with a wonky smile.

'No,' Mrs MacEndry said, shaking her head very definitely. 'I've rarely seen him that bad.'

Inside his office, Jack was leaning against the door, battling to control himself, his heart hammering in his chest. He was scared how much Ellie had annoyed him. He'd nearly caught hold of her and given her a good shake.

He breathed out slowly. What she'd said had hurt. Really hurt.

For if there was one thing Jack did understand completely it was loss.

CHAPTER 11

'Here you go, our Lord and Master wants you to do this.' Gavin plonked a brochure into Ellie's hand and she felt her life force drain away.

She turned the brochure round for Lesley to see and a few seconds later she too was making a 'Kill me now' face.

'Hurrah,' Ellie said bleakly, 'the yearly update to the Jubbitt & Jubbitt brochure, the poisoned chalice of the Creative Department.'

Gavin gave a large, false smile. 'And don't forget, they may be small but they have important friends on the board. So . . .'

'How come we're getting it again?' Lesley said so aggressively that Gavin took a little step backwards. 'I thought we had an agreement that each team took it in turns. We did it last year. I remember Ellie almost had a nervous breakdown.'

Ellie nodded. First there had been the usual battle with Jubbitt & Jubbitt to try to get them to produce something more attention-grabbing. Then there had been the copy. Jubbitt & Jubbitt did not believe that less was more. They liked lots of words in long, tortuous sentences.

Ellie suspected that they priced out every paragraph to ensure they got the right number of words for their money.

Gavin smirked. 'Not my decision, girls. Anyway, plenty to get your teeth into there, Ellie. Lots of lovely meetings with Jubbitt Junior and his wandering hands.'

Lesley gave Ellie a sympathetic smile and went to the mini-fridge and retrieved a bottle of lager. Wordlessly she handed it to Ellie, who held it to her forehead.

After a little pause Lesley winked at Ellie and asked Gavin very innocently, 'So how are things with you?'

Immediately Gavin's face clouded. It was common knowledge that 'things' were not good with Gavin, not good at all. He was now set on a collision course with Jack, who wanted him out of the Creative Department and out of the agency. Gavin might as well have had a line round his neck saying, 'Cut here.'

'Don't pretend you haven't heard,' he said as though he had something sour in his mouth. 'You know what happened at the suntan lotion screening.'

Lesley did. Everyone did. The screening of the Sunny Sol Mio advert had replaced the ill-fated knickers idea as the number-one topic of agency tittle-tattle.

Jack had been looking for one final excuse to show Gavin the door and unbelievably Gavin had served it to him on a plate. Ellie had not actually been in the screening room when Gavin proudly showed off the ad, but it had been a classic Wolfe moment.

Jack had gone into the screening with the knowledge that the sixty-second ad was massively over budget, and as soon as the lights dimmed and the ad started to play, things got very nasty indeed.

The ad had Gavin's hallmark self-indulgence stamped all over it. Palm trees threw shadows on the sand; little waves ran up the beach and back out to sea; sunlight glinted off the water. There was no music, only random clapping. The overall effect was not of a sensuous, sun-drenched holiday but of something sinister. It seemed that at any moment the happy sun-worshippers could be carried off by something unspeakable rising from the depths of the ocean.

And that was another problem. There was a distinct lack of sun-worshippers, despite the fact that Gavin had interviewed over fifteen bikini models and selected the three most expensive ones. They were on the screen for less than ten seconds and shot in such soft focus that they appeared as if they were melting.

But the final, final straw for Jack had been the almost non-appearance of the product in any size, shape or form apart from one hazy shot of the bottle lying half covered in sand. Unfortunately for Gavin, it was the wrong bottle; the client's packaging was being revamped at the same time as its TV advertising and Gavin had not bothered to keep up with the latest design.

After spending thousands of pounds of the client's money shooting the ad in the South Pacific, the agency now had to hire a studio in Slough, fill it with sand and reshoot part of the ad to feature the new bottle. The client was incandescent with rage and was refusing to pay a large percentage of the bill, and the agency was the butt of a load of nasty jokes within the industry. For Gavin, it was walk-the-plank time.

Those who had been in the screening session reported back that 'Jack had verbally grabbed Gavin by the testicles and swung him round the room.' He'd taken off his jacket and rolled up his sleeves to do it.

After the monthly board meeting the agency would be Gavin-less.

Gavin perched himself delicately on Lesley's desk, checking first that there was nothing on it that would besmirch his jeans.

'That's the trouble with advertising now, overrun by money men,' he said to nobody in particular. 'It's full of men who wouldn't recognise a creative idea if it bit them.' He perused his nails and rearranged a cuticle. 'What happened to the free spirits in us? What about poetry? What about art? What about ground-breaking design?'

'What about your ruddy expenses?' Lesley said under her breath.

Gavin ignored her. 'To tell you the truth, I'm not sure I can work with Jack.' He was talking as if he still had a choice. 'I'm thinking of going to Tuttlebacks.'

Lesley and Ellie tried to dredge up amazed and sad faces, but it wasn't news to them. Rachel had already told the entire agency.

'Much more *simpatico* set-up there. People who know what a creative idea looks like and are willing to spend the money on it. It's getting a good name for itself. And here . . . well, with the Yorkshire Axeman calling the shots, it's only a matter of time before we have fluorescent flashes saying, "Great product, cheap price," on every piece of work.' Gavin flicked something invisible from his jeans. 'I mean, this kind of set-up is fine for workmanlike creatives like you and Lesley, but I—' Gavin stopped abruptly.

Jack was in the doorway.

'Word. Gavin. My office. Now.'

Gavin went, nose in the air, an arrogant swing to his hips.

Jack watched him go and then turned back into the room. 'I see you got the brochure.'

'Yes,' said Ellie. 'We can't wait to get started.' She pushed the brochure along her desk as if it were a piece of radioactive waste. 'Lucky us, getting it again this year. So how come it isn't Jon and Zak's turn?'

'Gavin said you and Lesley have got spare capacity. Besides, nothing like keeping busy, eh? Take your mind off things.' Jack directed the last statement straight at Ellie. 'Oh, and you wrote too much copy last time. Try and rein yourself in this year, will you?'

He looked exceptionally pleased with himself as he left the room and Ellie felt the unfairness of his comment like a slap. Nobody had tried harder than she had to get that copy cut back.

'No problem, Jack,' she said loudly. 'I'll get Jubbitt Junior to cut it so that it will fit on the head of a pin. And while I'm about it, I'll go and find the Holy Grail too, shall I?'

Lesley stared at her as though she were insane, and then Jack reappeared in the doorway. His good humour had gone and Ellie felt the temperature inside the room drop.

'Meaning what?' Jack said extraordinarily slowly.

'Meaning I tried like mad to get him to cut it back last time and it was impossible.'

'Then why not simply say that?' Jack snapped.

'What?' Ellie said, knowing exactly what point he was trying to make but deciding to annoy him further.

'Why not just say that? Why go in for all that dramatic head of a pin and Holy Grail rubbish?'

Ellie chanced a smile. 'Oh, I'm sorry, Jack. I thought that you employed me to be good with words.'

Under the desk, Ellie felt Lesley's foot connect sharply with her leg.

Down went the temperature again, and Jack walked over to her desk. 'Yes, Ellie, I do,' he said, bending down so that his face was level with hers, 'but the thing is, you see, I pay you to be good on paper. Not to show your verbal brilliance by being sarcastic when you're not happy with the jobs you get.' He straightened up. 'And you know what? That little habit you have of always wanting to have the last word? I don't pay you for that either.'

Ellie bit down on her anger as Jack started to move out of the room. Reprimanding her like that in front of Lesley wasn't on. She waited until he had reached the doorway before saying softly, 'Are you sure that I always have to have the last word?'

Jack came to an abrupt halt and Ellie received another sneaky kick from Lesley.

'Yes, I'm sure,' Jack said without turning round. His tone was clipped and mean.

Ellie said nothing and Jack started to move again.

Ellie coughed.

Jack stopped walking.

Ellie kept quiet again and saw Jack's shoulders rise and fall rapidly before he left the room.

One, two, three.

'OK,' she shouted. 'Perhaps you have a point, Jack. I do always have to have the last word.'

There was a muffled noise, which may or may not have been Jack swearing, and then Lesley jumped up and raced to the door. She scanned the corridor before returning to her seat.

'You're lucky, he's gone,' she said, 'but, Jeez, Ellie, he looked really angry. Really hacked off with you. What are you doing?'

'I just don't like the way he dumped that Jubbitt & Jubbitt job on us.'

'Well, you made it seem like you were making fun of him, as if you're kicking against him being in charge.' Lesley selected a pencil from her pot. 'If you're not careful, you're going to make it seem like you're on Gavin's side.'

'As if.'

'That's what it could look like. You've already had two run-ins with Jack, haven't you? There's no way you're going to win.'

'I'm not trying to win. I'm simply standing up for myself.'

'Well, it's not really working, is it? Seems to me that he's proving a point by giving us the Jubbitt & Jubbitt brochure, and if you don't mind, I could do without you annoying him any more since I'm the one who now has to photograph the pug-ugly Jubbitt & Jubbitt team. Again.' She picked up the brochure and the brief and started to read them.

Later on Ellie apologised to Lesley.

'I'm being an idiot. I'll make a real effort not to stir Jack up again.'

Trouble was, even as she was saying it, a part of her knew she didn't mean it. There were bound to be further fights; how could she avoid them when Jack thought he could walk into the agency and pulverise everything in his path?

Three days later Ellie trailed up the road and pushed a strand of hair behind her ear. Half past pigging seven and she'd been discussing the position of full stops and semi-colons with Jubbitt Junior for the last two hours.

Jubbitt Junior? That was a joke: he was sixty if he was a day.

Some time ago he had discovered that Ellie had an English degree and had been beside himself with joy. Now there was nothing he liked better than to show her how her grasp of English was, in fact, inferior to his own.

'I'm a mere solicitor, Eleanor,' he would begin, and then point out what grammatical murders she had committed.

No matter how many times she tried to explain that she was writing selling copy and not an essay, he ignored her. Pulling his chair up close to hers, he would go through her copy with a red pen, destroying anything that was punchy, annihilating sentences starting with 'and' or 'but' and adding clauses, sub-clauses and extra paragraphs. And all the while taking every opportunity he could to touch her knee or her thigh. No amount of glaring on her part seemed to deter him, and Ellie was kicking herself yet again for letting him get away with it. She'd practised in her head over and over the little speech about respecting her personal space but always lost her nerve at the last minute. The man was a personal friend of Gerald Wiseman, one of the directors, and she wasn't ready to commit professional suicide yet.

Ellie dragged her feet and looked around her morosely. Jubbitt & Jubbitt's offices were in Epping, right at the end of the Central Line, and she'd got so fed up with the sweaty, packed Tube journey back into town after the meeting that she'd come up for air at Marble Arch. Even up here it felt pretty stale and muggy. Spring had arrived, but today it felt like there was a thunderstorm coming.

People barged into her as she moved along Oxford Street. The pavements were dirty. London didn't look so great this evening.

She'd been ravenous after the meeting and had just downed a chocolate brownie and a latte, some of which she'd spilled down her jumper. She picked at the stain with a nail and felt very, very tired. Ruddy Jack Wolfe; it was his fault she was trapped in the life-sapping Jubbitt & Jubbitt brochure. All because of one innocent 'girlfriends' comment.

She decided to cut away from the crowds still choking Oxford Street and head down a quieter side road. She had a long journey home ahead of her and only the wilted contents of her fridge to welcome her when she got there. No Sam to help her poke fun at Jubbitt Junior. If she was really lucky, Edith would turn up for some X-rated Scrabble.

She trudged on and then saw something that made her stop abruptly and nip into a doorway. There was Jack; Jack in a beautiful charcoal-grey suit with a tall, reed-like woman in a black dress. An aura of glamour hung about them and the woman's blonde hair moved seductively in the slight breeze. Ellie recognised her as Leonora Pritchard, daughter of the sushi king. Feeling tired and dishevelled as she did, Ellie had no wish to bump into this golden couple and was about to retrace her steps back on to Oxford Street when she slowed down. Then she turned round and started to walk, with great determination, towards them.

Jack had got himself into a bit of a tricky situation. He'd made the mistake of calling Leonora 'Sophie' for a second time and she had stalked out of the restaurant in a huge sulk. People passed by and looked at them as they stood on the pavement and he tried to smooth Leonora's ruffled feathers. He was hungry and thirsty and this wasn't how he wanted to spend his evening. His plans for good food, good wine and a good shag were rapidly disappearing.

'That's not the first time you've called me Sophie this evening. Who the hell is she?' Leonora's mouth formed itself into an ugly line.

Jack decided that if he was going to lie, he'd have a go at a big one, just for the hell of it. Should be easy enough with Leonora: although she had many impressive features, her brain wasn't one of them.

He shot her a wide smile that made his eyes twinkle. 'Come on, Leonora, you know who Sophie is. She's one of my sisters.'

Jack saw Leonora's gaze hold his and then flick to his mouth. 'I thought they were called something like Grace and Louise. Or was it Laura?' Her tone was slightly less sulky.

He moved his hand gently to touch her arm, following up on his hunch that she was willing to be convinced.

'Clever you,' he said in his best low and husky voice. 'You had the first name right – one is called Grace. But the other one is Sophie. And it's her birthday soon and I've been thinking what to buy her, so she's been on my mind and her name slipped out.' As he talked, he moved his hand very gently to Leonora's waist.

'Hmm, well, I suppose you know your own sister's name,' Leonora said peevishly, but Jack saw her wet her lips a little with her tongue. He was nearly there.

He pressed home his advantage by leaning forward and kissing her gently on her cheek. 'Come on, honey, I hate it when you're cross with me. Come back inside and let's have some champagne.' He gave her a tender look and then kissed her hungrily on the mouth, feeling her relax into him.

'OK, Jack,' she said, pulling away from him, 'I forgive you. This time.'

Jack chuckled at his own ability to turn the situation

around. Sometimes this was too frigging easy. He took the now smiling Leonora by the arm and they were about to re-enter the restaurant when he spotted Ellie walking towards them.

Despite her rumpled and stained appearance, she had a strange, triumphant look on her face, and Jack suddenly felt queasy.

'Hello, Jack,' she said, and then turned to Leonora with her hand outstretched. 'You must be Jack's new girlfriend, Sophie. I've heard so much about you.'

Seconds later Leonora was stalking racehorse-like down the road and Jack was rubbing his slapped face. Ellie opened her eyes wide and met Jack's glower with a glittering, green look of her own.

'Have a nice evening, Jack,' she said, and then pushed past him and was gone.

Jack stood there for a while and then laughed. Last word to her, he supposed.

So, she wanted to play hardball.

Fine.

CHAPTER 12

Mrs MacEndry contemplated Jack's office door with a worried expression.

'Are you sure Jack asked to see you right now, Ellie dear?'

Ellie nodded. Jack had been brusque and insistent on the phone and she suspected that he was going to chew her out for her little performance the evening before.

'Well, he already has somebody in there with him,' Mrs MacEndry said, straightening some papers on her desk that already looked pretty straight to Ellie. 'But I suppose if you're sure he told you to come ...'

Ellie knocked on Jack's door and pushed it open. A woman was sitting by Jack's side, her portfolio of work open on the desk. Her glossy red hair was very close to Jack's choppy, thick black hair.

Jack raised his head and shot Ellie a cursory glance. 'Yes?'

The woman turned to look at Ellie too, and as she flicked

her gaze up and down what Ellie was wearing, her blood-red lips formed into a little smirk.

'Ellie,' she said.

Ellie's brain froze. What the hell was copywriter Monikka Steel doing in Jack's office? Nasty, scheming 'Feral Monikka'? She must be thinking of leaving Rackman Jarvitt. Or even worse, Jack must be planning to tempt her away.

Ellie's eyes went to Monikka's portfolio again.

'Yes?' repeated Jack, a hint of irritation in his voice.

'You rang me. You wanted to see me.' Ellie could not wrest her attention away from Monikka's portfolio of work.

'Did I?' Jack's face showed innocent puzzlement. 'Can't think what it was about now,' he said, shrugging. Then he turned back to Monikka, who was examining him very closely. 'You were saying, Monikka?' he asked, shifting his chair a little nearer to her.

As Ellie backed from the room, she heard Monikka in full flow: 'Well, Jack, this was a difficult concept, yeah? But I came up with this clever way of combining the message with the medium, yeah, and it played very well. The judging panel loved it.'

Ellie all but ran back to her office, but there was no Lesley there to offer sympathy. She was currently reshooting metal flanges with a particularly truculent photographer.

Not that Lesley would have been able to help much.

Elle knew what was going on. Gavin's days were numbered and now it seemed that hers were too. She had been right: there was only one way of doing things, Jack's way. They'd had one too many arguments and now she was about to lose her job to a Monikka with two 'k's, a glossy femme fatale who wasn't invisible. Nobody would mistake her for a ruddy student.

She moved around the office, taking in all the things that she and Lesley had collected over the years. There was the chart on the wall showing how many people had made the 'Hey, your name's Les and you are actually a Lesbian' joke. She looked at the little figure of Frankenstein that they had christened 'Hugo', and at the posters and rude postcards. She thought back to the first day Lesley and she had moved in. Then she went downstairs to ask Rachel for some black bin liners.

Mrs MacEndry put Jack's cup of coffee on his desk. 'All I am saying is that she could not hide how very, very upset she was.'

Jack grunted and Mrs MacEndry retreated to her office, having learned through hard experience that this particular noise meant 'end of discussion'. Jack carried on looking at the papers on his desk and then sat back in his chair. There had been no mistaking the look of shock on Ellie's face when she had seen Monikka. Still, Ellie was a bright girl; she'd know it was a warning shot, a little message that he didn't take kindly to her mooching about like some lovesick Victorian, or dropping him in it with Leonora. Whatever the reasons she'd been engaging in this little power struggle with him, that should knock it on the head.

There was no way she could actually believe he'd let a viper like Monikka into the agency. God, the way that woman had simpered at him. She'd even run her hand up his leg at one point. He pulled a face and got on with his work.

He was considering packing up and going home when Ellie reappeared in his doorway. She was flushed and even more dishevelled than usual as she walked over to his desk and put down a little pile of papers.

'First draft of the copy for the Jubbitt & Jubbitt brochure. I've managed to beat him down to a sixteen-pager this time, but there wasn't a lot else he was willing to lose in the copy line. Lesley's got the photography arranged for next week.'

Jack tried not to look smug. He'd got the result he wanted quicker than he'd imagined.

'OK,' he said, picking up the papers and offering them back to her. 'But really there's no need to bring this to me – Gavin's still your creative director.' He hadn't expected her to cave in so quickly.

Except Ellie wasn't taking the proffered papers and she had a disconcerting expression on her face.

'No, you keep them, Jack,' she said in a very sweet tone, 'and have this too.' She placed a white envelope on top of the papers and then turned and walked out of the room.

Ellie was chucking the contents of her desk into a black bin liner when Jack reached her office. He held out the white envelope she had given him earlier.

'Ellie, this is stupid. I'm not accepting this resignation.'

She ignored it, ignored him and kept on filling the bag.

Jack lowered his head and came into the room, placing the envelope on the desk. He watched as Ellie kept sorting through her papers and winced as she stamped on a blow-up strawberry to get the air out of it.

'Come on, Ellie, stop being so dramatic.'

Ellie continued to ignore him. He looked at how she was holding herself, how she was moving and it all shouted, 'Manic woman,' to him.

'Look, I think you got hold of the wrong end of the stick with Monikka.'

No reaction, still the frenzied sorting and chucking.

'It's Gavin's job to keep up to date with the talent out there. He's not doing that, so I am.'

Ellie gave him a disbelieving look. 'Don't waste your breath, Jack. Besides, Monikka's an excellent writer. A crap human being, but an excellent writer. There might be a few personality glitches, like between her and everyone else who works here, but hey, I'm sure you'll sort them out.'

Ellie tied the top of the bag and then looked at the few remaining items on her desk. Picking up the wastepaper bin, she swept everything into it.

'Well, I'm off,' she said in a brittle voice. Hauling the bin liner into her arms, she turned and moved towards her handbag.

Jack got to it before she could.

'Right, stop this now,' he said. 'Calm down and talk to me.'

'Give me my bag, Jack.'

'Not until you've calmed down and we've had a talk.' Jack got himself between her and the door. He lowered his voice and tried to establish eye contact. 'Ellie, I would have hoped that we could sit down and discuss anything that was bothering you,' he said. 'You know I'm always willing to listen to any concerns that you have.' That sounded pretty reasonable to his ears.

'Ha,' Ellie said with some force. 'Ha bloody ha. Pardon me while my pelvic floor collapses.'

There was a little standoff during which Jack debated whether to try again, but then the decision was taken out of his hands.

'If you don't give me my bag back, I am going to slap your smug face, you arrogant Yorkshire git,' Ellie shouted at him. 'I'm going home. I don't care whether you think I should be handing in my notice or not. That's my decision. And stop pretending that you're put out about it.

You've been chipping away at me since you got here.'

Jack clutched her handbag tighter. 'Ellie, don't be so idiotic, and stop sodding shouting at me. All I've ever tried to get you to do is raise your game. You know I think your work's brilliant.' He went to take a step towards her, but she let out a strange, too-high, too-quick laugh and it made him hesitate.

When Ellie spoke again, she did it so quietly that he found it much more disconcerting than when she had shouted.

'Oh, come on, Jack,' she said. 'I'm never going to be good enough to meet your high standards. I'm not high profile enough, not glamorous enough, not Monikka Steel enough. Hey, and guess what, I'm not even German enough.'

Before he could stop her, she had wrenched the handbag out of his arms, and while he was still nonplussed by that, he felt the flat of her hand on his chest and she shoved him out of her way. Then she walked out of the door.

Jack looked at the doorway as if expecting her to reappear. What the hell? Nobody pushed him about. If there was pushing to be done, he did it.

And how had she managed to shift him, anyway? It must be all that fury. She was really boiling at the end; he could see it in her eyes.

He sat down heavily in Ellie's chair. He'd made a right mess of that, completely ballsed it up.

Looking around the office he noticed the mini-fridge on the cabinet. Had that always been there? Soon he had a bottle in his hand and was slamming it against the edge of the desk to get off the top. He took a long drink. That Monikka stunt was a mistake. Now he was a copywriter down and about to can the creative director. Why the hell had Ellie gone completely over the top like that when sacking her wasn't even on the agenda?

Didn't she understand how these things worked? You had a spat with your boss; he let you get away with it for a while; then he slapped you down and gave you a bit of a taste of how bad things could be. Result: you took the hint and toed the line.

How she'd managed to survive this long in the business when she was so blasted sensitive was a mystery. Everything he said to her she took the wrong way. He had another swig of lager.

Maybe, though, if he were honest, she did have a point about him chipping away at her. It was just so damned annoying seeing someone who was as good as she was not making more of herself. That's all he'd been trying to do, wasn't it?

He'd let her cool off for a couple of days, then send Lesley round to talk to her. She'd listen to Lesley.

How come she'd got him on the back foot when he was meant to have the upper hand? As he thought of the way he'd just got his back foot entangled with his upper hand,

Ellie's comment about 'a tortuous set of mixed metaphors' drifted into his head and he took another long pull on his drink.

Why did he feel as if he'd lost their little fight when she was the one with her possessions in a black plastic bin liner?

Jack frowned as he thought about coming into this office tomorrow and seeing Ellie's empty chair and all of a sudden he was back in his first-ever flat, the one he'd had in Leeds.

The memory came out of nowhere and made him put down his bottle on the desk with a clunk.

He sat there for quite a while trying to find some sense of calm before slowly bending down and retrieving the things that Ellie had swept into the bin. Carefully he put them back on her desk, trying to position them where she'd had them before, as if by doing so he could peg her back into place. Or perhaps, if he got the order exactly right, conjure her up again.

She had no right to leave him like that. No bloody right at all.

CHAPTER 13

Ellie threw the black bin liner on to the sofa and watched as it tipped over and the contents spilled over the carpet.

'So you decided to let yourself in and rifle through my belongings?' she said to Sam's back.

'Our belongings,' he answered, and carried on doing what he had been doing when she arrived: picking over the CDs on the shelves. 'We never got round to sorting them. You said I could come back and get them. I rang, but you weren't in.'

Ellie shook her head in disbelief, but Sam said quickly, 'Come on, don't look like that. It's still really my flat too, Ellie. I'm paying half the mortgage till the end of the month.'

Ellie did not need reminding of that, or of the fact that the flat was going to have to go on the market pretty quickly because she could not afford it for long on her wage alone.

Now it suddenly hit her that she would be looking for

a new job at the same time as a new home. She sat down on the sofa next to the empty bin liner and wondered how much worse this day could get.

There was a constant 'Tap, tap, tap' as Sam piled CDs into a cardboard box and she knew that she should see what he was taking, but she couldn't bear it. So many of those CDs they had bought together and trying to decide what belonged to whom would be too painful. Let him have what he wanted.

Sam paused and she saw him look at the black bin liner. 'Hard day at work?'

Ellie said nothing and struggled up off the sofa and walked out of the room into the kitchen. Her hand reached for the open bottle of red wine from the night before, and without bothering to find a glass, she started to drink from it.

Might as well get used to it: she'd be under the railway arches soon, homeless and cuddling a cider bottle.

'I won't take much longer,' she heard Sam shout. 'Lotte and I are off to a film.'

'Lovely,' Ellie said with as much sarcasm as she could. 'What's it called? *How to Come to England and Steal Somebody's Boyfriend*? Hope there are subtitles for the blonde.'

There was no reply from Sam, and Ellie shrugged and took another large slug of wine. What had happened to her promise to herself to act at all times with dignity? She only had to see Sam and she was like a vengeful witch. She hated what came out of her mouth, but she couldn't seem to stop. It was all about trying to inflict the same kind of pain on him as he'd inflicted on her, she knew that.

A few minutes later she heard him say, 'I'm going now.'

She didn't answer, couldn't be bothered.

'I'll let myself out,' he said.

Ellie waited for the front door to close and went into the living room. The denuded CD collection now looked like a gap-toothed grin. 'Here's to happy listening,' she said, raising the wine bottle in a mock toast before it percolated through to her brain what CDs Sam had actually left her with.

'No. No way. No,' she said out loud, slamming the bottle down on the table.

Within seconds she had snatched up the CDs and barged out of the room.

Sam was loading the boot of the car and telling Lotte that Ellie hadn't been 'too bad' when something sharp hit him on the back of the head. He spun round to see Ellie, eyes blazing with anger, standing on the pavement outside the flat, a stack of CDs held to her chest.

'Bloody Santana!' she screamed. 'I hate them. I've always hated them. You know that.'

Whoosh – another CD flew through the air. Sam picked up his briefcase from the boot and held it in front of himself like a shield. The CD bounced off it and landed on the road, the case breaking open.

A passer-by stopped to see what was going on.

'It was your seduction music,' Ellie screamed, throwing another CD. Sam batted it away easily with the briefcase, but Ellie was giving every appearance of just getting into her stride. 'Every time' – *chuck* – 'you felt romantic, you'd put it on.' *Chuck*. 'Boring guitar solos.' *Chuck*. 'Boring drum solos.'

Sam was having to work hard. The CDs were raining down and Lotte was shouting at him in German to get into the car, but Ellie had him pinned down.

Some people had now come out of their front doors and were trying to look as if they weren't staring. Ellie was making quite a noise.

'. . . and do you know what, Sam the Shagger?' *Chuck*. 'You always finished ages before the music.' *Chuck*. 'I had to lie there and listen to the stuff while you dropped off to sleep on me.'

Someone, in what was now quite a crowd, laughed and Sam was distracted long enough for one of the CDs to catch him on the side of his face. 'Stop it, Ellie,' he yelled, rubbing the place where it had caught him.

Just then there was a shout from further along the street.

Ellie turned. It was Lesley.

Sam took advantage of Ellie pausing and slammed the boot, wrenched open the passenger door and threw himself into the car.

Lesley was shouting something about knickers.

The crowd switched their attention from Sam to the woman racing down the street. This was good; this was worth every penny of the higher-band council tax.

'Our knickers are back on, Ellie. They're back on!' Lesley was shouting.

The crowd murmured. Wow, violence and sex all in one evening.

Sam and Lotte's car screeched away down the road.

'Back on?' Ellie let the last remaining CD fall from her hand.

'Yeah.' Lesley stopped and tried to catch her breath. 'Old Hetherington ... dropped dead ... in the company car park yesterday. He'd come back in for his retirement party. How ironic is that?' Lesley tried to look serious. 'I mean, it's terrifically sad.' She was silent for a few seconds and then her smile burst out again. 'But, Ellie, that woman, Pauline What's-her-name, has been on the phone to Jack. Says she wants us to present the knickers idea again.' Lesley grabbed hold of Ellie's hands and twirled her round before drawing her into a hug.

There was a ripple of expectation in the crowd ... These two might be going to kiss.

Ellie had a huge smile on her face too and then it died. She remembered she didn't work for the agency any more.

'We've got to get a move on,' Lesley was saying, 'because they want to see us tomorrow. We're going to have to work on it tonight. Jack's on his way. In fact, I thought he'd be here by now.'

'I am,' Jack said, and they turned round to see him leaning against his car, a little further down the road.

The crowd looked at him. Hmm, tall, craggy, handsome man. This was getting better and better.

'I've been watching the cabaret,' Jack said, as he moved away from the car and walked towards them. He raised an eyebrow. 'Will there be a second half where you throw bigger things, or was that it?'

Ellie made a point of looking past him.

'Oh, come on, Ellie,' he said, 'we've got lots of work to do. Which one is your flat?'

'We, Jack?' Ellie snapped back. 'Have you forgotten they aren't my knickers any more? I resigned, remember? Give them to Monikka – you might have to explain what knickers are, but I'm sure she'll do a good job.'

Lesley's eyes flared in surprise. 'Resigned? Monikka? Feral Monikka? What?'

'I'm really sorry, Lesley,' Ellie said, putting an arm round her. 'I didn't want to just leave a message on your voicemail. It's a long story. I'll explain in a minute.'

'No need,' Jack said, reaching into his jacket and pulling out Ellie's resignation letter. He ripped it up and put the torn pieces back in his pocket. 'Right, that's sorted, then.' He rubbed his hands together. 'Now, which one did you say was your flat? We need to get cracking. We're in with a shout here. Think of that, Ellie, all those people with your song in their heads.'

Ellie crossed her arms. 'Do you really think it's as easy as that, Jack? That I'm that much of a pushover?'

The crowd looked from Ellie to Jack. Lesley looked from Ellie to Jack.

Ellie raised her chin as if she were waiting for something.

'What do you want me to do?' Jack asked. 'Get down on my knees and beg you to come back?'

By one in the morning they were all running out of energy. Jack had divided the presentation between the three of them, as Hugo was currently away shooting something feathery in Northumberland. When Ellie asked what Gavin's involvement would be, Jack simply made an 'O' shape with his finger and thumb.

They had gone back over the storyboards, the song and the business case for the approach, and then they had practised, practised, practised until they didn't think they could make the presentation any better.

Ellie surveyed the empty coffee cups and bits of sandwich and grinned as her eyes strayed to the two dirty patches on Jack's knees. She wondered if he would sack her after the presentation for forcing him to get down on his knees in the street and beg.

Beside her, Lesley was wilting and every now and then

she gave a huge yawn. After a particularly jaw-stretching one she said, 'Ellie, can I doss down here tonight, save me having to hack over to my place?'

Ellie nodded and then felt she had to offer Jack a bed for the night too. 'Stay if you want, Jack,' she said, 'but I guess you'll need to go home and change.' She stared pointedly at his knees.

'No, don't need to go home,' he said cheerfully. 'I've got spare clothes and things in the car.'

Ellie supposed that when you spent as much time as Jack did in other people's beds, you probably needed to carry most of your possessions around in your car.

'OK, well, you can have the spare bed. Lesley and I will share mine.'

Jack nodded and got to his feet and Lesley started to laugh. 'Go on then, Jack, say something.'

'About what?' he said, a puzzled look on his face.

'About Ellie and me sharing a bed. Most of the other men at the agency usually end up dribbling down their shirts if they find Ellie and me even hugging each other. Or they ask if they can watch.'

'Or they try to get in the middle,' Ellie added, wondering if it was actually a wise idea to tease Jack.

Jack studied them both, letting his eyes travel from one to the other. 'No,' he said slowly, 'I won't be making any comments about that. Not about two beautiful bodies, caressing and pleasuring each other ... about soft lips meeting soft lips . . . gentle hands running over and under and around yielding flesh . . . No, nothing like that.'

Lesley and Ellie stood as if bolted to the floor while Jack gathered up the dirty cups and plates and took them out to the kitchen as though nothing had happened.

'Jeez.' Lesley put a hand on her forehead. 'That was like being humped by Ted Hughes.'

'Makes a change from Heathcliff,' Ellie said, and tried to give a dismissive snort. It got stuck in her throat.

By the time Jack returned, Lesley had skittered off to bed and Ellie was attempting to look engrossed in the task of rearranging the sofa cushions.

Jack stood in the doorway with his shirt sleeves rolled up and Ellie tried not to think about the way he was watching her. Now he was in her home, he seemed bigger, more real. More man. She fumbled with a cushion and heard Jack move into the room to take his jacket from the back of a chair.

'So, Jack, let me show you where you'll be sleeping,' she said as breezily as she could.

He stepped to one side to let her pass, but she was still acutely aware of where he was in relation to her. 'Along here,' she said, her voice sounding too high and too loud even to her. It was the voice of a nervous woman and she thought she saw Jack palm a smile at her discomfort.

Why did he have to walk so close behind her?

Ellie opened the door of the spare room and pointed

in the direction of the bed. 'There's a towel for you there, and you know where the bathroom is. Do you need anything else?' She folded her arms defensively and then quickly unfolded them in an effort to look nonchalant.

Jack shook his head and did not speak.

'Well, night, then. See you in the morning,' she said very quickly.

'Ellie?' he said suddenly, his voice a whisper.

She raised her eyes to meet his. 'Uh-huh?'

'Try not to make too much noise, will you?' He jerked his head towards the room where Lesley and she would be sleeping. 'I'm a very light sleeper.'

Ellie moved away from Jack as if she'd been burned and was in her own bedroom in seconds. She leaned against the door, her heart hammering in her chest. Very funny, Jack. And he'd had the last word.

'You OK?' Lesley said in a drowsy voice from the bed.

'Yeah, fine. Fine. Getting a bit nervous about tomorrow.'

She stood there for a while longer, thinking about going to the bathroom to clean her teeth, and then decided against it. You never knew what was prowling around out there.

In the spare room, Jack was still laughing softly to himself as he got undressed. He chucked his clothes on a chair, narrowly avoiding causing a landslide to one of the many piles of books stacked up on the carpet. He ran his finger down the spines of a couple of paperbacks and smiled ruefully. She'd actually read them. Yeah, every one he picked up had little tell-tale creases.

That shouldn't surprise him, should it? As she'd said herself, that's what he paid her for, to be good with words.

As he slid himself under the duvet, he thought about the way Ellie had insisted that he kneel in the street to apologise to her. He had expected to find it humiliating. Instead he'd found it kind of erotic. His mind went back over what he had said about Ellie and Lesley sleeping together and he suddenly felt very aroused.

He lay down and closed his eyes and soon he was back at work and Ellie was in front of him. Very gently he bent her face down over his desk, pulled aside those pale-gold knickers and pushed himself into her over and over again.

But somewhere in his dream a cold foot was touching his leg and then someone started to scream. Jack sat upright in bed, his heart hammering. It was pitch black, and what was that smell? Gin ... and ... and ... moth-balls? Over the high, warbling scream he heard footsteps and the sound of a door opening. A light came on and Jack winced and closed his eyes.

He heard Ellie shout, 'Edith, what on earth are you playing at? What time do you call this to turn up?' and the screaming stopped.

Jack opened his eyes to the sight of an extremely old lady in a thermal vest snuggled down beside him in the bed. In the doorway, Ellie was standing with her hand over her mouth. Behind her, Lesley was doubled over with laughter.

'Well,' the old lady said, running her gaze over his broad shoulders and bare chest, 'you're rather a fine physical specimen, aren't you?'

It had taken Ellie a while to persuade Edith that she could not keep on sleeping with Jack. Ellie set about making up a bed for him on the living-room sofa and listened to Edith chatting on in the bedroom. At one point she heard Edith say, 'You're not at all like Mr Magoo,' and then laugh. She couldn't make out what Jack said in reply.

Ellie was not sure that if she were in Edith's position, she would be so unselfconscious. Sitting up in bed, his hair all messed up and in his eyes, Jack had not, indeed, borne any resemblance to Mr Magoo. She tried not to dwell on the way the duvet had been pushed down round his waist to reveal a chest that had made Sam's rugby-honed one look completely puny.

She realised that she was standing looking at the sofa and biting the skin down the side of her thumbnail, so she took a deep breath, smoothed down the sheet and tucked the edges under the sofa cushions. She supposed he'd got muscles like that from doing press-ups over all those women.

Still, at least now she knew he wasn't covered in fur all

over his body. But even without fur he'd looked disturbing. What was it about him? She cast around for the correct word. It seemed incredibly important to attach a label to Jack, as if by doing so she could pigeonhole him neatly and put him away on a high shelf.

She picked up the duvet, gave it a good shake and then dropped it on the sofa. No, that word still wasn't coming. She could settle for 'powerful' or 'intimidating', but there was a better word out there somewhere and she couldn't reel it in. 'Sexy' would certainly apply, she had to admit that, especially how he looked right now, half wrapped in duvet. But it wasn't *the* word.

She punched the pillows into shape. What was that ruddy word? It had something to do with the way he had been sitting there chit-chatting with Edith and Lesley, completely unfazed by the whole thing. Apart from a confused squinting into the light when he had first realised that Edith was in bed with him, his only other reaction had been to look faintly amused.

Ellie looked down at the sofa and gave the pillows one last thwack. This was weird; she always had the perfect word on the tip of her tongue.

Jack would have to stay unlabelled until she could find it.

Her pre-presentation jitters hadn't been helped by all this. Pulling back her shoulders, she put on a bright smile and went back into the bedroom to rescue Jack.

When she finally managed to get Edith to settle down, they all averted their eyes while Jack got out of bed, wrapped a towel round his waist and padded off to sleep on the sofa.

Except Ellie was not convinced that Lesley and Edith had totally averted their eyes. In fact, when Lesley and she were back in Ellie's room, Lesley admitted that she hadn't.

'And let me tell you, Ellie,' she said with a little giggle, 'as an objective observer, I can tell you that the bottom half is just as impressive as the top half.'

Nearly twenty-four hours later Jack was unsuccessfully trying to manoeuvre Ellie out of his car. She seemed all arms and legs.

Arms and legs made of jelly.

Apart from the odd passing car, the street was silent and deserted. He guessed the silent bit was about to change.

'Has she always been able to drink that much?' he asked Lesley.

'Yeah,' she said, falling up the kerb. 'Sam was a rugby player, so Ellie's had years of practice – pre-match, during match, after the match. She brought home a supermarket trolley once after a night on the town, you know. Got it up two flights of stairs.'

Jack pulled Ellie to her feet and she started to sing 'Barnacle Bill the Sailor'.

'Oh God,' said Jack, 'not again. Come on, you.'

Between them, Lesley and he managed to get Ellie to her front door, and as Lesley started to hunt for Ellie's key, Edith opened the door from inside.

'Hello, you big hunk,' she said to Jack. 'Back for more?' Then she noticed the way Ellie was being held up. 'Well, what have we got here?'

'It's me, Edith,' trilled Ellie. 'I've had a few little drinks.'

'We had a good presentation, Edith,' Jack said. 'It's more or less a cert they're going with the idea. So we stopped for a little celebration on the way home.'

'And you've been plying these poor girls with drink and staying sober yourself, you devil,' Edith said in a way that had probably been the cutting edge of flirting back in the 1950s.

Jack was distracted from replying by Ellie, who was slowly starting to slide to the floor. He lifted her up into his arms as if she was a small child, her head on his shoulder, and carried her over the threshold. Lesley wobbled along behind them, before tripping over and ending up on the floor in a giggly heap.

Jack tut-tutted, but he was having a job keeping a straight face.

'I'll put this one on her bed, shall I, Edith?' he said.

As Jack laid her down, Ellie's eyes fluttered open and Jack realised that they weren't uniformly green, they had tiny flecks of some other colour in them. What was it, brown or gold?

'I had a lovely time today, Mr Wolfe,' Ellie said softly.

'Felt good, did it, Ellie, being on the winning side?'

'You bet your hootanooty-tooty it did. And you were such an impressive boy . . . even after a bad night's sleep on a too-small sofa.'

'Well, I've slept in stranger places.'

Ellie laughed up at him, her hair spread around her on the pillow. And then suddenly she raised a hand and trailed it gently down his face.

A jolt of desire hit Jack squarely in the groin and for one wild instant he was tempted to bend and kiss the soft skin of her throat. He stood up abruptly and stepped back.

'Nunnight, Mr Wolfe,' Ellie said in a whisper, rolling on to her side and closing her eyes.

Jack walked slowly back into the hall.

'Lesley has passed out,' Edith said with a smirk, 'but if I am not very much mistaken, there will be vomiting and headaches later.'

Back outside in his car, Jack returned his rear-view mirror to its original position. Lesley had been too befuddled to notice that he'd changed the angle earlier so that he could see Ellie in the back seat. She'd been so animated, so alive. He hadn't even minded the singing. Quite a revelation seeing her relaxed when he was about. She normally acted as if she was on her guard.

If he concentrated hard, he could still conjure up how

she felt in his arms when he'd carried her into her flat. His hand had inadvertently connected with a breast and he had felt its weight and warmth like an electric shock up his arm. Damn it, she'd looked inviting lying on that bed. And when she'd reached up and touched him, he hadn't just been tempted to kiss her; he'd wanted to lie on top of her to feel all that softness against him.

He thought about those flecks in her eyes again and blew his breath out slowly and sat motionless for a while. This was not good. On so many levels. Ellie was someone who worked for him, someone he couldn't dump in a hurry if things got too serious.

What was the point in having a perfectly good 'no mixing work and sex' rule all these years and then tearing it up?

Mind you, she'd been great in the presentation today. Fired up, really selling the idea, charismatic. He'd hardly had to do a thing.

Still a scruffbag, but that was kind of growing on him.

Hang on. Jack ran his hand down his face. It was 'kind of growing on him'? Where had that come from?

Too much adrenalin still coursing around his body, that was the trouble. Probably post-presentation euphoria.

He reached for his mobile and punched in a number.

'Sophie darling . . . Yeah, I know it's late, but I was

wondering if you felt like ... You do? Right. I'm on my way.'

Jack ended the call, smiling a thin little smile. Then he threw his mobile on the passenger seat and drove off.

CHAPTER 14

'I think this would be better if we changed the comma to a semi-colon,' Jubbitt Junior said, positively hyperventilating with excitement. Ellie fumed as he destroyed her lovingly crafted copy but made sure her 'You are a complete idiot but you are a client' smile was still on her face. It had been plastered there for so long it was making her ears hurt.

Now she was going to have to go back to the agency and knit the brochure copy together tonight if they were to meet the printer's deadline.

Jubbitt Junior pored over the brochure again and Ellie let her mind drift back over the week. Things had moved quickly since Pauline Kennedy had rung and green-lighted the knickers idea. They'd already had a preliminary meeting with the animation company, and yesterday Lesley and she had spent the whole day with Dave, the guy composing the original music for the knickers song. They had auditioned ten singers, searching for the best voice for each pair of knickers. It had been a long day, but all in all exactly the kind of experience that had attracted Ellie to advertising in the first place.

Unlike today. The voice of Jubbitt Junior brought Ellie back to the present for a few seconds as he made a particularly unfunny joke about hanging participles and then she returned to thinking about the way Dave had lunged at her to say goodbye after the auditions were over. Even she, who had spent years out of the dating pool, had recognised that he seemed a bit keen and was probably aiming for her mouth.

She hadn't been sure how she'd felt about that at the time and she wasn't quite sure now either. She still missed Sam, his physical presence around the flat, their easy companionship. You couldn't simply forget all those years of shared experiences. And the humiliation of being cheated on still felt like a shameful burn somewhere inside her.

But since the excitement of getting approval for the singing knickers and all the work that had brought, she'd lost touch with those intense emotions she'd felt when Sam had first left her. How could that be possible? All those years together and now, a matter of weeks later, she could only dredge up regret and sadness.

Ellie focused on Jubbitt Junior momentarily to make him believe that she was actually listening, and noticed with unease that one of his hands was deep in his pocket. Eeew, that was a new trick.

She retreated back into the relative safety of thinking about lost love. Was Sam right? Familiarity and habit had been the only glue keeping them together?

Ellie decided to stop thinking about it any longer or she'd spiral off into the deep, brain-frying question of 'What is love?' She had no ready answer; all she knew was that if Sam turned up at her door now and begged to come back, she wouldn't have him. What would be the point? Whatever they'd had was over; there was no way of reheating it.

Ellie flinched as she felt Jubbitt Junior's hand on her knee. Yeuch, was that the hand that had been in his pocket?

'Oh look, Eleanor my dear,' he said as though he had discovered a rare and exotic animal, 'I think that we can put another colon here.'

Ellie smiled politely, imagining in great detail what she would like to do with Mr Jubbitt Junior's colon should she ever get her hands on it.

It was already eight o'clock when Ellie got back to the agency, and reception was deserted. Ellie didn't mind. There was something about the place at this time of night that was inherently exciting to her, more so than when it was full of people. It was almost as if she were part of some special little group within the agency that made it tick – people who worked late to produce the raw material by which the agency stood or fell.

Either that or she was a deluded workaholic.

She walked over to Rachel's desk to see if there were any messages, smiling at the make-up bag carefully positioned out of view. Then the lift doors opened and out came Jack in a dinner suit.

'Bit posh for the pub, isn't it?' she said, trying not to stare.

Jack did a mock yawn. 'Trade do at the Dorchester.'

In his dinner suit he didn't look like the customary penguin, more like some dangerous panther that had been partially tamed but could turn nasty at any minute. He didn't smell nasty, though. The smell of him curled its way into her consciousness and she couldn't place what it was. No doubt, in her breathy way, Rachel would say, 'Essence of Man'.

'Working the night shift on the Jubbitt thing?' he asked.

'I toil at night so that the world can rest easy that not a piece of punctuation will be out of place.'

Jack laughed. 'I heard yesterday went well, though. You got some good voices. You happy?'

'Yes, it was really good. I learned a lot. So now, once I've got this brochure out of the way and Jubbitt Junior's handprints off my thighs, I'll be ecstatic.'

Jack went very still. 'Jubbitt Junior's what?' he said, barely moving his mouth.

'His handprints ... He's a bit of a hands-on client, if you know what I mean.'

Jack stared at her and for the briefest of moments she saw his gaze travel down her body and then back to her face. His look was deep, unfathomable, and Ellie felt she had done something wrong. Then he gave her a curt nod and walked away.

'Bye, then,' she said to his retreating back, and went off to tackle the Octopus Man's amends.

The next morning Ellie looked at Jubbitt Junior standing in front of her in the meeting room and wondered what fresh hell he was about to subject her to. Her eyes were still tired from the marathon session she'd put in last night to deal with all the changes he had flagged up yesterday and she'd had the amended brochure biked over to him first thing. All he needed to do was check he was happy with it, sign it and have it biked back. If he didn't approve it today the printers would go ballistic.

So what was so important that he had turned up at the agency? Perhaps he'd decided he wanted copperplate writing instead of type, or maybe he'd like the whole ruddy thing printed on parchment and not paper.

He was acting very strangely. He'd leaped to his feet when she'd walked in, and there was a crumpled look about him. Sweat beaded on his top lip and his forehead, and he was executing a strange little movement from one foot to the other.

He looked as she imagined Mr Collins did in *Pride and*

Prejudice just before he proposed to Lizzy Bennet. It was a thought that made Ellie take a couple of surreptitious steps backwards.

'Um, Eleanor, I mean, Miss Somerset, I have approved the copy amends.' He pointed towards a large folder on the glass-topped table. 'You must have worked very hard yesterday after we met, very hard indeed. I wanted to say how pleased I am with it. We're all very pleased with it.' Jubbitt Junior plaited his fingers as he talked.

It couldn't be that simple. If he fell on one knee and asked her to marry him, she was going to have to kick him in the groin, despite having promised herself she was never going to get anywhere near Jubbitt Junior's groin.

She saw him lick his lips nervously.

'I also wanted to say, Eleanor, that I have always been a very tactile person and it may be that sometimes I am tactile in the ... ahem ... wrong situation.' Jubbitt Junior's blinking was reaching worrying proportions. He stumbled on, 'If this ... um ... tactile approach should have occurred in any of our meetings' – more blinking – 'I'm not saying it has, of course, but if it has, I unreservedly, without any further preamble, straight to the point, want to say I'm sorry.'

Good grief, the dirty devil was apologising. Ellie was unable to comprehend why he should realise right now that he'd been a lecherous old goat. Even more perplexing was the way he was looking at her as if pleading with her to say something.

She should leap down his throat and tell him exactly what she thought of his fondling ways, but he already looked scared half to death. All those things she had rehearsed to say to him dissolved. Next Christmas she was definitely asking for a harder heart.

'Well,' she started hesitantly, 'I have found that maybe you don't respect people's personal space as much as you should.' She waited for him to deny it, but he looked more terrified. 'And with you being one of our clients, it has made it very difficult for me to say anything to you about it.'

Jubbitt Junior's words came out in a torrent. 'Right. Yes, well, good point, Eleanor. A lesson learned by me there, Eleanor. Yes. Say no more. A lesson learned. Thank you.'

Ellie could hear his laboured breathing and actually started to become concerned about him having a heart attack or a stroke.

She was going to say something else, but he abruptly stopped dancing from one foot to the other and made a huge detour round her to get to the door.

'I'm glad that's clarified,' he said hurriedly, and gave her a grotesque little half-bow, half-curtsey before wrenching open the door and leaping out into the corridor.

Most odd. Ellie collected the folder from the table and walked quickly to reception. Rachel was looking up under her eyelashes at a courier who was dressed in an extremely tight pair of cycling shorts and a vest.

'Sorry to bother you, Rachel,' Ellie said, interrupting the cyclist and trying to keep her eyes from straying to his crotch. 'Did Jubbitt Junior simply turn up this morning?'

'No, Jack asked me to call him in. He was in with the creep for about half an hour before you.'

Ellie decided to take the stairs back up to her office. She needed time to think about this. Jack had stepped in and had words with Jubbitt about his inappropriate behaviour, that much was obvious. Why was she surprised? Probably because Gavin had never lifted a finger to help her. She'd spent so long working for a self-obsessed oaf she'd forgotten what a good boss was meant to do for his staff.

After all, hadn't Jack brained that guy who had been rude to Mrs MacEndry?

So if Jack was only doing his job, why did it make her feel as if she'd had a warm blanket wrapped around her shoulders?

She ran up the last few stairs and decided not to beat herself up about it. If someone did something for her, why shouldn't she feel pleased?

'What are you grinning about?' Lesley asked when she walked into the office.

'Oh, nothing,' she said, and wondered if not telling the truth was the same as telling a lie.

CHAPTER 15

The producer counted out, 'One, two and three,' with his fingers and then the sweet sound of the singer's voice filled the studio: 'With Sure & Soft you've got everything covered.'

Penny was a pale girl with washed-out blonde hair almost hidden by the headphones, but boy, did she have a voice. She was the singer they were using for the last lines of the song and her voice was so good that Ellie and Lesley had decided to fade out the music right before she started to sing. It gave more emphasis to the product name and they were convinced that the sound of Penny's voice singing out on its own would really stick in people's brains.

The producer asked Penny to sing the lines again a couple of times and then shouted across to Ellie, Lesley and Dave, 'I think that last one was the best. You three happy?' They all nodded. 'Well, in that case, ladies and gentlemen, I thank you. Our work here is done.'

There was an outbreak of cheering from the musicians,

who had finished recording some time before but had hung around drinking the free coffee and snaffling all the biscuits. The saxophone player, a guy with a straggly goatee, said loudly, 'Hallelujah! There's a ton of dust in my mouth needs watering.' There was general laughter and a move to pack up and leave.

Recording studios had always seemed like glamorous little worlds to Ellie, even though the people who inhabited them were usually dressed more casually than she was. And some were definitely borderline geeks. She supposed the glamour bit came from all those decks and switches and microphones. And every now and then you could catch a glimpse of a famous face coming in to do a voiceover for an ad or a documentary.

On top of that was the thrill Ellie got from knowing that somebody would read out her words here in this room and soon they would be heard by people all over the country. Ignored possibly, but still out there on the airwaves.

Ellie was relieved that it had been a glitch-free day. The producer and Dave had overseen everything; all she and Lesley needed to do was ensure that the spirit of what they wanted had come through.

'You going to the pub?' the sound engineer asked them.

'Just for a quick one,' Ellie replied. 'I've promised someone I'll meet them for dinner tonight.'

Lesley gave her a funny look but didn't say anything

until they were out of the building and some way down the street. Ellie guessed that, like her, Lesley was a little disorientated after being in the studio for so long. It was easy to lose track of everything when you were in there concentrating so hard, particularly as there were no windows anywhere to remind you of the outside world. To come out into the street and find that life was carrying on as normal and it was nearly dusk took a few minutes to absorb. Ellie hoped that Lesley wouldn't pick her up on her comment about dinner, but soon she felt Lesley's hand on her arm pulling her to one side.

'Who are you meeting?'

'Edith.'

Lesley flicked her eyes skyward and clicked her tongue. 'Well, why didn't you say that? You made it sound like a date. It really wiped the smile off Dave's face.'

'Dave?' Ellie said, trying to sound as if she didn't know what Lesley was getting at, even though the way the guy had been behaving all day had confirmed her earlier suspicions that he liked her. Every time she'd moved, he'd been right behind her.

'Look,' Lesley said, 'I know you won't have noticed this, not having dated since Magna Carta was signed, but Dave really fancies you. Play your cards right and I think he's going to ask you out.'

'Really?' Ellie realised she'd overplayed the innocent bit when she saw Lesley's eyes narrow.

'Hang on . . . you wanted him to think you had a date.'

Ellie started walking again. 'Yeah, well.'

'What's the problem? He's really keen.'

'I don't know, Lesley. I—'

'What are you afraid of? That you'll have a bad time?' Lesley gave her a playful pinch on the arm. 'Or that you'll have too good a time? Afraid he'll dislodge Sam the Slug out of your brain for a few hours?'

Ellie stopped and faced Lesley. There was no shutting her up when she got her teeth into something. 'I don't feel ready for—'

'For what? Look, we're not talking about finding a replacement for Sam. All you need is someone to give you a quick re-bore.'

Ellie grimaced. 'Oh, Lesley, lovely poetic thought.'

'Never mind my poetic thoughts. Come on, put him right about your dinner date and get his phone number, eh?'

They had reached the pub, and as Lesley went to open the door, Penny and the keyboard player came back out. He had his hand on her backside and she had one of hers on his thigh.

'That was quick,' Ellie said. 'Must be off for a bit of organ practice.'

Lesley sniggered and pushed her in through the pub doors.

Half an hour later Ellie was on the bus to meet Edith

with Dave's phone number on a beermat in her handbag. He hadn't seemed to mind when she'd told him that she had recently come out of a long-term relationship and wasn't sure she was ready for anything else yet.

'Well, when you are, make sure it's me you ring first,' was all he'd said.

His goodbye kiss had had a lot of heat in it and it was only Ellie extricating herself from it as tactfully as possible that had stopped it bursting into something much hotter.

When Ellie got to the restaurant, Edith was already sitting at the table, a large gin and tonic in front of her. She seemed preoccupied and Ellie suspected that she was up to something. The restaurant was all starched table-cloths and even starchier waiting staff; the waiter who greeted Ellie had done a little camp shudder at the sight of her jeans.

Somewhere there was a string quartet sawing its way through Lloyd Webber hits.

When Ellie saw the prices on the menu, her suspicions that Edith was buttering her up grew stronger.

'Edith, it's mind-blowingly expensive here. I'm only going to have a first course and a pudding.'

Edith waved her objections away and, as if to prove some kind of point, ordered an expensive bottle of wine.

Over on the other side of the restaurant, a couple of diners were smirking at Edith's outfit and probably trying to work out which short transvestite in London was currently missing a velvet catsuit with sequinned belt. Edith gave them one of her dowager stares and they looked away hurriedly and became engrossed in the wine list.

The first part of the meal passed without event. As the large white plates bearing tiny portions arrived, Ellie and Edith chatted about nothing in particular and whispered about the people at the next table, who had not said one word to each other since they had been seated. Even so, Ellie knew that Edith's mind was elsewhere, and after the puddings had been placed in front of them, Edith put down her spoon and fork.

'Ellie darling, I have not been entirely honest about why I invited you for dinner tonight.' Edith's tongue darted out and made a nervous pass over her lips.

'Well, I was curious, Edith. I mean, you're always generous, but this is way beyond that. Come on, spill the beans.'

Edith's fingers were now playing with the buttons down the front of her catsuit. She gave a delicate cough. 'Well, Ellie, I know, of course, that your flat is up for sale and I couldn't help noticing when I was staying with you recently that you have lots of details of other flats. From estate agents. Lots.' She gave Ellie a concerned look.

'Too many, Edith. I'm getting bogged down trying to decide which ones to go and see. But with Sam . . .' Ellie still couldn't bring herself to say 'gone'.

'Yes, I understand, dear. On one salary you can't afford the flat you're in.'

'Not just the flat, Edith. I can't afford the area either. I'm looking much further out. It will cost me more to get to and from work, but . . . Anyway, there are a couple of flats in Harrow on the Hill that sound good.'

'Harrow on the Hill!' Edith made it sound like Hades.

'They're still slightly outside my budget, but what with the knickers thing, I was thinking of asking for a pay rise soon.'

Thinking about it, but not fully intending to do anything. That would mean going in to see Jack, whom she'd been avoiding since the Jubbitt Junior incident. It had been much easier to see Jack as a testosterone-driven power freak than a decent person who protected his staff. And she still couldn't quite understand that deep look he had given her when she had first told him about Jubbitt Junior's wandering hands. It had made her feel at the time as though she was at fault; now it made her feel unsettled, like . . . Well, she wasn't sure. She couldn't name that emotion, like she couldn't name the word that would describe Jack perfectly. Just when she needed words, they seemed to be failing her. Jack was making her feel like a dictionary slowly being wiped of its contents.

Ellie realised she had been daydreaming when she heard the tail end of Edith saying, 'And I did notice, Ellie, that many of those flats only have one bedroom . . .'

Ellie had a light-bulb moment. 'Don't worry, Edith – I'm going to get a sofa bed. When you want to stay, you can have my bed and I'll sleep on that.' She reached across and gave Edith's arm a squeeze. 'Nothing will change. It will just be a bit further for you to travel. I can always come and collect you, keep you company on the bus.'

Edith picked up her spoon and pushed her chocolate mousse *à la* Bavarois around the bowl. She had her lips pursed and Ellie noticed how she had managed to overrun the edges of them quite dramatically with her lipstick. Edith put down her spoon again.

'This flat business, Ellie. There is an alternative you might like to consider. My house is very large, too large for one ... I wondered ... why not come and live with me?'

Ellie's mouth formed itself into a little 'no' shape. There wasn't any way she could live with Edith. The thought was a kind one, but completely mad. Every time she visited Edith's house she came away depressed. With its swirly carpets and epileptic-fit-inducing wallpapers, it was a homage to all that was wrong with 1970s décor. The kitchen was a nightmare of old and unreliable appliances, and the garden was completely overgrown.

Surely if she moved in with Edith, it would only be a matter of time before she starting wearing support stockings and buying a 'nice piece of fish' for her tea.

That 'no' wasn't coming out, though. She made another

effort to say it. Then she made the mistake of looking directly at Edith and saw the hope burning in her eyes. Ellie pictured Edith among all those empty, echoing rooms in her house and felt intensely sad. She thought about all those times Edith had pitched up at her flat, unannounced and looking for company. How was she going to manage that when she wasn't living right round the corner?

Ellie heard herself saying, 'You've been thinking about this a lot, Edith. How would it work?'

'Well, you would have the top floor as your own. You've got a bathroom up there and two other good-sized rooms. You can have a sitting room or a study as well as your bedroom, arrange it as you like.'

'I could get it redecorated, get some new carpet?'

'Of course, and I've done a bit of research into having a shower installed.' Edith reached down for her handbag and extracted a sheaf of leaflets from bathroom suppliers. 'It would take a few weeks, of course, but you could use my bathroom while it was being done.' She held out the leaflets.

'Mrs Radjewzki at the day centre, her nephew Stanislaus is a plumber and he's already given me a quote. Very reasonable, and he could fit us in almost at once.' Edith's eyes twinkled. 'He's very fond of his aunt, and luckily his aunt is very fond of me.'

Ellie put the leaflets on the table and couldn't hide her amusement. First Lesley and now Edith: this was the second time today that she had been mentally mugged by small, doughty people.

She looked at Edith again, at all that hope, and before she could change her mind, said, 'Edith, that's a brilliant idea.'

Edith stared resolutely at her pudding, and after a while Ellie handed her a napkin and Edith gave her eyes a good wipe and blew her nose.

The meal turned into a bit of a celebration after that; it was like a light had gone back on inside Edith.

Later, with Edith snoring happily away in the spare room, Ellie went back over her decision and convinced herself it was a good one. She was getting to stay in an area she liked and her rent would be more or less what she was paying for the flat before Sam went. Being able to keep an eye on Edith would take a whole lot of worry off her mind too. She could subtly make sure she was eating properly and actually getting some rest.

Edith hadn't seemed to mind the few stipulations that Ellie had set. On Monday morning Ellie was going to ring some cleaners to come and blitz the whole house, and Ellie had already been on the internet and ordered a new cooker and fridge. All Edith had to do was find somebody to run a flamethrower over the garden.

Ellie had no idea why she was feeling so elated. Perhaps it was all about making a fresh start in a place where she had never lived with Sam.

She looked around the sitting room, at the empty spaces that marked where Sam's possessions had been. It already felt half lived in; the entire flat did. There were too many reminders of the fact that a couple used to live here.

She stood up and started turning off the lamps.

She'd always thought that when she moved from this flat, it would be into a house with Sam, the next stage in their life together. That thought should have upset her, but she found herself having very few feelings about it at all.

She pulled the sitting room door closed behind her and walked towards her bedroom.

Time to move on.

Her brothers would tell her she was mad. Lesley would tell her she was mad. Everyone would tell her she was mad. But sometimes being mad was the most sensible thing you could be.

Two weeks later and Ellie was putting her books on her new shelves in her new home, the swirly carpet and hideous wallpaper a distant memory. Everything past the turn of the stairs was pale and calm, except for the bathroom, which was currently ripped out but would be back gleaming and white by the end of next week. Stanislaus had promised, and what Stanislaus promised, he delivered. Usually ahead of schedule.

Ellie wandered through her rooms and that feeling of

elation sprang up inside her again. It was all hers. Nobody to negotiate with over what went on the walls or what colour the bedding should be. Queen of all she surveyed.

Down in the garden, two lads were sitting reading newspapers and smoking, their backsides on a couple of boxes, their legs stretched out in front of them. A few square yards of lawn could now be seen among the brambles, but it looked like it was going to take a while. Shame Stanislaus didn't do gardening; he'd have had it cleared and an ornamental pond in by now. With hot and cold running water.

Ellie heard the front door open and Edith's voice waft up the stairs. She went out on to the landing and peered down. 'Hello, Edith. I'm sorting out my books.'

Edith shouted something back that might or might not have involved putting the kettle on and Ellie went back to cosying D. H. Lawrence up with Jane Austen and had a good laugh over what that particular pairing would have been like. The next book she pulled out of the storage box was *Wuthering Heights*, and she held it away from her as though it was somehow dangerous. She wasn't going to open it and look inside. She didn't need to. There was already a large, unpredictable Yorkshireman rampaging around her head.

She put the book between Gertrude Stein and Virginia Woolf and gave a nod of satisfaction; that would keep the bugger in check.

Edith called up the stairs about biscuits and Ellie called back. It felt good to be living with another heartbeat again, and so far Edith had proved to be a surprisingly easy housemate, certainly easier than Sam. She had a better social life than Ellie's, so she wasn't in a lot, and she didn't seem to expect Ellie to do anything at all for her. When Ellie did, though, she was delighted, but there was no 'poor little old lady' act. They had fallen into an easy routine and Ellie knew that she was getting as much out of the arrangement as Edith. Sam leaving had brought home to her how much she needed Edith to make her feel part of something that had slipped away with the death of her parents. Ellie had her brothers, of course, but they had families of their own now, other pressures on their time. Edith was her link with her past. She was happy to sit and listen to Edith's stories about growing up in Canterbury and then India and delighted to discover things about her father's childhood that she had never got around to finding out from him herself.

If Sam leaving had made her feel as if she was drifting, all familiar points of reference gone, Edith was anchoring her again.

Ellie straightened a few more books.

Yes, it had been a brainwave on Edith's part, this living together.

Ellie had even got used to everybody and anybody calling them 'the odd couple'.

She walked back out on to the landing to retrieve her clothes from the black plastic bags they had been stored in while her wardrobes were being built. Edith had got the guys doing the garden to bring them up from the 'glory hole' next to the kitchen, where everything in Edith's house got dumped until she could find a place for it.

As she untied one of the bags, Ellie froze. She stared at the jumble of old crockery and saucepans inside. Moving quickly to the next bag, she ripped it open with her nails and pulled out an old lampshade and a moth-eaten sari. Tearing the other three bags revealed more of the unwanted stuff she and Edith had sorted out last weekend to go to the charity shop.

Ellie grabbed a statue of the Taj Mahal and hurtled out of the room and down the stairs into the kitchen, where Edith was arranging bourbon biscuits on a plate.

'Edith,' she said breathlessly, 'when do the guys from the charity shop come for the jumble stuff?'

'Oh, they've already come, dear. Came this morning while you were at work.'

Ellie sat down. 'They took the stuff from the glory hole?'

'Yes, dear, except for your clothes, of course, silly thing.' She gave a little grin. 'I got those moved beforehand. Didn't want any silly mistakes happening.'

Ellie put her hand over her eyes. 'And my clothes in the tumble-dryer? Tell me they're still in there . . .'

'No, dear, I took them out and put them into one of

your clothes bags so everything would be together for you.' As Edith finished talking, her eyes strayed to the Taj Mahal in Ellie's hand. A look of consternation spread over her face and she sat down quickly in the chair next to Ellie. 'Oh dear,' she said in a tiny voice.

In her head Ellie counted up the items of clothing she still had. There was the stuff she had on – jeans, a sweat-shirt and her most broken baseball boots, which she wore for decorating. There was the silk kimono dressing gown. Her denim jacket was hanging over a chair in her bedroom. And then . . . nothing.

She groaned. Then somehow the groan turned into a giggle and once it had started, she couldn't stop. Edith watched her horrified, as if she were worried that Ellie was becoming hysterical and should be slapped. Ellie kept right on laughing. The giggling turned into full-blown laughter and soon she had her head down on the table. Her poor clothes, unloved by Jack and Sam and goodness knows who else, had been hauled off in a van and were now being picked over in a charity warehouse. That had to be worth a laugh, didn't it?

After a while Ellie felt Edith's hand on her arm and raised her head.

'Ellie dear, I cannot apologise enough. You must let me help you buy some more clothes.' Ellie waved away the suggestion, but Edith was adamant. 'And perhaps you should go to Selfridges, use one of their personal shoppers. That way you could get some help, buy something different than you normally choose.'

Ellie started to howl with laughter again. Good grief. How bad had her dress sense become that a woman currently wearing a canary-yellow cardigan with a purple sparkly skirt was offering her fashion advice?

Jack was driving back from a meeting thinking about how Gavin would take being fired. Could go either way. Devious git was already rubbishing the agency at every opportunity. If it had been down to him, he would have got rid of him before the board meeting. Perhaps via a second-floor window.

Jack stopped for the lights. The weather was warming up and he wound down the window, enjoying the feel of the sun on his arm. He watched the people rushing by and caught a glimpse of a woman walking by the park. Lovely legs. She was wearing a skirt that did a nice little flip along the hemline every time she took a step. Pretty top from what he could see of it and quite spectacular hair. Bit like Ellie's. The clothes all had a kind of French look. Perhaps she was French. The traffic edged forward. Jack continued to watch the woman as she swayed her hips, her skirt doing its little flip and her hair bouncing gently.

As the car drew level with her, Jack turned to see whether the view from the front was as appealing as the one from behind.

Damn. He had to slam the brakes on to avoid crashing. It was Ellie. Ellie not wearing jeans and a shirt. What was all that about? The last time he'd seen her look so hot was when she went off for that supposedly dirty weekend in Barcelona.

Jack watched her as far as the park entrance and then she disappeared from view. Why did she have to go through the park? Why couldn't she have stayed walking down the road?

Jack turned his attention back to the traffic, but in his head he was still seeing those hips swaying hypnotically. Perhaps hinting that she should smarten up hadn't been such a good idea after all. He could feel himself growing excited imagining getting hold of those hips and running his hands round ... Jack swore softly as a cyclist veered in front of him. He needed to stop thinking about this, stop thinking of Ellie like that. Stop thinking of Ellie at all.

Even in her bag-lady phase it had been pretty difficult to stop himself from imagining her naked. How the hell had she done that to him? How had he careered from being irritated by her to this?

Time to nip it in the bud. This was getting too tricky, making him do unprofessional things. Like with that slime-ball Jubbitt Junior. If Mrs MacEndry hadn't talked him out of it, he'd have sent that letter telling him where to stick his account. As it was, he could barely hold himself back from pinning the guy to the wall and shouting at him every time he thought of the little pervert touching Ellie's thighs.

Jack shifted in his seat and cast a wry glance at his groin. Exactly what he needed when he walked through reception. Rachel never missed a trick. He'd have to be extra clever in the way he arranged his briefcase and jacket.

This was definitely not good. He might have turned into someone he didn't quite recognise outside of work, but he wasn't ready to start seducing his employees yet. Especially not when this particular employee had a hot brain to go with that body. The kind of brain that could get you to tell it things. Get you to open up and before you knew it, you were hooked.

Jack flicked on the indicator.

Getting hooked, caring about someone. That only led to one place.

He concentrated on negotiating the tricky entrance to the car park and nosed his car into the space reserved for him. Time to think about something else, something calming. Like sacking Gavin. Not about grabbing Ellie by the hips, sinking himself into her and making her hair bounce on her naked shoulders.

CHAPTER 16

Gavin put his face close to Jack's. 'You know what you are? You're a complete Philistine.'

Jack surveyed him coolly. 'Actually, I'm from Yorkshire. Similar, but we have a much better cricket team.'

'Yeah, cricket and rugby,' sneered Gavin, 'and whippets and pigeon racing. That's what passes for culture oop North, eh, Jack?'

Jack briefly considered decking Gavin. The idiot had seemed to take his sacking on the chin in front of the other directors – he'd had long enough to see it coming – but then he'd ambushed Jack as he was going out for lunch. He was spoiling for a fight. Well, as much as a designer-clad fashion-plate who didn't like physical contact could spoil for a fight.

Now there was quite a little audience, which was presumably what Gavin wanted: a nice dramatic exit. His creative David against Jack's soulless Northern Goliath.

'Look, Gavin,' Jack began, 'I don't know what point you're

trying to make here. You got a good deal. The board has been more than—'

'Blah, blah, blah,' shouted Gavin. 'Listen to you with your facts and figures. You're turning this agency into a sausage factory. Put good ideas in one end and they all come out the other end looking the same.'

Jack scowled, which was usually enough to send people scurrying, but Gavin seemed determined to have his time in the spotlight.

'I'm going where people really appreciate creativity,' he said loudly. 'I'll be there at the award ceremonies next year, up on the stage, and do you know what, Jack, I'm going to piss on you.'

'I'll look forward to that,' Jack said.

Gavin was getting bolder and Jack sensed that he wanted to be hit. The stuck-up git had even taken off his Prada glasses and put them in his top pocket.

Gavin took a step towards Jack and gave him a hefty push. Jack, caught off guard, stumbled back and then stopped.

Grabbing hold of Gavin by the throat and shaking him until the buttons fell off his Paul Smith shirt was very tempting, but then Gavin would do him and the agency for assault. Better to weather the tantrum.

Gavin gave Jack another shove.

Jack stood his ground.

Gavin pushed Jack again and then clicked his fingers

under his nose. 'Not so macho now, then, Jack the lad, eh?' Gavin spat out. 'Do you know I'm really enjoying this, Jackie boy. I've got the upper hand. And do you know what I'm going to do with it?'

Before Jack had time to answer, Gavin had waved one of his hands around dramatically and then used it to give Jack another hearty push. Jack didn't even flinch this time, but he was finding the temptation to lay Gavin out on the floor harder and harder to resist.

Ellie, watching from near the lifts, felt uneasy. Why couldn't Gavin see that this was the calm before the storm? Jack had lowered his head slightly, but more ominously he was standing as though he had moved all his weight forward. It reminded Ellie of the way her mum's cat used to look when it had caught a mouse and was deciding whether to eat it or chase it some more.

Gavin carried on, seemingly unaware of the danger. 'You know, Jack, I'm going to be delighted when you get kicked out of this agency. I will laugh myself sick when the scales fall from people's eyes and they see you for the uneducated, domineering jerk you are.'

Suddenly Jack's head snapped up and he said, 'Finished,' and Gavin said, 'No,' and Jack said, 'It wasn't a question, it was a statement of fact. You. Soft. Idiot.'

Gavin tutted contemptuously.

'Right, Gavin,' Jack said, folding his arms, 'you're going

to pick up your box of toys and walk out that door right now without saying another word. You've had your little hissy fit, now sod off.'

Gavin played up to the audience and folded his arms too. 'No,' he said defiantly. He gave a little centre-stage smile. 'What are you going to do about that, then, Jacko mate?'

Jack flashed Gavin a look that was all teeth and no smile. 'First I'm going to strip us both naked. Then I'm going to fight it out with you here, man to man, like in the film *Women in Love* . . . You must have seen that, Gavin . . . cultured man like you.'

There were a couple of nervous giggles around the room, but then people realised Jack wasn't laughing. His eyes were dark and glittering dangerously.

Ellie saw Gavin shift uneasily. Doubtless the script he was acting out had ended with Jack hitting him. Nowhere was there anything about nude wrestling. He gave a nervous-sounding laugh.

Jack put his head on one side. 'Don't believe me?'

Gavin stuck his chest out and tried to look unconcerned.

'OK,' Jack said, and slowly took off his jacket. He walked over and laid it on the reception desk. Then he returned to Gavin and started to roll up one of his shirt sleeves, folding the striped, crisp material over and over up to his elbow.

The fact that he was doing it all so slowly seemed to unnerve Gavin and he moved back a few steps.

Jack started on the other shirt sleeve, his long fingers working deftly as he rolled the material back to reveal his forearm. The muscles in his other arm moved rhythmically as he worked.

Then slowly Jack reached up and pulled the knot loose on his tie.

Nobody was laughing now; the only movement was from Gavin as he unconsciously flexed one of his hands.

Once the tie was off, Jack walked back over to the reception desk and coiled it on top of his jacket. Rachel followed his every movement, wide-eyed.

Ellie could see tension now in the faces of the people watching. Even the women who had initially thought that all their birthdays were about to come at once were not so sure they wanted to witness this; the whole spectacle was too toe-curlingly embarrassing because Jack was so very, very calm. If he'd been exhibiting anger, it would have been understandable. This was like a small boy pulling the wings off a fly.

As Ellie was thinking this, the word that she had been groping for to describe Jack plopped into her mind fully formed. It was 'detached' and it wasn't at all the one she was expecting, but she knew it was perfect.

It was what made him able to sit there naked in bed with Edith as if he were simply seeing where it would lead. Perhaps that was what enabled him to cut a swathe through all those women without seeming to feel a thing.

And it was what was powering him now, long after anybody else would have said, 'OK, joke over. Let's sort this out in private.'

Jack had started something without really caring how it would finish. If Gavin gave in or ended up naked, she guessed it was all the same to Jack. He didn't give a stuff.

It was almost as if there were a plate of glass between him and normal emotions.

That thought made Ellie feel extremely sorry for Gavin. The idiot had no understanding of what he was dealing with.

The level of tension hiked up again as Jack pulled his shirt free from his trousers.

Gavin audibly gulped. Up until then he had, perhaps, been unable to comprehend that Jack would do exactly what he said he was going to do, but there was something so menacing about the way in which Jack executed the movement with his shirt that caused Gavin to twig that he was in deep trouble.

Jack started to unbutton his shirt, very, very slowly, never letting his eyes move from Gavin's. He reached his last button and now it was possible to glimpse his chest.

The girl standing next to Ellie made a kind of 'Gorr' noise.

Gavin took another step back, his once-smug expression replaced by dawning horror.

For all she disliked Gavin, Ellie wanted this to stop now.

It was probably already too late, though, because Jack gave a dry laugh and said, 'Hang on, Gavin, what am I thinking? I'm getting too far ahead. You need to catch up.'

Terror flooded Gavin's face at about the same time as Jack's hand shot out and grabbed his wrist.

Gavin let out a bloodcurdling scream and flapped around trying to get free, but Jack had him fast. Panic and shock flashed across Gavin's face.

'I'll go, I'll go,' he shouted, gulping in great mouthfuls of air.

Jack pulled Gavin close. 'Good decision,' he hissed. Then he let go of Gavin's wrist. 'Shame, though. I was looking forward to throwing you on to your back.'

That sent Gavin completely over the edge. With a little whimper he darted round Jack and stooped to pick up the box containing the contents of his office, the ones he hadn't already squirrelled away at home. Jack's hand shot out again, this time grabbing hold of the box.

'Those design directories . . . yours or the agency's?' he said.

Gavin scooped the large books out of the box and threw them on the floor. Stumbling over his feet, he headed for the door, but couldn't get it open with his arms full. Jack strode across and pushed it open for him.

'You're a sick bastard,' Gavin shouted back over his shoulder once he was safely down the steps. 'You've got too much testosterone and you're a sick bastard.'

Jack didn't reply and calmly buttoned his shirt back up, rolled down his sleeves and went and collected his tie and jacket from the reception desk. Within moments he had gone for his lunch.

'Oh my God,' Rachel said, standing up unsteadily, 'I think one of my ovaries has just exploded.'

Upstairs in the ladies' toilets, Ellie was in a cubicle leaning against the wall. She couldn't breathe properly, she could feel her heart pounding in her ears, and she felt jittery. But more than that she was on fire between her legs and right up to where? Her stomach? Her womb? She didn't know. All she knew was that as Jack had buttoned up his shirt, he had given her a dark and brooding sidelong glance that had knocked the wind right out of her and made her feel desired and dirty at the same time. He had been high on his victory and the look had only lasted a second or two, but it had been enough.

Ellie realised she was gnawing at the skin down the side of her thumbnail and took her hand away from her mouth. Then she sat on the edge of the toilet seat and closed her eyes. She tried to get her breathing back under control and think straight. She could handle this. He probably wasn't even looking at her.

She needed to avoid him completely from now on.

After a while she felt calmer and even able to replay the scene in her head as she set off back to her office.

Who was she kidding? Moments later she was back in the toilet cubicle with her cheek pressed against the cool wall of the partition.

By the time Ellie got back to her room, word had gone round that Gavin's wouldn't be the only departure.

In offices throughout the building people waited for the phone call from Mrs MacEndry that would summon them into Jack's office and then out on to the job market again.

Lesley passed the time by arranging and rearranging her pencils; Ellie sat there and debated whether getting sacked would be such a bad thing. At least she wouldn't have to see Jack every day.

A knock on the door made them both jump and Juliette and Mike were in the room, faces lit up and so excited they could barely talk.

'Jon and Zak—'

'Just came out of Jack's room—'

'And a security guard—'

'Big chap, built like a brick wall—'

'Escorted them out of the building—'

It felt wrong to jump up and down and punch the air, so they fought the urge for a couple of seconds and then did it anyway.

As the afternoon wore on, the atmosphere became more

hysterical. Nobody knew how long the culling was going to last.

Ellie tried to apply herself to the ad she was writing for a new theme park ride. Lesley and she had been on it the previous week for research purposes. Afterwards they had both thrown up. Ellie wasn't going to mention its vomit-inducing properties in the ad; best to concentrate on its other unique selling points.

But her mind couldn't leave the sackings. 'The G-Force Phantom is designed to take you on the ultimate thrill experience,' she wrote, 'through P45 degrees of mind-blowing . . .'

She balled up that bit of paper and tried again on a fresh sheet. This time her mind went back to that glittering, dark look Jack had cast her way as he had buttoned up his shirt. She took a deep breath, pushed the thought away and wrote, 'Take your senses to the edge as you hurtle through forty-five degrees of mind-blowing, G-spot-punching excitement.'

That piece of paper ended up in the bin as well, and then Juliette and Mike were back in the room.

'That's nine gone now, not counting Gavin.'

Ellie didn't like to say, 'I told you so,' but Jack was doing his usual fat-trimming exercise.

'What happens to all of Zak and Jon's accounts?' Mike asked. 'Will we be expected to do all their work and all Gavin's work as well?'

'Yes,' Jack said from the doorway, 'you'll be working all the hours there are. In fact, I wouldn't bother going home most nights if I were you.'

None of them was quite sure if he was joking. Even when he laughed, they still weren't certain.

He ducked his head and came into the room and sat on the edge of Ellie's desk with his back to her. She was looking at an expanse of charcoal pinstripe and she knew that if she reached out, she would feel the heat of Jack's skin under the material.

She sat back in her chair. She was in trouble if even looking at his back made her feel light-headed. This had been creeping up on her ever since that night in her flat, ever since the Jubbitt Junior thing, and now what had happened down in reception had made it pounce on her.

'Sorry I left you till last,' Jack said. 'It's been a busy day.' Ellie could picture his wry smile even though she couldn't see it. 'But now everything else has been sorted, I can tell you that you're going to see some massive changes in the Creative Department over the coming weeks. The first one is the appointment of a new creative director. He starts on Monday.' Jack gave a little laugh. 'You might have heard of him. Ian Armstrong.'

There was a stunned silence in the room and then somebody said, '*The* Ian Armstrong?'

'Yup. I've poached him from McWhirters, who are

mightily hacked off about it, but Ian and I worked together years ago. He's looking for a new challenge.'

Still nobody said anything. The thought of actually working with Ian Armstrong was too big a concept to take in. Would someone that good really join their agency? Since he'd come down from Manchester, he'd had a meteoric rise. Ellie had been to award ceremonies where Ian seemed to wear a path in the carpet because he was called up to collect so many awards. More intriguing than that, though, was his attitude. He didn't do the tantrums or the keeping all the glory to himself. He had a reputation for bringing his staff on along with him and fostering new talent. Sure, he was a hard-nut Geordie who called a spade a 'fucking shovel', but if he liked you, the sky was the limit.

Lesley was the first to speak. 'Ian Armstrong is coming here?'

'Ian Armstrong is coming here,' Jack said again, very slowly as if he understood that they were finding it hard to believe.

Suddenly everyone was talking at once, except for Ellie, who had stopped looking at Jack's back and was now concentrating on the hand he was resting on her desk. Long fingers, a smattering of hair, neat nails. Her own hand had gone to her mouth and she was punishing that little strip of skin again. She put her hands in her lap.

Jack swivelled round to face her. 'You're very quiet. Not

like you to miss an opportunity to make a couple of wise-cracks. Anything wrong?'

Ellie's heart gave a huge thud and she found her eyes drawn to the way Jack's choppy black hair sat on his collar. She wondered if it would feel soft or wiry if she ran her fingers through it.

'No, everything's fine. It's just a big surprise,' she said, focusing on a point somewhere above Jack's head. 'I'm a bit shell-shocked.'

It wasn't a lie. She was. Completely.

CHAPTER 17

'It takes hundreds of individual movements to create one minute of film,' Craig the model-maker said, while demonstrating what he meant by moving Ellie's hand almost imperceptibly, finger by finger.

Ellie marvelled that a man could have such soft hands.

She worried vaguely whether anyone needed her, but a quick look round confirmed that Lesley was deep in conversation with Ian Armstrong and the director of animation filming. On the first day of the shoot everything was a flurry. The studio was full of people either huddled together in intense discussions or rushing about with lights and cables. Everyone's ultimate focus was on a little section of the studio where a small garden had been created, complete with a plasticine clay model of the career girl's knickers pegged on a line. Ellie had spent a long time looking at it; everything was so beautifully executed. The garden even had a patch of worn-out grass and a tiny dandelion.

Ellie turned back to Craig. He had moved a little nearer, his blue eyes concentrating on her hand, and Ellie found herself enjoying the attention. There was something hypnotic about the way Craig was moving her fingers and she wondered if he made love that slowly. Was animation sex like tantric sex: hours and hours of delicate little movements?

She felt quite hot.

'Perhaps I ought to go and pay some attention to what's going on, Craig?'

'Oh, don't bother, Ellie. Everyone starts off thinking this stop-motion animation is going to be fascinating, but after eight hours watching someone make the tiniest changes to the position of a knicker leg, you'll be begging to escape.'

Craig had put quite a bit of stress on that word 'begging', Ellie noticed, and also seemed to be getting even closer. At one point she saw him look down the front of her dress. She waited for the usual wave of embarrassment to roll over her, but instead felt eerily calm as Craig continued to rub and manipulate her hand. It really was hard to drag her eyes away from his long, tapering fingers.

Jack held open the door of the studio for Pauline Kennedy and her team. They'd been keen to see at least part of the ad being filmed and Jack was always happy to involve the clients as much as possible. Pauline was good company, a bright cookie; he knew she wouldn't get in the way or change the brief halfway through. He spent some time introducing people to each other and was congratulating the director on his last piece of work when he spotted Ellie on the far side of the studio.

Jack stopped in mid-word and felt something twist in his guts. Some bloke was stroking Ellie's hand and she didn't look particularly unhappy about it. Jack looked away and tried to concentrate on his conversation, but very soon his gaze had travelled back to the other side of the studio.

Now the little sod was looking down the front of her dress.

'Who's the guy with Ellie?' Jack asked, pretending to find something riveting on the sleeve of his jacket.

The director turned to look. 'Oh, that's Craig, one of our best model-makers.'

Jack nodded and wondered how good a model-maker Craig would be with two broken hands. He stood there a little longer and then made an excuse about needing to check something and started to walk across the studio.

What was going on with this bloody woman? He'd heard Rachel chuntering on about that musician guy trying to get hold of Ellie's number, then there was Jubbitt Junior pawing her, and now this Craig was sniffing around.

He slowed down. Why was it any of his business if men found her attractive? Where was all this anger coming from? He should turn round, go back and talk to Pauline and Ian, and leave Ellie to get on with it. Jack took another look at the way Craig was manipulating Ellie's fingers and speeded up again.

As he walked, he spied the model for the sex kitten's knickers laid out on a bench not far from where Craig and Ellie were standing. He drew level and bent down, hands on his thighs, and looked as though he was inspecting the knickers closely. He let a disturbed look settle on his face.

'Something wrong?' Craig asked, dropping Ellie's hand quickly.

Jack sucked in a breath noisily. 'Well, I'm not sure. These look slightly weird to me. Aren't they going to be a bit out of proportion to the stiletto you're planning to lie them on?'

Jack saw Craig's calm demeanour change into one of irritation, the kind of irritation felt by a man who had spent a whole week on the gusset of the knickers alone.

'I don't think so, Mr Wolfe,' he said, coming closer. 'I think they're perfectly fine.' He got down level with the model and peered at it. 'I have been doing this an awfully long time, you know,' he said with a patronising laugh.

'Yes, of course, I realise that. I realise I'm only a layman with something like this.' Jack flooded his speech with smiles and reasonableness. 'I'm sorry. I know you're intending to shoot these later, but I do think there is something wrong here.'

Craig still looked unconvinced, so Jack said, 'What do you think, Ellie?'

'I think they look fine, Jack. Perhaps it was the angle you were seeing them from?'

Jack pretended to be assessing the model again before shaking his head. 'No. Look, Craig, mate, I know it's a sickener and it's going to be a bit of extra work, but can you go and do something about them?'

Jack guessed that Craig probably wanted to tell him where to shove the knickers; he was eyeing him up and down as if trying to pluck up the courage to insist once again that the model was fine.

Then Jack saw all the fight go out of Craig. 'You know, you might be right, Mr Wolfe. I'll ... I'll just go and do some more measurements.' Craig lifted the board on which the model knickers were sitting as carefully as if they had been made of glass. He gave Ellie a regretful look. 'See you later, Ellie, yeah?'

He wandered off and Jack ignored the look Ellie was giving him.

'Seems a nice boy, that Gromit.'

'He's called Craig.'

'Ah, yes. Gromit's that other, furry one.'

'That's not even funny, Jack,' Ellie said, but Jack could see she was struggling not to laugh. He tried not to think about the beautiful effect that had on her cleavage.

He gave a businesslike cough. 'Right, well, sorry to drag you away, but we've got to get back.'

'Back? I've only just arrived.'

'Sorry,' Jack said unconvincingly.

'Why do I have to go? I've been looking forward to this for ages. Why can't I stay?'

Jack considered saying, 'Because I don't want you anywhere near Craig's hands,' but settled for, 'Look, Ellie, you can come back later in the week or even next week. You must see that we don't need Ian, Lesley and you all here now. Not on the first day. And with the clients here too it's swamping the place.'

Ellie crossed her arms and Jack sensed the start of a fight and decided to play the 'trouble back at the agency that only you can sort out' card.

'There's a problem with the copy for that yoghurt ad.'

'There is no copy for the yoghurt ad,' Ellie protested.

'That's the problem. Client's getting a bit anxious, thinks there should be.'

Despite her confused look, Jack saw that Ellie was wavering, and before she could really protest, he had manoeuvred her out of the building, only stopping to give his apologies to Pauline.

The atmosphere inside the car on the journey back was claustrophobic. Jack didn't like what he'd done in the studio, another unprofessional act. Craig certainly wasn't going to be sending him a Christmas card this year. And that idiot idea about the yoghurt ad, how was he going to explain that when they got back?

Ellie was looking out of the window and Jack heard her mutter something about 'mouldy milk in a pot'.

He decided to say nothing, but then got distracted by the way the seat belt cut between Ellie's breasts. He turned his head back quickly to concentrate on the traffic, but seconds later his hand brushed against her leg when he changed gear. That jolt of desire was back, rushing up his arm and into his chest.

He saw Ellie squash herself into the corner of her seat and cross her legs.

This was stupid; he needed to calm down.

'How are you getting on with Ian?' he said, desperate to say anything.

He was rewarded with one of her groin-stabbing smiles and a slight thaw in the atmosphere. 'He's wonderful, Jack. I mean, tough and nobody's fool, but I already feel I've learned more from him in the two weeks he's been here than I ever did from . . . well . . . before. He's so generous with his knowledge. He doesn't make you think you have to apologise for thinking of mad ideas. He even encourages it. I really, really like him.'

'Good,' Jack said, and suddenly, completely, hated Ian.

He wanted to accidentally touch Ellie's leg again. Even though his brain was telling him he must seem like a pervert, his baser instincts were egging him on to have another go. He fought the urge, ransacking his mind for more small talk.

'That's a nice dress,' he blurted out, and then wished he could have bitten right through his tongue. Too personal, too guaranteed to get him thinking how well she filled every little bit of it.

He could see from Ellie's body language that she felt uncomfortable about his comment. She moved even further away from him, the furthest it was possible to go without actually climbing out of the car. She seemed to be chewing her thumb as well.

Jack opened his mouth again and hoped for the best. 'You've obviously been treating yourself lately, lots of different clothes . . . I suppose you'd been waiting for that pay rise last week.'

'No, I bought the clothes before then.' Ellie clasped her hands in her lap. 'I had to. Edith accidentally gave all my clothes to the charity shop.'

Jack gave his brain one more chance to redeem itself. 'Well, at least it all went back where it came from,' he heard himself say, and watched appalled as a hurt and ashamed look passed over Ellie's face. He saw her hunker down even further in her seat.

Jack gave up after that and tried to concentrate on driving and breathing without annoying the hell out of her.

When they got back to the agency car park, he went

round to open the car door for her, but she had already climbed out. They stood facing each other and Ellie did an awkward little side shuffle to get round him. He sensed she was avoiding looking at him, and who could blame her?

By the time Jack had collected his briefcase and jacket, she was quite a way ahead.

Funny how that morning after he'd met her in Cavello's she had walked at a snail's pace. Now she was doing some kind of power walk. Jack covered the distance between them easily, but they walked into the agency without Ellie even acknowledging he was there. She had her head down and he couldn't think of anything to say to her that didn't involve asking her to come up to his office right now and let him peel her dress off.

He tried to appear impassive as he walked up to the reception desk, but his heart was thudding away in his chest. The thought of having to go and sit in his own office, knowing that Ellie was only a couple of floors away, was making him feel incensed, like it wasn't fair. He had to grip tightly on to his briefcase to stop himself from doing something stupid.

He saw Rachel's eyes flicker knowingly over him and then over Ellie. She might not be quite there yet, but it wouldn't take her long to work out something was going on. He might as well have a damn great sign over his head saying, 'I want to kill every man who looks at Ellie Somerset and quite possibly her as well for making me feel like this.'

He checked on Rachel again. Perhaps when she did work out what was going on, she could tell him, because at this moment he didn't know his arse from his elbow.

Rachel was twiddling with her hair and continuing to give him a searching stare. He pulled his face into a frown and turned on Ellie.

'And it would be a nice change if every time I asked you to do something you didn't come across like a truculent school kid,' he said. Ellie looked at him as though he had kicked her. Ignoring the fresh set of inappropriate feelings that stirred up, he turned back to Rachel. 'I told her she couldn't sit and watch the filming today, that there were more important things to do here, and she's sulked all the way back in the car.' He reached out and picked up the stack of messages that were waiting for him on the desk, hoping Rachel didn't notice the way his hand was not quite as steady as he would have liked.

'Shame not everyone can have your sunny personality, eh, Rachel?' he said, before winking at her and walking away.

That should put Rachel off for a while. All he had to do now was stay away from Ellie.

And fit a cold shower in his office.

CHAPTER 18

'So, what's the big secret, then?' Ellie said, settling herself down next to Lesley in the pub. 'Why couldn't you tell me whatever it is in the office?'

'Well, I wanted you on your own.' Lesley reached for her purse. 'Can I get you a drink?'

'I'd rather have the secret first.'

'Nah, got to wait for Megan. What are you having?'

'Red wine, a small one.' Ellie caught Lesley's disbelieving look. 'No, really, I'm trying to cut back. I've been a bit out of control since Sam left.'

'Cheers,' Lesley said when she got back. 'Here's to us and our knickers.'

'Cheers,' echoed Ellie, and then saw Lesley's face light up. Without turning round she knew that Megan must have arrived.

The two of them embraced tenderly and Ellie had to hide her own smile. She knew what Lesley's little secret was going to be, had known days ago when Lesley had taken to staring off into the distance and then doodling Megan's first name next to her own surname. Any minute now she was going to tell her and Ellie was going to have to be a good actress and pretend to be very surprised.

'OK,' Lesley said when they were all settled back down.

'OK,' Megan said, clutching Lesley's hand.

Lesley gave Megan a nervous smile that made her look like she was about to go in and see the dentist. Ellie was tempted to put them both out of their misery.

'We wanted to tell you first, before anybody else,' Lesley began. 'I mean, we've invited some other people from the agency to the pub, but we wanted to talk to you on your own first.'

'About what?' Ellie said sweetly.

'Well, Megan and I . . . me and Megan . . . we're . . .'

'You're what?'

'We're . . .' Lesley was looking desperately at Megan.

'You're getting a puppy? Moving to Neasden?' Ellie didn't know how long she could keep this up without laughing.

Megan shook her head. 'No, Ellie, it's much more—'

'Life-changing,' Lesley chipped in.

'Oh, no, tell me you're not getting matching tattoos.'

Suddenly Lesley's expression changed. 'You know, don't you?'

'Know what?'

'That Megan and I are going to get married,' Lesley said loudly. There was a pause while Lesley realised what had just happened and then Ellie gave a huge shriek and was on her feet and grabbing them both into a hug.

'Of course I know, you big romantic idiot – you've been humming the "Wedding March" for the last three days.' They were all laughing and Megan started to cry and the men on the next table suggested they get a hotel room.

When they had quietened down a bit, Ellie went to the bar and came back with a bottle of champagne.

She gave them another hug each. 'Oooh, I'm so happy for you both, so happy. But, Megan, what a challenge you're taking on. You have no idea what you're letting yourself in for.'

Megan gave the kind of smile that showed she did know and she didn't care. Lesley poured the champagne.

'You should have seen my mum, Ellie. You know what she's like for crying at the best of times. Well, she was practically floating after we told her.'

'Happy tears, though, weren't they?' Megan added quickly.

'And what about your family?' Ellie asked Megan. She saw their good mood fade.

'Oh, not so good.' Megan touched Lesley's arm as if for reassurance. 'In fact . . . awful.'

'They'd only recently got used to the idea of Megan being what they call "one of those",' Lesley explained.

'They'll come round, though, Mam and Dad, before the

wedding. It'll just take time.' Megan's accent made the whole speech sound even more morose.

'I'm sure they will,' Ellie said quickly before the happy atmosphere disappeared altogether. 'Here, drink up and tell me what you've got in mind for the ceremony. Oh, and the honeymoon ... It's got to be Graceland or the Pencil Museum in the Lake District. Time's going to fly, Megan.'

Lesley chucked a beermat at her and soon they were laughing again and the men on the next table joined in and then slowly people from the agency started to arrive. The little announcement was repeated over and over again and there were more hugs and more drinks bought and soon the noise was deafening and it looked like it was going to turn into one of those evenings where anything could happen and nobody knew quite where they would end up.

After her first glass of red wine and a glass of champagne, Ellie stopped drinking. She'd been honest with Lesley about wanting to cut back, but had skimmed over the real reason: Jack. Being even slightly tipsy around him was not a good idea. She needed to have all her wits about her.

More people piled into the pub, slamming the door back against the wall as they came in. Ellie tried not to acknowledge the disappointment she felt when Jack was not among them. She was out of her mind. He'd dragged her away from filming, spoken complete insulting gibberish to her in the car and then torn her off a strip in front of Rachel. Yet here she was hoping he'd walk in and do it all again.

Every time she even thought about him these days it got the blood roaring around her body.

Pathetic, Ellie, part of the Heathcliff Fan Club.

The door opened again and she couldn't help scowling when it was only Mike.

The noise level rose and Rachel swayed in wearing a kind of silver handkerchief thing that she said was a dress. The men on the next table immediately sat up a bit straighter. At one point they tried to persuade her to go on to a club with them, but she had no time for them. She grabbed Ellie by the arm and pulled a rolled-up copy of *Ad Infinitum* magazine out of her bag. The source of all knowledge about what was happening in the world of advertising, it ran a catty little gossip column that dished the dirt, only just staying vague enough to escape any libel action.

Rachel was always the first to get her hands on it, receiving an advance copy every week from one of its journalists who still had fond memories of a short but glorious fling he'd had with her a couple of years earlier.

'Listen, listen,' Rachel said, looking around to check she had their attention. She unfurled the magazine, found the page she was looking for and started to read: '"He's one of ad land's biggest, scariest lads, but are his days as a lone wolf numbered? Not content with living up to his reputation for being a hatchet man and nearly scaring the pants off one of London's most stylish creative directors, it now seems as though he might be settling down. His girlfriend, herself a well-known advertising figure, has been dropping heavy hints to friends that she can hear wedding bells. We fully expect the female population of ad land to be wearing even more black than usual when the happy date is announced."'

Ellie felt as though somebody had kicked her in the heart.

Rachel was in full flow. 'It's obviously Jack, isn't it? Lone wolf, hatchet man and that bit about scaring the pants off Gavin.'

'My hero,' Mike said, looking gutted, 'about to get married.'

'More women for you, then, Mike,' Juliette said with a barely concealed snigger. 'Perhaps he'll pass you his little black book.'

Rachel looked immensely sad. 'That sucks, doesn't it, Ellie?' she said.

Ellie settled for a non-committal shrug, knowing that she wouldn't be able to keep her true feelings from seeping into her voice if she spoke.

The door opened again and her heart executed a little pattering drum roll. It was Alec from Finance.

Mike was slowly tearing up a beermat. 'Perhaps he's actually doing it tonight. Proposing.'

'No, Ian and he are at some graduate fine art thing . . . some prize-giving,' Rachel said, putting the magazine back in her bag. 'I need another drink. Jack getting married, what a bummer.'

Ellie went to sit in the toilets. There was too much noise in the pub and she needed to think. As Rachel had read out her little scoop, Ellie had not been able to stop thinking about that glittering danger she'd seen in Jack's eyes and how it was soon going to be lavished on somebody else. Permanently. She'd never see it again. Never get the chance to find out if his hair was soft.

The thought of him kissing Sophie and asking her to share his life with him made the tears come and she angrily blotted them with some toilet paper. This was ridiculous. Why was she so upset? Jack hadn't paid her any more attention than any other woman who worked for him. He'd been worse to her, in fact. It was a stupid, stupid crush and she was way too old for those.

She sat there torturing herself by returning again to that hot, dark look Jack had given her and soon her poor thumb was getting chewed again. She forced herself to go back out into the pub and concentrate on Lesley and Megan's happiness. When the door of the pub opened again, she steeled herself not to look.

'Boo!' a voice behind her said, and she turned round to

see Dave. He seemed shorter than she remembered and his eyes didn't look quite so brown or his face so attractive. But he was here and right now Jack wasn't, and even if he was, what on earth would that have to do with real life?

'You here by chance?' she asked him.

Ellie saw a look pass between him and Lesley. 'You want a drink?' he said, heading for the bar.

'Large red wine,' she shouted over the noise. She couldn't take the news of Jack's impending marriage completely sober. She watched Dave struggle through the crowd and went to talk to Lesley.

'You told him to come, didn't you?'

'Well, you took his number and you never rang him.'

'So now you're all hooked up with Megan, you're thinking of a double wedding?'

'Only looking after you. And you've got to admit it's funny, Ellie. All the time I was playing the field, you were settled down, and now, well . . . I'm giving you a helping hand.'

'He seems cute,' Juliette said.

'Nice bum,' added Rachel.

Ellie turned back to look at Dave and had to admit that everything they said was true. She should give him a chance. Why not? When he came back, she took her drink from him and he started to tell her what he'd been up to and how well his music was going and how close he was to getting a chance to pitch for some work for one of the major television companies. Ellie listened and nodded and every now and again tried to tell him about what had been happening to her, but they always came back to talking about him. Ellie gave up trying to get a word in edgeways and decided to relax into her wine.

Then all at once her feeling of wellbeing dissolved and she felt like there was only her in the pub and the man who had at that moment come in through the door. She knew he was there even before she heard Lesley shout out, 'Hey, Jack, come here! I've got some news,' and she waited for the first sight of him. Charcoal suit, black choppy hair, long legs, broad shoulders. He was only inches away from her. Even in here she could smell him. She saw him look down at Lesley and Megan and then bend to kiss them. She tore her gaze away, only to bring it right back to watch him go to the bar. He moved through the crowd easily, gracefully, and she couldn't take her eyes off him.

'Penny for them,' Dave said, grabbing back her attention. Ellie tried to concentrate very, very hard on what he was saying, but when he was in full throttle again her eyes sought out Jack and at that moment he turned round at the bar and stared right back at her. It felt as if he was removing every item of her clothing.

She saw his eyes flicker over her and then over Dave and she had the urge to push Dave away from her and pretend she wasn't with him. Then someone got in her sightline and Jack disappeared from view. The next time she saw him he was handing a bottle of champagne to Lesley with another kiss.

Dave was telling her about his newest guitar and Ellie shifted slowly so that she was facing away from Jack. Get him out of sight and out of mind. But it didn't matter which way she was facing. She knew exactly where he was. He moved to chat to a group off to her left and she still managed to look straight into his eyes. He wandered over to talk to Mike and Rachel and the same thing happened again.

The effect of the wine had worn off and she felt trapped and distracted. It was as though she were listening to Dave in some kind of fog. Her body might be standing in front of him, but all her senses were tuned into Jack. How come nobody else in the pub could hear the crackle of tension between them?

Because you're bloody well imagining it, Ellie. It's all in your head, not in Jack's. Get. A. Grip.

Ellie concentrated on Dave's mouth in an effort to make out what he was saying and she saw him smile and lean in to her.

'I feel the same, Ellie. Do you want to get out of here?'

His eyes were shining expectantly and she realised what he meant. It was decision time. She could go with him and see where it led, or stay here, her stomach tilting and pitching, being tortured by a stupid crush.

'OK,' she said, and put her glass down on the nearest table. 'I need to go and say goodbye to Lesley and Megan.' She didn't – she could have left and Lesley would have understood – but she desperately wanted Jack to see her leave.

Lesley told her how very much she loved her and how much she loved Dave and of course Megan too and that Ellie was her best, best friend ever. Then she fell sideways off her seat.

Ellie kept her head down as Dave led the way to the door. She was positively not going to look at Jack. She would have managed it too if Lesley's voice had not boomed out across the pub, 'Let yourself go, Ellie. Lie back and have a good time.' Amid the laughter Ellie's head whipped round to look at Lesley, but she got Jack instead. It sent her stumbling out of the door.

As soon as she was out in the fresh air, she began to feel better. Then as Dave launched himself at her, she felt rapidly worse again. She tried to relax into his arms. She could do this. It was time. He kissed her enthusiastically and she responded, trying to concentrate on the feelings he was stirring up in her.

Except he wasn't stirring up anything. She felt his tongue poke at her lips and she opened her mouth. Still nothing. He might as well have been checking her teeth. After a while she broke away, expecting him to ask her what was wrong.

'Wow, Ellie, I've been wanting to do that for ages,' he said, his eyes bright, and before she could object, he had clamped himself back on to her mouth.

After what seemed like hours, he removed his mouth from hers. He had a glazed expression that made her feel intensely guilty that she wasn't able to summon up any matching emotion.

'I know you're going to think I'm pushing you a bit fast,' he said, sounding short of breath, 'but I fancy you like mad, Ellie. You want to go somewhere more private?'

What she wanted to do was go home to curl up on her bed and try to make sense of what was happening to her. But that would lead her straight back to thinking about Jack.

'Why not?' she said, and then thought of Edith at home. 'But it will have to be your place.'

'No problem. It's a bit of a walk to my bus stop, I'm afraid, and a bit of a walk the other end, but there's a bus soon.'

'Couldn't we get a taxi?'

'No. Waste of money,' he said, and started to walk.

Every now and again he would stop to kiss her and she would do her best to be interested. When he wasn't kissing her, he was telling her more about his music and how he knew he was on the brink of some kind of breakthrough. Ellie let him talk, glad for an excuse to stay quiet. She didn't have the right shoes on for a long walk and his comment about taxis being a waste of money was niggling away in her brain. People who were tight with their money were way up there on her personal hate list. She knew she ought to cut him some slack; he was a struggling musician after all. But then there was all this stuff about him, him, him. Not once had he asked her anything about her work.

Did all that matter? Shouldn't she be like Rachel and switch off her brain and just enjoy it? Plenty of people did. At least he wasn't intimidating. He wasn't likely to laugh when she took her clothes off.

But if his horizontal performance was anything like his vertical one, he probably wouldn't stop talking all the way through, and he wouldn't care if she was having a good time.

She wasn't so sure now that she could do this.

He had her in another clinch when his phone started to ring. She saw his eyes widen as he listened to the caller and every now and again he made an enthusiastic little 'Uh-huh' noise. At one point he looked at his watch and said, 'No problem. I can be there by eleven. OK. OK. Bye.'

He switched off the phone and gave a huge whoop of laugher and punched the air.

'That was Greg Southern. Greg frigging Southern. The guy I've been trying to get through to for weeks . . . head of Lionmark Music. He wants to see me, like, now.' He reached in his jacket for his wallet. 'I'm really sorry, Ellie, got to go.'

'Now? But it's after ten.'

'Yeah, brilliant, isn't it?' He scanned the road and then rushed to the edge of the kerb and stuck his arm out. A taxi had just come round the corner. 'This could be the big break, Ellie,' he shouted back at her as the taxi came to a stop. 'Give you a ring, yeah?'

Ellie's annoyance that he had miraculously found money for a taxi battled with her relief that he had gone. Then she gave a little jump: someone had put their hand on her arm and she knew it was Jack.

'You all right?' he said, and Ellie felt an electrical storm eddy its way up her arm and right into her body. How was it possible that one man could stick his tongue right down your throat and leave you bored while another could simply put his hand on your arm and make your knees tremble?

'I'm fine,' she said, stepping away from him. It was a good move, or would have been if she had not turned her ankle over doing it.

'Steady.' Jack caught hold of her arm again as she righted herself and the small electrical storm started up again.

Ellie tried to subtly disengage herself, but he was holding on tight and the look he was giving her was filled with real warmth. No, no, no. She shifted her gaze to his tie.

'Not very gallant,' he said, 'going off like that.' He nodded in the direction Dave's taxi had gone.

'Gallant?'

'Yeah, abandoning you in the street, late at night.'

'Well, he had to go, and so do I.'

Jack's hand was still on her arm and he seemed angry. 'Him having to go is no bloody excuse. Anything could happen to you in the street at this time of night.'

'Jack, you're squeezing my arm really tightly,' she said, trying to draw away.

He looked down as if he hadn't realised what he was doing and she felt his grip relax a little, but he didn't take the hint when she tried, again, to pull her arm free.

Ellie wanted to run, get as far away as possible from the overwhelming feeling that she was going to throw herself at him.

'I hope you're getting a taxi,' he said forcefully.

'Um . . .'

'Ellie, I can't hear you with your head down like that, and why do you keep looking at my tie? Is there something on my tie?' Jack put his hand to his tie to check and Ellie took the opportunity of being free of him to take another step backwards.

'I'm going for the bus. I was going to go when you came along. The bus. Just along here. Bus.'

Suddenly his hand was back on her arm and for the second time he wasn't being particularly gentle with it.

'Are you bloody mad? This time of night? It'll be full of people even more drunk than you are.'

She should have walked away then, when he was mad

at her. She could cope with him being angry. But something made her unable to resist answering him back.

'I have had three drinks tonight. I'm not drunk. Didn't take you long to start having a go at me again, did it?'

Jack dropped his hand from her arm. 'Don't be ridiculous. I'm simply trying to point out that lurching around London at this time of night isn't a good idea.' He reached into his jacket and pulled out his wallet. 'You know the agency has an account with a cab firm.' He held out a card for her. 'This is the number. Give them a call.'

'I can't,' she said. 'My mobile needs topping up.'

She waited for Jack to make some sarcastic remark, but he surprised her by laughing softly and then his hand was rubbing her arm. It was a gentle, consoling gesture, but she fully expected to see sparks fly up from her sleeve.

'Oh, Ellie, what the hell are we going to do with you?' he said, and there was such tenderness in his tone that she couldn't help looking directly at him. The tenderness was in his eyes too. It would have been so easy to take a step forward and lower her head on to his shoulder and keep it there.

Jack broke away first. 'I'll give them a ring, then,' he said brusquely.

While he was making the call, Ellie wandered down the road a little distance, aware she was trembling. Actually trembling. Best to put some space between her and all those out-of-control feelings. Why couldn't he go away? Her hand strayed to her mouth, but she put it firmly back down by her side.

When he'd finished phoning, he came and stood by her.

'What are you doing now?' she said.

'I'll wait until it comes.' He was being gruff and domineering again.

'You don't need to.'

'I know,' he said, and crossed his arms.

More waiting. More awkwardness. Where was that taxi?

Then she saw him shift his feet. 'I watched the rough edit of the ad.'

'Yes. It looks quite good, doesn't it?'

She heard him sigh. 'You want to work on that.'

'On what? Work on what?'

'That irritating modesty. It's a brilliant ad. You should be talking it up, not muttering about it being "quite good".'

Ellie shook her head. How did he do this every time? Nice and nasty, nasty and nice. It was like being batted about by some temperamental toddler.

Those eyes were mocking her again. No longer pools of grey tenderness.

She would keep her mouth shut, say nothing.

No, she couldn't.

'Sorry, Jack, I think we've had this conversation before about how I never seem to quite come up to your high expectations.'

He stared at her. 'That's what you think, is it, Ellie? That I find you . . . not quite good enough?'

She wanted to shout that she didn't know. He had her so confused she didn't know anything.

She was bone tired now with all the emotion zinging about inside her. Please, please let that taxi come round the corner. Lusting after Jack was humiliating her, changing her into a woman she didn't recognise.

She shrugged. 'Yeah, well, we can't all be like Sophie.'

Jack gave her a funny look. 'What?'

'Nothing,' she said, and then saw the taxi turning the corner. Hallelujah. She started to walk towards it. 'Thanks, Jack,' she called back over her shoulder, only to find he was right behind her. He opened the door of the cab and her face was right next to his. She was looking into his eyes and what she saw there made her stop completely still. She wasn't even sure she was breathing.

She'd been over and over this. It was madness. It was temporary insanity brought on by lust. The Heathcliff effect. Fight it and it would pass.

Then Jack leaned forward and kissed her very gently on the cheek, the lightest of touches. His lips were warm; his hair touched her eyebrow.

'Night, Ellie,' he said gently. 'Look after yourself. Ask the taxi driver to wait until you've gone into the house.' His hand was on her arm helping her.

She sat down on the seat, stunned, looking ahead, not

daring to glance back at him, and soon the taxi was out of the street and away.

All the way home she tried to unravel the threads of Jack's behaviour towards her. It was impossible; all she knew was how he made her feel. Like she was wrestling with something she couldn't control that might turn round and bite her at any minute. Was he simply being kind? All that stuff about being careful, those looks. Was this why he was so successful with women, because he made you feel as if there was no one else alive as important to him as you were? It was a good skill, a neat trick.

But what if it wasn't a trick?

Edith was still up when she got in and Ellie told her all about Lesley and Megan and they opened a bottle of wine to celebrate. She gave her edited highlights of the Dave incident too and mentioned that Jack had got her a taxi home.

Edith sat looking at her with her head on one side.

'What's up, Edith? You look like you want to say something. Is it about Megan and Lesley? Don't you approve?'

'Good gracious, Ellie dear, I couldn't be more delighted for them. Splendid news.' Edith took a large sip of wine. 'Modern life is so much more sensible than in my day. I had an aunt Rose who lived with another woman, Jessica, all her life and they had to pretend they were just friends.'

'Perhaps they were just friends.'

'No, dear. When Rose died, quite a few years after dear Jess, we found certain things that suggested otherwise.'

Ellie didn't dare ask what kind of things they'd found.

'No,' continued Edith, happy that all was now clear about lesbianism in less enlightened times, 'I am very pleased for Lesley and Megan. It was Dave I was going to ask about.'

'Uh-huh.'

'Well, I haven't heard you mention him before.'

'No? Well, he wrote the music for the knickers ad and I've been working with him quite a bit. He gave me his phone number a while ago.'

'Hmm,' Edith said.

'Hmm, what?'

'But you hadn't rung him?'

'No.'

'But when he turned up tonight, you were glad to see him?'

Sometimes Ellie wished that Edith was starting to lose her marbles. She decided to pretend she hadn't heard.

Edith carried on, 'And Jack happened to wander past as Dave left?'

Ellie kept her lips tightly clamped together, but Edith wouldn't be deterred. 'Did Jack ask you where Dave had gone?'

Ellie gave in and shook her head and Edith started to laugh.

'What's so funny?'

'Oh, Ellie darling, you're such an innocent. First that filthy Jubbitt man apologises to you after a meeting with Jack; then there's that incident with the model-maker where Jack dragged you away; and now this.' Edith's eyes were bright with mischief. 'Dave gets called away; Jack appears on the scene and doesn't even ask where he's gone?' Edith finished her wine and leaned back with a satisfied grin.

'What are you saying, Edith?' Ellie asked, starting to nibble at her thumb without realising it.

'I'm saying that Jack didn't need to ask where he had gone because he knew already.' Edith leaned forward again. 'I'm sure Jack is a good friend of this music man who called Dave, aren't you?'

'Edith, I think you're putting two and two together and coming up with completely the wrong number.' Ellie was quite brisk; she wanted to shut this conversation down as soon as possible – it sounded too much like the one she'd had with herself in the taxi home. 'If you're hinting at what I think you're hinting at, there's one big flaw in your theory.'

Edith said nothing, simply cocked her head a little.

'Jack doesn't care two hoots about me. Every bit of nice-ness from him is always followed by something nasty. Always. You wait, come Monday he'll tear my head off about something to make up for getting me a taxi. He might have dragged me away from the shoot, as you so rightly pointed out, but he ended up humiliating me in front of Rachel.'

Edith was still doing that irritating cocking-head thing.

Ellie ploughed on, 'He simply made up a whole story about me sulking. I mean, I was a bit put out about having to come back to the agency, but it wasn't a sulk. Turned on me and savaged me. I stood there like a muppet while Rachel simpered at him.'

Ellie was pretty pleased with herself. In the course of trying to show Edith how cross she was with Jack, she'd actually made herself angry with him all over again.

All Edith said, with rapier-like clarity, was, 'And it bothered you, Rachel simpering at Jack, did it?'

Caught off guard, Ellie said, 'No, of course not,' much too quickly, and then added, 'That wasn't the point I was trying to make, Edith.'

Edith's eyes were twinkling mischievously again. She tapped the side of her nose. 'Say what you like, Ellie, I still think that there is a pattern emerging and you refuse to see it. Your Mr Wolfe seems to be keeping an eye on you.' She stood up slowly. 'I may look like a desiccated prune, but I do know a little bit about men. I had five brothers, remember? And quite a few boyfriends.' She bent to kiss Ellie on the head. 'And you, my dear Ellie, are an open book. Every time you mention Jack Wolfe these days you end up nibbling the skin down the side of your thumbnail.'

'I do not,' Ellie said, hurriedly covering up her thumbs.

'Ellie, don't fib. I was a drama teacher for years. Body language is my subject.' She patted Ellie on the shoulder. 'You should be happy. You're at the start of a big adventure.'

Ellie was on her feet. 'No, Edith, I'm not. I'm sorry. You've been reading too many romances. Jack is my boss and he's a serial womaniser. He's domineering; he insists on getting his own way . . .' Ellie became aware that she had raised her voice and made a conscious effort to lower it. 'Look, I admit I find Jack attractive, but nothing is going to happen. I'm not going to let it.'

Edith continued to smile at her and Ellie felt like shaking her.

'Don't smile at me like that, Edith. I'm serious. People are attracted to one another all the time; they don't have to do anything about it. And I'd have to leave the agency if . . . Look, it's always the woman who has to leave.'

'Ah, so you've thought about it, then?' Edith said triumphantly, and started to move towards the sitting room door.

Ellie made one last attempt. 'Edith, listen. Nothing is going to happen. For lots and lots of reasons. But the main one is . . . Jack is getting married soon. A girl called Sophie.'

Edith stopped. 'Sophie and Jack,' she said, running the words slowly around her mouth. 'S-o-p-h-i-e and Jack.' Eventually she shook her head. 'No, no, that doesn't sound right at all. That's not going to happen.' Giving Ellie a cheery wave, she left the room.

'Bugger,' Ellie said softly to herself, and very soon her thumb was back in her mouth.

On Monday morning Mrs MacEndry was leafing through *Ad Infinitum* when she came to the gossip column. She started to read and with each word her eyebrows disappeared further into her hair. She put down the magazine and gave a tiny, ladylike snort, then got up and went into Jack's office and placed the magazine, open at the appropriate page, on his desk.

Jack arrived at work about ten minutes later and said in a confused tone, 'Lydia, have we won some awards over the weekend that I don't know about? Three people on the way up here have offered me their congratulations.'

Mrs MacEndry smiled. 'I think you need to look on your desk.'

Jack went into his office with the confused look still on his face and shut the door behind him.

Mrs MacEndry sat very still and waited. When Jack's door flew open and he stood there, magazine in hand, he was looking murderous.

'For God's sake,' he said, and threw the magazine into Mrs MacEndry's wastepaper bin. 'Get Sophie on the phone for me, will you? She can hear wedding bells, can she? Well, she must have better hearing than I've got.'

He went back into his office and stood looking at the phone. Marry her? Hell had frozen over, had it?

He thought back to Friday night. Well, that explained Ellie's comment about Sophie.

Jack sat down at his desk and let his mind linger yet again on the particularly satisfying memory of how Ellie's cheek had felt against his lips. Soft, warm, incredibly inviting. Thank God he hadn't managed to get to her mouth.

The way her beautiful eyes had flashed at him when he'd annoyed her was worth replaying too, along with all those little electrically charged glances that had passed between them in the pub. But the absolute top moment had been that look she'd given him right before he'd put her in the taxi.

Had she guessed he'd had something to do with dull Dave buggering off? Had she worked out what she was doing to him?

He was stuffed if she had.

But then again, he was stuffed if she hadn't. Right now he was stuck in some kind of no-man's-land where he didn't dare do anything about claiming Ellie for himself, but he was damned if he was going to sit around and watch any other man get his hands on her.

He cast a look at the phone, willing it to ring so that he could escape from having to go over all this yet again.

Perhaps he could persuade her to go into a nunnery.

That was the only solution. Because making a move towards her would be like embarking on some chemical experiment that you knew was going to blow up in your face and leave you lying among broken glass.

He put the heels of his hands over his eyes and tried to stop thinking completely, and then the phone was ringing.

He took a deep breath. 'Ah, Sophie darling,' he said when he picked it up. 'Look, there's no nice way to tell you this . . .'

CHAPTER 19

Jack was standing very close to Ellie in his office.

'Ellie,' he said, 'we have a real problem with the ad. The client has decided that they don't want knickers any more. They want model aeroplanes with huge wings.'

He was rubbing her arm with his hand. 'You have to go to the model-makers and get them to make some planes.'

'Planes, Jack? But none of the song will make sense,' Ellie said, starting to cry. 'I'll have to write a new song and get new music and I can't because I kissed Dave and now I wish I hadn't.'

'What?' snarled Jack. 'You were kissing someone else?' He grabbed her by both arms, pulling her close. 'You know that's wrong. You know it's in your contract that you have to kiss me.' He moved his mouth to her ear and whispered, 'What's wrong with me? Don't I turn you on enough yet?'

'No, Jack ... yes ... I,' she tried to say, but he was looking at her with such intensity that she took his face in both her hands and started to kiss him. Deep, searching kisses. She could feel his stubble on the palms of her hands.

They were down on the floor now under his desk, his hands undoing the buttons of her blouse, and then she felt his hot mouth on her nipple, hot even through the material of her bra.

'Oh God, Jack, yes . . . yes,' she said, but he probably couldn't hear her over the sound of somebody hammering on the office door.

A voice shouted, 'Ellie dear, I heard the most dreadful thump. You haven't hurt yourself, have you?'

Jack disappeared and Ellie found herself face to face with a pair of shoes. She was lying on the rug by her bed. Several bits of her hurt.

'Ellie dear?' shouted Edith through the bedroom door.

Ellie sat up slowly. 'No harm done, Edith. I think I must have fallen out of bed. I had a bad dream, that's all. Sorry.'

Edith muttered something and went downstairs, and Ellie hauled herself back into bed and lay there looking at the ceiling.

Sleep wouldn't come again, though, no matter how hard she tried. Jack wasn't just disturbing her days; he was prowling through her dreams with his glittering, dangerous looks. She was being stalked and there were only two things she could do about it.

One was too embarrassing even to think about, and the other would involve leaving an agency she liked and people she had grown to love. She couldn't go on much longer like this, though, acting like some schoolgirl. Perhaps she had to face the fact that it was time for a move. Once the knickers ad was on TV, she and Lesley were bound to be more in demand.

She climbed out of bed, got dressed and went and had a look at the 'Situations Vacant' in her copy of *Ad Infinitum*.

CHAPTER 20

Ellie could pinpoint exactly when she knew the Sure & Soft ad was going to be a success. It was at 8.35 a.m. on 5 June, when the woman next to her on the bus started to hum 'The Thong Song'. It meant more to Ellie than all the slaps on the back at work and gave her a similar thrill to the one she'd felt when she and Edith had watched the ad on TV for the first time.

She still had a spring in her step when she walked into the agency, although as always she scanned reception nervously to make sure Jack wasn't around. She'd become pretty expert at avoiding him over the past weeks and now there was only one day to go before her holidays. Two glorious Jack-free weeks. Two weeks of not having to worry about whether to move agency or not. Although, seeing as she hadn't mentioned anything about that to Lesley, the whole plan had proved to be a bit of a non-starter so far.

'Hi, Ellie,' Rachel said, as she passed by. 'Looking forward to your break?'

'Can't wait. I'm going to kick back at home and take it easy.'

She would have liked to have stayed and chatted longer, but Rachel's eyes took on an extra-warm sheen and Ellie guessed she'd spotted Jack arriving. Rachel was back on Jack's trail since *Ad Infinitum* had broken the news that Sophie had 'counted her wolves before they were hatched and had now returned to the singles' market'.

'See you, Rachel,' Ellie said, and scooted towards the stairs. This was a doddle. Now, if she could get the great hulking Yorkshire guy out of her dreams, she could return to normal life.

Upstairs in her office, Lesley and Ian were waiting for her.

'Here she is,' Lesley said, jumping up from her seat. 'Ellie, this photo shoot looks like it's going to go on all day. I'm probably not going to see you again before you go off.' She wrapped Ellie in a hug. 'Have a great time and don't get up to anything too wild with Edith.'

'I'll try not to, although she has promised to introduce me to the delights of bingo and that can get pretty cut-throat.'

'Hey, you're not wrong. Megan has a cousin who ended up in A&E after the woman next to her elbowed her in the eye while she was shouting—'

'Hey, when you two have finished fannying on,' Ian said, rummaging about in his shoulder bag, 'perhaps we can go?' He pulled out his diary and started to flick through it. 'So, nothing I need to know about before you go off tonight, Ellie? No nasty surprises you've left for me?'

'No. I've shredded everything I didn't get round to doing.'

'Good lass,' Ian said, scanning a page in his diary. 'That's the spirit . . . Oh sod it.' He slammed the diary on the desk before looking a bit shamefaced and picking it up again. 'You know what it is?' he said with some force. 'I need my own Mrs MacEndry to keep me straight. Then I wouldn't keep doing this double-booking thing.' He held the diary up for them to see. 'Look, I wrote the details of the shoot down in ink right over the top of the pencil scrawl about this meeting that starts after lunch. I'm knacked . . . unless . . .' Ellie saw his gaze shift to her. 'That's a really nice dress you're wearing, Ellie. Did I mention that earlier?'

'Very subtle, Ian,' Ellie said, shaking her head. 'Completely unpremeditated flattery. But go on, I'll do your meeting for you. Who's it with?'

'Those medical suppliers, Cratchbull & Weston. Nice bloke, Bill Weston, very enthusiastic, very friendly. Jack needs another brain in the room with him and yours is the best brain there is. After mine, of course,' he added.

Ellie stared at him. 'Jack's going to be in the meeting?' She knew her voice had gone up a couple of octaves.

'Yeah.' Ian put his diary back in his bag. 'So there shouldn't be any problems. He's got all the background info on the company. He'll soon bring you up to speed.'

'No, look, Ian, I'm really busy this afternoon.'

'You said you'd do it, Ellie. What's wrong with you, woman? You look like you've heard you're going to have some teeth out. It's only a meeting.' He tapped his watch. 'Are we going to this shoot? God, I don't know, you two haven't been the same since you got famous. One great campaign and you think you can arse around all day.' He shepherded Lesley out through the door and Ellie stood there and watched them go.

She could do this meeting with Jack. She could. It wasn't what she wanted, but she could do this. She could cope with the jolting-stomach thing. And the breathlessness. She was getting good at it now. All she had to do was steer clear of those grey eyes. If she didn't, he'd take one look at her and know. He'd just know.

She leaped to the door. 'What's the product?' she shouted down the corridor after Ian. 'I forgot to ask.'

His voice drifted back. 'Fantastic new scalpel, the Whispedge.'

'Pigging perfect,' she said, wandering back into the empty room. 'Absolutely pigging perfect.'

Jack knew that the feeling in his stomach was guilt. He'd been unfair to Ellie, no doubt about that. Even from where he was sitting, he could see she was definitely going a funny colour and that smile on her face looked more and more strained.

Perhaps he should have listened to her when she'd told him she was squeamish about blood and needles. If it had been any other member of staff, he'd have been sympathetic, but he'd thought it was another of Ellie's ruses to avoid being in the same room as him.

He was sick to the back teeth of seeing her disappearing round corners every time he got anywhere near her. Much as he loved the sight of her sweet backside, that was the only part of her he'd seen for days, swaying temptingly as she moved out of reach.

And if she did catch sight of him, she glared at him as if he were carrying something contagious. The one or two times he'd got close enough to talk to her, she'd hardly answered. That staring-at-the-carpet thing was getting worse too, really hacking him off. And that damned incident in the pub last week had been the last straw. He'd gone over to sit by her and congratulate her on how well the knickers ad was going down with the public. Well, to be honest, he'd used that as an excuse to get close to her. He was going to go on and ask if she wanted something to drink, even though he was finding it hard to think in a straight line what with the way she smelled so good and how she'd piled her hair up beautifully so there was a little tendril curling down her neck.

And what had been her reaction? She'd shifted along the seat as if she were afraid he was going to bite her and then got up and disappeared off home without a word. Unbelievable.

So when she'd come up with all that 'I'm afraid I'm going to make a fool of myself and faint' stuff, he'd talked right over her.

Bit tricky, though, when she'd tried to win his sympathy by asking him straight out whether there wasn't something that he was scared of. Cue great crashing waves of panic.

Luckily she hadn't noticed. He smiled bitterly. His reputation as 'fearless Jack' was still intact.

Anyway, if he'd had to pick her up and carry her into the meeting, he'd have done it.

Damn. That wasn't a good image to have in his head, not when he was meant to be concentrating on Bill Weston and his amazing Whispedge scalpel. He took another look at Ellie and saw her reach up and tuck her hair behind her ear with a hand that was definitely trembling.

The feeling of guilt in Jack's stomach intensified. He'd let his determination to get close to her take priority, he could see that now. And his behaviour in their little pre-meeting briefing session hadn't been much better. As he'd outlined Cratchbull & Weston's credentials, he'd been thinking about kissing Ellie all the way down her neck until he ran up against that silky button at the top of her dress.

When he'd got to the company's management buy-out,

he'd mentally undone all of her buttons. Explaining how the client was poised to break into the Far East market saw him slipping her dress from her shoulders. He'd even imagined the little scattering of freckles she would have there, the perfect match for the ones across her nose.

By the time that Bill Weston had actually arrived, Jack had to welcome the poor guy with a weird hunched-over half-rise from his desk to conceal how turned on he was.

It was a damned good job Ellie was off for the next two weeks. It would give him the chance to calm down a bit, maybe find a hot replacement for Leonora and Sophie. Or probably two replacements.

Jack checked on Ellie again.

Her knuckles were clenched white round her pencil. If she didn't relax her hand, she was going to snap the thing.

Jack turned back to Bill Weston. Unfortunately for Ellie, Bill was a man completely in love with his products. Jack had expected him simply to bring along some samples of the Whispedge and talk them through its revolutionary design. But not good old Bill.

Instead he had hauled out his laptop. 'I can't actually perform an operation to show you just what this little baby can do,' he'd said, chuckling, 'but I've got the next best thing.' And with that he'd started to play a lovely film of a particularly tricky bowel operation.

Once or twice already Jack had seen Ellie close her eyes,

but that hadn't really helped her because Bill was also providing an enthusiastic and very colourful commentary: 'See, Ellie, the way the scalpel goes through that layer of muscle like butter? See, see? Marvellous, eh? And because we've got the balance of the blade exactly right, it means there's much less exertion involved. That can make a real difference to the surgeon's dexterity, of course, especially when you're talking about a three- or four-hour operation.'

Jack saw Ellie nod mutely and could hear her breathing coming in short gasps above the squelching and slopping sounds on the little film.

'Now, you don't want to miss this bit, Ellie,' Bill said, pointing out a deep incision that the scalpel was making.

Jack heard a crack as Ellie snapped her pencil in two.

'Bill, I think we've probably seen enough now to give us a good idea of the product,' Jack said hurriedly.

Bill's forehead creased in a little frown. 'Oh, it's no bother, Jack. I don't mind seeing the whole of this through, and if we turn it off now, you won't see how the sleeker design enables the surgeon to get a sharp, clean cut even when the angle is tricky.' Bill turned back round to face the screen and jabbed at it with his finger. 'This is it coming up. Bit hard to make it out clearly until the blood gets swabbed out of the way, but there, you see?'

Jack fully expected Ellie to crumple forward on to the table, but she was still sitting upright, a sheen of perspiration now covering her face. He had the sudden urge to go to her and put his arm round her and take her out of the room.

If the film didn't finish soon, he was going to have to ask Bill to turn it off. He'd think of some excuse or other. He leaned forward and poured a glass of water and pushed it towards Ellie, but she didn't seem to notice.

Finally, twenty-five blood-soaked minutes after it had started, the film was over and Jack managed to engage Bill in a discussion about market share and positioning and the opportunities in the Far East. At some point Jack saw Ellie reach out and take the glass of water and slowly raise it to her mouth.

He relaxed a little; she appeared to be coming back from wherever the gore fest had sent her. Jack started to wrap up the meeting, arranging a date when the agency could take a tour of the manufacturing facility. Bill got to his feet and so, Jack noticed with amazement, did Ellie. She had determination, he had to give her that. True, she'd got up fairly unsteadily, and she still looked a strange shade of green, but she was doing her best to smile and nod at Bill. That feeling of wanting to wrap her in his arms came back. He wasn't sure if it was lust or an urge to protect, but it made him want to tell her everything was going to be all right, even though that was a sentiment he'd ceased to believe in years ago.

Suddenly Bill struck his forehead with the palm of his

hand. 'What am I thinking of?' he said. 'I never gave you this.' He rummaged about in his briefcase and came out with a slim wooden box.

'Here you are, Ellie,' he said. 'It's no good simply talking about it and looking at it – to really appreciate the Whispedge, you have to feel it in your hands.'

Bill took the scalpel from its box and put it into Ellie's hand. Jack saw Ellie's jaw tighten. Quickly he manoeuvred Bill out of the room, talking rapidly to cover Ellie's silence. He still wasn't quick enough to stop Bill telling him a final anecdote about the early days of surgery. When Jack chanced a look back over his shoulder, Ellie was staring down at the scalpel lying in her hand as though it were a loaded gun.

Eventually Jack managed to hand Bill over to Lydia and walked back into his office.

It was empty.

'Ellie?'

No reply.

And then Jack noticed a foot sticking out past the end of the desk.

'Shit, Ellie,' he said out loud, and got himself round to where she was lying.

She was entangled in the legs of her chair, her dress hitched up around the tops of her thighs. Jack lifted the chair off her and then knelt down at her side. He tried not to look at her thighs as he pulled her dress back down;

it somehow seemed unfair. Placing his hand on her face, he felt how clammy her skin was.

'Lydia, give me a hand here,' he shouted towards the door.

He tapped Ellie lightly on the cheek. No response. She looked dreadful. What a bullying jerk he was. She told him she couldn't do this and he'd made her go ahead and do it. Gavin was right: too much testosterone.

'Lydia, are you there?' he shouted again, this time more urgently.

Ellie stirred and moaned and opened her eyes and Jack saw them flare in shock. She sat up abruptly.

'Hey,' he said, holding her by the arms, 'take it easy. You fainted. Don't try to get up.'

Ellie pushed his hands away and, using the seat of the chair to help her, got unsteadily to her feet.

'No, you shouldn't be getting up yet. You look dreadful. Stay here.' Jack tried to get hold of her again.

Ellie batted his hands away and started to move round the desk, clutching at it for support. Jack followed a couple of steps behind her.

'Ellie, you still look really pale. Come and sit down.' Jack put his hand on her arm and tried to steer her to a chair. 'Lydia, where the hell are you? I need help here,' he bellowed.

'No, I'm fine, I'm going,' Ellie said shakily, and removed his hand from her arm. She launched herself away from the desk and blundered towards the door, but only managed a couple of steps before Jack saw her knees buckle. He rushed towards her, just managing to catch her round the waist before she fell.

'Lydia!' he shouted, trying to get a firmer grip on Ellie, who felt like a deadweight, even to him. He struggled to turn her to face him and then half lifted, half dragged her over to the desk. Perching her bottom on it, he leaned her against his chest and got his breath back. Easier to carry when she was drunk than unconscious.

He was about to call for Lydia again when he stopped. Ellie felt soft against him, her breath warming a little patch of skin beneath his shirt. Damn it. He brought his arm round her waist and held it there, then bent and placed his face against her hair. Damn, damn, damn. Slowly he pulled Ellie to her feet so that her body was pressed right against his. It was completely the wrong thing to do. He should be lying her down, putting her in the recovery position.

But he didn't want her to recover, not yet. And really, there was another position he would prefer to have Ellie in right at this moment.

Jack pulled her even closer and felt the breath catch in his throat. Her breasts were pressing into his chest, her thighs were on his, and together, those contact points were sending a surge of lust right into his stomach and then into his groin. He closed his eyes and rested his chin on the top of Ellie's head. She was all softness and curves and he wanted to protect her.

He tentatively brought his other hand up to Ellie's hair and ran his fingers through it. He wound a curl round his index finger, smiling at how silky it felt, looking at the reddish glint of her hair against his skin.

Nothing else in the whole building registered with him any more except the feeling of her body against his. Holding her like this probably put him in the same league as that serial fondler Jubbitt Junior. No, he was worse than that creep: even Jubbitt hadn't leaped on Ellie when she was unconscious.

He should at least loosen his grip and sit her back down on the desk, but that meant losing how gorgeous the weight of her felt against him and how vulnerable she looked. He couldn't move.

Everything was silent except for the soft sound of her breathing. He had no idea what he was going to say to Lydia if she walked in. And how was he going to explain himself to Ellie? Then he looked down at her face, the way her eyelashes lay against her cheek, the curve of her mouth.

Everything else could go to hell. She'd fallen into his lap; he'd be a fool not to stand here and hold her.

Too soon he felt Ellie start to stir and her eyes opened. She lifted her head, still half conscious and half not, and Jack groaned and tried to look away and concentrate on something calming, like icebergs or white doves. Icebergs, white doves. White doves, icebergs.

Nope, wasn't working. Ellie made a little 'Oh' sound and the icebergs melted and the doves drowned.

Slowly he bent down, tilted his head slightly to one side and kissed her very softly on the mouth. He felt her breath against his lips and whatever had been making him behave himself vanished. He moved his hands down over her beautiful backside and kissed her on her soft mouth again, this time running his tongue along between her lips.

For an instant he felt Ellie's mouth yield to his tongue and then her eyes finally focused. She looked appalled and shot back from him as though he had thumped her. Her chest was rising and falling in a way that was both alarming to him and deeply, deeply exciting.

'No, no, no,' she cried out, and before he could put out a hand to stop her, she had run out of the room, ricocheting off the doorframe in her panic to get away.

Jack stood there motionless for a while and then slowly turned and fumbled for a chair. He sat there until Lydia came into the room.

She looked concerned, puzzled. 'Jack, are you feeling all right?' she said.

'Not really, Lydia,' he replied, and then stood up and reached across the desk for Ellie's notebook and the two halves of her pencil.

CHAPTER 21

Ellie sat in her office trying to disappear into the cool, white art pad on her desk. She hoped that if she stared at it long enough, the memory of what had happened would stop replaying in her head. So far that plan wasn't working. Her heart was still thumping so hard she was surprised the people in the next office couldn't hear it.

She reached forward and moved a pencil sharpener slightly to the left, a rubber slightly to the right and then put her hands back in her lap and resumed her staring. Jack Wolfe had been kissing her and it was as if bits of her dreams had come to life. Ellie put her hand out to move the pencil sharpener back to its original position and then stopped. My God, it had been such a wonderful kiss too. A millisecond longer and she did not know how she would have responded.

The red-hot shame of that thought made her want to get up from her chair and go and plunge her head into the mini-fridge. She concentrated on getting her breathing back into some recognisable pattern.

Everything would be fine if she could sit quietly and think about the cool, pure paper.

The building went quiet around her as people headed home. She wanted to go home too, but she was worried about bumping into Jack. Her hands fluttered up from her lap and started moving the pencil sharpener and rubber about again. She couldn't forget how lovely Jack smelled and how warm he had felt. But mainly it was the look in his eyes that had been unsettling: not amused or mocking, just scorching.

She didn't know how she was going to be able to cope with seeing him again.

And then suddenly there he was standing at the door.

Jack couldn't remember the last time he had seen anybody look so terrified of him. Except Gavin when he had threatened to wrestle him naked. The sensible thing to do would be to go home now; apologise abjectly and go home. Blame it all on the moon or the weather.

Except that the instant he walked into her office and saw her, he wanted to feel her softness against him again. No, correction: he wanted to feel it wrapped all the way around him. What was the bloody point in pretending any more? It was a mistake, it was a mess, and he shouldn't be doing it, but what the hell. There wasn't any mess that couldn't be sorted. He was fed up with tiptoeing around like some randy schoolboy, engineering chance meetings with her. Well, that was going to stop. You couldn't get that close to somebody and then pretend nothing had happened.

Jack put Ellie's notepad and bits of pencil on her desk and cleared his throat, feeling it was a show-off thing to do even as he did it.

'Look, Ellie,' he said, 'I should apologise for what happened in my office. I was completely out of line. You weren't even conscious.'

Ellie made a funny little noise that might have been a 'no' or a 'yes'. Jack squinted at her, but she didn't say anything else.

He started again. 'I'm sorry, Ellie, for how it happened, but not that it did happen.'

He saw her lower her eyes. She seemed to be finding her art pad fascinating. Well, she was going to listen to this next bit whether she wanted to or not. He took a step nearer. 'I've been wanting to do that for weeks. It was going to happen sometime, you know that.'

No response.

'It's madness, I know. I mean, I've never mixed work . . . and . . .'

Ellie flinched and Jack stopped, stumbling over the cliché. He should have known that he couldn't get away with that with Ellie. She'd picked up on how it made her sound like she was some kind of passive thing that he could either choose to treat as a colleague or a theme park ride. He groped around for something better to say, but Ellie blurted out, 'Forget it, Jack. It was nothing. Forget it.'

There was a pleading tone to her voice that should have made him nod and turn round and leave the room. Instead it made him want to prove to her that she was wrong. He wanted to haul her out of the chair and taste her on his lips again.

'Sorry, I can't do that,' he said flatly, and saw her drop her gaze back to that damned pad. So she wanted to look at it? Right. He reached for a pen and started to write across the pad. 'This is my address,' he said as he wrote. 'I'm going home now and I'll be there all evening. I want you, Ellie. I'm sorry if that scares you, but I do. If you want me ... well, that's where you'll find me.'

In any other circumstances the look on her face would have made him laugh. It was terror mixed with complete bewilderment. Perhaps she was worried about what would happen to her at work if she took him up on his offer ... or if she didn't.

'Look, I'm not a complete bastard, Ellie. I'll understand if you don't come round. I won't mention this again ... I'm not the kind of man who ... If you do or don't want to do anything about this, it won't make any difference to anything here. Understand? Somehow we'll work around it.'

She didn't look convinced, was still peering at him as though he were some particularly poisonous creature.

'At least think about it before you decide "no".' He gave what he hoped was a self-deprecating laugh.

He couldn't do any more; it was up to her now. He had no idea if she was going to rip the paper into shreds once he had gone. All he could do was go home and wait.

Jack had barely left her office before Ellie reached across and tore the page off the art pad and threw it into the wastepaper bin. Women who slept with people at work were stupid; women who slept with people who were their boss were suicidal. It always ended in tears. And with Jack that was almost guaranteed. She would just be a new sensation for him, a flavour that he hadn't tried before.

That was even before she thought about that worrying air of detachment that hung about him. No doubt he would stay sitting on the emotional sidelines whatever happened and that would be that. If she wasn't careful, she'd be hurtling towards heartbreak and misery, followed swiftly by the search for a new job.

She ignored the voice in her head telling her that she was going to have to move on anyway now, even if she didn't end up in Jack's bed.

She got up, put on her jacket, picked up her bag and left the office. As she entered the lift, she told herself that she was doing the right thing. She walked through reception, now thankfully empty of Rachel, and then left the agency and hurried towards her bus stop.

She wasn't going to think about it any more. She was going to go home, enjoy her holiday and then work out how to persuade Lesley it was time for a move.

She wasn't going to become another notch on what was bound to be a bedpost already whittled down to matchstick proportions.

Ellie raised her chin. A warm breeze blew along the street and a smell of something cooking reached her. The evening sun glinting off the office buildings made everything look bright and exciting, and around her the sound of traffic ebbed and flowed. That tingle of anticipation that always hit her when she came out into a London evening started in her stomach and worked its way down to her toes and up into her chest. Everything in life was sitting out there waiting for her to grab it with both hands.

Including Jack.

Ellie walked on towards the bus stop for a few more paces and then stopped. Timid and stale, Sam had said. And out there was a glittering, dangerous man who wanted her. It would be madness to go back on her decision, though. Complete madness.

But the way his mouth had felt on hers had sent a spark of lust right down her body. She could still feel the heat of his hands on her bottom.

Where was it written down that she always had to do the sensible thing?

Well, there were other ways to make a decision. She could let fate decide. Taxis were impossible to get in this part of London at this time of night. If one came along before her bus, it would be a sign that she should go and find Jack. She was perfectly safe; there was no way there would be a taxi free within the next few minutes. Soon she would be safely on the bus and at least she could comfort herself that, for a few seconds at least, she had toyed with doing something she'd regret later.

Anyway, she wasn't even certain she could remember the address he had written on that art pad. So even if by the wildest chance a taxi did turn up, she'd never be able to find her way to his flat.

She stuck her arm out.

There was a screech of tyres and a volley of beeping horns as a taxi executed a kamikaze U-turn in the middle of the road. Its yellow 'For Hire' sign shone brightly.

'Where'd you wanna go, love?' shouted the driver.

CHAPTER 22

Jack opened the door to his flat and Ellie's pulse leaped way off the scale. When she had played this scene in her head in the taxi, she had never got any further than ringing his doorbell, but now there he was with his jacket off and his tie undone and his shirt sleeves rolled up and he looked much bigger and more dangerous than she remembered.

Ellie was vaguely aware of a huge window behind Jack that looked out on to the river, of a pale-wood floor and a huge black sofa. Everything else was a bit blurry.

What on earth was she thinking? She couldn't do this.

'I-just-came-to-say-I-can't-do-this-and-I'm-sorry-but-I-have-to-go-home-now.' She took a step backwards.

'Oh, no, you don't.' Jack reached out, grabbed her by the arms and pulled her inside the flat.

His hands were so warm that she could feel them through her jacket. It brought a tight feeling to her chest.

Then she saw him take a step nearer and could not stop

herself from looking up into his face. Suddenly the fear that he would see how much he affected her didn't seem to matter any more. His grey eyes were filled with such longing that it felt as if he had actually reached out and caressed her.

Jack started to undo her jacket and Ellie stood there and let him, unable to think what else to do. She, Ellie Somerset, was standing in Jack Wolfe's flat. She had come here for the express purpose of having sex with him. Putting it into words like that spooked her, and as Jack finished with the buttons and started to push the jacket down her shoulders, she made a little move away from him.

Jack put his hands on her shoulders, like he was about to give her a pep talk. 'Relax, Ellie. You did the difficult bit deciding to come here. Just relax now.'

'No, Jack, I can't stay, honestly . . . I . . . I . . . don't have the qualifications for this . . . I . . .'

'Nice try, Ellie,' he said, and pulled her jacket right off, 'but this is one thing you can't wisecrack your way out of.'

Ellie heard her jacket fall to the floor and Jack was standing right up close. He smelled intoxicating. Then, without warning, he pushed her gently against the wall and his mouth was on hers, soft but insistent. She felt his arms go round her and pull her closer in and the heat between her legs spiked all the way up into her belly. His tongue was pushing between her lips and she opened up and let him in. As his tongue touched hers, she found herself touching it tentatively back with her own.

'Bloody hell, Ellie,' he said accusingly, breaking his mouth from hers, 'you've been eating liquorice.'

'Yes, in the taxi,' she gasped, as she felt his leg move between hers and nudge them further apart. 'I . . . I had garlic chicken for lunch and I couldn't find any mints, so—' Jack bent to kiss her neck and Ellie felt her throat constrict and she was unable to say anything else.

Jack's mouth found its way back on to hers, and this time when she touched his tongue, she heard him make a little sound that vibrated through her and set off an unbearable urge to cling on to him and push her hips against his groin. In response she felt his hand cup her breast through her dress. He gently rubbed her nipple between his thumb and forefinger and Ellie didn't seem to have internal organs any more, just meltwater. She tried to pull his shirt free from his trousers so that she could feel his skin, but had no strength. Jack's hand and mouth were tormenting her so that all she could think about was trying to get hold of a sensation that was dancing and shifting in a maddening way.

She didn't know if the ragged breathing she could hear was hers or Jack's, although she wasn't aware of breathing at all. And then Jack started to undo the buttons on her dress and she heard herself make a noise that sounded something like 'Ahargh.'

She'd expected him to rip at her clothes, but she found the determination and skill he lavished on her buttons infinitely more sexy. She watched each one being slowly undone and then glanced up. He dropped the darkest of looks on her. A look that told her exactly how much he wanted her and what he was going to do to her. It made her reach her hand up, put it behind his neck and pull his mouth back down on to hers.

Jack had other ideas, though. He kissed her once on the lips and then moved down her neck, pushing aside the material of her dress. Through her bra he began to caress and suck and nibble her, his hand on the small of her back trapping her under his mouth.

She could barely stand up under such a battering of sensations and closed her eyes and just let him hold her together as he took her apart.

'This underwear,' Jack said softly, 'worth every penny,' and then he pulled her dress from her shoulders and pushed it down past her waist and hips. The material of his trousers felt rough against her thigh and she found his desire to get her naked while he was fully clothed turned her on even more.

Jack kicked her discarded dress to one side and reached round and undid her bra. Very slowly, as if he were strip-teasing her with the removal of her own clothes, Jack drew the straps of her bra down her arms and then whisked the whole thing off her.

'Oh, Ellie,' he said with feeling, his eyes growing darker as he looked at her, and then she was on the floor flat on her back and Jack was straddling her on all fours. Ellie grabbed hold of his tie and pulled him down on to her. She didn't care that she was panting away beneath him or that his fingers had found their way between her legs and now he would know exactly how excited he had made her. All she wanted was to catch that feeling that was still tantalisingly slipping away from her.

She felt him tug at her knickers and she lifted her hips to help him get them off. Then she closed her eyes and hung on to him, her arms round his neck, as she felt him start to touch her exactly where she needed to be touched. Of course Jack would be good at this, she should have known. She moved her hips slowly, trying to tap into the rhythm Jack was setting.

'Don't shut your eyes, Ellie,' she heard him say, and as she opened them, she felt his fingers push into her. 'That's it, Ellie,' he said softly, dropping little kisses on her neck, 'just feel, nearly there.'

Ellie could barely remember her name, let alone feel. How did he know she was nearly there? Jack's thumb continued to trail over the place where every nerve ending in her body now seemed to live and she pushed against him, wanting more.

Then she heard Jack's voice again, distracting her from the delicious and maddening feelings he was stroking up.

'I need a word, Ellie.'

Through the layers of impatience and heat building in her groin, Ellie wondered what he meant. Was it something about work? Was this really the best time for him to bring this up?

Wasn't he the one who had told her off for always wanting to have the last word? Why was he demanding one from her now?

'A word?' she said in a weak voice, as the things he was doing with his hand made her arch her back. 'What ... like in Scrabble, *Countdown* ... what?'

Jack laughed into her neck and followed it with a kiss. 'No, just a word, a little word you will say to me if I start doing something to you that you really don't like.'

Ellie knew then that she was out of her depth and should get out from under him and grab her clothes and run, but her body was too far gone.

'Can't I simply say no?' she half said and half cried out.

She saw Jack shake his head. 'That won't work, Ellie. Sometimes you'll be saying no when you really mean yes.'

The thought of that punched Ellie right between the legs, until that yearning, grasping feeling was unbearable. She had to reach that thing they were both chasing or she would die right here on Jack Wolfe's floor. And then there it was rushing towards her.

She felt her body clench around Jack and, as she shuddered, the perfect word spun into her mind.

'Barcelona!' she cried out, and heard Jack laugh and felt his arms come round her and hold her until she lay still.

'Barcelona it is, then,' he said, kissing her on the cheek. 'I'll do my best to remember that.' He got to his feet and started to take his clothes off and Ellie sat up groggily to watch him, bringing up her knees and folding her arms over her breasts. Neither of them spoke as Jack slowly unbuttoned his shirt, never taking his eyes from Ellie's.

'I feel like Gavin,' Ellie said with a nervous laugh.

'You don't bloody look like him,' Jack replied, raking her with a glance that made her toes clench. 'Not that I can see much of you any more,' he added pointedly, and Ellie found herself unfolding her arms, putting them behind her and leaning back. It felt right. Jack rewarded her with another gusset-soaking look and undid the last button on his shirt. He tugged it out of his trousers, pulled it open and shrugged it off.

Ellie was not quite able to cope, all at once, with the sight of that flesh and muscle again. When she did glance up at him from under her eyelashes, she felt very little and unprotected. Soon that chest was going to be pressed against her. She felt everything below her waist dissolve into heat again.

Jack unlaced his shoes and soon stood there barefoot. His eyes sought hers and he came over and knelt by her side.

'You still with me? You look a bit . . . dazed.'

She thought that 'concussed' might have been a better description, but she simply said, 'I'm fine, Jack.'

Before his name was out of her mouth, he had undone his belt and the top button of his trousers and pulled down the zip. Ellie watched his chest rise and fall and reached out to touch him. He was warm and solid, and she was about to bend forward and place a kiss on his skin when he stood up decisively and took off his trousers and pants.

Ellie had been hoping for some kind of gradual introduction to what was in Jack's pants. She'd got a fair idea of what was in store when she'd come out of her faint and felt him hard against her hip, but now he was naked. With no clothes on. All skin.

Once she'd actually seen . . . him . . . she couldn't escape from the fact that she was here, in this room, waiting for Jack Wolfe to have sex with her.

He knelt down again and she tried to stop time by looking into his eyes, but he got hold of her hand and pressed something into it. She felt the smooth, square shape of a wrapped condom and from there her gaze was drawn to Jack's erection.

Right. So it wasn't only Sam's chest that now seemed puny in comparison. Jack had been right about the size of his tail. Before she could think it through properly, she had reached out and wrapped her hand round him. She heard Jack suck his breath in through his teeth and he gave a little lurch forward. Then she stroked him lightly and Jack groaned and put his hand on her shoulder to steady himself. Ellie continued to stroke him, simply staring down at him.

She heard Jack say urgently, 'Ellie, for God's sake, do something else with it. Stop looking at it with that worried expression. I haven't killed anybody with it yet.'

Ellie continued to stroke and heard Jack's urgent tone again. 'I'm from Yorkshire, for Pete's sake – everything's bigger up there.'

'Uh-huh,' Ellie said. 'Good joke, Jack. I wish I'd thought of it.' And then she was running her hand more roughly over him. Such an intimate thing to do to Jack Wolfe.

His hold on her shoulder tightened. 'Ellie,' he gasped, 'I am about to really embarrass both of us. Help me here. Please.'

Ellie looked up at Jack asking for help and knew then that everything was going to be all right. She didn't care how rubbish she was probably going to be or how he'd guess she was completely clueless. He needed her to do this. She let go of him and tore open the square, shiny packet and enjoyed the effect of what she did next on his eyes and his mouth. All that power in her hand.

Jack gathered her up to him and gave her a look filled with such hunger that it made her stomach flip. And then his mouth was covering hers and his tongue was inside her and she was on her back again. He kissed a line down her belly far enough to make her hips rise up to meet him and then he lifted his head and looked at her from under his dark brows. 'Uh, you might want to open your legs at this point, Ellie,' he said, and when she did, her heart ramming against her ribs, he was inside her in one fierce, quick movement that forced the air out of her lungs.

Somebody was making a whimpering noise and, as it wasn't Jack, Ellie guessed it must be her.

She brought her legs up and Jack pushed deeper, sometimes slowly, sometimes fast, until Ellie wasn't sure she could stand the anticipation any more. When Jack stopped supporting himself and brought his weight down on her, it made her feel completely possessed and that thought drove her to kiss him back with more passion, digging her nails into his shoulders.

She was already heading for sensory overload when he put his mouth close to her ear and started to growl obscenities at her in his roughest Yorkshire accent. They were filthy, filthy rude.

That was it. She was gone again and crying out something, but she never knew what. It certainly wasn't 'Barcelona', because Jack kept right on thrusting into her until she felt him tense too and then groan deep down in his chest. A few more thrusts and he lay still, breathing into her hair.

Ellie lay under him, feeling his heart beating against

her, and then very gently she reached up and ran her hand through his choppy black hair. It wasn't wiry at all, just soft and thick.

Jack turned his head and looked at her. 'Am I squashing you?'

'A bit.'

'Good,' he said, and she felt his hand snake up her hip and start to caress her breast again.

CHAPTER 23

'Hello, sleepy girl,' Jack said, turning away slightly from the cooker and smiling at Ellie.

She stood in the doorway to the kitchen, blinking a little in the light. Behind her, he could see the duvet and pillows on the floor of the darkened sitting room.

Just for a second he wasn't sure if she was sleepwalking, she looked so disorientated, and then he realised that she couldn't be, unless she'd managed to sleep-dress as well. When he had left her under the duvet, she had definitely been naked.

She came a little further into the room and he heard her say, 'Hi,' and felt her gaze travel swiftly over what he was wearing: jeans, a dark-blue shirt, nothing on his feet. Then he saw her frown.

'Something wrong?' he said.

She shook her head and sat down on the nearest chair and Jack studied her a little longer before turning back to the cooker. He pushed the steaks in the frying pan around with a fork. They spat and fizzled in the oil.

'They're nearly ready. Well, if you like them rare. Do you like yours rare?'

'Rare is fine.'

He turned back to look at her again. 'I bet you thought I ate them raw?' he said, and then laughed.

She just smiled wanly and Jack heard his laugh fade.

He thought about what might be wrong with her and went back to looking at the steaks. He cooked them a little longer and then, turning off the heat, lifted one out of the pan, letting the excess oil drip from it before putting it on a plate waiting on the work surface. He did the same with the other one and then brought them both over to the table.

Ellie wordlessly took the knife and fork he handed her.

Jack sat down and stared at his own steak, sitting in its puddle of pink juices, and was thinking about a suitably bland thing to say when Ellie cut in.

'What time is it?'

'Mr Wolfe?' he said, raising an eyebrow and smiling.

Ellie expression was blank and he swallowed his smile and said, 'About two.'

They sat in silence with the moonlight spilling across them, eating steak while everyone else slept.

Jack watched Ellie eat – decisive cuts and little bites – and he slowed down his own eating to keep pace with her. It took a great effort on his part. He was ravenous, always was after he'd had sex. If she hadn't woken up, he had fully intended to eat both of the steaks.

'Is it how you like it? Not overdone?' he asked, and suddenly wanted to ask her those questions about the sex too.

She nodded, but there was no masking how miserable she seemed, as if he'd disappointed her or hurt her. He grimaced. He'd never had any complaints before. He was sure she had been enjoying herself. He'd been really careful to make sure she was. Perhaps he'd gone too fast, or too far.

Jack put the last piece of his steak into his mouth and laid down his knife and fork. The 'clunk' they made resonated around the kitchen.

'Could I have a drink, please, Jack?' Ellie asked, and he got up and fetched her some water.

When he sat back down, he put his finger out and wiped it through a smear of steak juice left on his plate. Ellie was still frowning, just sitting there sipping her water.

She was obviously having second thoughts about what they'd done. That frown said it all. Well, that might not be so bad; that could work in his favour. If she wanted to forget all about it, that could make it less complicated. He wouldn't have to break it to her gently that it was only a fling, and she wouldn't be tricky with him about it all when she came back from her holiday.

But he was in uncharted waters here: he'd never had to cope with having sex with anyone at work before.

No, that wasn't true. He had in fact had sex at work before: that time in his Manchester office with a soft-drinks client. Bubbly, he remembered, like her products. But sex with a client wasn't the same thing at all.

He checked on Ellie's expression again. Still frowning. Shame she felt like that, though, a big shame.

Jack lifted his finger to his mouth and absentmindedly licked the juice from it. Still, at least Ellie wasn't a blabber; there was no way she would spread this all over the agency; that was Rachel's role in life. So perhaps it was for the best, this misery. They could both remember it as one mad night, a way to clear all the sexual tension that had been fizzing and crackling between them.

Bloody wonderful night, though.

Jack wiped his finger round his plate again. And bloody wonderful body. She definitely wasn't a xylophone girl with the kind of ribs you could feel as you ran your hands over them. No, Ellie was soft and curvy and ... what was the word? Jack lifted his finger to his mouth again. Yielding. Yeah, definitely yielding. And it looked like she didn't have any underwear on under that dress now either. He popped his finger back in his mouth. Probably on to a loser asking her to stay a bit longer when she obviously wanted to get the hell out, but the thought of having her one more time was very, very tempting.

Jack sucked his finger deep into his mouth and then happened to look up. Ellie was watching him. Her eyes, focused on the finger in his mouth, were heavy with a look he recognised.

Lust. The realisation that she was feeling it too stirred his groin back into life, but before he could do anything, she gave a kind of half-gasp, half-sob and turned his guts to water.

'Jack,' she said, 'I'd become so stale, so timid. Thank you.'

He was on her in seconds, lifting her on to the table and ripping her dress from her shoulders. Very soon he had his jeans down and he was inside her, his thighs straining against the table. He heard a clatter and a crash as they knocked a plate on to the floor; he felt the empty condom packet crinkle under his foot. Nothing mattered but getting as far inside Ellie as he could. She was warm and sexy and funny and right at this minute it didn't matter that he should be running like hell in the other direction.

Jack saw her throw her head back, her curls like a mane around her shoulders and the moonlight bathing her in silver. She looked wild and ethereal and he couldn't stop himself. Bending forward slowly, he gave a low growl and bit her very, very softly on her neck.

CHAPTER 24

Jack stood on the pavement outside the agency, watching the traffic go by. A group of girls giggled past him. A young boy ran across the road and tripped on the kerb. Pigeons pecked in the gutter.

He put his hand into his pocket and felt for the slip of paper. Pulling it out, he read the phone number on it and remembered the look on the woman's face when she had handed it to him earlier in the day. Hungry, promising. She was probably sitting in her chambers right now. Perhaps she was even waiting for his call. It was only round the corner; he could be there in no time. Perhaps she'd keep on her wig and wear nothing but her gown and he could chalk up another first: a judge. Or had he already had one of those?

Jack squinted up at the sky and pursed his lips, then rolled the slip of paper into a tight ball and put it back into his pocket.

What was he playing at? He should forget the mad

weekend he'd had with Ellie and ring that judge. It was Monday now and everyone knew mad weekends ended when you dropped the girl back at her house on Sunday night.

It had been a fantastic weekend, though. No, more like mind-blowing. Jack grinned. Really surprising, very energetic, very erotic. Bit of a slow burner, Ellie. From dazed to downright dirty in forty-eight hours.

But it had to be just a weekend nonetheless. Monday was back to work, real life and on to pastures new.

He stood there a bit longer looking at the traffic.

But sometimes people had long weekends, didn't they? Ones that included Monday. He put his hand out abruptly and a taxi veered towards the kerb. He would see if Ellie was in. If she wasn't, he'd ring that judge.

What difference would it make, in the end, if he grabbed one more night? It still gave them both time to calm down before she came back to work.

Jack ignored the very faint sound of an alarm bell in his head and got into the taxi.

Ellie lifted up the carrier bags and negotiated her way through the crates of oranges and onions to get out of the shop. Edith trotted along behind.

'No, I enjoyed it, Edith,' she said, as she gave Mr Arundi from the launderette a wave.

Edith waved at Mr Arundi too and then turned her

attention back to Ellie. 'Even the bit where the vampire impaled the girl with the—'

'Yup, OK, no need to go back over it.'

'Only, even in the dark of the cinema you looked a bit green. I remember your mother didn't like blood and sharp things and—'

'Honestly, Edith, I enjoyed it. Now, do you need any more rice?'

'No, dear, plenty of that, enough to feed an army.'

They continued to chat as they passed the last of the shops and turned round the corner to the house. Ellie let Edith go ahead to open the gate and promised herself that she'd come out later and give the front hedge a bit of a haircut. She was busy thinking about whether Edith might have some shears anywhere and did not notice, until she had bumped into her, that Edith had stopped walking up the path. The word 'sorry' died in her mouth when she saw who Edith was looking at.

Jack was sitting on the doorstep, reading the evening newspaper and eating a bar of chocolate.

'Hello,' he said.

'Hello,' Ellie replied, trying not to grin.

'Been somewhere nice?'

'*Zombie Maidens and the Vampires of Death,*' Edith said.

'A tender portrayal of blood, guts and carnage,' added Ellie.

Jack nodded and folded up his newspaper.

'Have you been waiting long?' Ellie asked.

He didn't answer, simply took a last bite of chocolate and then gathered up his paper and his briefcase and stood up. There was a little hiatus, which Edith ended by saying, 'I was about to make tea, Jack. Would you care to join us?'

Jack made a doubtful face.

'It's one of my proper curries, Jack, made from scratch, all the genuine spices. It'll blow your brains out.'

'Well . . .' Jack said, shoving the chocolate wrapper in his pocket.

'Go on,' Edith said, pushing past him to open the front door, 'and then you and Ellie can go upstairs and discuss those things you advertising people are always discussing.'

'What's that, Edith?' Ellie eyed Jack warily.

Edith hesitated on the threshold as if she had forgotten what she was trying to say. Then her expression brightened. 'Unique selling points, that's it. Yes, you can go and discuss each other's unique selling points.'

Behind her, Ellie heard Jack snigger.

Later that evening Ellie dragged herself up off her bedroom floor and stood with her back to her full-length mirror. She turned her head as far as she could to try to look over her shoulder and down her body.

'Sorry,' Jack said, smiling up at her from the floor, where he lay naked and propped up on one elbow, 'bit over-enthusiastic.'

'That's fine, Jack.' Ellie flinched as she found the carpet burn and touched it delicately with her fingers. 'Not sure if it was the high quality of your technique or the low quality of my carpet.'

'Back to the wisecracking, eh?'

A look passed between them.

'What do you mean?' Ellie said hesitantly.

'You do it a lot. I think I've worked out that it's not you wanting to show off. It's actually some kind of defence mechanism.' He grinned. 'Bit late to try to keep me at arm's length, Ellie.'

Ellie dropped her gaze. 'I'll go and put some cream on this,' she said, and walked quickly from the room so that she didn't have to tell Jack he was a clever swine.

When she came back into the room, Jack was lying down. He seemed distracted and vaguely sad.

Perhaps he regretted coming round? Or found her as dull as Sam had?

'Jack,' she said softly, sitting down on the bed, 'I didn't expect you to come round ... I mean, you shouldn't feel that ...'

Jack didn't appear to be listening and Ellie worried if it was that plate of glass between him and his emotions that was making him appear so distant. Then she saw his eyes clear and he stood up. Here in her room, he looked so tall that it made the ceiling appear too low.

'So, all the rooms up here are yours?' he said. 'No swirly

orange carpet, no china figurines or footstools in the shape of Indian elephants?'

Ellie had seen him survey Edith's sitting room earlier with an amused expression.

'No, Jack, this floor is mine and Edith has very kindly let me decorate it as I please.'

Jack nodded and picked up Ellie's dress from the floor and wrapped it round his waist before going over to the window. Ellie's eyes lingered on the magnificent view he presented, even dressed as he was now, in what looked like a floral miniskirt. Long, long legs, slim hips and broad shoulders. More like a swimmer than a rugby player. She supposed that was what gave him his grace. She wondered if Jack did lots of swimming and then thought about him wet and forgot what they had been talking about.

'Nice view,' he said, bending down to look out of the window.

Ellie had to agree that it certainly was, although she guessed that Jack was actually referring to the garden.

'We eat out in the garden a lot now the weather's better.'

He nodded and, turning away from the window, went over to the door. 'So, what else is up here?' he said.

'I'll show you. Hang on, I'll put on my kimono-ey thing.'

Jack was already out on the landing. 'No, come as you are,' he called back. 'You're not going to be able to improve on that.'

'Is that a compliment?' Ellie felt a blush spread up over

her face; stupid, really, to get embarrassed after what they'd been up to on the carpet. 'Or are you having another go at my dress sense?'

'It's a compliment, Ellie,' Jack said, his voice now coming from her sitting room, 'although since I've seen Edith with her clothes on, I can see where you get your sense of style.'

Ellie grabbed her kimono and tied its belt as she went to follow him. 'Cheeky swine, I've improved a lot recently.'

'Still like you better without anything on, though,' he said, as she joined him.

'Right.' Ellie smiled at him and for a moment he smiled back and then he was off round the room peering at the book titles and picking up the pebbles and shells she had lying around. Ellie decided that he was looking for clues about her, but whether that was a good or bad thing she had no idea.

'So, this living with Edith thing . . .'

'Go on,' said Ellie, folding her arms.

'Don't you have any friends your own age?'

'Yeah, I have plenty of friends my own age, thank you. I didn't do it because I was a Billy no mates. I needed to find somewhere to live quickly after Sam . . . after Sam . . . Anyway, Edith suggested it and it made sense.'

'Why did it make sense?' Jack was staring at her intently again.

She sighed, probably a bit too dramatically, but he was

starting to remind her of how he was at work, always trying to dominate her.

The way he was working to prise out little details about her was becoming disturbing. What would he do with these nuggets of information once they were both back in their normal roles at work? That 'wisecrack' observation had been a little near the bone.

'So,' Jack asked again, 'why did it make sense to move in with Edith?'

'Because I wanted to stay in this area, I like it a lot, and because it meant I could keep an eye on Edith.' She glared at him, defying him to make something of that, and then added, 'Besides, she was spending about three nights a week at my old flat anyway.'

Jack sat down in an armchair. 'And does Edith have any family of her own? I mean sons, daughters?'

'Yes, two daughters, Constance and Pandora. They've got their own families. And, well, she's a bit of a disappointment to her daughters I think. They don't come to see her very often, just Christmas, Easter, her birthday, that kind of thing.'

'Poor Edith.'

'I don't think of her like that. To be honest, she and her daughters don't have much to say to each other when they do meet up. I think they bore her. And I suppose from Constance and Pandora's point of view, she's best kept at a distance. There they are, pillars of their local community, and then Edith totters into view dressed in a leopard-print trouser suit and reeking of gin. It's not the image they're after.'

'Doesn't bother you, though?'

Ellie waved a hand dismissively. 'She's not my mother, it's different. I actually like the fact she's a bit unpredictable. I'm sure she's pushing eighty, you know, though she'd rather tear out her tongue than admit it. Yet she still keeps on going out, having fun, making new friends. I hope I'm like that at her age.'

Jack cast her a look that she couldn't decipher and said nothing. She began to feel uncomfortable, but there was something about the way that Jack was looking at her that made her stay quiet.

'I'm sure that you will be like her,' he said eventually. 'And good luck to Edith – she's got the right attitude.'

'I suppose so, but I do worry that she's doing too much. I'd like her to slow down.'

'It won't matter whether she sits down in her slippers or dances the flamenco,' Jack said very gruffly. 'It won't make a scrap of difference. You don't get extra years added on for good behaviour.'

Again Ellie sensed that Jack was and was not in the room and couldn't understand how the conversation had so quickly become so serious. How had they backed themselves into this particular verbal cul-de-sac after a lighthearted discussion about Edith and her *joie de vivre*? She was going to ask him if there was anything in particular that was wrong, when he said, 'So, you're only living with Edith because it makes sense?'

'Yes.'

He laughed. 'Few things I've noticed about you, Ellie. Good at one-liners; always like to have the last word; dreadful liar.' He leaned forward in the chair. 'In all that about Edith you haven't mentioned being kind. That you're doing it because you're kind.'

'I'm not particularly,' she said, trying to deflect his attention. It all felt so un-Jack-like, somehow.

'Cover it up all you like, Ellie, but you can't fool me. So, the question is, how did you get to be so kind?'

Ellie blinked at him. He somehow made it sound like a fault.

'Good genes, I guess,' she said with a shrug.

He nodded and then her heart did that flip thing because as she watched, his eyes were changing expression again and it was that dark, dangerous look that was holding sway now.

The melancholy that had filled the room earlier had been replaced by something that was making Ellie's heart beat faster.

She saw his gaze travel down her body. 'Your genes haven't only made you kind, have they, Ellie? They've given you all kinds of other lovely things too.'

'Well, I—' she started, but never got to finish, as Jack

was out of the chair and standing right next to her. She could feel his breath on her cheek.

'Take this off,' he said, tugging at her kimono. 'Let's have a good look at how well you did in the gene pool.'

How could he get his emotions to turn round like that? Ellie was still a step behind. But if he was trying to confuse her, she could do the same to him. She looked at him and yawned. 'Sorry, Jack, I don't feel like taking anything off. That interrogation about Edith has quite worn me out.' She dodged away from him and out of the door.

She only got as far as the landing before he caught her and had her down on the floor. Her skin prickled all over as he touched her, but he was going to get a fight. Jack tried to pin her down and she was wriggling ferociously and managed to tug her dress from his hips. He pulled her kimono off one shoulder. She grabbed some of his flesh and pinched it. He didn't even seem to feel it and simply flipped her over on her front and got her other shoulder bare. Ellie reached back and grabbed his thigh and started to squidge her fingers about on it. The effect was instantaneous. 'No, no, no,' Jack shouted, and directed all his attention to stopping her hand from tickling him.

She rolled over, pulled her kimono back together and attacked another part of him, 'Damn it, Ellie, stop it!' he said, trying to catch her hand.

Ellie got two more good attacks in before Jack managed to catch both of her hands and pin them over her head.

A slight readjustment to his position and he was lying on top of her and she couldn't move at all.

They were both out of breath, chests heaving against each other and laughing, and then Jack put his mouth over hers and really took her breath away. It was a long, sensuous kiss that made every nerve-ending right down to her toes sizzle.

He pulled his mouth from hers and gave her a stern look. 'If you promise not to do any more tickling, you can have your hands back.'

Ellie briefly considered that and nodded.

'Promise?' he said.

'Promise.'

Jack let go of her hands and immediately ripped open her kimono and lay on her again, his naked chest against her bare breasts. She felt his hands move down her body and his knee nudge her legs apart.

'Oh, no, not the carpet burns again,' she said in a weak voice.

Jack stopped what he was doing and rolled off her. 'Fair enough. You go on top, then. But you'll have to do all the work. Don't just sit there thinking of England.'

Ellie narrowed her eyes and before he could stop her, she had him in her hand, holding him perhaps more tightly than was absolutely necessary.

'Be very, very careful with that,' Jack said in a strangled voice. 'I use that all the time.'

'Oh, I will, Jack, don't worry,' she said, teasing him and enjoying the way that he had shut up and stopped being so domineering.

'Trouser pocket ... condom,' he said a few moments later in a broken voice.

Ellie found Jack's trousers and then, when she had made him ready, she manoeuvred herself over him, holding herself out of reach.

'You know, you could do with being less bossy,' she said.

'Uh-huh.' Jack took her hips in his hands and tried to pull her down to get some contact, any kind of contact.

'Yes,' she said, resisting his efforts. 'Try negotiating a bit more. Don't be so bullish.'

'I'll try and remember that, Ellie,' he said, his face screwed up with frustration. 'Now, will you stop talking and damn well sit on it?'

She swayed her hips and moved a little lower. 'Would there be a "please" anywhere in that last statement?' She started to laugh and then laughed even louder at the sight of Jack grinding his teeth and glowering at her.

Suddenly she stopped laughing and sat down on him in one quick movement and Jack winced and said, 'Ah,' and then closed his eyes. She felt his strong fingers splayed out around her hips and it seemed to her that this was the only place in the world where any woman with any sense would want to be sitting. The sensation was incredible; she didn't think it was possible to get any closer to him than she was now.

Ellie could not explain how, in less than three days, she had got herself into this, sitting astride Jack Wolfe's groin absolutely naked and not giving a fig about it. She didn't know, but she felt wanton and wanted and right at this minute she wasn't going to think about next week or even tomorrow. She was going to concentrate on showing him what she was made of.

'Right, Jack,' she said, 'I'm thinking of England now.' She gave a little jiggle and was pleased to see his eyes shoot open. 'Yeah, I'm really thinking of England.' She leaned down and kissed him. 'But you know what, Jack? I can only bring to mind the dirty bits.'

Jack walked along the road and kicked a drink can out of the way. It was nearly dawn and there was nobody else about. No damned taxis anyway.

It served him right that he had to walk most of the way home. He must be completely stark, raving mad. That was meant to be a shagging visit. Not a sitting in the garden eating curry visit, or a talking about Edith visit, or even a rolling around on the carpet giggling visit.

He was starting to lose it here.

He dug his hands in his pockets and walked on. And he had carpet burns all over his backside that hurt like hell. Mind you, he'd got them in a good cause ... That was something, the way she'd looked naked and jiggling about. He'd envisaged a quick, hard ride, but she'd kept him just off the boil for ages. He was practically begging her at the end. He'd been on the point of yelling out, 'Barcelona,' himself.

Jack shook his head. It was a good last workout, but that was it. It was over. Finished. *Finito.* If he stopped it now, he could walk away without it bothering him.

He wished he hadn't got bogged down in all that stuff about Edith, though. And then telling Ellie how kind she was ... Mind you, she was, incredibly. Sort of old-fashioned in a way how she cared about Edith. Completely unselfish and—

He came to a halt. What the hell was he talking about? This was exactly why this had to stop.

Tomorrow he'd ring her and explain that he was calling it a day and he expected her to be a grown-up about it when she came back to work.

He had no choice: all the danger signs were there. When you started wanting to find out more about them, that was definitely time to bail out.

Yeah. That was it. Definitely.

CHAPTER 25

Ellie remained in her seat with her eyes closed after the rest of the audience had left. She didn't want to lose this feeling. It had been brilliant from the moment the actors had walked on to the stage until the last one had stepped off again at the end. A magical evening: Regent's Park in summer, the sun going down and a Shakespearian comedy in the open air. It had chased the thought of Jack away for a couple of hours, apart from when the lovers were reunited at the end. Then he'd shot straight back into her mind and she'd found herself wondering what he would look like in a doublet and hose.

When Ellie did get to her feet, she bent down to scoop up her programme from where it had fallen on the ground. She had told herself she was not meant to be thinking about Jack. It had been a fantastic few days, but anybody who thought they were going to get more from Jack than a very good seeing-to was crazed. She guessed the next time she saw him would be at work and they would both have to pretend nothing had happened.

Ellie left the theatre, walking through the groups of people milling about outside. She was glad she hadn't invited anybody else along. Even Jack. Going to the theatre on her own was a great big treat. Sometimes you didn't want to paw over it afterwards, listen to other amateur critics dissecting something you'd loved.

She turned towards Baker Street tube station and found she was thinking about Jack again, wondering what he was up to. Madness. Judging by his non-appearance last night, their liaison had been a three-and-a-half-day wonder. That probably put her just above the legion of women who had enjoyed one-night stands with Jack. She pulled a face at how she had managed to end up joining Jack's army of admirers. Pathetic.

Still, at least she'd gone into it with her eyes open. Jack sleeping with her and then losing interest wasn't like finding out Sam had become bored with her. Jack had merely done exactly what he always did. Ellie rolled her programme up tightly, shoved it in her bag and decided not to let the thought of Jack ruin a lovely evening.

And then there he was walking towards her. Ellie tried not to look surprised, tried to look as though it was a natural place to bump into him. She felt the soppy smile slide on to her face and could not get it off.

'I was just passing,' he said, 'and I remembered you'd

be here tonight. I was basically just driving by.' He fixed her with a look that dared her to point out that Regent's Park was not on his way home unless his satnav was seriously confused.

They stood there as people jostled past them and Ellie wondered what the hell was going on. She was exceptionally pleased to see him, her stomach was churning about already, but what did it mean?

'I was going for the Tube,' she said as casually as she could.

'Well, OK, but I've got my car here, you know, if you want a lift.' He looked away from her while he was speaking, as though it was nothing to him, one way or the other, if she took him up on his offer.

'Well, I could, I suppose,' Ellie's voice said, while her brain shouted, 'Yessss!'

They walked off side by side and Ellie made polite conversation about the play and every now and again Jack asked a question about the actors. Once they were in the car, though, the conversation died and Jack appeared to be getting angrier and angrier about something. He was frowning more than normal.

'I didn't realise the upholstery in here was red the other day,' she said eventually to fill the empty space between them.

'It wasn't. This is a different car. I only got it yesterday.' He shook his head as though he couldn't quite believe that she was so stupid. 'Didn't you notice it's a completely different model? Not to mention colour?'

'Evidently not,' she said softly to the window.

They drove on and her conviction that Jack was fuming about something grew stronger and stronger. Finally she said, 'Jack, have I done something wrong?'

She thought he hadn't heard her, or wasn't going to answer, and then he simply said, 'No. Forget it. I've had a bad day, that's all.'

Ellie turned to look out of the window again. She wasn't going to ask him about work. If she asked him about work, then the knowledge that she had done a foolish thing would come rushing back into her head. While she was on holiday, she could keep that uncomfortable thought at bay. She could view Jack as a bit of an adventure. Work would come hurtling towards her soon enough; she wasn't about to rush and meet it.

Thinking about the play and the warmth of the sun on her skin was the safest thing to do. Then she realised that nothing she was seeing out of the window looked at all familiar.

'This isn't the way home,' she said.

'No.'

'Where are we going, then?'

'I wanted to see what the car could do. It's a nice evening – I thought we'd go for a drive in the country.' He scowled. 'Is that a problem?'

'No, it's fine,' she said gently, to try to disarm his scowl, and then she lowered the window and closed her eyes as the wind blew her hair around.

When Ellie felt the car slow down, she opened her eyes. They were driving down a lane off the main road and after a while it turned into a dry dirt track. And then Jack stopped the car. Ellie thought that they might be visiting someone who lived at the end of the track, but then Jack turned to her and asked, 'Ellie, have you ever had sex in the back seat of a car?'

He was giving her that dark, dangerous look.

'What? You can't mean here? Now?' she squawked at him.

'Yes. Right here, right now.'

'Just like that?' she said, wide-eyed.

Jack nodded and undid his seat belt before reaching round her and undoing hers.

'It's dark out there ... What's the worst that can happen?' he whispered in her ear. 'Some guy walking his dog is going to go home with a smile on his face.' Jack's voice was low and husky, like grey smoke. He had his hand on her seat and she could feel the heat of his skin against her own. 'C'mon, Ellie, look me in the eye and tell me you're not tempted.'

It was pointless trying to lie to him. The thought of having sex with him on his new red leather upholstery out here in the countryside scared her, but the minute he'd said it, she'd felt herself getting aroused. So when she did look him in the eye, she said nothing. He held her gaze and she thought it was one of the sexiest looks anybody had ever given her.

Jack laughed softly and brushed his lips against hers. 'OK, then. You better climb in the back first.' Ellie made a move and Jack shot out an arm. 'Take your knickers off here. There's not much room back there for undressing.'

Panic and excitement roared through her and from the smile on Jack's face Ellie felt that he was somehow pushing her, testing to see how she would react and whether she would keep pace with him.

She lifted up her skirt, hooked her thumbs in the top of her knickers and wriggled until they were down past her thighs. Then she pulled them right down and off. Jack held out his hand and she dropped them into it.

'Wow, Ellie,' he said, 'they're almost on fire. Strange how that could be considering how damp they are.' That glittering look burned into her and Ellie blushed and felt a spasm of lust thread its way right through her belly.

Jack slowly pocketed her knickers. 'Over you go, then, don't dawdle.'

With some difficulty Ellie scrambled into the back seat, her legs wobbling, and soon Jack was on top of her and they were having sex like frenzied teenagers. One of Jack's arms was braced against the headrest of the driver's seat and she couldn't move much, but it felt tight and sweaty and wonderful. They were both noisy and demanding and impatiently grabbed at whatever bits of flesh they could wrench free from clothing. It was over too quickly and it was the naughtiest, filthiest thing Ellie had ever done in her life. She lay under Jack panting and laughing until she got the hiccups.

Later, when they were back in the front seats and Ellie had done up the buttons on her blouse, Jack said, 'See, the sky didn't fall on your head.'

There was something about his tone that annoyed her, something a little too smug, as though he were the teacher and she some inhibited pupil.

It had too many echoes of Sam's 'timid and stale' quote, and she wasn't having it.

'Jack,' she said sweetly, as he put the key in the ignition, 'can I drive home?'

'Very funny, Ellie,' Jack said, and went to turn the key.

'I'm not joking,' she said firmly. 'I'd like to drive home. I've done something I was really quite scared about and now it's your turn.'

There was a look of disbelief on Jack's face. 'You must be joking. I've only had this since yesterday.'

'I want to drive home, Jack,' she said again with more determination.

'No way.' Jack started the car. 'Put your seat belt on.'

'No, I want to drive home.'

'There is no way I am letting you drive my new car.' He

gave a laugh that got Ellie even more annoyed, the kind of laugh that seemed to say, 'Only an idiot would let you drive this car.'

'Why? Are you afraid I'm going to mess it up? You didn't seem to care whether I messed up the back seat.'

'That's different.'

'Ah, I see. So you're the kind of man who doesn't mind having sex with a woman in the back seat of his car but wouldn't let the woman actually drive his car? Interesting. Very enlightened. Perhaps you'd be happier if I got out and walked home? Got any laundry I can do for you when I get there?'

Ellie saw Jack take a deep breath and then turn the engine off. He slammed both his hands on the steering wheel and muttered something and Ellie had to look out of her window to hide her smile.

'OK,' Jack said at last, 'you can drive home, but if you scratch her, if you dent her, I will personally take both your—'

'I get the picture,' Ellie said, and was out of her seat and racing round to the driver's side in an instant.

Jack unfolded himself from the car and walked round to the passenger door as if his feet were made of lead. Ellie saw him run his hand sadly over the bonnet as he passed.

'Right, she's very responsive,' Jack said when they were ready to set off. 'Be gentle.'

Ellie didn't move and after a while Jack said, 'Well, come on, let's get it over with. Start her up.'

'I can't. I never learned to drive.' Ellie started to giggle. 'I just wanted to see if you would let me, that's all.'

Jack's face was impassive, although Ellie thought she saw his mouth twitch at one point. Then she definitely saw him narrow his eyes and it made her stop giggling.

'Ellie,' he said in a silken tone she hadn't heard before, 'have you ever made love in the open air up against a tree?'

Jack dropped Ellie off and watched her go into the house, thinking how dishevelled and downright gorgeous she looked. That was most definitely it now. The final fling. Well, two flings. His suit had grass stains on it, or whatever it was that grew on the bark of trees, and his thighs ached like hell. Then he thought of Ellie pulling that stunt about driving home and laughed out loud. She'd wrapped him right round her little finger, really had him on the back foot, making him out to be some kind of Neanderthal.

Which was another reason to get the hell out. She was getting inside his head. If he called an end to it now, they both still had over a week to let it all die down.

She was bloody gorgeous, though, and when she'd hitched up her skirt and taken her knickers off . . . Jack turned the engine off and slid down slightly in his seat and closed his eyes. She's been scared and she'd still done it; he'd felt her trembling underneath him. That almost sent him over the edge before he'd even got inside her.

Yeah, our Ellie had layers and layers waiting to be unpeeled. Feistiness, then vulnerability, then ... Jack opened his eyes and sat back up abruptly. Well, those layers were going to have to be unwrapped by somebody else. Tonight was a bad idea and now that was most definitely it.

He'd stop it right now and then Ellie wouldn't get the wrong idea, try to make it into some kind of relationship. And he could get back to thinking about her as one of his copywriters. Tomorrow evening he was busy with a client meeting and then he'd probably give that judge a ring. He was sure he still had her number on that screwed-up piece of paper in his suit. She had nice eyes and she was definitely up for it. It was exactly what he needed: a no-strings-attached encounter. No danger of getting his emotions tangled up.

Jack tried to imagine the judge naked but couldn't quite conjure her up, and then suddenly someone rapped on the car window and he jumped in his seat and nearly choked himself with the seat belt. It was Ellie. Hell, what did she want now? Jack wound the window down.

'Please, sir,' she said, and gave him a sexy smile that kicked in near his stomach, 'can I have my knickers back?'

CHAPTER 26

Ellie watched the river flowing past and sipped her wine. It was so cold it was giving her a headache. Or perhaps the real reason for her headache was currently sprawled out asleep on the sofa. Ellie turned to look at Jack lying under a black throw and then decided she'd better not. She turned her attention back to the river, but Jack's slow, steady breathing invaded her thoughts and she found herself sitting on the arm of the sofa looking down at him.

Without those grey eyes boring into her, it was possible to make a frank assessment of him. Really, that nose was too big and sharp, and his lips were a little too narrow. But they were beautifully effective lips; if Ellie concentrated, she could still feel them moving, slow and hot, down her belly. And those eyelashes ... she'd had to fork out £12.68 in Boots to buy a pair like that.

Ellie reached forward and gently sorted out the little peaks and ruffles in his hair.

Sitting here looking at Jack was a bad idea. An extremely

308

bad idea. Ellie stood up and went around the room picking up bits of her clothing. Hard to believe it was only a week since she'd been here the first time, ringing the bell and waiting for him to open the door. And then getting beautifully ground into the carpet under him.

Ellie remembered how nervous she had been. Now she was still nervous but for entirely different reasons. She was thinking about him all the time, forgetting that he was, at the end of the day, her boss. She was turning a blind eye to his 'slash and burn' approach to women. Yesterday he had done his disappearing act again, but today, one call from him late into the evening, an invitation to 'come round', and she'd been in a taxi like a shot. How stupid.

And when she'd arrived, he had barely spoken to her except for a few gruff commands. Although he had made up for it during the sex bit. Well, more than made up for it. Ellie let a little giggle escape, remembering the way Jack had hit his head on the overhead light fitting.

But really, it was no laughing matter.

She wandered over to have another look at him and knew that she was immeasurably glad that there was a face like that in the world.

Then she tut-tutted at her own romantic stupidity.

She took herself off to the bedroom, got dressed and let herself out of the flat.

But she might as well still have been in his flat looking

down at him rather than sitting on the Tube wishing that she was.

Saturday night and Ellie had a couple of failed attempts to get the key in the front door before she managed it. That last round of flaming sambucas had been a mistake. Whose idea had it been? Liz's? Caroline's? Julia's? Then Ellie remembered. It had been hers.

Still, good night out. Nice to catch up on the gossip, although they could have probably done without Liz's rant about her boyfriend. They'd heard it all before. Liz told them what an inconsiderate turnip he was, they agreed, and then next time they saw her, she was still with him. It was like a loop she couldn't get out of.

Ellie had thought about dropping in something about Jack a couple of times to distract Liz, but decided against it. Everyone would ask her what was going on and she had no answer to that.

Ellie tiptoed along the hallway, bumping gently against the walls and trying not to look at the swirly wallpaper. For once, she wanted to get upstairs without seeing Edith. Plain walls and a soft bed were what she needed, and perhaps a couple of paracetamol and a pint of water. Or a stomach pump.

Ellie could hear voices coming from Edith's sitting room. That settled it. She definitely couldn't face making polite chit-chat.

She concentrated very hard on how she was going to climb the stairs, but before she had even got past the sitting room door, she heard Edith call out, 'Ellie darling, is that you? How was your girls' night out?'

Ellie hesitated and then turned round and pushed open the door to the room. 'It was good, Edith, very enjoyable. Liz went on a bit, but I think—'

Ellie figured she must be absolutely paralytic because Jack appeared to be sitting down next to Edith playing Scrabble. He had a look of deep concentration on his face and was rubbing his bottom lip slowly with his thumb.

'Hello,' he said without looking up. He was wearing jeans and that dark-blue shirt again that made him look about ten years younger than he did at work. Flip-flap went Ellie's stomach, and she fully expected to see the flaming sambucas again.

'Come on now, Big Jack,' Edith said, 'you've got to put something down soon or you'll have to miss a go . . . and can I remind you that I only have four letters left and I can see a place where I can make a really good word.'

'Not so fast, Edith,' Jack said, taking a sip from his drink.

Ellie could see, even from where she was standing, that the words on the Scrabble board were so filthy that it should have been placed immediately in a sealed container and buried at sea. All at once she felt very, very sober.

'Edith,' she said, 'some of these words are terrible. Truly awful.'

'Well, they're not all mine. That one and that one, oh, and particularly that one are Jack's.' Edith tapped Jack on the arm playfully. 'He has quite a wide vocabulary, hasn't he?'

Ellie sat down, unsure whether she felt more perturbed by the sight of Jack or by Edith's flirting. Before she could decide, Jack leaned forward and put all his letters down on the board one by one. Edith let out a little 'Oh' noise and went quite pale and Ellie looked at the word Jack had made and was sure she had turned scarlet.

Jack grinned. 'There you go, Edith, an eight-letter word on a triple-word score. That's a hundred and twenty, plus an extra fifty points for using up all my letters.' Jack reached for the score-pad. 'So, let's see . . . You got two hundred and one, minus the letters you still have . . . plus the one you've got hidden up your sleeve.' He gave her arm a little shake and a 'Q' fell out on to the floor. 'Which gives you a total of a hundred and eighty-five and I have three hundred and forty. Sorry, Edith, you're stuffed.' Jack put down the pad and pen, drained his drink and then got to his feet.

Ellie saw that Edith was sucking her teeth. She hoped she wouldn't do that thing where she actually took them out to do it.

'Well played, Jack,' Edith said finally. 'I bow to your superior skill.'

Jack gave her a half-bow back. 'Right, then,' he said, clapping his hands together, 'time for bed,' and he lifted

Ellie on to her feet and pulled her behind him out into the hall.

Ellie wanted to ask him what he was playing at, besides Scrabble, but he dragged her towards the stairs and pushed her up them ahead of him. He was humming to himself and then he started to sing, patting her on the bottom in time to the song: 'Ellie, Ellie, show us your belly.'

Ellie stopped and turned. 'Jack, how many of Edith's gin and tonics have you had?'

He smiled up at her, his eyes sparkling. 'I have had four.'

'Oh dear. That means you've had one gin and tonic and three neat gins. Edith's measures are a bit haphazard.'

Jack came up a step so his mouth was level with hers. 'Don't worry.' He lowered his voice to a whisper. 'It will have absolutely no effect on my ability to pleasure you repeatedly until morning.'

Ellie still had her mouth open when he lifted her up and put her over his shoulder. 'No, Jack,' she shouted, 'I'll be sick. I'm full of pizza and wine and sambucas.'

'Shut up, wench,' Jack said, stumbling slightly on the top stair before heading for the bedroom. 'You're going to be full of something a lot bigger in a minute.'

When Ellie woke up, Jack had gone and there was no sign that he had ever been there at all. She struggled up from the floor and wondered what Jack had against using a bed.

She got herself under her duvet and lay there for a while thinking about him. Since that first weekend he'd sought her out nearly every day. What did that mean? That he liked her? That he liked having sex with her? Both? She turned over and pulled the duvet right up around her neck. What would Rachel do in this situation, besides put up a billboard announcing the news? She'd lie back and enjoy it, of course, and not read too much into it. Just go with it and not look to the future. That's what any savvy woman would do.

She turned over again and wriggled about until she was comfortable, ignoring how the muscles all the way up the insides of her legs hurt. The important thing was not to look too far ahead. Not to make plans, any plans that involved Jack. Yes, she had to remember that. Really.

Ellie went out to the cinema with an old school friend that evening and came home and wandered around downstairs for a bit, rearranging things that didn't need rearranging. In the end Edith told her to sit down and watch some television, but Ellie only managed a few minutes before she was up on her feet again. She checked the answerphone and then decided to sort out her handbag and have a look at her mobile. Then she wandered off into the garden and rushed back in at one point because she thought she had heard the front doorbell ring.

'I think you need to calm down,' Edith said, looking a little weary.

Ellie took herself off to bed and tried to guess what Jack was doing now, and even while she was wondering, she knew it was madness. He was probably out having a good time. Or even worse, staying in and having a good time.

That he didn't need her tonight was obvious.

The thought of that made her curl up into a tight ball under her duvet and force herself to think about what would happen when she went back to work. Was she really the kind of woman who could sit opposite Jack in a meeting and forget all the times they had made love?

She sat up abruptly. Made love? Made love? How had it gone from 'having sex' to 'making love'?

She hurtled out of bed and started sifting through the piles of paper on her desk until she found the latest copy of *Ad Infinitum*. Then she took it back to bed with her and looked again at the job adverts she had previously circled in red.

CHAPTER 27

Letting Edith go into the Hampton Court maze on her own had probably been a bit of a mistake. She had been gone twenty minutes already. If she didn't come out soon, Ellie was going to have to go in after her.

Ellie wandered about a little longer, trying not to keep checking her watch. Honestly, this must be what it was like when your kids were late home.

It had seemed natural to come here today when she needed distracting. If she couldn't forget about Jack here, she wasn't going to do it anywhere. This had always been one of her favourite places, the Tudor bit of it especially. Maybe it wasn't as elegant as the later bits closer to the river, but that red brick, the massive gateway and the secret, cobbled courtyards all cast their magic over her.

She didn't need to close her eyes to imagine Henry VIII and his court living here; she could still feel them, almost see them.

There was Henry beating everyone at tennis, his white

shirt sticking to his skin; here was Anne Boleyn, her hand tracing the wood panelling as she walked and casting a look over her shoulder at some man she had bewitched. But the one she could see most clearly was poor Catherine Howard. The story went that Henry had been told of her infidelity in a note he had been given at chapel. Whenever Ellie visited that part of the palace, she imagined Catherine screaming and being hauled away by the guards as she tried to reach Henry to somehow convince him she was innocent.

Among all this grandeur, all this history, it still came down to sex and betrayal.

Ellie gravitated back to the entrance of the maze, moving into the shade to stop the back of her neck from burning in the sun, and then spotted a couple whom she recognised as having gone into the maze slightly before Edith. 'Sorry to disturb you,' she shouted, 'you didn't by any chance notice an old lady in there who might have got a bit disorientated?'

'Wearing bright-red Crocs?' said the man.

Ellie nodded. They were Edith's latest acquisition and she teamed them with everything.

'She was sitting on the seat right in the middle when we last saw her,' said the woman. 'She was talking to some French students about India. She seemed perfectly happy.'

Ellie thanked them and rushed off, hoping that she would be in time to stop the French students from dying of confusion. She had not got very far when Edith appeared, surrounded by a group of young men chatting animatedly.

'Ah, here is my great-niece now, the one I told you about, the one with the singing knickers.' The men turned to look at Ellie as though they actually expected her underwear to burst into song. Perhaps something had got lost in Edith's translation.

'*Bonjour*,' Ellie said, and gave a little wave.

'We have been discussing the similarities between the role of the British in India and the role of the French in Indo-China. Quite, quite fascinating,' Edith explained.

The students nodded enthusiastically.

'But now I must go, my dear friends. It has been an absolute pleasure. Thank you for helping me find my way out of the maze. Really, it's a wonder I ever found my way back from India.'

There was much laughter and then Edith and the students exchanged kisses and hugs and they all gave Ellie a kiss on both cheeks too.

Edith and Ellie watched them wander off, a little group of bright T-shirts and jeans and olive skins.

Ellie put her arm round Edith. 'You know, you keep right on surprising me.'

'Thank you, dear,' Edith said, reaching up and patting Ellie's hand. 'Is that when you're not surprising yourself?'

'Me? Surprising myself?' Then the penny dropped. 'Ah, with Jack, you mean,' she mumbled.

'Yes, with Jack.' Edith prodded at the dusty path with one foot. 'I seem to recall somebody telling me that although she found him attractive, nothing was going to happen. Judging by the noises that were coming from your flat last week, a lot seems to have been happening.'

'Well . . .'

'He's very different from Sam, isn't he? Are you glad you weren't too scared to leap into that particular pool?'

They walked on. Ellie didn't want to talk about Jack and she certainly didn't want to think about all the ways in which he was different from Sam. She had only seen him once more since that night she'd discovered him playing Scrabble with Edith. He had arrived on the doorstep, been monumentally taciturn – except when they were actually entwined round each other on the floor, when he had been very vocal indeed – and then stomped off into the night. Tomorrow, she knew, he was flying out to New York.

Filling her days with retail therapy and trips out with Edith had not stopped her wondering what he was up to and whether he had now lost interest in her.

It worried her that he was still rampaging around in her head. She had kind of imagined that when she got to know him better, she would like him less.

Ellie tried to distract Edith with a visit to the kitchens, set out as they would have been at the time of a Tudor banquet. They marvelled at the sheer quantity of food needed and agreed that it would have been hell to work in this part of the palace. They chewed over what peacock would have tasted like. And then all their energy left them and they were filled with the desire to sit down and eat something processed and modern.

'Sam was very much what I call a boy-man,' said Edith mid-sandwich, as though there had not been any delay in the conversation since her last utterance about him.

'A *boy-man*?'

'Yes. It's not a criticism. He was grown-up, but still a bit boyish, you know. Whereas Jack, well . . . Jack's lived. He's a man, isn't he? You won't catch him lighting his farts.'

'I don't recall Sam doing that, Edith.' Ellie stirred her coffee a bit too vigorously and watched it slop over the side of the cup.

'Don't get cross, dear. It was a theoretical example, not an actual one. All I'm saying is that Jack is a man and, well, now I know him, I can see there are depths there. Quite substantial depths, I'd say.'

Ellie took a large bite from her sandwich and was happy it gave her an excuse not to answer.

She tried to avoid Edith's gaze, which was, for somebody her age, extremely penetrating, but Edith took her by the hand. 'All I'm saying, dear, is that you have really only ever been with Sam. You're not very experienced with men. You need to be careful with Jack. Don't expect too much. Just try to treat it as fun.'

Ellie didn't respond with anything more than a weak smile. It was painful to hear somebody else voice what she already knew about Jack. She realised that up until that moment she had been holding out some feeble hope that maybe, maybe she might mean something more to him than the rest of his harem.

And that, as even Edith knew, was foolish.

She had, indeed, become like all the others, doing the very thing of which she had accused them: hoping that she was the one who could burrow under all that stone and find a soft centre. All those brooding silences, that unpredictable temper, it was almost as if Jack had followed some guide to being the classic tortured hero.

Whereas Ellie had evidently ingested a study of romantic self-delusion.

Unfortunately, knowing all this didn't make it any easier to be living through it. Ellie felt tears threatening to come and so made an excuse about getting some more milk and went off and took a long time to fetch it. When she got back to the table, Edith was busy studying her guide-book and for the rest of the visit they kept to the safer topic of Henry VIII beheading his wives.

CHAPTER 28

By the time they were finished with Hampton Court, Ellie decided that there was no way that Edith could handle the journey back on public transport, so she found them a taxi and they sat in comfort all the way back to the house. Ellie had kept half an eye on the huge fare they were racking up and then decided life was too short to worry. The early-evening sun was infusing even the shabbiest bits of the route with a warm golden glow. It seemed as if all of London were sitting out on a pavement with a drink in its hand. Edith were singing gently and every now and again waving at people.

It might as well have been raining as far as Ellie was concerned. Jack had wormed his way into her heart and now all she had to look forward to was the humiliation of rejection and the hassle of finding a new job.

Oh, plus a few weeks of pretending absolutely nothing had happened between them and knowing another woman would be kissing those lips and messing up his hair.

She was going to be hopeless at pretending nothing had happened, she just knew it.

Ellie thought about Jack's habit of putting his head down slightly when he came into her office and it made her stomach twist and turn. She remembered his arm braced against the headrest when they had made love in his car and the way he had of putting his jacket on and then shrugging his shoulders. Little details she was stuck with now for the rest of her life.

She closed her eyes and rested her forehead against the window and tried very hard not to cry.

When they arrived back home, Ellie helped Edith from the taxi and was handing the driver the contents of her purse when she heard Edith talking to somebody in the front garden. Her heart leaped and she almost ran through the garden gate to see if it was who she hoped it was.

'Been somewhere exciting?' she was in time to hear Jack ask. All of Ellie's gloom melted away and she was standing in a sun-dappled street in London, with endless possibilities of happiness spreading out before her.

He was sitting on the step, and if Edith had not been there, Ellie would have got down beside him and put her arms round him. She smiled down at him, knowing that what she felt at seeing him must be obvious.

Except Jack wasn't even looking at her.

'We've been to Hampton Court,' Edith said.

Jack hauled himself to his feet, looking hot and cross. He had a crumpled carrier bag in his hand.

'It's wonderful, Jack. They've made it so interesting,' Edith went on, looking uneasily from Jack to Ellie. 'It's changed such a lot since I was there last.'

Ellie took a step forward, desperate for Jack's attention. 'No wonder it's changed, Edith. When you were last there, Anne Boleyn was still making eyes at Henry.'

Jack gave her a withering glance as though he were personally offended by that joke.

Edith mouthed, 'Oh dear,' at Ellie behind Jack's back and started to fuss around opening the front door. Ellie tried again to smile at Jack, but he turned away from her.

She scrutinised the expanse of charcoal suit in front of her, taking in how well it fitted him and how it accentuated the breadth of his shoulders. Well, she had a full understanding of what lay beneath that suit now, but was none the wiser about what was going on in his brain.

'Are you both going to stay in the front garden or come in?' Edith was holding the door open.

Jack went into the house and Ellie followed, feeling dizzy because she couldn't take a full breath. When Edith wandered off to the kitchen, leaving Jack and Ellie standing very close to each other in the hallway, Ellie automatically looked down at the carpet.

'You're doing that carpet-staring thing again,' Jack said.

'Sorry.'

He coughed. 'This is for you.' He pushed the carrier bag at her and walked off to the kitchen.

She heard him asking Edith how she was, how the Scrabble was going, what she was having for her tea. He sounded amicable, relaxed.

Ellie opened the bag and looked inside. It was her dress, the one she had been wearing that first evening in Jack's flat. She felt unable to think. It couldn't be that dress: it had been ripped so badly across the front that she had thrown it out.

Jack was back. 'It's the same size as the last one, I think.' He stood watching her and then strode back into the kitchen. A warm feeling welled up in Ellie's chest. He had bought her a new dress. Did that mean something? Surely that meant something?

He was back again. 'Well?' was all he said.

At that moment she needed to feel his skin against hers so much that she reached out her hand and ran it tenderly down his face. Immediately his eyes looked hard and he jerked his head away. This time when he returned to the kitchen, you could see how angry he was with every step.

Ellie felt as though he had punched and winded her. She waited to see if he was going to come back and then went upstairs and hung the dress in her wardrobe. What had just happened? She caught sight of herself in the wardrobe mirror: hair awry, eyes huge and worried-looking. This was what he was doing to her.

When she came back downstairs, Jack was sitting in the garden with Edith, drinking a beer.

This was worse than him never coming back at all.

She placed both of her hands on the work surface and pressed down, expecting the tears that had been threatening all day to fall, but there was anger instead, rolling and turning inside her. What had she done to be treated like this? Why give her something with such bad grace and then look as though her very touch was repugnant? All she had ever done with him was be herself and it obviously wasn't bloody good enough.

She set about cooking the salmon, dividing the two large pieces so that they would now feed three, and steaming the vegetables. Every now and again she moved to the window to watch Jack chatting to Edith. He was laughing at something she had said and Ellie felt betrayed. It was ridiculous, she was jealous of her great-aunt.

When they sat down to eat, Ellie gave it one last go and tried to ask Jack how he had been. He glowered at her as if she had asked him if he'd ever had piles. After that she gave up, and if it had not been for the fear of upsetting Edith, she would have picked up her plate and launched it at him. As it was, she left it to Edith to try to string together some kind of conversation. By the time they had finished the strawberries and cream, it was obvious that even Edith was struggling. She got up slowly and Jack stood up too.

'Ah, dear boy,' Edith said, patting his chest, 'such lovely manners.'

Ellie couldn't help giving a little snort and Edith speeded up her exit, pleading some prior social event at the pub that was news to Ellie and probably to the pub as well.

When she had gone, they sat with the dirty plates in front of them. The air was heavy with the smell of the honeysuckle on next door's fence, and a bee was fussing around the flowers. It would have been lovely if all Ellie's nerve endings did not feel as if they had been rubbed up the wrong way. She was so sick of this grumpy wall of testosterone. If Jack wanted to tell her it had all been a horrendous mistake, why didn't he do it? Why string out the torture?

'I think you had better go, Jack,' she said, even though every part of her was screaming out for him to stay.

'I don't want to go,' he shot back.

'Well, you could have fooled me.'

'Why? Why could I have fooled you?'

'Because you're acting like a bad-tempered jerk again.'

'I gave you a new dress.'

'You can have it back.'

Jack looked exasperated. 'That's pretty ungrateful.'

'I'd like you to go now, Jack,' she said, standing up. 'I'll go and get the dress. You can take it away with you.' She paused, trying to hang on to her anger, which seemed to be disappearing with every word. 'I don't want you here again. It's too . . . too unsettling. You'll still be in New York when I get back to work, won't you?' She saw Jack nod. 'Well, that will give me a few days to get back to normal. Get sorted. We'll never mention this again, Jack.'

She left the garden and went upstairs. It had been a good parting speech, except that she hadn't meant a word of it and now she was really struggling not to bawl her eyes out.

How dull was life going to be from now on without that body to hold? Without that complicated, taciturn, reckless man down there wanting her.

She took the dress from its hanger and shoved it back in the carrier bag. Why did he have to come round at all? Why did he have to keep reminding her how gorgeous he was, how he made her want to hold him and care for him?

Ellie took a deep breath and, turning to leave the room, walked straight into Jack. She stepped backwards and he caught her by the arm, ripped the carrier bag out of her hand and pulled her into him. Then he was kissing her hungrily and she could not help responding. The parts of her not preoccupied with feeling and touching and yielding sneered at how easily she had caved in again. But soon she was down on the floor with him and then wrapped around him as he hammered into her as though it was some kind of cure for his bad mood.

She lay there on the floor afterwards in a patch of sunlight, staring up at the open window. Way off in a garden somewhere, children were giggling and shouting. Normal life was going on all around, but she didn't know what it meant any more.

Was it normal to be lying on the floor with a man who obviously didn't want to be here? With someone who seemed to be blaming her for something?

It would be so much easier if he told her what he expected of her.

She turned her head to look at him and saw that he had his eyes screwed up tightly as if he were in pain.

'Are you going to tell me what's going on, Jack, or is this how you normally conduct your relationships?'

The speed with which he got to his feet surprised her. 'Relationship?' he said with a deeply sour expression. 'Oh, it's a bloody relationship now, is it?'

That felt like another punch.

'Tell me what's wrong, Jack. Please.'

She heard him sit on the bed.

'It's nothing,' he said. 'Leave it. I'm a bad-tempered swine sometimes.'

Ellie shook her head. 'No, that's not good enough. You weren't bad-tempered with Edith. You were all smiles and laughter with her. It's me you have a problem with. Even when I made that joke about Anne Boleyn you acted as if you wanted to rip my head off.'

'I said leave it, Ellie.' His tone was sharp and he got off the bed and started to pick up his clothes. Ellie went back to staring out of the window, and when she looked at him again, he was getting dressed.

'I can't leave it, Jack,' she said. 'When I think I've made some headway with you, when I think there's something real under all this sex, you treat me like some kind of irritant.'

Jack went on knotting his tie, checking the ends of it were the right length as if that were the most natural thing to do when a naked woman was asking him to tell her what was going on in his brain.

Ellie did the only thing she knew would get a reaction from Jack.

'Been anywhere nice recently?' she said with a cheesy, earnest expression.

He didn't disappoint her. His head shot up and he said tersely, 'What is this, "get-to-know-Jack night"?'

'No, only the normal kind of conversation that normal people have. Remember, you asked us earlier where we'd been today and now I'm asking you if you've been anywhere nice recently. Of course, because you've got some deep psychological problem with me, it's bugged the hell out of you, but hey, at least you're talking.'

She saw his shoulders rise and fall as if he were sighing, but he did answer her: 'All right, I had a quick trip to see my parents, just overnight.'

'Lovely. And where do they live?'

'In a house,' he snapped.

That was it. Ellie stood up, ignoring the way he was glowering at her from under his brows. She'd tried; she'd really tried to find out what was wrong and to make things better. How dare he come round here and treat her like a piece of meat. And how dare she let him. It was like he was only nice to her when he wanted to have sex. No, when he was having sex.

'Tell you what, Jack,' she said softly, 'why don't you simply pay me for sex? Why don't we start being honest? You come round, pay me, we'll have sex, and then you won't have to do all that messy pretending that you think I'm a person worthy of your conversation. Even better, we'll have sex first and you only pay me if you think I was good enough.'

Jack continued to keep his head down. No reaction at all. The tension between them was like some ugly, un-invited guest in the room.

Ellie bent down and gathered up her discarded clothes and then walked out of the room and went and locked herself in the bathroom to dress. Her limbs felt like they were someone else's and she had to force them into her clothes. She turned on the cold tap, putting her wrist into the water and waiting for it to cool her down.

The cure for being obsessed with someone was easy. You got to know them well and then the mystery went. But what if the person you wanted to get over didn't want to tell you anything? What if they insisted on remaining a mystery? Managed to keep you hanging on with a perfect balance of disinterest and passion?

She turned the water off and heard a knock on the bathroom door.

'Go away, Jack,' she called, and started to clean her teeth. When she turned the water off this time, she heard him say something. 'What?'

'Scarsdove,' he said through the door. 'My parents live in a place called Scarsdove. It's a market town between Leeds and Halifax.'

Ellie put her toothbrush back in the cup and kept silent.

Jack's muffled voice came through the door again. 'My sisters, all my family, they still live around that area.'

Ellie pressed her lips together.

'Ellie, are you still in there? Ellie?'

'What?'

'Oh, I see. You're not talking because you're sulking again. Well, I didn't have you down as a sulker.'

Ellie knew she was being played, but she couldn't stop herself from answering back. 'Really, that surprises me. Didn't you tell Rachel I liked a good old sulk? Anyway, you've got a nerve. The man who looks as though he could sulk for Britain. Mr Granite-Faced Yorkshire Bastard himself.'

Ellie heard Jack laugh and it did that thing to her stomach that it always did, even through a door.

'How many sisters?' she asked.

'Two. Older. They're called Grace and Louise.'

'I have three brothers. I mean they're great, but a sister would have been wonderful.'

Nasty then nice, she knew that it was happening again, but the fact that he was actually confiding in her made her grin like an idiot.

Ellie heard Jack move, and the next time he spoke, it sounded like he was sitting down. Ellie sat down too.

'Older or younger, your brothers?' he said.

'All older.'

'Right.'

Ellie put her fingertips to the door as if she could feel Jack's heat through it. 'They must have spoiled you, your sisters, what with you being the baby and the only boy.'

'A bit. When they weren't getting me to run errands for them or teasing me, yes, I suppose they did.'

Ellie leaned her head against the door and imagined Jack as a little boy. She wondered what he had looked like before he grew into his nose.

'So you weren't brought up by wolves?'

There was another laugh. 'Sorry to disappoint you.'

'Wish my brothers had spoiled me. They always used to put me in goal or make me wicketkeeper. Or get me to keep an eye out whenever they were doing anything bad. And I was always the one they pushed forward to take all the flak. They said I could get away with more, talk my way out of it.' Ellie put her cheek against the wood. 'Must be nice going back to the family home, going back to Yorkshire. We sold the house we grew up in when Mum and Dad died.'

There was a pause and she heard Jack move.

'Both your parents are dead?'

'Yes. Dad had heart problems for years, so, well, we were expecting it, but Mum got ill not long after he died. I think she'd been ignoring all the signs, concentrating on Dad. She died within a year of him.' Ellie felt tears come into her eyes and that horrible lumpy feeling in her throat.

She'd had years to get used to her mum and dad no longer being around and now she had to cry in front of Jack. She was always crying in front of Jack. She didn't know whether it was because he made her feel vulnerable or because she wanted him to comfort her.

She waited for Jack to say something gruff, something that would get her back to her original anger. She needed to start disliking him enough to see that this was going nowhere. He'd be nasty again in a minute and then ignore her for days, and God knew how he would treat her back at work. She had to start putting all this behind her.

'Open the damn door, Ellie,' Jack said. 'You shouldn't be alone and talking about this. You should have somebody holding you. Don't stay in there being sad.'

Ellie stood up quickly, slid back the bolt on the door and Jack came in and without a word wrapped his arms round her. Ellie disgraced herself totally by blubbing all over his shirt. When she looked up into his eyes, his expression was so kind that she felt she would tell him anything if he would only ask her.

Jack let her cry for a while and then led her by the hand back to the bedroom and sat her on the bed and began kissing her gently, starting with her mouth and telling her how beautiful it was. Every part of her body he kissed and told her why he particularly liked it. He started to undress her, gently, slowly, kissing every inch of her that he uncovered and she lay back on the bed and let him. It felt like being bathed in warm honey, and every now and then he would move back to her face and look into her eyes and murmur how much she turned him on, how he couldn't get enough of her, how she made him want to hold and protect her. It made Ellie ache, but she could not have said where the ache was centred; it was simply a longing for him and for this moment to continue indefinitely.

When she was completely naked, Ellie helped him undress and, as she did, she knew she had to tell him how she felt. It all came tumbling out – how she had fought the feelings she had for him, how he made her feel so sensual and wanted. And then, before she could bite it back, how she suspected that she was falling deeply in love with him.

When he finally took her, it was slow and tender and in bed. Not on the floor or spread across a chair or on a table, but deep down in the bed with her hair tangling on the pillow.

Afterwards Ellie sat up to look at Jack and knew she was completely lost. It had been like falling into quicksand; she had fought and fought to get out, but in the end she had been sucked down into him.

She'd said things to him that she couldn't take back now. She didn't know what would happen when they were back at work together, but it didn't matter. She would cope; they would cope. She loved him. And what she saw in his eyes told her that he felt the same way. She might not know much about men, but she knew the difference between lust and love, and that was a loving look.

She lay back down and felt his arm round her, protective and strong.

Jack lay with his arm round Ellie and knew he was in deep, deep trouble. She loved him and he was damn sure he loved her because it felt like the last time he'd been in love. He thought all the way around that and tried to swallow down the panic that was winding up from his stomach.

This had all been inevitable somehow; there was nothing to be gained from beating himself up about it. Ever since that presentation when that swine Hetherington had savaged her. That's when it had started. That had made him feel like looking after her and opened the door to all those other feelings. When he should have been retreating, he'd advanced.

She was exactly the kind of woman he'd done his best to avoid all this time. She was his 'sort': feisty, bright, funny and with a direct link to his libido. It was like she'd tied a string round him and could drag him away from wherever he was in London to bury himself in her.

He hadn't even meant to come here tonight. How many times had he said that to himself over the last two weeks? Where she was concerned, it hadn't worked. And this evening had been a nightmare. He'd come all prepared with his speech about it being great but being over, how they had to be adult about this, blah, blah, blah, and she'd wrong-footed him at every turn. Everything she'd done had cranked him up another gear. Jack closed his eyes. Why did her parents have to be dead? That did it. Lost.

His innards squirmed as he went back over all the loving things he'd said to her. How much worse was that going to make what he was going to do to her next?

There was no getting away from it; the whole thing was a great big mess. A mess he needed to sort out quickly.

He opened his eyes again and thought with anguish of that look she'd given him just now. It had been pulled right up from her heart. And why had he said all that stuff about wanting to protect her? The very thing he was unable to do.

But it didn't matter. He was going to run. Let her think

it was because he couldn't handle a relationship with someone he worked with.

She need never know he couldn't handle a relationship full stop.

Jack lay there a bit longer, relishing the way Ellie's leg was lying between his own and the feel of her hand cupped on his neck.

He should really tell her to her face that it was over, but there was no way he could do that. He'd be down on the floor with her five minutes later and back to square one. Keeping on confusing her was a bastard's trick anyway.

He felt Ellie's other hand move lazily on to his stomach and then relax, and suddenly, appallingly, he was crying. He blinked furiously and got himself back under control.

Well, her being lovely and loving didn't count for anything in the long run. In fact it made it worse.

He wasn't leaving himself open to all that crap again. To all that pain.

The Sophies and Leonoras of this world were the ones he should be concentrating on. Shallow, self-obsessed, put-downable, safe.

Jack ran his hand over Ellie's hair and heard her sigh. He bent his head to kiss her and said softly, 'Ellie my darling, I am so, so sorry.'

She was already half asleep and just mumbled, 'What for?'

'Everything from here on in,' he said into the dark.

CHAPTER 29

The text Ellie had just received from Jack made her frown. She had heard nothing from him since he had flown to New York, and now all she had was this one-word message: *Fine*. Two days, one word, and she'd had to drag that out of him by sending him a text first. She'd tied herself in knots composing it, trying to strike a light, jokey tone. Finally she'd come up with, *How is the city that never sleeps?* when what she really wanted to say was, *I miss you. I love you.*

She'd comforted herself yesterday with thinking that he was probably too busy to call, but then Ian had been going on and on about the long chat he'd had with Jack on the phone and how he was off to a party at the Waldorf Astoria. That's when she'd felt the first stirrings of unease.

She was aware that there was a silence in the office and Lesley was shaking her head.

'You haven't been listening to a word, have you?' she said. 'I've been pouring my heart out, telling you how

Megan's family won't even talk to her now and you've been more interested in that phone.' Lesley picked up her bag. 'I have waited and waited for you to get back so that I could talk to you about it. I wanted to ring you up at home, but I thought, No, let her have her holiday. Now you can't even be bothered to listen. Thanks a bunch, Ellie.' She got up and left the room.

Ellie put her head down on the desk. Coming back to work had been fine on Monday. She had held the secret about all that she and Jack had shared like a lovely bright jewel in her palm. Nobody knew Jack like she knew Jack. But as Tuesday came, the reality of who Jack was and who she was had started to crowd out the memories of that lovely last night in bed.

If he had only been in touch, it would have made every-thing fine. Now here she was acting like a lovesick adoles-cent and ignoring her friends. After all the hours Lesley had sat and listened to her talk about Sam, the way she had looked after her.

She got up and went to find Lesley to apologise, but she was still wondering about Jack, still trying to work out if it would look too needy to actually give him a call.

How's the weather in Manhattan? she texted the next day. *Sunny*, came back the reply. She tried again: *Seen anybody famous?* Hours later she got a curt *No*. Finally she plucked up her courage – *I miss you, Jack* – and sat and waited. And waited.

There was still no reply when she got to work on Thursday. No matter how many times she checked her mobile or her email, there was nothing.

Black, black fear took hold of her.

She stared at the copy she was meant to be editing and it might as well have been hieroglyphics. She got up and made a cup of coffee and tried to look at the copy again, but her hand kept straying to her mobile even though she knew that she would have heard if a text had arrived.

When Lesley walked in, Ellie shoved the phone in her drawer and put on her brightest face to listen to the latest developments in the Megan saga. At least she and Lesley were talking again. Lesley had been her creative partner and friend for years and she'd known Jack for how long? She despised how sad and stupid she was being but couldn't shake herself out of this thing that appeared to be clamping on to her.

At lunchtime she went to find Ian so that she could work the conversation round to Jack.

'So, how's New York suiting Jack, then?'

'Pretty well, I think. The negotiations with the American agency are going OK.'

'What's it called? Something Bootle?'

'Bar Bootle.'

'Well, don't suppose Jack has seen much of the city itself, probably too busy.'

'I think he's been out and about quite a bit,' Ian said, searching on his desk for something.

'Right. What, being wined and dined?'

'Knowing Jack, it will be wined, dined and that other thing ending in "ed" and starting with "f".' Ian sat down and smiled at his own cleverness and Ellie reassessed whether she did actually like him after all. 'And if you'll pardon me being crude, Ellie, I hope he is getting his end away. Might put a smile back on his face. He's been walking around here like a bear with a sore arse for the last two weeks.' Ian gave a loud laugh. 'Perhaps he was missing you while you were on holiday, eh, Ellie?'

He continued to laugh uproariously at what he saw as the preposterousness of the suggestion and Ellie slunk back to her office doubly wounded: Jack had not only been socialising in New York, but during the time he'd been seeing her, he had been spectacularly miserable.

By Saturday, when Jack was due back in the country, Ellie was almost hysterical. A nasty little voice had taken up residence in her head saying, 'What did you expect?' over and over again. She stayed in bed most of the weekend, gnawing at her thumb and pretending she had a cold. It was hard to fight the urge to go to Jack's flat and talk to him. If she could only see him, all would be well again; they could go back to what they were like before he'd left.

Edith was very kind and tactfully did not ask her about Jack.

On Sunday night Ellie could not sleep. Everything about that last evening that she and Jack had spent together told her that they were meant to be together, that he had developed deep feelings for her.

But everything about the past week told her that he had lost them pretty sharpish.

Her thoughts drove her out of bed and down to the kitchen to make toast. She took it back upstairs and couldn't eat it. She fell asleep and dreamed of Jack, woke up again and thought he was in bed with her. Around about 5 a.m. she fell asleep, and when she woke up, it was past ten and she was very, very late for work.

By the time Ellie got off the bus, it was lunchtime. She hesitated outside the front entrance to the agency and wiped her hands down her skirt. Only one thing would be worse than bumping into Jack and that was not bumping into him.

Rachel was on her feet before Ellie had even reached the reception desk.

'What a morning for you to be late, Ellie – you missed all the fun.'

'Bit of a rush, Rachel.' Ellie said, feeling too exposed. There was no way she could bump into Jack here and pretend nothing had happened.

She tried to get past Rachel, but she put out her arm

and stopped her. 'You've got to listen to this, Ellie. We've bought that agency, Bar Bootle, and guess what? Jack's moving out to New York to run it.'

Ellie didn't hear the rest of what Rachel said, all the details of when he was going and how sorry everybody would be to lose him.

She would not accept this version of reality. It was not the one she'd seen in that bed.

One last hope was left. 'Is he taking anyone with him, Rachel?' she said, straining to make her voice sound normal.

Rachel gave her a confused look and then said, 'Oh . . . I see. No, Jack's tried to persuade her to go with him, but Mrs MacEndry says she's too old for New York. She's been thinking of retiring for a while, so this has made her mind up.'

Ellie wanted to scream, 'I don't mean Mrs MacEndry, you stupid bitch. I mean me. Is he taking me?' She stumbled across to the stairs and started to climb them. With every step the little house of potential happiness that she had built came crashing down.

That snide voice was back inside her head too. This time it was shouting, 'What did you expect, a white wedding and lots of Jack-shaped kids? You knew what he was like.'

The 'Jack is going to America' story was all that people talked about that day, and every time she heard it Ellie wanted to strangle the person who was speaking. Even

Lesley never shut up about it. She kept providing little updates with such glee that Ellie had to press her lips together to stop herself from screaming. Lesley had bumped into Jack coming out of the big board meeting and he'd told her he was going next week and had already found an apartment. They'd laughed that he had already started calling it that and not a flat. He'd seemed happy. And he was going to have a big leaving party at Zucchinis and everyone was invited. It was going to be a joint party with Mrs MacEndry to mark her retirement.

'So, lucky old New York, eh, Ellie?'

'Yes.'

'That's all you've got to say? I mean, I know you and Jack have had your ups and downs, but you were getting on better recently. It's going to be quiet around here without him.'

'Yes. Look, sorry, Lesley, I've got a thumping headache.'

'Thought you were off colour. Only a headache, is it?'

Ellie nodded slowly. 'Didn't sleep very well last night. Feel a bit wobbly.' She got up and went to the mini-fridge to get the one bottle of water she knew was still in there and, while she was facing away from Lesley, asked, 'When do you suppose Jack decided he was going to move to New York? I mean, has it been on the cards for a while?'

Before Lesley could answer, Ian stuck his head round the door.

'Big creative meeting in Jack's office in ten minutes.

Catch up on the New York stuff and what's happening on all the accounts.'

Ellie put the bottle back in the fridge and walked down to Jack's office with all the enthusiasm of a woman going to stand in front of a firing squad.

'Right, any more questions about New York and the oper-ation there?' Jack asked.

Juliette raised her hand. 'Only, can I come with you, Jack?'

There was laughter around the room and Jack smiled down at the desk.

'Hey, I get first refusal,' Ian said.

There was more laughter from everyone and Ellie wanted to smack their stupid faces for them.

When she had first walked into the room and seen Jack, she knew that there must have been a mistake. He was going to turn round and come to her. They had been so close, so intertwined that he couldn't possibly shrug her off like all the others. They had connected at some deep level that made another person seem somehow part of you. He'd felt that too, she was sure of it.

Well, he had turned round, but he hadn't even glanced in her direction. She'd had to find a seat quickly to stop herself from falling down. Now all she could do was look at him. He seemed taller and stronger and even sexier than she remembered. Knowing every inch of his body made it even more appealing. But the sudden realisation had hit her that she was probably never going to hold him in her arms again, or get to know him any better, and the bitterness of that thought made her lower her gaze.

Back to staring at the same old carpet, but for a whole new set of reasons.

Jack started to speak again. 'OK, as this is our last get-together, we'll have a quick run-through where we stand on the major accounts and what's in the pipeline. But first I think Ian has some news about the Sure & Soft campaign . . .'

Ian did a little drum roll on the desk with his hands. 'Figures for audience recall of the ad are very high – it's in the top five – and I had Pauline Kennedy on the phone this morning saying they are pleased . . . No, correction: they are delighted with the latest sales figures. She's given the nod to roll out the poster and press campaign, and has changed her mind about the radio – she's up for it now. We need to get the twenty-second ones polished up.' Ian gave a sharp laugh. 'I stopped myself from saying, "I told you so." She's also going to liaise with our Web guys about the design of their existing site . . . If you'll pardon the pun, it's pants. She's keen to explore their Facebook presence too . . . Twitter . . . you name it . . . Bring them into the twenty-first century in fact.' He turned to Ellie and Lesley. 'So well done, you two.'

There was a little round of applause before Ian went on, 'Also, of course, it's had a good reception from everyone in the industry, which bodes well, come award season. Better get yourselves some posh frocks, girls.'

Ellie gave a little half-smile and then started to feel disconnected from everything around her. She was aware that Jack was talking them through various accounts and then there was something about being chosen to do work for a council in Yorkshire.

Just then she happened to glance up and caught his eye and there was absolutely no glimmer of anything there for her. No warmth, no guilt, no embarrassment. He was a stranger to her. His gaze passed right through her and he was on to the next subject.

She stood up abruptly and walked out of the room, only pausing in Mrs MacEndry's office to say, 'I'm sorry you're retiring. I'll miss you,' before going up to her office, collecting her bag and going home.

Back in Jack's room, Lesley explained how Ellie had been feeling ill since she'd got in and shouldn't really have come to work at all. Jack nodded along with everyone else and then filled them in on what had happened with the yoghurt account.

CHAPTER 30

Jack opened the door of his flat and Ellie sensed that he wasn't surprised to see her. Which made her feel worse: like he believed she was the kind of woman who habitually stalked men who chucked her.

'I thought you'd gone home. Lesley said you'd been feeling ill.'

'You made me feel sick.'

He regarded her coolly. 'Sorry.'

'That's it? You're sorry?'

She saw his hand go to the knot in his tie. 'If you've got something to say spit it out, Ellie. I'm a bit busy.'

She could not believe that this was the same man who had held her in his arms when she had been crying. He seemed to have had all the warmth sucked out of him.

'When did you decide to go to New York?'

His hand strayed back to his tie, but he said nothing.

'And all that lovey-dovey stuff the last night we were together, that was what?'

'People say things in bed they don't mean, Ellie. Come on, you're an adult, you understand that.'

She didn't know why she was doing this to herself; it was like picking at a sore. 'I never tell people I love them if I don't, Jack,' she said, and heard the tremor in her voice.

He wouldn't look at her. 'I don't know why you're here, Ellie. We had a great time, a great two weeks, but these things don't always work out.'

'You aren't going to let it, you mean?' she shot back.

Jack didn't answer.

'I'm asking you again, when did you decide to go to New York?'

'I don't see what relevance that has to anything.'

'It makes a difference to me whether you knew before we got together or not.'

He wasn't going to give her an answer to that, she could tell. She swallowed rapidly, determined she was not going to cry.

'It was just sex, then, was it, Jack? Another notch?'

He nodded.

'You're lying, Jack. You're not that good an actor. You're running away from me for some reason and I don't know what it is. The things you said, the way you looked at me—'

Jack cut across her impatiently. 'Look, Ellie, I'm sorry if you thought that there was more to it than there was.'

That was the point at which she lost her resolve to be dignified and calm. 'But you don't normally have sex with the women you work with,' she wailed.

She saw Jack take a step back and there was a nasty set to his mouth. 'True,' he said, 'but perhaps I'm psychic. Perhaps I knew we wouldn't be working together for much longer.'

'I don't recognise you like this, Jack. It's as if you're thinking of the cruellest things to say to drive me away.'

'Cruel to be kind, Ellie. No use giving you false hope. It's over.'

Ellie could feel the tears running down her face. Her breath was coming in big gasps. 'I . . . I . . . have deep feelings for you, Jack. You know that. You let me tell you that the last time we were together. And you said you couldn't get enough of me, you wanted to protect me. Yet now you do this? I don't know why you're being so cold to me. If you wanted to end it, why not be honest?'

Jack turned away from her and went to go into his flat. Ellie reached out and grabbed hold of his arm and yanked him back. She couldn't even speak now, she was sobbing so hard.

'Ellie,' he said without looking at her, 'it was a mistake. I shouldn't have got involved with you. Having sex with someone you work with is always a bad idea. They start to read too much into it. They think that they know you better than the other people you work with.' He shook her hand from his arm. 'Well, you don't know me, Ellie. All you know is what I'm like in bed and there's a long list of women who know that.'

It was too brutal and Ellie tried to reach out for him again. He dodged away from her and folded his arms and watched her cry.

At some point he said, in a matter-of-fact tone, 'You'll feel better about this soon. Nothing has altered at work. I still think you're a brilliant copywriter and there are more big changes coming to your department. I can't tell you what yet, but changes for the better. For you and Lesley. You deserve what's coming.'

'What, for sleeping with you?' she managed to blurt out.

The look he gave her was filled with distaste. 'I'm not even going to bother talking to you, Ellie, if you're going to be stupid like that.' He moved quickly into his flat and slammed the door behind him, leaving her standing there.

When he looked out through the spyhole a few minutes later, she had gone.

Ellie never made it into work the following day, and when she did return, she kept to her office. She didn't want to see Jack and she certainly didn't want him to hear she was moping around. She couldn't bear him to feel sorry for her. Although judging by his performance outside his flat, he actually didn't feel anything at all for her any more.

She put her head down and surreptitiously wiped her eyes. Her official line was that she had some kind of virusy-cold thing. A virusy-cold thing that made her eyes red, her bottom lip wobbly and plastered a look of permanent misery over her face.

She wished she could talk to Lesley, but everything was too raw to put into words. Having any kind of conversation about it seemed impossible.

She had to go through the motions of being a fully functioning human while, two floors down, the man she loved got ready to leave her behind.

She couldn't even comfort herself that she'd got over Sam and it was only a matter of time before she started to feel better about Jack. She was never going to feel better about Jack. Simple as that, she knew it in her bones. A part of her had been missing before he'd come along and it would go missing again when he went.

She had only managed to write two words of copy since she'd got into work. Not a great output, especially as one of them was a ground-breaking 'and'. Any minute now Lesley was going to notice that she wasn't in fact doing anything and ask her for the third time in an hour whether she should have come back to work so soon.

Ellie put down her pen and took herself off to the toilets for some solitude and yet another chance to gnaw away at her thumb and at all those things about that last night together with Jack that didn't make sense. Did she have to face the fact that it had all been an act on Jack's part? She definitely wasn't ready for that yet.

When she returned to the office, Ian was sitting in her chair waiting for her.

'Ah, Ellie, Ellie, Ellie,' he said with a 'little boy in trouble' look on his face. 'That's a lovely top you've got on today. The red kind of matches your eyes.'

'What do you want, Ian?' she said abruptly.

'Got another little problem. I'm meant to be going up to Yorkshire, preliminary talks with these council people. It's that account Jack was talking about, the one he got through his old contacts?' He stood up to let her sit in her chair and then perched on the edge of the desk. 'It'll be a quick visit – up in one day and back the next – going tomorrow. But my wife has rung. Looks like Josh has come down with chickenpox, and what with the baby not being weaned yet, she's demented. I don't suppose you fancy a trip?'

It was a gift, the chance to get out of the office and away from Jack. 'Where's the council again?' she asked, giving the impression that she'd known and simply forgotten rather than not been paying attention in the first place.

'Scarsdove,' Ian said, pinching one of the biscuits from their tin on the filing cabinet. 'It's a nice little market town between Halifax and Leeds. You know, the place Jack comes from.'

CHAPTER 31

Ellie liked Scarsdove on sight, and not just because it was where Jack was born and grew up. It had a main street of shops, little independent ones, not the big names, and it sat slap-bang by the moors. Half wild and half civilised. A bit like Jack.

Ellie had decided not to fight the need to think about him while she was there. She wanted a good wallow and there was no better place to do it. So, after a very friendly and productive meeting with the council representatives, she wandered around the town. Over a cup of tea in a little café with white tablecloths and china teacups, she found herself looking out for strong noses. There appeared to be quite a few in this part of the world. After that she sat on a seat in the square and wondered if Jack had ever sat there and toyed with the idea of going to find his old school. Then she spotted the library. They would have copies of old newspapers and perhaps she'd come across a picture of him.

She was a lost cause, but at least she was only hurting herself.

The library was deserted except for a bored-looking librarian, whose eyes lit up when Ellie walked in. She directed Ellie to the local history section, indicating a curving metal staircase up to the first floor. Evidently the newspapers were still on microfiche and the librarian was very eager to come and help Ellie find what she was looking for. Fortunately at that moment a man with a nylon shopping bag came in through the library doors. Ellie saw the librarian go a little pale and skulk off behind the large-print section. Ellie left her to it and headed upstairs, her heels making a loud tapping noise on each of the steps as she went.

Fitting the microfiche in the machine was fiddly and her eyes soon began to ache, but she found the steady cycle of agricultural shows, nativity plays and summer fêtes comforting. She felt close to Jack here, or at least to his past. After a few minutes there he was, a smiling schoolboy, holding up a trophy for winning a long-jump event. Even all these years later she felt proud of him and sat there with her fingers lightly touching the photograph for a while.

A few more pieces of microfiche and there were other photographs of him: one as part of a school group off to Rome and another announcing his departure for Leeds University. He was more recognisably Jack in that last photo.

She jumped forward a few years to when she figured he would have graduated and then realised she'd gone too far. She was about to reverse when a small headline leaped out at her. Her obsession must be particularly acute: she'd picked Jack's name out from a whole page of small type. As she started to read, her heart rate speeded up. Her eyes scanned quickly through the article, barely able to believe what she was reading. When she'd finished, she went right back to the beginning and read it again more slowly. Then she sat back, not seeing anything.

It was some while before she reached down into her handbag, pulled out her notebook and pen, and started to write.

Jack was heading home for the evening when it struck him that he hadn't had a pint for a while. Very soon he wouldn't be able to simply pop into a pub and get one. He bumped into Ian at the bar and bought them both a pint of Tetley's.

'I can't stop long,' Ian said, lifting his glass to his mouth. 'I'm on daubing-the-spots-with-cream duty tonight.'

Jack made a face. 'How's it going?'

'Early days. We're waiting for the rest of the kids to come down with it now.'

'Probably better they get it when they're little. That's what they say, isn't it? And we're quiet at the moment if you do need to nip off early some days. Even when I'm gone.'

'Thanks, mate . . . and that reminds me . . . When you're gone, can I have your office? Not for me – I was thinking of turning it into a games room – you know, basketball hoop, table tennis, that kind of thing. Break down the barriers, get the creative juices flowing.' He took a sip of his beer. 'Mind you, Ellie's going to have an unfair advantage when it comes to basketball. Have to make sure we put the hoop as high as it'll go.'

Jack felt the familiar lurch in his stomach at the mention of Ellie's name. 'I haven't seen her for a couple of days . . . Is she still sick?' He knew if she was, he was to blame.

'No.' Ian scraped at something stuck on the bar with his nail. 'She's doing that Scarsdove Council meeting for me. She's up there now.'

Jack brought his pint down heavily on the bar and felt a ball of queasiness roll around in his stomach.

'Yeah,' Ian continued, returning his attention to his pint, 'she was quite keen, and I told her to do a bit of research while she was there. You know, get a feel for the place and the people. I've noticed she's good at that, getting stories out of people.'

'Great,' Jack said, and stared at the bar until the unease stopped threatening to turn into something more uncontrollable. Then he reached out very slowly and lifted his pint back to his lips.

CHAPTER 32

Jack watched Ellie come into his room on Monday morning and knew with complete certainty that it was payback time. He didn't like the way she was smiling at him. It wasn't an Ellie smile; there was absolutely no warmth in it.

'I told Mrs MacEndry I wasn't to be disturbed.'

'This will only take a minute.'

Jack's eyes were drawn to the notepad in Ellie's hands. 'Go on, then,' he said, knowing that he really didn't want to hear this.

'It's amazing what you can find out if you look in the right places,' she said innocently, sitting down.

Jack lowered his pen and tried to look unconcerned. Deep breathing, that was the secret.

Ellie's eyes were gleaming. 'Fascinating place, Scarsdove. I spent a few hours in the library going through old newspapers and guess what I found out ... ? Besides the fact that you were very good at the long jump.' Ellie laughed, but Jack couldn't hear any amusement in it.

He felt his hand stray to his tie and forced himself to bring it back down to rest on the desk, but not before he had seen Ellie register the movement.

She gave a covert little smile and looked down at her notebook. Jack would not have been surprised if she had stopped and dramatically cleared her throat. She started to read: '"Mr Jack Wolfe of Harbiston Avenue, Leeds, pleaded guilty to a charge of threatening behaviour at Leeds Magistrates' Court this week. The charge followed an incident outside the home of Mr Dean Wilkinson in Burland Crescent on 22 May when Mr Wolfe repeatedly threatened to castrate Mr Wilkinson, a camera operator with the BBC in Leeds. PC Armitage, one of the police officers who attended the incident, said that Mr Wolfe was 'extremely agitated by the presence of Mrs Helen Wolfe in Mr Wilkinson's house'."'

Jack didn't need to listen to the story; he knew it off by heart. He waited, every muscle tight with tension, for what else Ellie might have ferreted out, but she closed her notebook and sat there with her hands in her lap. Jack let out a breath very slowly and stopped gritting his teeth.

Ellie flashed him a triumphant look and smiled again, although Jack felt it actually belonged more to the smirk family.

Her tone was light and assured when she spoke. 'So, Jack, I'm putting two and two together and guessing why your wife was in Dean Wilkinson's house that night. Basically your wife had an affair with another man. The great Jack Wolfe, not able to keep his own wife satisfied.' Ellie shook her head. 'Shame there wasn't anything about your divorce, it might have made for juicy reading. Although I think what I found out told me everything I needed to know about you.'

Ellie got up and sauntered over to the desk. She was definitely enjoying herself. 'This explains so much, Jack. Why you're such a serial womaniser. Why you find it hard to commit to any kind of long-lasting relationship. Why you say one thing and do another. Why, most importantly, you drop women in the cruellest, most callous way.' She folded her arms. 'It's absolutely classic get-your-own-back behaviour.' She shot him a poisonous look. 'Well, I'm sorry your wife was a two-faced, shag-somebody-else-behind-your-back tart, but it really isn't an excuse for treating other women badly.'

Jack felt sick at the mention of Helen's name next to all those cold descriptions of her. He wanted desperately to stand up and tell Ellie she was wrong, but then he'd have to tell her everything and there was no way he was ever doing that. He had to shake her off. He had to get her out of the room before he did something stupid. Even with her looking at him in such a mean way he still wanted to throw her down on the floor and bury himself in her.

He had missed her so very much these last few days and if she stayed near him any longer, he wasn't going to be able to fight that longing for her.

'Finished?' he said, giving her a look that he was relieved to see wiped the smile off her face. 'Is that the best you can do? What happened to your dignity, Ellie? Scrabbling around for sordid little details about my life. What are you going to do, get them published in *Ad Infinitum*?'

He saw her look confused. 'No, of course not. I just—'

'What? You just wanted to tell me what a horrible bastard I was?' He picked up his pen and examined it. 'Pretty pointless exercise. I already knew the Helen story and you already knew I was a bastard. Face it, Ellie, it's the action of a sad little woman scorned. Not a pretty sight.'

He turned his attention to the paper in front of him and started to write. He didn't know what he was writing: anything so that he didn't have to see the look in her eyes or watch as she hesitantly turned round and then left his office. He wasn't even going to think about the horrible gulping noise she had made.

When he was sure she had gone, he went out to have a word with Lydia.

'I thought I said I wasn't to be disturbed.'

'Did you?'

'You know I did. This isn't like you. What are you playing at?'

'I like Ellie,' she said very precisely. 'A great deal. I think you do too. She's a nice girl.'

Jack grunted. 'London's full of nice girls.'

'Possibly . . . but I think you're being an idiot, Jack. And I think Helen would agree.'

'Lydia,' Jack said softly, 'watch your step. Or you're going to find yourself getting sacked right before you retire. We've never had a cross word, let's not start now.' He turned round and headed back to his office before Lydia could say anything more.

He wasn't really surprised that she'd picked up on there being something between him and Ellie, but one thing he did not need was someone telling him how nice Ellie was. Like he didn't already bloody know that. Like that counted for anything in the end.

Ellie had carried her little bit of news about Jack and his wife around with her like a hand grenade all weekend. She wanted to pay him back for his callousness; stop him seeing her as a victim he could merely use without any consequences. She had relished the thought of telling him she knew why he had become the man he was.

Then it had all gone wrong. Ellie put her head against her old friend the cool wall of the toilet partition. All that stuff she'd said about his wife, all that venom spilling out of her. He still cared for Helen, judging by that look of pain he'd had on his face. He'd covered it up pretty quickly, but it had been there. Hurting him had been horrible; she didn't care if he deserved it.

It was a completely hollow victory; she'd come across like some bunny-boiling maniac.

She'd made things worse and now he would hate her as well as thinking she was pathetic. Putting in even a cursory appearance at his leaving do was out of the question. She'd have to pretend to be ill again and come back when he was safely in New York.

Ellie made it out of the ladies' toilets before realising that she'd just seen Jack for the last time. She managed to get herself back into a cubicle and stayed there crying as quietly as she could until a worried Lesley came to look for her and then put her into a taxi and sent her home.

CHAPTER 33

The agency was quiet when Ellie finally returned to work the morning after Jack's leaving party. When she passed the reception desk, Rachel had on her sunglasses.

'You missed a great night, Ellie. Really awesome,' she croaked.

Every office Ellie passed was deserted. The quiet seemed to emphasise the fact that Jack was gone; the excitement had passed on somewhere else.

Ellie opened the door to her office and immediately spotted the white envelope on her desk. The thought that it might be a leaving note from Jack made her leap at it and tear it open, but as she read it, she saw it was confirmation of what he had hinted at. It was promotion. From now on she was to be senior copywriter, and as Lesley had a similar envelope on her desk, Ellie guessed she must be getting promotion too.

A few weeks ago she would have been overjoyed; everything she'd wanted from work was falling into place.

Promotion and a successful ad campaign, probably even some awards later.

She put the letter on the desk and went to fill the kettle.

Lesley crawled into the room later and the genuine surprise on her face when she opened the letter was priceless. Promotion had come out of the blue for Lesley and her happiness was uplifting. She threw herself at Ellie and almost squeezed the breath out of her and then she was on the phone to Megan. Ellie picked up the phone too and rang round the agency and soon their office was full of people, all hung-over but all willing to have one more drink to celebrate the good news.

Ellie felt guilty that they were so concerned about how she was feeling. She was a coward and a fraud.

'You missed a cracking night,' Ian said. 'Even Mrs MacEndry was up and giving it hell on the dance floor.'

'And Mike, you missed Mike,' Juliette said, a brilliantly mischievous smile illuminating her face. She reached out and ruffled Mike's hair.

There was a volley of catcalls and someone slapped Mike on the back.

'Go on, big boy,' Juliette said, poking him with a finger, 'tell your Auntie Ellie all about it.'

Everyone looked as if they were about to burst into laughter and Mike mumbled something in Ellie's direction.

'Speak up, Mike, don't be shy,' Juliette said, enjoying his discomfort.

'I got off with Rachel,' Mike blurted out.

The catcalls and whistles started up again and one of the studio jocks said, 'Hey, what's it like to be her first?'

'Shut up, shut the fuck up,' Mike shouted, glaring round at them all. 'I don't care what you think. I like her. I've liked her for months. Anyone says anything like that again and I'll—'

Suddenly Ian was standing next to Mike. He put his arm round his shoulders.

'Come on, lad, calm down. It was a bit of fun. Nobody meant anything. We all like Rachel.'

Somebody sniggered and Mike glared again.

Ian held his hand up for quiet. 'That's enough. We're a team. Save that kind of sniping for people at other agencies. Cut it out.'

Nobody spoke. Ian might not have Jack's size, but he had the same air of danger about him at times. And this was one of those times. When he calculated that his message had hit home, he gave Mike's shoulder a consoling squeeze. 'You've got to admit, though, it was pretty funny the way you both disappeared for a while and then she came back with her blouse done up all wrong.'

'Yeah . . . well . . .' Mike said, grinning.

There was a barrage of raucous laughter and then the

conversation veered off to other scandals from the party. Ellie waited to hear something about Jack, steeling herself for the news that he'd ended up wrapped in someone else's arms. She didn't have to wait long.

'What about Jack, though, eh?' Ian said, shaking his head, and Ellie's antenna was on full alert. 'Arrived drunk, drank himself back sober and then got completely bladdered again.'

'When he was dancing with me, he could barely string a sentence together,' Lesley said.

Ian went over to the biscuit tin and took out a handful of shortbreads. 'He held me much too tight when he danced with me. I couldn't even breathe most of the time. Daft great lump.'

'He danced with you, Ian?' Ellie said, confused.

'He danced with everyone. Including the bouncers at one point, I think. Completely out of his tree.' Ian went to pop a biscuit in his mouth and then stopped. 'I had to pour him into a taxi and take him back to my house in the end. Doesn't look too clever this morning, though. Especially with Josh bouncing up and down on him.'

Ellie pretended to check whether there was anything in the mini-fridge and fought her murderous jealousy of a five-year-old boy with chickenpox. But at least Jack hadn't gone home with a woman. It was a little chink of light.

'He's going to have a hard time pulling himself back together by tonight,' Ian continued, in between mouthfuls of biscuit. 'Hot date with a hot judge evidently. Helping her with her briefs, I expect.'

There was a sudden crash that made them all jump and then Lesley dashed from her seat to help Ellie put the mini-fridge back on top of the cabinet.

The agency emptied out early and no one went to the pub after work, but Ellie stayed a bit later and, when everyone was gone, wandered down to Jack's old office and sat in his chair. Soon it would be the games room.

She ran her hands over his desk and then turned the chair round to look out of the window. Two pigeons were mating on the windowsill, the male every now and again pecking the female on the neck. Ellie fully expected to see the male pigeon throw the female off the ledge when he'd finished with her. Or perhaps males in the bird world were kinder than human ones.

Her thoughts came back to Jack and where he was now. If he was with that judge woman, had he completely wiped her from his mind? Detached Jack, moving through the female population without a second thought. One woman had completely screwed him up and so the rest of them had to pay.

Tomorrow he would be in New York. She closed her eyes and concentrated on trying to commit his face to memory.

When Ellie opened her eyes and swivelled back round to face the room, Mrs MacEndry was standing there.

'I never had a chance to thank you for my beautiful flowers, Ellie,' she said in answer to Ellie's quizzical look. 'Peonies, my absolute favourites. And so thoughtful to have them delivered to my home.'

'You didn't need to come all the way back in to thank me, Mrs MacEndry.'

Mrs MacEndry smiled. 'You can call me Lydia, you know, and I didn't just come back in about the flowers.' She pulled a chair up to the desk. 'I also wanted to say goodbye to you properly. I was so sorry you weren't well enough to come to the leaving party.' Mrs MacEndry sat down. 'Are you feeling better now?'

Ellie was about to make her usual bland reply when something about Mrs MacEndry's body language stopped her.

'You knew about Jack and me, didn't you?' she said.

Mrs MacEndry nodded. 'Yes, although not definitely, not until you left that meeting abruptly the other day. But I suspected before that.' She laughed. 'Sometimes I feel like one of those old ladies in an Agatha Christie novel, picking up little snippets of information here and there, piecing together clues, building the full picture.'

Ellie started to sniff. 'What gave it away?'

'Oh, I don't know, lots of little things. You going a shade of beetroot anytime you were close to Jack. Him strutting about losing his temper with you like a rutting stag. That day he looked so strange when I went into his office after that meeting with the scalpel man.' She stopped, reached down for her handbag, extracted a handkerchief and handed it to Ellie with a smile. 'Oh, and the mystery of why he should return from lunch with a carrier bag containing a brand-new dress that was exactly the same as one you already had.'

'You're good,' Ellie said, dabbing at her eyes.

Mrs MacEndry made a little dipping motion with her head. 'Thank you.'

'You must think I'm a complete idiot. I mean, me and Jack, what was I thinking?'

'You're not an idiot at all, Ellie,' Mrs MacEndry said, shaking her head. 'You wear your heart on your sleeve, and you're a bit too trusting, but neither of those things are faults. And you are most definitely not the idiot in this case.'

'Thanks, I think, Mrs Mac— Sorry, Lydia.'

Mrs MacEndry leaned forward and lowered her voice. 'I would never do anything to hurt Jack, you know, Ellie. He has been more than a boss to me.'

Ellie's skin goose-bumped all over. Not Mrs MacEndry too?

Mrs MacEndry caught Ellie's expression and quickly said, 'No, no, not in that way. I meant he has been a good friend to me, a person I could really depend on.'

Ellie felt a rush of love for Jack that necessitated some serious handkerchief work again.

'Jack took me under his wing when my husband died. You know he died quite young, don't you?'

Ellie did.

'Well, I felt like giving up totally . . . work, eating, life, everything. I was working for Jack at the time in Manchester. He was so kind, and when he decided to head south, he said I should come too. I thought he was mad, but in the end he persuaded me.' She raised her eyebrows. 'As you know, he can be very persuasive. He said if I stayed in Manchester, I would never be able to move forward. Horrible expression, but I knew what he meant. There were too many reminders of happier times up there. Jack understood it all perfectly. I came south and made a new life. Everything was so different here I had to get on with living.'

Mrs MacEndry came to a stop, but Ellie got the distinct impression there was more to come and that Mrs MacEndry was having some kind of internal tussle with herself. She sat very quietly until Mrs MacEndry was ready to start again.

'I am not sure whether I am doing the correct thing here, Ellie, talking to you like this, but . . . but I think that you need to find out some things about Jack that he would never tell you.' Mrs MacEndry had said the last part of her speech very quickly, as if she were getting something out into the open before she had the chance to reconsider and perhaps stop herself.

'What kind of things?' Ellie was clutching at the hope that whatever they were, they might bring Jack back to her.

Mrs MacEndry's smile returned. 'Well, I think it best if you find them out for yourself. That way, when Jack tortures me, I will be able to say with a clear conscience that I didn't actually tell you anything.'

Both women laughed, but Ellie could see that Mrs MacEndry was concerned that somehow Jack would be angry with her. It was obviously a big secret.

'What you need to do, Ellie dear, is go back up to Scarsdove,' Mrs MacEndry said.

'Back?' Ellie was confused and then decided that perhaps Mrs MacEndry was not aware that she had already found out that Jack was married. 'I don't think there's any need for me to go back, Lydia. If the big secret you're talking about is that Jack had a wife who cheated on him, I've already found that out.'

Ellie expected Mrs MacEndry's face to register surprise, but instead she kept smiling that calm smile of hers.

'There's a man called Bryan North you need to talk to, editor of the local paper. He was Jack's first boss. I believe he doesn't work Thursdays, but any other day you should be able to find him.'

CHAPTER 34

Ellie waited for someone, anyone, to come and open up the *Scarsdove & District Advertiser* offices. What time did these people start working? It was ten o'clock already. Ellie watched a Land Rover reverse into a parking space not far from the seat on which she was sitting. A solitary jogger skirted round the square and disappeared up a side street.

Ellie supposed this was what constituted the rush-hour. Still, she was here and it was warm and all she had to do was wait.

But that was the hardest part, waiting. She took a look at her hands. She was still chewing the skin down the side of her thumbnail and now she had also started on her nails. They'd been lovely and long, even after Jack had dumped her, but since Mrs MacEndry had hinted at there being something else she ought to know about Jack, Ellie had decimated them. She didn't need to revisit her psychology A-level notes to know what that meant. She was afraid she'd got something very wrong somewhere.

A bird started to peck at a discarded pie not far from her feet and Ellie wondered if she looked like that: gobbling up anything she could find out about Jack. Pray God Ian never found out the real reason he was funding another trip north. He'd assumed she was being her usual diligent self when it came to researching the client.

Unlike Lesley. She hadn't seen the point of Ellie's return visit. The people from the council were due at the agency soon; they could get all the background information they needed then. Ellie had tried to change the subject, but Lesley had definitely been suspicious. There'd been a bit of an atmosphere between them since then. Which was another reason why her nails were bitten to nothing.

Ellie had another look at the newspaper office. Bingo. The lights were on.

'Oh, yes, she was a researcher at the BBC in Leeds. Lovely girl. Great sense of humour. Fantastic legs.' Bryan North sucked the end of his pencil as he remembered Helen, Jack's wife.

Ellie sipped her coffee and tried not to fall to her knees and beg Bryan to get to the end of the story.

'They met at university. Here, I've got a picture of her and Jack somewhere. I'll go and find it.' Brian disappeared 'out the back', as he called it, and Ellie looked around at the clutter in his office and thought it highly unlikely that Bryan could ever find anything. She and Lesley were mere amateurs at being messy compared with Bryan. The room was large, but they were sitting in the only tiny space left uncluttered. On every available surface were piles of old newspapers, many yellowing and torn, and an assortment of boxes labelled with dates stretching back to the 1970s. The floor, which Ellie guessed had not been cleaned for a long time, was also covered in random piles of paper.

Most impressive, though, was the large stuffed rat on a plinth that for some reason was sitting right in the middle of the floor. Ellie found it hard to take her eyes off it and wondered if it was Bryan's lunch.

Still, Bryan was a fund of information – about the area, about the council and now, hopefully, about Jack. She had supposed he would think it strange that she had turned up out of the blue with so many questions, but he gave every appearance of being happy to oblige. Perhaps it got lonely with only the piles of paper and the stuffed rat for company.

Brian bustled back into the room. 'Here you go,' he said, handing her a framed photograph, and Ellie was looking at a younger version of Jack with his arm around a girl.

'That was taken at our Christmas do. Made a handsome couple, didn't they?'

Ellie nodded. The girl was very pretty, with shoulder-length dark hair, delicate features and a big smile. From what Ellie could see of her figure, it was voluptuous. To Ellie, she looked friendly and open – not at all the sophisticated, cool woman Ellie had steeled herself to see on Jack's arm. But then Jack didn't look like Jack either. It wasn't simply that he was younger; it was something about the way he was smiling, like he hadn't a care in the world. It wasn't a smile Ellie had ever seen on his face. She handed the photograph back to Bryan, unable to look at it any longer.

Surely now Bryan would notice her hyperventilating and wonder what the hell she was up to. But Bryan wasn't looking at her. He stared down at the photograph and whistled softly. 'Jack and Helen . . . haven't thought about them for a while. Mind you, all credit to him – he still sends me a card at Christmas.' Bryan put the photograph down on his desk. 'He was only here for about two and a half years in all. Plus a couple of summer holidays when he was still at school. 'Course, we were a bigger set-up then. Everything was done from here. Now there's me and a couple of part-timers. Technology, see. All our sales and admin staff are on an industrial estate on the Leeds ring road.'

'So you were Jack's first boss?'

'Yes, for my sins, of which there are many. He was a good lad, quick learner, but I knew he wouldn't stay long. Bigger fish to fry. I could see that it was the advertising side of it that fascinated him. He got more interested in the ads in the paper than the articles. This place was never big enough for him.'

'Well, he's in New York now.'

Bryan's eyebrows shot up. 'Is he? Is he really? Well ... it doesn't surprise me. He was always ambitious, driven.'

Ellie waited for Bryan to go on, but he was staring at one of the piles of paper. She gave a little cough to bring him back. 'So, Helen and Jack met at university ...'

Bryan gave a start and focused on her again. 'Yeah, first day if you can believe it. After university they had a year off travelling. Extended honeymoon, I think. Then he came to work here and she got a job in Leeds.' Bryan laughed. 'God, he was a soppy bugger about her. Mind you, she wasn't much better. Bit of a mutual-admiration society going on there. She used to write little notes and leave them in his wallet. And he could have had his pick of women any day of the week. They were throwing themselves at him, but he just laughed and went home to Helen.'

Ellie digested the information that Jack hadn't always been a serial womaniser and then simultaneously felt happy for Helen and jealous of her.

She waited for Bryan to resume, but he had drifted off again. This drip, drip, drip of information was torture. She couldn't take much more of it. She had hoped that Bryan would come out with everything she was desperate to know, but it looked as if she was going to have to ask him straight out. She juggled the question around in her mind until it sounded as sympathetic as possible.

'Poor Jack,' she said, 'he must have taken it badly when she cheated on him ...'

Bryan stared at her and seemed offended, as if she had affronted him.

'Where did you hear that?'

'I stumbled on the court report of the disturbance outside Wilkinson's house.'

Bryan continued to stare at her until he said, in an annoyed tone, 'Yeah, well, I wouldn't have written it up in such detail, but our tight-arsed owner said we had to be impartial. Couldn't pussy-foot around because Jack was one of our own.' Bryan snorted. 'I buried it on page eight, though. You did well to find it.'

All of a sudden Ellie didn't feel so proud of her investigative skills.

'How Jack didn't kill that little shit Wilkinson I don't know,' Bryan said. 'He'd been after Helen for ages, slimy git. Told people who didn't know him that he was a producer, but he was really a cameraman. Helen couldn't stand the sight of him. Not when she was well.'

The tiniest snake of unease began to uncurl in Ellie's stomach. 'When she was well?'

Bryan picked up his pencil and stared at it as if he had never seen one before. There was a pained look on his face. 'Of course, she was already quite ill when she went back to Wilkinson's house that night. Jack didn't know it, though. Nobody did. Not even Helen. It didn't come to light until a week or two later.' Bryan added gloomily, 'The mackerel incident.'

The snake of unease was steadily uncoiling in Ellie's stomach.

'Mackerel incident?'

'Yeah, Jack got a call saying that Helen had been caught shoplifting in Morrisons. He got down the police station to find her sitting with fifteen cans of mackerel in front of her. She'd put them in her bag and walked out of the store. Hadn't even tried to hide them and had chatted happily with the store detective when she'd stopped her. He knew then that something was badly wrong.' Bryan rolled his eyes. 'I mean, Helen didn't even like mackerel.'

Ellie knew what was coming next, from the tone of Bryan's voice, from the way he was sitting, from the expression in his eyes. Everything told her how this story was going to end, but she had to push on and hear it for herself. She had to hear those words that would make that snake in her stomach turn round and bite her for the stupid woman she was.

'What was wrong with her, Bryan?'

'Brain tumour. Made her act erratically. She got forgetful too, even a bit aggressive, which wasn't like Helen at all. That incident with Wilkinson was part of it. I was convinced she didn't even know where she was that night.'

'And . . . ?' Ellie held her breath.

'Died. Four months start to finish. Aggressive type, you see. Advanced already and beyond surgery. We gave Jack all the time off he wanted to . . . well . . . to get her through it. He came back for a few weeks afterwards, but it was too hard for him being back here. So he buggered off to Manchester, then took off south.' Bryan sighed. 'Poor Jack. Not got married again. Or what is it nowadays? A partner?'

Ellie shook her head. For the first time in her life she hated herself. Every spiteful, petty, self-absorbed bit. All this time she had been convinced that this was her love story when really there had been a bigger, more heart-breaking tale underneath.

And now she knew what had put that big plate of glass between Jack and any normal emotions.

She tried to get on to her feet but couldn't. So she sat there opposite Bryan in silence, thinking of the last time she had seen Jack and wishing that she could unsay all those terrible things she had said to him about Helen and hold him in her arms.

CHAPTER 35

Ellie stood in the queue for a cab and swallowed over and over again, trying to get rid of the pain in her ears. The queue shuffled forward and the man behind her rammed the back of her legs with his luggage trolley. She was going to turn round and give him her best disapproving face when it occurred to her that he might be armed. Everyone in New York was armed, weren't they?

She went back to trying to unblock her ears. Still, at least she was on solid ground at last, not circling above JFK Airport for twenty ear-popping minutes waiting for a landing slot. And she hadn't had to stand in the huge queue to retrieve her luggage. She didn't have any – just a handbag crammed with a clean pair of knickers, some paracetamol and a toothbrush.

One ear cleared, the queue moved forward, and the late-summer heat wrapped itself around her. She was weary from the journey, but most of all she was exhausted from thinking about what she would say to Jack when she found him. It had been madness to come here, but adrenalin had got her this far. Now, standing amid the mayhem and building work that was JFK Airport, she was beginning to lose heart.

A cab drew up and the big, sweating man organising the taxis bellowed at two Japanese people to get a move on.

Jack was out there somewhere, perhaps standing on a sidewalk feeling the same heat. All she had to do was find him. Not that difficult, then. Simply hunt him down in a city of nearly eight and a half million people and then apologise for calling his dead wife a slut and try to win him back. Easy-peasy. She closed her eyes and tried to go back over the haphazard plan she had been brewing in her head ever since Bryan North had dropped that bombshell about Helen.

Get a taxi to Bar Bootle, talk her way in, find Jack, get down on her knees and apologise. Happy ending.

The person in front of her was suddenly whisked off into a cab and the big, sweating guy was bellowing at her, 'You wanna ride or what? Come on. Where you goin'?'

'Roosevelt Hotel,' Ellie shouted back.

'OK, then,' he said, and shouted her destination at the driver.

Ellie pulled open the door of the cab and a smell of exotic spices hit her, swiftly followed by the pulse of Arabic music.

'Hello,' she said, but the driver didn't even turn his head.

Ellie took in the multitude of little charms and pendants hanging from the rear-view mirror. She sat behind the partition and grille separating the driver from the back-seat passengers and felt like she was in a tank.

'Which way you wanna go?' the driver said, not turning his head.

'Um . . . the quick way?' Ellie guessed.

The driver nodded and set off with a lurch. Then he started saying something and laughed uproariously.

'I'm sorry,' Ellie shouted, 'I didn't catch that.'

It was only after he carried on talking and laughing that she understood he was chatting to someone else on his radio. Feeling very naïve and very lost, she sat back in her seat. Of all the stupid ideas she'd ever had, this was perhaps the stupidest. What did she think she was doing? This wasn't a Richard Curtis film. Jack wasn't going to run towards her with his arms out when he saw her, touched by the fact she'd come all the way to New York to find him.

She decided to try to stop thinking for a while and let the sights and sounds wash over her.

Everything here was like London and nothing was like London. Except for the traffic jams. They came to a halt and then started to inch their way down the express-way. She looked out at the billboards and low wooden houses and frustration and anger welled up inside her. She just wanted to find Jack and try to put right the damage that her big mouth and her small brain had done. She didn't need this.

She went back to thinking about her plan. It stank. Sure, she knew where the agency was, but it was already after 7 p.m. What if he'd gone home? She had no idea where he lived and trying to worm it out of anyone at work would have alerted them to why she wanted it in the first place. So then what? Spend a sleepless night in her hotel and try again tomorrow?

She realised she had been chewing the skin along the side of her thumbnail again. If she went on like this, she'd have eaten herself completely by Christmas.

She took her thumb away from her mouth but couldn't get her mind off her plan, or lack of it. What if she couldn't actually get into his office? What if he'd told people a madwoman called Ellie Somerset was never to be allowed in? She had one evening and one day to find him and then she had to go home. It was hopeless.

Then she thought of the look of pain on Jack's face when she had said those things about Helen, and knew she had no choice. She had to find him.

A few more minutes and she had moved on to berating her own stupidity. How could she, Ellie Somerset, have cocked things up so badly? She had a reputation for researching the far end of a fart when it came to her work.

It was unbelievable that she'd confronted Jack with only half of his story.

She thought back to him accusing her of acting like a sick cat when Sam had left her and felt deep, deep shame. Of course it had made him angry when he had been through such real pain.

She was gnawing her thumb again. She sat on her hands and then realised the driver was talking to her. 'Rush-hour,' he said in a tone that suggested she must be mad trying to get into New York at this time of day. He waved his hand at the road ahead. 'This road is called the LIE, the Long Island Expressway, but it's a *lie* because it's not express at all.' He started to laugh. 'You get it? *Lie* because you can't go fast . . . express lane . . . fast . . .' He was slapping his thigh now with the hilarity of it.

Ellie ripped the boarding pass she was still holding into as many tiny pieces as she could.

When he'd stopped laughing, he turned his head slightly. 'You should have come into LaGuardia Airport. You'd have been there one and one half, maybe two hours ago.' He smiled at her in the rear-view mirror as if he had been incredibly helpful.

'Thank you so much,' she said politely. 'I'll make sure that I remember that for next time.'

Why couldn't he shut up? Why did she have to wade through all this when the only thing she wanted was to find Jack?

Slowly, slowly they moved towards New York, along the Grand Central Parkway and then across the Triborough Bridge. Halfway across, there was a little sign saying, 'Welcome to Manhattan.'

'Are we really in Manhattan now?' Ellie asked like a little girl, feeling excitement despite all the other emotions weighing her down. It looked so familiar, like a film set.

The driver caught her eye. 'Good, eh? Anything you want, anything you want, it's out there. The good and the bad. All there. You come here for something special?'

'Yes,' Ellie said, lowering her head to try to see to the top of the buildings they were driving past. 'I've come to find the man I love. I'm going to apologise for calling his dead wife a two-faced slapper and then explain that I understand why he keeps running away from commitment and that I want to make it all better for him for the rest of his life. And hopefully when I've done all that, he'll say, "OK, Ellie," and come home with me.' She had started to laugh even before she saw the expression on the driver's face. It was probably the start of jet lag or post-flight hysteria, but once she'd started, she couldn't stop and she sat back in the seat and let it happen, watching the buildings flick by and wondering whether the driver would charge her extra for being a mad Englishwoman.

Later, after checking into her hotel, Ellie walked out into a hot, sticky Manhattan evening. She wandered along the street for a while and then stuck out her hand for a cab. Her little stash of ready cash was fast disappearing, but what the hell. She'd already cleared out her bank account to buy the plane ticket. Hard to believe she was actually standing on a New York street. Two days ago she had been in Scarsdove. No wonder her arms and legs felt like lead.

A yellow cab drew up and she went to open the door when another hand reached out for it too.

'Oh,' she said, and automatically stepped back. The other hand belonged to a man in a suit. A really attractive man in a suit.

'Which way you goin'?' he said, hauling open the door.

'Um . . . Midtown?'

'You wanna share?'

'Share?'

'Yeah, I'm goin' that way too.' He gave her a look. 'Tourist, huh?' He didn't wait for her to nod. 'It's OK,' he rattled on. 'It's a New York thing.' He held up the hand that wasn't carrying a briefcase. 'See, I'm not armed . . . It's just that it's hard as hell to get a cab down here.' He gave her a large smile. Good teeth.

'You two gonna get in or dance on the sidewalk?' the driver said.

'After you,' the man in the suit said, and so, against her better judgement, Ellie got in.

She studied the man as he settled himself next to her.

He really was very good-looking. Psychopaths probably weren't that handsome. The man stared right back.

'So, you here on your own?'

'No,' Ellie said rather too quickly, 'with a huge group. Judo experts. Well, all martial arts really.'

'Oh yeah? Or you sayin' that because you think I'm a psycho?'

'Because I think you're a psychopath.'

The man chuckled and held out his hand. 'Steve Martin.'

'But not *the* Steve Martin?' she said, giving the hand a quick shake.

'If I had a dollar for every time—'

'Sorry. I'm Ellie, Ellie Somerset.'

'Pleased to meet you, Ellie. So, here on vacation?'

'Short trip,' Ellie said, and felt Steve's thigh connect with hers.

'OK. Need someone to show you the sights?'

'Um. No.'

'Shame. I was gonna offer.' His arm came along the back of the seat.

Ellie tried subtly to pull her dress down to cover her knees. 'You're quite direct, aren't you?' she said. 'In fact, everyone here seems quite direct. I thought New York was meant to be ...' She was going to say 'unfriendly' and then thought better of it. She didn't want to be rude and she didn't want to give Steve an excuse to show her how friendly he could be.

He seemed unperturbed. 'Hey, we're all in a rush. Busy, busy. We got no time for the slow build.' He brought his thigh into even closer contact with hers. 'This is only a short cab ride, so I gotta move fast. And it's not every day you get to share it with a beautiful Englishwoman.'

Ellie felt herself blush. There wasn't much room in the back of the cab and now there didn't seem to be much air either.

'Actually, I'm here to meet my boyfriend.' It felt nice to describe Jack like that, even if it was a total lie.

Steve removed his arm from the back of the seat.

Ellie decided to change the subject, 'So, you going home?'

'Nah. Back into work. Need to check on somethin'.'

'Right. And what do you do? As a job?'

'Account director. Advertising firm – Schneider & Linklan. You know it?'

Ellie was wide-eyed. 'No. But that's amazing. I work in advertising too.'

'Yeah? Cool coincidence. Well, we gotta pitch tomorrow and I'm goin' back in to check on the creatives, lazy sons of bitches. If you don't watch 'em, they'll louse up and go off to the bar. Whaddya do? Account director too?'

'I'm a copywriter,' Ellie said, and watched with some satisfaction as Steve's face crumpled in embarrassment.

'Do you have that expression "puttin' your foot in your mouth" in England?' he asked.

Ellie reached out and patted him on the arm. 'You are speaking to a master of the art.'

When the cab had dropped them both off, they walked a little way along the street together until they arrived at Steve's building. Ellie could see it was only a few doors down from Bar Bootle. 'So there are a lot of agencies round here?' she said.

'Yup. All sizes. Some on the way up, some on the way down.'

'What about that one?' Ellie indicated Bar Bootle.

Steve laughed. 'Well, it was on the way down. Big time. But now, who knows? Been bought by some English agency and they've got some fierce bastard in. One of your fellow countrymen. British accent, but not like yours. Now he's got them falling over themselves to show who can work the hardest.'

Ellie imagined Jack striding through the office sizing everyone up and picking off the weakest.

'OK,' Steve said, 'I'm goin'. But, hey, take this.' He handed her a card. 'If you get bored with that boyfriend, gimme a call.'

Ellie watched him walk away. Why couldn't the pigs in suits back home look anything like that? She put the card in her bag and walked along the street to peer through the smoked-glass window of Bar Bootle. She could see the receptionist's desk and a wall of art, but nothing else. Even though she had expected it to be closed at this hour, it was still a crushing disappointment. The thought of having to wait another whole night with that apology burning in her brain was depressing and she turned away from the agency and began to walk. She could smell the excitement on the streets here, just like in London, but somehow more dangerous.

She walked for a couple of hours, clocking up the sights. She looked in the windows of the Fifth Avenue shops and chatted to a man outside St Patrick's Cathedral who gave her a leaflet and tried to convince her that Charlemagne was the rightful king of America. She got moved on by a security guard when she tried to sit on a wall at the Rockefeller Center. As she explored, the conversations she overheard made her feel like she was in a Woody Allen film – 'Well, I said to her, "You're just gonna walk away from this. I'm the one with the therapy bills"' – and sometimes like a Martin Scorsese one – 'Yeah, he gave me that look, you know, the baseball-bat one.' Everything was frantically alive.

An old man dressed in a tuxedo was doing a soft-shoe shuffle on the sidewalk, his dog barking along to the music. Ellie thought of Edith and how, if she had been with her, she would have walked forward and joined him. It made Ellie feel very alone and very far from home.

She pushed on to Times Square and burst out laughing. It was the naked cowboy, not quite naked but wearing a pair of pants and a cowboy hat and serenading people with his guitar. She'd travelled three thousand miles and here they were: the singing knickers.

The evening got hotter. She gawked at the advertising signs; she bought a huge pretzel and a soda; she ignored the couples walking together with arms entwined. Sirens wailed, and steam really did come up through the manhole covers.

Finally she headed for Grand Central Terminal, her feet throbbing, and worked her way into the middle of the concourse and stared up. There were constellations of stars on the ceiling and impulsively she made a wish on one of them. When she brought her gaze back down, everything had gone blurry.

Eventually she pushed through the milling people to find the passageway leading back to her hotel. She was alone in a big foreign city, but Jack was here too. Whoever he was with tonight, tomorrow she would see him. What happened after that would be down to fate.

And you had to have hope, didn't you?

CHAPTER 36

'Oh, what a shame, you've just missed him,' the receptionist at Bar Bootle said, and Ellie tried not to show the disembowelling disappointment that she felt. 'Mr Wolfe will be so sorry. We know all about you, Mrs MacEndry.' The woman smiled a smile that was all perfect teeth and carefully applied lipstick. 'Mr Wolfe always says he's looking for another one of you over here to keep him organised.'

Ellie tried to look flattered.

'Do you want to see Rosa? She's normally on the desk here. You talked with her a couple of times on the phone, I think?'

Noooooooo.

'No, no, don't bother her—'

'It's funny,' the girl cut in, frowning, 'I had the idea you were much older. Mr Wolfe said you'd retired.'

Ellie did her surprised face. 'Did he? Well, he calls it retirement – it's his little joke. No, I'm taking a break. I've worked for Jack . . . Mr Wolfe since leaving school and now he's gone, it's time for me to have a rethink.'

The woman nodded. 'Constant reassessment is essential,' she said earnestly.

'Quite. Anyway, this New York trip, bit last minute. Thought while I was here, I'd drop in and surprise him.' Ellie heard her own voice sounding clipped and upper class, like some pastiche of a frightfully posh British matron. She wasn't certain how that had happened, but it appeared to be doing the trick: the receptionist seemed satisfied and the lovely smile came back. Ellie wondered how much it had cost or if all American people were born with perfect teeth.

'So,' she said, rushing on before Miss Colgate could ask her any more questions, 'Mr Wolfe's not here?'

'No, I'm sorry. He was going back to his apartment and then he was meeting . . . well . . . he was . . .' Ellie sensed the woman was reticent to discuss what else Jack was doing that day.

'He's out with some woman, I expect?' Ellie said in a chortling 'Isn't he a lad?' voice.

It seemed to be the prompt the receptionist needed. 'Well, yes, yes, he is. One of the models from a catalogue shoot we've completed. I think Mr Wolfe is taking her out to lunch.'

'Quite a one for the ladies, our Jack,' Ellie said, laughing over the top of a black wave of despair seeping into her.

'Uh-huh.'

'Oh well, you better tell him he missed me.' Ellie turned to go and then, as if she had just had a brainwave, she turned back. 'Or . . . if I rush, I might catch him at that apartment of his. I've got the piece of paper with the address on somewhere here.' She scrabbled in her bag, careful to keep her left hand out of sight and then dropped the bag deliberately on the floor. The receptionist was round the desk in a shot helping her scoop everything back up.

'Sorry,' Ellie said, 'jet lag.'

The receptionist retrieved Ellie's pen from where it had rolled under a chair and handed it back to her. 'Oh, don't worry, Mrs MacEndry. Here, let me write it down for you.' She jotted the address on some paper and handed it to Ellie.

Ellie was out of the door calling her goodbyes over her shoulder before the receptionist got suspicious. She felt mean and shabby about the deceit and hoped the receptionist didn't ring Jack and tip him off, but hell, all was fair in love and war, and fortune favoured the brave.

She was on her way.

Ellie arrived at Jack's apartment block to find he wasn't there. Or so the doorman told her. He was an old guy with medals on his chest and she guessed that he was used to protecting the residents in the building from unannounced callers. She tried to engage him in conversation, but he wasn't having any of it. And the longer she stood there, the more attention she was getting from people passing through the lobby.

She made a move to go to the lift and he told her politely but firmly that she couldn't go up. Mr Wolfe was not at home. He didn't know when he was expected back. She could leave a message, but it was a waste of time remaining there.

And then Ellie felt the atmosphere in the lobby shift and she turned round to see Jack. She needed all of her self-control not to run across the marble floor and throw herself at him. Instead she waited for him to see her. Please God let him look pleased.

Jack looked utterly horrified. He stood completely still and stared at her before walking somewhat unsteadily over to the doorman.

'It's one of those Velcro women I told you about, Lou,' she heard him say. 'Hard to prise off, you know?'

Ellie felt physical pain at the words. 'Jack,' she said, 'listen to me—'

'No,' he said. He didn't look at her, but the doorman was watching her as if she were some kind of lunatic.

'Can you deal with this?' Jack asked him, placing a hand on his arm.

'No problem,' the doorman said, almost standing to attention. 'You carry on, Mr Wolfe.'

Jack started to move towards the lifts and Ellie tried to

get to him, but the doorman simply positioned himself in the way. Short of pushing him over, she couldn't do anything.

'Jack, please,' she called, but the lift doors were already shutting.

There was quite a little scene after that where Ellie refused to go and the doorman told her what would happen to her if she didn't. As it involved calling the police and being put on the first available flight back to London, Ellie slunk out of the building and went and stood round the corner.

Now the skirmish was over, she realised that she was shaking. She hadn't expected Jack to welcome her with open arms, but what she'd just witnessed was ... She couldn't think of the word. Callous? Cruel? He'd more or less had her chucked out. The man who had kissed every part of her body had brushed her off like some kind of insect. Ellie sat down on the kerb. She was tired, she was hungry, but most of all she wanted to give up.

Only the thought of flying back to England without having talked to Jack made her stand up again. She took a deep gulp of air and tried to think what to do next.

Plan B.

If only she had a Plan B.

She walked back round to the front of the building as the door opened and Jack emerged, looking neither to left nor right and striding determinedly towards the cab that was waiting at the kerb. Ellie ignored the doorman advancing towards her and only had time to shout out the words 'Wait, listen!' before Jack slammed the car door behind him and the taxi sped off.

The doorman kept on coming and Ellie had a surge of inspiration. She raced out of his reach down the road and then jabbed out a hand.

It was probably the only time in her life she was ever going to say, 'Follow that cab,' and so she made the most of it, even though the cab driver looked bored to tears when she said it.

The lunchtime traffic was vile and at one point they lost sight of Jack's cab, but Ellie waved a fifty-dollar bill at her driver and promised him it was his if he caught up with Jack. In response he jumped a red light and dropped her round the corner from the restaurant as Jack walked in through the front door.

Ellie followed him at a distance. Catching sight of her reflection in a window, she paused to twist her hair up and secure it with a clip from her bag. She smoothed down her clothes as best she could and bit her lips and pinched her cheeks. Now all she needed was the British matron's voice.

'Jack honey, tell her to go away – she's starting to bore me.' The blonde woman with the pneumatic breasts put her hand on Jack's arm. Ellie could see that under the restaurant table Miss Plastic Tits' foot was slowly rubbing Jack's ankle.

The urge to grab hold of the woman by her perfectly cut hair was nearly overwhelming.

'What the bloody hell are you hoping to achieve here?' Jack said to Ellie. 'I thought I made it clear at my apartment block that I didn't want to speak to you. Stop making a fool of yourself and go home.'

Ellie ignored the glowering Jack in front of her and tried to focus on the one she had known back in London. The funny Jack, the one who was kind to Edith, the one who had talked to her through the bathroom door and then cradled her in his arms.

'Jack, I came all the way here to talk to you. I'm not going to be put off. I can't go home without telling you what I have to say. You must see that?'

In reply Jack swore loudly and slammed the menu he had been holding down on the table.

The other diners were pretending not to take any notice. But cool New Yorkers or not, Ellie could see the looks surreptitiously darting her way, the heads turned slightly. She tried to pour all the love she felt for Jack into her eyes so that he would know that he should leave the blonde by his side and come home with her. But the adrenalin pumping through her body was making her feel shaky, and her close proximity to Jack was having the usual effect on her body. She couldn't concentrate, couldn't get beyond wanting to sit herself in his lap and feel his arms come round her.

'Jack, please. I am trying to apologise for being so horrible about Helen. I'm trying to explain that I got hold of the wrong end of the stick. I didn't know the full story until I talked to Bryan at the paper. If I could take back those things I said about her, believe me I would.'

'And I have told you that I'm not interested in apologies or anything else from you,' Jack shot back. 'We had a fling, it was OKish and it's over.'

That 'OKish' rammed into Ellie's chest and she had to get hold of the table to stop herself from giving in and sliding under it. The blonde woman giggled and Ellie felt her hands twitch as if they had decided quite independently of her that they wanted to be round the woman's neck.

Ellie tried again. 'Jack, please listen to me—'

Jack slammed his hand down on the table. 'No, I have told you before. I am not listening to you. Everything we had to say to each other we said in London. You're being pathetic chasing me across the Atlantic like this.'

Ellie could see the other diners openly staring now. There was a general murmuring. No doubt they had her down as a pathetic stalker, a pathetic scruffy English stalker in their nice, cream-coloured restaurant. She was interrupting their lunches and talking over the jazz track. Ellie saw the blonde pneumatic woman yawn elaborately.

She stumbled on. 'I am so sorry about Helen, Jack. I cannot begin to understand the pain you have been through. I wish I could take every piece of it away from you. I love you, Jack.'

'Right, that does it.' Jack rose abruptly to his feet. 'You've got a choice here, Ellie. You either stop making a tit of yourself and go, or I get you chucked out.'

Ellie saw the blonde woman run her hand up the back of Jack's thigh. She smiled at Ellie like a cat that had all the cream and wasn't handing it over anytime soon.

'I'm sorry, I can't go, Jack. Not until I've said everything I have to say. Stop fighting me and listen. If you listen, I'll go, I promise, but listen.'

Jack folded his arms. 'Go on, then. Amaze me.'

Ellie glanced round at all the faces looking at her. This scene wasn't meant to go like this; she was meant to be talking to Jack somewhere private, just the two of them. She felt like she was some kind of freak in a show. She took a deep breath. 'I got it wrong, Jack, but so have you. All this' – Ellie waved in the blonde woman's direction – 'it's not you. It's not who you used to be when you were happy.'

Jack laughed. 'Well, bugger me. You're not only a copywriter, you're a psychologist too.'

'Jack, please ... I ... I think that you've got stuck somehow at the point you were at when Helen died. I think you're scared to move on, to really work at a relationship in case you find someone you love as much as Helen. It would make you feel like you'd forgotten her, like you were being disloyal. If anybody gets close to you, you run.'

Jack snorted. 'Oh, I get it. You think that you were getting too close, so I ran away?' He looked down his nose at her and then leaned forward. 'Perhaps when you've had more experience of men, you won't take a little fling like we had so much to heart.'

Ellie gripped the edge of the table more tightly and made one last effort. 'I wanted you to forgive me for what I said, Jack, but if you won't forgive me, please at least think about what you're doing with your life. I can't bear to think of you carrying on like this, being permanently lonely and going from one mindless fling to the next.'

'Gee, thanks,' said the blonde woman.

'I know I've blown my chances, Jack, but please, please find someone who will look after you and love you and . . . and give you a family and security and everything you deserve.' It was a great speech and she managed to get to the end of it without faltering. But hearing herself say she had blown her chances finally brought it home to her that she had.

Jack's face was stony, empty. 'Go home and stop humiliating yourself, Ellie. You're hardly qualified to lecture anyone on relationships. Didn't your last boyfriend have an affair for months without you even noticing?'

That was it, a final killer blow delivered in front of everyone, her deepest secrets aired at the freak show.

The blonde woman leaned forward. 'Face it, honey, you're the type of girl that men cheat on.'

When Ellie felt a waiter's hand on her arm, it was almost a relief. The torture was about to end. 'I'm sorry, ma'am,' he said, 'you're disturbing the other diners. I'm going to have to ask you to leave.'

She was aware of Jack sitting back down, of the blonde woman raising her hand to his cheek, and then she let the waiter lead her from the restaurant and out into the street. There was no parting, mind-changing wisecrack, no final romantic declaration that would melt Jack's heart. The last look he had given her had been one of intense anger.

Down in the men's room later, Jack splashed cold water on his face and then braced his arms against the back of the sink. It was pointless going back over every word he'd said. He knew he'd inflicted pain on her as effectively as if he'd punched her. Hell's teeth, if he'd heard any other man talking to a woman like that, he would have gone over and decked him. No question.

What choice had he had? She had to stop thinking he was a good guy. When she got over the shock and sat and thought about it, she would definitely hate him. And that was good; hating him was good. She could move on from that, get over it and get on with her life.

Damn it, though, she'd come all the way out here to apologise. How much had that cost her? And she looked so sad, so ill. Jack turned on the cold tap again and rubbed his wet hand over his face. Why did she have to make it so hard? Why keep turning up and telling him how much she loved him? He took a big gulp of air and kept his head down until his throat stopped tightening.

Better to leave it like this. She'd get over him soon enough.

He ignored the pain that thought brought with it and stood back up straight and smoothed down his hair.

He'd got a free afternoon and piranha woman upstairs in the restaurant had already made it more than clear she was his for the asking. So he was going to ask and then he was going to bury himself in her and forget all about Eleanor Somerset.

Jack went back up into the restaurant, paid the bill and escorted the blonde woman to his apartment, where he had sex with her against a wall and tried not to compare her plastic hair and plastic conversation and plastic breasts to Ellie's.

It didn't work. He just felt like a cheap, dirty bastard and sadder than he had since Helen had died.

CHAPTER 37

'You and Jack Wolfe?' Lesley said, her eyebrows doing a manic dance. 'Jack Wolfe and you?'

She said it a few more times until Ellie put her hand on her arm and said, 'Yes. Jack Wolfe and me.'

They were sitting on a bench in the park, eating lunch. Ellie had known it was the right time to tell Lesley about Jack, out in the open, without any flapping agency ears listening.

Lesley moved on to, 'Jack was married and his wife died?' which she repeated quite a lot while Ellie looked at the ducks and ate her prawn and avocado wrap.

Telling Lesley hadn't been easy, but she couldn't go on pretending everything was fine. She'd given Lesley the very edited highlights in the end, and hadn't mentioned Helen's fling. It didn't seem relevant to the woman Helen had been or to her marriage. In some crazy way Ellie felt protective towards Helen and even more protective towards Jack.

Lesley finally ran out of astonishment and settled on, 'Jeez, you should have told me earlier.'

'I know,' Ellie said, 'but you had your own problems with Megan and her family back in Wales and well, it was too big to talk about.' Ellie reached over and took hold of Lesley's hand. 'It wasn't because I didn't want to tell you. It was too painful. And I felt so stupid.'

Lesley shook her head. 'Right under my nose and I couldn't see it. No wonder you threw that sickie when he came back from New York.'

Ellie let go of Lesley's hand and took another bite of her wrap, and they sat there looking at people walking their dogs and a group of small children kicking a football.

Lesley broke the silence with a self-mocking laugh. 'I wish you'd told me before his leaving do. I made a right arse of myself telling him he was the best boss I'd ever had. And I put a tenner in his leaving collection. Bastard. If I'd have known, I'd have got even more drunk and kneed him in the groin.'

'Thanks, Lesley, you're a real friend.' Ellie threw the last of her wrap on to the grass and watched the ducks start to run towards it. 'Anyway, it doesn't matter now. It's over, finished. It was just sex for Jack and I built it up to be something more. He's still in love with his wife as far as I can see.' She brushed the crumbs from her skirt to cover up the fact that her eyes had started to fill up. It was a little while before she felt composed enough to say, 'Why can't I be more sophisticated and slip in and out of relationships without getting so involved?'

Lesley gave her an incredulous look. 'Why should you? It's a hideous way to be, believe me. I mean, great for a while, but, Jeez, in the end it's like stuffing yourself stupid at some kind of all-you-can-eat people buffet and then making yourself feel sick. And . . .'

'And what?'

'Well, it's no wonder you got confused with Jack. He isn't meant to have sex with anybody he works with. It's a Jack rule – everyone knows that.'

'He knew he was going by then, so I didn't count.'

'He said that?'

'More or less.'

Lesley shook her head. 'I really, really wish I hadn't put that tenner in now. What a git.'

They watched the ducks fighting over the wrap and Ellie waited for the one question that she knew Lesley was dying to ask.

'Um . . .' Lesley said.

Ellie wasn't going to help her out.

'Um . . .' repeated Lesley with the addition of a querying look.

'Um, what?'

Lesley shuffled her feet about a bit. 'Well, we've

established that Jack was a bastard out of bed, but . . . uh . . . in bed?'

Ellie had formed some witty reply and was about to deliver it when a picture of Jack and her entwined on her bedroom carpet came into her mind. She saw Lesley's face disintegrate into a watery blur as her tears came properly this time. 'He was lovely, Lesley, completely lovely,' she sobbed. 'Filthy and tender both at the same time.'

'Oh, Ellie,' Lesley said, and scooted along the bench to put an arm round her.

Eventually Ellie got herself under control.

'I'm really sorry, Lesley. I miss him so much and I got it so wrong and I don't feel I can trust myself to understand anything any more.' She scrabbled in her pocket for a tissue. 'When it ended with Sam, when I got over the shock of the Barcelona thing, I realised there were loads of signs that we'd been on the skids. Loads. But with Jack, it seemed to be getting better and better. Just before the end I felt we'd got really close, crossed over some kind of line. He said such wonderful things to me.' She blew her nose fiercely. 'I was so trusting, such an idiot.'

'C'mon, you've got to stop putting all the blame on yourself.' Lesley gave her another hug. 'Someone like Jack's used to getting women to believe that they're the centre of his world for a night, or a couple of nights.'

'Or a couple of weeks.'

'Yeah. Look, you're talking to the queen of getting it wrong here. Till I met Megan.'

Ellie gave Lesley a waterlogged smile. 'But I thought Jack was my Megan. Do you remember when you met Megan for the first time and you said you realised it was a face you'd been waiting for your whole life? Well, that's how I felt about Jack. Everything I knew about him told me to run away, but I couldn't. I fell deeper and deeper into liking him and then loving him. He was who I'd been waiting for.'

Lesley gave her shoulder a squeeze. 'Poor, poor Ellie. You don't deserve another swine, not after Sam.'

Ellie wiped her face dry and put the tissue back in her pocket. 'We better get back. I've still got the copy for the Whispedge pack to polish up.'

They started to walk across the park, Ellie aware that people were looking at her blotchy face.

'You've got to promise me, Lesley, hand on heart, that you won't tell anyone anything about this. I couldn't stand having it all raked over by Hugo and Rachel and the rest of them.'

''Course I won't. Except . . . can I tell Megan?'

'Yeah, you can tell Megan. But no one else. Tell anyone else and I'll let Megan know about that sandwich-delivery girl last year and what you did to get that extra filling.'

Lesley made a 'cross my heart' sign and for good measure

a 'zipping up my mouth' sign too and then they went over the road and headed back to the agency.

That evening Ellie couldn't think of another single word to make with the Scrabble tiles in front of her. Edith was playing to her usual high and bawdy standards, but so far Ellie had only managed 'wig' and 'top'.

Ellie was aware that Edith was studying her. Up until now Edith had been extremely understanding about the whole Jack thing, not once saying, 'I told you so.' For her part, Ellie had tried her hardest to do her mourning for Jack in private and had worked on her bright and breezy act, the one that she had been perfecting at work. Even when Edith had caught her yesterday standing in the garden with tears streaming down her face, Ellie had tried to pass it off as hay fever.

'Ellie, Ellie, Ellie,' Edith said suddenly, real sadness in her voice. She got up and poured them both another gin and splashed the tiniest bit of tonic on top. Then she set the glasses back down, gave Ellie a little consoling pat on the hand and disappeared out of the room. A few minutes later she was back with a battered old biscuit tin. The lettering on the side revealed that it had once held custard creams costing one shilling and six old pence. Edith set it down on the Scrabble board with a flourish.

'Now, Ellie,' she said, taking a big gulp of her drink, 'tell me exactly what happened with Jack.'

'Oh, Edith, no, you don't want to hear it. You warned me and I didn't listen.'

'Tell me. I want to help you. Come on, drink up and talk.'

So for the second time that day Ellie spilled out everything about Jack and how much she loved him. She even told Edith something that she had not told Lesley: that for a brief period of time she had felt that Jack understood her better than anybody, even her family.

Edith listened and nodded and drank some more, and when Ellie had finished, she reached across and took the lid off the biscuit tin.

'Ellie, I know you feel dreadful, but . . . well, things will get better . . . if you let them. Sometimes you have to realise that somebody is not coming back and there will be no happy ending. You don't get the prince, you get the frog. And sometimes after a while the frog doesn't seem so bad and you realise that the prince was not in fact that much of a prince.'

Ellie was slightly concerned that Edith might not have taken all of her medication today and was steeling herself to move the gin a little further away from her when Edith put her hand into the tin and pulled out a black-and-white photograph.

'Meet Flight Lieutenant Henry Simpson,' Edith said, and handed her the photograph.

Ellie looked down at a young man, broad and blond, wearing an RAF uniform.

'He looks handsome,' was all Ellie could think to say, confused about what this had to do with her and Jack.

'Oh, he was, Ellie, he was. Very handsome. Not only that, he was completely filthy and very tender.'

Ellie looked up sharply. She hadn't mentioned those words to Edith when she'd described Jack; she'd only used them to Lesley. Before she could think any more about that, Edith dropped another bombshell.

'He was the love of my life,' she said, and took the photograph back.

Ellie tried to get her mind around the idea that Edith had a lover that she hadn't known about.

'So, Henry was before Great-Uncle George?' she asked.

'Before, during and, if I'd had my way, forever after too,' Edith said, not looking at all embarrassed. She put down her glass and ran a finger tenderly over the photograph. 'Henry was stationed in India during the war, that's when I saw him first. I was a girl then, well, a teenager I suppose, and he was a good eight years older than me. Managed to persuade him to pose for this though.' Edith continued to hold the photograph, smiling down at it. 'He went back to England after the war, of course, and I thought about him from time to time, never really expecting to see him again and then, just after I'd turned twenty-one he strolled into a party in a friend's house. Unbelievable. Liked India so much, he'd come back. Still flying, this time cargo planes.' Edith paused. 'I'd already started going out with

George by then, but it was awfully hot and Henry was awfully funny and he had a stomach on him like a washboard. He was hung like a donkey too,' she added cheerfully, and Ellie almost choked on her gin and tonic.

'I'm sorry to say that I started to go out with him as well as George.' Edith giggled, a lovely throaty sound. 'Actually we didn't go out much at all. He was a marvellous, marvellous lover.' She placed her hand in the tin and ran her fingers over the envelopes and notes there. 'Wrote such beautiful love letters too. But he was a wild one. I suspected I wasn't his only lady friend.'

By the look on Edith's face she was currently back in Henry's arms in India.

'So . . .' Ellie said.

'So, I tried to give him up, especially when George proposed. I mean, I knew the thing with Henry wouldn't come to anything – he wasn't the marrying type. He told me that. So I accepted George's proposal and determined never to see Henry again.' Edith paused and rummaged around in the tin for another photograph. She handed it to Ellie. In this one Henry was older and stripped to the waist by the side of an aircraft. Edith was right about the washboard.

'Then, one evening, not long after I got married, Henry came round to bring some papers to George. He wasn't in and, well, it all started up again.'

Edith caught Ellie's eye. 'I never imagined I'd be an

adulterous wife . . . well, not so soon after getting married. And of course it was so stupid. I knew I could get found out. I knew I was hurting George. But I couldn't stop myself. And by then Henry was telling me he loved me, wanted to look after me. He'd tried to stay away but he couldn't.'

Ellie heard the echoes of her own story and didn't like it. She finished off her drink and resisted the urge to go and pour herself another one. Edith reached across and took the second photograph back from Ellie and stared down at it. 'I was completely at a loss to know what to do, Ellie. I was in love with Henry, but I was a married woman. And then, well, then the problem solved itself.'

Edith slowed to a halt before resuming. 'One afternoon, about six months after we'd taken up again, he was due to take a plane up to Delhi. When he walked out of my bedroom door that afternoon I never saw him again. Didn't ever get the chance to say goodbye.'

All these years later Ellie could see the pain in Edith's eyes. She got up, went and sat next to her on the sofa and held her hand.

'So he was killed? In his plane?'

'No.' Edith snorted. 'He wasn't going to Delhi at all, the little shit returned to his wife and family. In Torquay. It appeared he was the marrying type after all.' She threw the photographs back into the tin.

This was not turning out to be the poignant love story Ellie had imagined.

'The point I am trying to make, very badly, Ellie dear, is that I had to come to terms with the love of my life just going. He left me to pick myself up and get on with living with George. And I did. George may not have been Henry, but he was a good man and, well, we rubbed along.'

'You're telling me that I will have to do the same, aren't you?'

'Yes. Jack was a lovely, lovely man, but I think you have to accept that he is not coming back to you, Ellie. Jack either can't or won't sort himself out enough to fall for someone again. Particularly somebody like you.'

'Why *particularly* somebody like me, Edith? What's so strange about me?'

'Well, you don't really do half-hearted, do you?' Edith said in a matter-of-fact way. 'You have never been . . . what do you call it? Cool? I remember your mother bought you the most beautiful frilled knickers when you were about three and you walked around all day with your skirt held up looking at them. You were completely oblivious to people laughing and even to your mother's embarrassment. You loved them so much you couldn't bear not to see them.'

There they were again, knickers. Whatever happened in Ellie's life, it always came back to them.

'There was no way you would accept half-measures from Jack and share him with someone else.' Edith patted Ellie's hand. 'Look, I'm not saying that Jack is exactly the same as Henry, but they did both have wives they forgot to mention. And in Henry's case, he decided not to leave her for me . . .' Edith's meaning was clear: Jack wasn't going to leave Helen.

Edith put the lid back on the biscuit tin. 'I know this won't have cheered you up, Ellie dear, but it should give you hope. I never thought I could be happy again after Henry went, but I was. Maybe not the ecstatic kind of happiness I had with Henry, but it was enough.' She picked the tin up and looked at it. 'And at least I had something to remember Henry by.'

'Yes,' Ellie said with a sigh, 'all those love letters and photographs.'

Edith grinned. 'No, dear, I was thinking of your aunt Pandora. She's the spitting image of him.'

For the first time in her life Ellie did a double-take. *Whaaat?*

'She doesn't know, of course,' Edith said, getting up. 'Nobody does. Only you.' Edith stooped to kiss Ellie and then toddled off to bed, her biscuit tin clamped firmly under her arm.

Ellie could not believe it. Aunt Pandora, linchpin of the WI and the local Conservative Party, was a love child. She started to laugh, thinking of the expression on Pandora's face if she ever found out, and then abruptly stopped laughing. She wished that Jack had left her something, anything, to remember him by.

Climbing the stairs to bed, she tried to concentrate on Edith's message that life would go on and things would get better.

But that night she dreamed that she was carrying Jack's baby, and when she woke up, the realisation that it was only a dream left her feeling empty and cheated.

CHAPTER 38

It was positively uncanny. The more power and prestige you got, the funnier your jokes became. Hugo was almost bent over double at her story about the beaver and the vicar. In fact, since she had become senior copywriter, he'd found everything she did side-splittingly funny or deeply, deeply impressive.

Still, Jack had been proved right: her opinion of Hugo and the other suits had improved since she'd taken a little time to get to know them better. Hugo could still be an arrogant swine at times, but he'd earned his wages on the Scarsdove account.

He had taken the jittery council, worried about spending money on anything that looked too flashy or expensive, and led them gently through the case histories of other councils who had successfully rebranded. He'd even accompanied them on hearty, back-slapping tours to some of the best ones. Ellie could not help but be impressed by the way he had handled it. Somehow Jack had worked his magic on Hugo as well.

Except, as far as she knew, he hadn't slept with Hugo, told him he wanted to look after him and then dumped him.

So, once Hugo had got the council used to the idea of going for something a bit more radical, Ellie and Lesley had come up with a look and a tone of voice that they could live with. The council had now convinced themselves that it had been exactly the kind of thing they had been looking for all along.

Much against her usual instincts, Ellie had since found herself saving Hugo's bacon on quite a few occasions. Being a pig in a suit, he was extremely grateful.

Ellie let Hugo laugh a bit longer and then gave him a playful punch on the arm. 'Come on, Hugo, it wasn't that funny. Now, where are you taking our Yorkshire friends tonight?'

Hugo went red and started to fiddle with the pencils on Lesley's desk.

'I see,' she said. 'You're taking them to a lap-dancing club, aren't you?'

'Well, um, yes, Ellie, yes, I am. They asked specifically. They don't have one in Scarsdove.'

'Tut, tut. Do the taxpayers of Yorkshire know how their public servants spend their time?'

'Well, strictly speaking it's their own time. I mean, it is after working hours.'

HAZEL OSMOND

'I was pulling your leg, Hugo.'

'Oh, yes. I knew that. Yes. Ha, ha, ha.'

She gave him another friendly punch on the arm. Hugo seemed to respond to 'chap-like' behaviour from girls, probably a result of his years at a single-sex boarding school.

'Seriously, though, Hugo, thanks for doing this tonight. If I had to watch Adam Adamthwaite's impersonation of a hippo dating a giraffe again, I might die.'

Hugo winced. 'Yes, palls a bit, doesn't it? Well, perhaps the Thong Throng will take his mind off it.' He stood up. 'OK, see you later. Think I might have time to thrash Ian at table tennis.'

When he'd gone, Ellie sat back in her seat and let her mind roam to Jack. In the five weeks since she had returned from New York, her recovery from him had been virtually non-existent. A part of her was still over on the other side of the Atlantic.

She kept finding herself replaying every detail of that first time they had made love, and the time he had allowed her to give him carpet burns on his bottom, and the time he had slung her over his shoulder and carried her off to bed. She let her mind travel over every detail of his body, from his long fingers and his strong arms to the flat sweep of his muscled belly. If she was feeling particularly masochistic, she would remember how she had wrapped her legs round him and how he had cried out into her hair.

But it was that look in his eye on their very last night

together that still haunted her. If it had been a lie, then all her senses were redundant, her gut reactions misplaced. Never again could she trust herself to see something and interpret it correctly.

She leaned forward and clicked the mouse on her laptop to open her emails and paged down to find the only communication she had received from Jack since she had seen him in New York: *Congratulations on the ideas for the Whispedge account. Saw them yesterday and thought they were great. Jack.*

As love letters went, it lacked something. Like love.

She'd dithered for days about replying. In the end she had simply typed, *Yes, we're pleased with them. Best wishes, Ellie and Lesley.*

She was satisfied with how professional it sounded, and the inclusion of Lesley was a masterstroke. He'd see how she had put it all behind her now.

Or he'd guess that as an advertising copywriter she was really good at bending the truth.

She sat for a while and thought about him mourning Helen, unable to go back and unwilling to move forward, and felt incredibly sad. He was living some kind of half-life and now, it appeared, she was too.

The only difference in their two situations was that her love had rejected her, not died. Somehow there was not as much comfort in that thought as there should have been.

Her particular grieving process had not been helped by having to hear about Jack every day. He was doing well, transforming the American agency, helping them win new accounts. Same old story, same old Jack.

She checked the clock and packed up for the evening. No point in hanging around. Lesley would not be back from her 'get to know the future in-laws' holiday in Crete until tomorrow. Apparently Lesley was now the second daughter that Megan's parents had always wanted. The thaw had happened when one of Megan's married uncles disgraced himself with his secretary. The ensuing scandal meant that Megan and Lesley had been demoted from the top sinners spot and Megan's family had decided that Lesley was, after all, not that bad a catch. Apart from her lack of a penis. The wedding looked as if it might take place before the end of the year, and Megan's grandfather had stopped threatening to put Lesley in his leek trench.

Ellie closed the office door behind her and headed for the lifts. She wanted to get home and check on Edith, cook her a proper meal, perhaps even persuade her to stay in for one evening. Edith showed no signs of slowing down; in fact she was even more manically busy. Yesterday it had been a tea dance, today it was carpet bowls, and tomorrow she was on a coach trip to Brighton.

Wandering through reception, she waved at Rachel. Mike was in his customary position, leaning on the desk worshipping her. There had been a general agency bet on the number of weeks the whole thing was going to last – even when the two of them announced that they were moving in together. Almost everybody had laughed behind their hands, but Ellie wished them luck. She was holding out for romance.

Outside on the street, it was hot and sticky and London was crying out for a good downpour of rain to clean and rinse everything. Ellie sniffed the air, but all she could smell was petrol fumes. There was nothing to excite her here this evening. The only thing that excited her was thousands of miles away, probably planning to cook steak for some other woman by the light of the moon.

CHAPTER 39

Among the presents that Lesley had brought back from Crete were a liqueur that tasted of ash, a statue of a man with an enormous penis, and a blow-up aubergine. Ellie was trying to find room for them in the office. They'd have to have a good clear-out when they decamped to the bigger room along the corridor, but for now Ellie balanced the items on the mini-fridge and hoped nobody asked for a beer.

'. . . Ooh, and this one is of me and Megan's mum at a restaurant in Chania,' Lesley said, clicking through the photos she'd already downloaded on to her computer. 'And this is Megan's dad trying to teach the waiter Welsh.'

Lesley's happiness was infectious, and they spent the morning chatting about the holiday and the fast-developing wedding plans. Ellie was glad to lose herself in somebody else's life. Over a second cup of coffee Ellie filled Lesley in on what had been happening in the agency while she had been away, especially the latest develop-ments in the Rachel and Mike romance.

'Yeah, Rachel's already backed me into a corner to tell me. She was hinting she might make it to the altar before me. Mike stood there with a soppy grin on his face.' Lesley frowned at her pencils. 'Has someone been touching these?'

Ellie remembered Hugo playing with them. 'I knocked them over, sorry.'

'Oh, that's OK. I don't mind if it was you.' She hurriedly started to rearrange them and then said hesitantly, 'Talking of office romances, how are you feeling about "he who cannot be named"? I've been building up to ask you.'

Somehow the nickname Lesley had given Jack always made Ellie laugh. And laughing felt good, like she was exercising muscles she hadn't used for ages. 'Well, concerning Voldemort, there is nothing new to report. Heart still smashed, pride still trampled, still zero interest in other men.'

Lesley gave her a searching look. 'You don't have to do that light-hearted thing with me, Ellie.'

'No, I know, but—'

'You're allowed to be sad for as long as you want.' She reached out and brushed her fingers over Ellie's hand. 'But remember, the hating-him stage will kick in soon. It's got to. Law of physics, you know.'

Ellie laughed. 'Well, if I think of how he talked to me in that restaurant in New York, then I think I do hate him a bit. Especially when I remember how he let that woman he was with join in. But ... when I think of everything else about him, then, pathetically, no, I can't hate him.'

Lesley asked a few more questions about Jack, but Ellie didn't want to linger on the subject. What more was there to say? It was over; even she could see that. If she had been starring in a romantic comedy, Jack would reappear and say it was all a mistake on his part. Unfortunately this was real life, her life, and she had somehow to get on with it. Just as Edith had said.

At this moment, though, the thought of what 'getting on with it' meant filled her with dread. In a few years' time would she have 'settled' for someone else, some kind of approximation to Jack? Or even worse, would she be half of a couple like the one Edith and she had whispered about in the restaurant, sitting there with nothing to say to each other? Bored, bad reflections of each other?

Ellie steered the conversation round to other things, and soon they were both buried back in the Scarsdove annual report. Ellie enjoyed the easy silence as they worked. At least losing Jack meant that there was no more sneaking around behind Lesley's back, hiding things from her.

The morning moved along and the only sounds were the tapping of Ellie's nails on the keyboard and the squeak of Lesley's pen on the paper. About an hour before lunch there was a knock on the door and Rachel walked in.

'Ooh, nice tan, Lesley. I'm surprised to see you've got one. I didn't think you'd get out of the bedroom.'

'Very good, Rachel – that was almost a joke. Nice to see you haven't lost your sense of humour when you're going to need it most.'

Rachel looked puzzled.

'Now you're living with Mike. Jeez, you'll need a sense of humour for that.'

'Ha, ha, very funny. Look – I'm cracking up.' Rachel made a weird, googly-eyed face and then turned to Ellie. 'Anyway, it's you I came to see. There's a guy from Scarsdove downstairs.'

'Well, can't Hugo see him?'

'He says he wants to speak to you. Just you. It's important.'

Ellie sighed and stood up. It must be something about last night. Perhaps Hugo had reverted to default plonker mode and got the entire council arrested. 'OK, where is he?'

'Meeting room,' Rachel said, and disappeared out of the door.

Ellie trudged down the stairs wondering whether she should have brought the draft copy for the annual report along with her to give the guy a taste of how it was going to read. Too late now – she wasn't walking all the way back up the stairs.

She pushed open the door and suddenly thoughts of

annual reports and holidays in Crete and Rachel living with Mike left her mind and all of her attention was focused completely on one spot in the room.

A spot where a tall, dark-haired man with broad shoulders was standing totally still.

CHAPTER 40

Ellie felt her heart thump and then speed up.

'A man from Scarsdove,' she said. 'Rachel said there was a man here from Scarsdove.'

Jack nodded. 'I am a man from Scarsdove.'

Of course he was. A big, handsome man from Scarsdove, but was he actually here? After dreaming about this happening for so long, Ellie could not trust that this wasn't some kind of fevered imagining on her part. The man looked like Jack, though; a tired, more crumpled version of Jack, but Jack nonetheless.

'How have you been?' he said.

Well, even if her brain couldn't quite accept yet that he was in the room, her senses all knew it. Every part of her was feeling wired.

How had she been? She had no idea how to answer his question. 'Devastated' sounded too dramatic. 'A bit upset'? She shrugged.

Jack raised a hand and ruffled his hair but didn't smooth

it down again and Ellie wanted to do it for him. All those little boxes in her head filled with happy memories of him were beginning to open up again. Him in the car, in her room, sitting outside the bathroom door. She'd tried to seal them down and keep them shut, but that wasn't working.

Jack had been unable to sit and wait for Ellie to come into the room. He'd been pacing up and down until he'd seen the door handle move, and when he saw her, he could tell that Rachel hadn't warned her that he was there. Good old Rachel, finally able to keep a secret.

He couldn't trust himself to move towards her, though, and in truth he had no idea what she would do if he did. The look of surprise on her face had gone and now her expression was unreadable. She hadn't answered him when he'd asked her how she was, but he didn't need an answer really. She was wonderful.

Why had he ever thought she looked like a student? She looked exactly like she was: funky, slightly dishevelled, soft. She had that flippy little skirt on again and a top with a neckline that gave a hint of where the swell of her breasts started.

The thought that he might never get to kiss her there again made him swallow hard.

He might actually have left this too late. He backed to the table and sat down on it more heavily than he had intended. He knew Ellie was watching him, but there were no clues about what she was thinking. She was normally so animated; he could read what she thought simply by looking at her. She'd never hidden anything.

Now she was asking him how he was, and it seemed to him that it was the same kind of tone she would have used for somebody she'd met in the damn street.

He felt sick. He was an idiot; he needed to say something to her before he found he couldn't say anything at all any more.

'I'm great, Ellie. Great.' His reflexes were carrying him along.

'And New York?' It was that same damn polite tone. It was so, so detached.

'Great too. It's . . .' Jack stopped. Time to end all this formality, all this chit-chat. He'd been up for twenty hours. He was going to fall over soon if he didn't say what he had to.

'Actually, Ellie, it's not great, it's rubbish, complete rubbish.' Jack looked at Ellie's face again, but there was no reaction, nothing. He took a deep breath. 'It might as well be sodding Halifax in the drizzle, Ellie.'

Jack wondered whether Ellie had actually heard him, her face was so impassive. He felt his heart rate go to buggery. There was a nasty metallic taste in his mouth. He had to get this out, come clean.

'Ellie, I cocked up big time . . . I . . . What you said in

the restaurant in New York . . . Well, it wasn't completely right, but it was near enough.' Jack paused and then restarted all in a rush: 'I don't know how you feel about me any more, Ellie. I've been a jerk, a complete jerk.'

Why wasn't she saying anything? Why was she just standing there looking at him like he was someone she used to know? Jack felt panic grab at his skull, the same kind of panic he'd felt when that doctor had taken him to one side and explained about Helen. Why the hell had he left it so long? He should have given in before now and come back to her.

He wasn't certain what to say next, where he was going, and then he was talking and he couldn't stop the words. 'Look, I fought this. I'd got my life under control. I didn't want to ever be out of control again . . . I didn't want this, Ellie.' Jack came to a halt as he saw Ellie's eyes flare at him. He could not believe what he had just said, that wasn't what he had practised all the way on the flight over the Atlantic; he was meant to tell her he loved her first. That was meant to be first. Sod it, perhaps if he could hold her, he could get it right.

Jack took a step towards Ellie and saw her take a definite step away from him.

A lovely warm feeling of hope had spread through Ellie when Jack had talked about New York being rubbish. He must mean that it was rubbish without her. That's what he was trying to say. Maybe, just maybe, she hadn't been imagining what he felt for her. When he called himself a jerk, he had seemed so sad that despite everything he'd done, she was tempted to tell him to stop talking and come over and hold her.

Then everything changed. He was being horrible to her again, telling her how he didn't really want this. He didn't want to be out of control. The lids on all those happy boxes were slamming shut again and her mind was pulling forward all the nasty things he had said and done to her, turning them over and seeing how ugly they were. Casting her to one side and not even having the guts to tell her; deciding to move to New York and her being the last to know; humiliating her in front of all those people in that restaurant.

He'd come all this way to tell her he didn't want her messing up his ordered life.

So why the move towards her? Well, he could forget that.

'Sod you, Jack,' she shouted.

Ellie saw Jack make another move towards her and he was trying to say something else, but there was nothing in the world that was going to stop her screaming it all out now. She'd been so reasonable, so understanding; she'd made herself sick.

'You were a bastard to me, Jack,' she yelled at him, her hands balled into fists, 'and I never did anything to deserve it. Nothing. You made me feel used; something you could wipe yourself in and then throw away, like a piece of old tissue.'

Jack's mouth was moving, but she could only hear her own voice. 'And those things you said in that restaurant, the way you humiliated me in front of everyone and I took it because I was so desperately sad about Helen dying. I let you and your stupid girlfriend laugh at me. Have you any idea how much that hurt to hear you say those things? Have you? I was on my own in a foreign country, I was begging you to listen to me, and you just cut me down.'

She saw Jack lift his hand as if he was going to reach out for her. No. She didn't want to feel his touch ever again.

Ellie whirled round and strode towards the door. She felt hot and wobbly; the blood was pounding in her ears. She heard Jack shout her name in a tone she had never heard him use before; it had a pleading, desperate sound. It almost stopped her, but her anger was carrying her forward and she had to get right away from him.

She was reaching for the door handle when she saw it turn of its own accord and Lesley barged into the room.

Her gaze went first to Ellie and then to Jack. She gave a little 'Oh' and her brow furrowed, and then her attention was all back on Ellie. Her eyes were huge behind her glasses.

'It's Edith,' she said, and Ellie could see the panic in her expression. 'She collapsed at the coach station. They've taken her to St Thomas's. She had you down as her next of kin.'

CHAPTER 41

Edith hardly made any kind of bump in the bedclothes. Her whole body seemed to have shrunk, her skin grown more translucent.

Seeing Edith without her make-up and her bright clothes, those sleights of hand that had distracted people from her real age, was gut-wrenching. Ellie sat down in the hard chair next to the bed and scolded herself for not being more insistent that Edith should slow down. Why hadn't she treated her more like the old lady she was?

'Talk to her, love. Let her know you're here,' the nurse said, as she pulled the curtains round the bed.

Ellie leaned forward and put her hand over Edith's. It felt cold and bony and very small. 'Edith sweetheart, it's Ellie. What have you been doing to yourself?'

There was no response; Edith lay quite still, her eyes closed.

Ellie looked around at the grey locker, the plastic water jug and the garish curtains and wanted to take Edith away from it all. She didn't belong here. She should be back home with the stools in the shape of elephants and a gin and tonic in her hand.

'Now come on, Edith,' she tried again, moving to sit very gently on the bed, 'you can't keep lying around like this, not in the middle of the day.'

Nothing.

'I was looking forward to thrashing you at Scrabble tonight.'

Edith's eyelids fluttered open and Ellie squeezed her hand.

'That's it, Edith. Come on, it's me, Ellie.'

Edith's eyes looked misted, unfocused, but Ellie saw her mouth twitch slightly on one side.

'You're going to be all right, Edith. You've had a bit of a turn. You've been doing far too much.'

There was no change in Edith's expression, but Ellie felt the slightest movement in the hand on the sheet, so she lifted it up and sandwiched it gently between her own. It seemed so fragile she was afraid she would shatter it if she pressed too hard. There was definitely movement there, though. She smiled down at Edith, trying to encourage her back from wherever she was.

Ellie thought about telling her that she had called Constance and Pandora, but decided against it. Edith would know things were serious if her daughters were on their way. So softly she talked about Lesley's holiday and the liqueur that tasted of ash and the figure with the huge penis. Then she talked about the weather and what was on television that night and about how they would be missing her down in Brighton. She didn't mention Jack, couldn't trust herself to say anything about that.

All the time Edith's face remained impassive, as if she were there but somehow frozen, and Ellie was finding it more and more difficult to remain cheerful; a feeling of dread was creeping over her like a shadow over a lawn.

'Edith sweetheart, please try to listen to me.' Ellie fought to keep the desperation out of her voice. 'I'm going to stay here with you and hold your hand and keep on talking and you're going to have a little rest. You're going to need all that energy of yours. There's a double-feature *Dracula* at the Forum on Tuesday and then we've got that talk on the Indian hill stations.' Edith's eyes were still unfocused, but her hand continued to make little movements between Ellie's.

'That's it, Edith, come on. The house is going to be pretty dull with you in hospital. I don't want you in here any more than a couple of nights.'

Ellie kept talking, but Edith's eyes drooped closed and for a second Ellie stopped talking and watched Edith's chest. It was still rising and falling. She started talking again, quicker this time, as if by talking she could keep at bay whatever was lurking, unmentionable, just out of view.

She wished Pandora and Constance would get here soon, and then as quickly unwished it. When they arrived, she would have to take a back seat. They would be the ones holding Edith's hand. The thought of that made Ellie hold Edith's hand tighter and tell her how much she loved her and that she wouldn't leave her.

But the movements of Edith's hand were getting less frequent.

The sounds of the ward were all around, she could hear people talking on the other side of the curtain, but her world seemed to have shrunk to the length and width of the bed and the woman lying in it. This woman who had taught her so much without trying and entrusted her with the biggest secret of her life.

And then something about Edith changed and Ellie knew that she had gone. There was no major event, no crisis, just a slipping away of all that zest and energy. It went like a whisper, but it was definitely gone.

Ellie could not move, could not believe it. Edith was indestructible. Surely she would sit up in a minute and ask why the hell she wasn't on the coach to Brighton. Reaching out her hand, she very gently ran it down Edith's face and her fingers felt what her brain could not digest.

Ellie continued to sit there holding Edith's hand. She was unwilling to let go or leave Edith alone in order to fetch a nurse. The rest of the world would be barging in soon enough. She needed some time to say her goodbyes to Edith in her head, even if there was no point in saying them out loud.

In Edith's face she saw traces of her own father and of herself, but no trace of the real Edith any more.

When she felt able, she bent forward and kissed Edith gently on the forehead. Then she thought how cross Edith would be about anybody else seeing her looking so un-Edith-like and reached for her handbag and got out her comb. Methodically she tidied up Edith's hair for her.

Then the silence broke and the room was suddenly full of Constance and Pandora with their husbands in tow complaining about the price of hospital parking. The nurse was walking towards the bed.

As quickly as they had all burst in full of chat, they stopped, each one of them transfixed by the sight of Edith. Five pairs of eyes turned to Ellie.

'I'm sorry,' she said, 'she's gone.' She let go of Edith's hand and got up off the bed. The nurse became all action and concern. Ellie couldn't stand it. 'I need some air,' she said, and snatched up her handbag and ducked through the curtains.

Outside the hospital, she sat down on a bollard. Edith was dead. The impossible had happened.

Someone came and stood in front of her and she looked up to see Jack.

'I was in the waiting room,' he said. 'I saw you go past ... Edith ... ?'

That was when Ellie started to cry properly. Jack tried to put his arm round her, but she swatted him away. She was aware that he was still standing there as she sobbed and wiped her nose with the back of her hand. Here she was, crying in front of Jack again, but this time she didn't give a damn what he thought.

Jack mumbled something about calling a taxi, and when it came, she climbed in and he sat next to her. Ellie looked out of the window. Everything seemed the same; the sun was shining; the streets were full. But London was one feisty old woman short.

Jack's thoughts were on that other trip he had made home from hospital in a taxi and how he had hated every smiling fool he had seen out of the window. Now here he was in another taxi, watching someone else suffer, and he couldn't even comfort her. He couldn't even help the woman he loved because he'd magnificently, stupendously stuffed everything up. He tentatively moved his hand over Ellie's and she didn't pull away. But she didn't look at him either.

CHAPTER 42

Jack watched Ellie buttering the piece of bread as if she hated it. He wanted to offer to do it for her, but she hadn't spoken to him since they'd got back to Edith's house and there was no reason for him to believe she would talk to him now. She'd walked into the house and disappeared upstairs, leaving him to sit in Edith's sitting room and go over, yet again, how much he'd messed everything up. She'd only re-emerged when Constance and Pandora, with husbands, had arrived back from the hospital.

This was the nearest he had got to her since the taxi ride, standing in the kitchen pulling together something for everyone to eat.

Ellie tore open a packet of ham, put some of it on the bread, then sliced up some cucumber and placed that on top of the ham. After she'd rammed another piece of bread on top, she cut the whole thing roughly into four triangles. Jack picked up a bottle of red wine from the counter and, as he was uncorking it, continued to watch

Ellie uneasily. She'd been crying upstairs, but now she was angry. He guessed it was at death, he knew that feeling, but probably it was also at him.

He was about to have another go at talking to her when Constance came into the kitchen and shooed them both into Edith's sitting room.

Sitting in there on his own before, he'd remembered that night when he'd been playing Scrabble with Edith and Ellie had come home tipsy. Tipsy and beautiful.

Now here he was, balancing a plate on his knees and making small talk with a long streak of a guy called Gerald who was Pandora's husband. Across the room sat Frank, a man who talked constantly about money and was about half the size of his wife, Constance.

Ellie didn't look his way once. Mind you, she wasn't looking at anybody else either. Just staring ahead of her, knocking back the wine. Constance and Pandora started to reminisce about Edith's eccentricities and Jack saw Ellie cast a venomous glare in their direction.

'Do you remember that speech day when she turned up in that appalling coat with the fox heads still attached at the neck?' Constance slipped her court shoes off her large feet. 'Terrified the first-year pupils. They had to be rounded up and frog-marched out of the hall.'

Pandora snorted and helped herself to more wine. 'How could I forget? Or that skirt she wore the next year. Totally inappropriate.'

Constance nodded. 'Totally.'

'We could probably sell her clothes collection to a museum, or a travelling circus,' Gerald said, and then sniggered.

'Probably make a bob or too,' added Frank.

Jack wasn't sure, but he thought he could hear the sound of Ellie grinding her teeth.

'Wasn't only the clothes, though, was it, Pan?' Gerald said, taking a massive bite out of a sandwich and then proceeding to talk with his mouth full. 'Remember when she turned up at our silver wedding with that salsa band she'd met in the pub?' Gerald turned to Jack. 'She got completely plastered and ended up trying to limbo under the dining-room table. Made a hell of a mess.'

'Oh, don't,' said Constance. 'I've lost track of the number of times I had to apologise for her. Remember that disgusting thing she suggested to Mr Hunter? How Father stood it I don't know.'

Jack saw Ellie's hand reach out for the wine bottles again. That was her third glass and he hadn't seen her eat anything yet. He picked up the plate of sandwiches and took them over to her. She shook her head and waved him away.

'So,' said Frank, his eyes glistening, 'what are house prices like around here?'

'Had a quick scout when I went out for some matches,' Gerald said. 'Still look pretty buoyant. Reckon you're looking at around eight hundred and fifty thousand for this.'

There were appreciative noises all round, which didn't quite mask the sound of Ellie putting her glass down on the table with some force.

Jack felt Frank tap him on the arm. 'Where do you live, then?'

'Down by the river. Greenwich.'

'Flat or house?'

'Flat. Warehouse conversion.'

Frank whistled appreciatively. 'Bet that's worth a bob or two now, then?'

Jack glanced uneasily at Ellie. 'Well, I bought at a good time . . .'

'Bet you did. You look like a man who knows a good deal. What line of business you in? The City?'

'No. Advertising and marketing.'

A cheeky smile spread over Frank's face. 'Advertising and marketing. Same as Ellie, eh? You two don't work together, do you?'

'Well, we used to.'

'Office romance, eh?' Frank said, jabbing Jack with his elbow. 'Boss and secretary?'

Jack wondered if it was acceptable to slap the husband of a recently bereaved woman.

'Ellie wasn't my secretary. She's a senior copywriter and—'

'Secret's safe with us,' said Gerald.

Jack chanced another look at Ellie. She had filled her wineglass yet again.

'Leave Ellie alone,' Constance said, and then patted Ellie's knee. 'We all know that you were very fond of Edith. We're very grateful for the way you looked after her. She was such a worry to us before you took her under your wing.'

'Not such a worry that you got off your backsides and came to visit her,' Ellie snapped, standing up so abruptly that she sloshed wine on to the carpet. 'I mean, God knows it's hundreds of treacherous miles from Surrey to here. Shame it took her dying for you all to pay her a visit.'

Ellie stood there glowering and then shook her head. 'Sorry. I'm sorry,' she said quietly, and walked unsteadily out of the room.

After a sticky silence Constance and Pandora started to mutter about how easy it was for Ellie because Edith hadn't been her mother.

Jack figured that Ellie needed to be alone for a while to pull herself together. And really, what help was he going to be? He had no idea how things stood between them. Anything he wanted to say to her she wouldn't want to listen to tonight. He should leave her alone.

He got up slowly, excused himself and went to look for her.

He found her out in the back garden on her knees. She

appeared to be digging a hole in a flowerbed with a large soup spoon.

'Don't you have a trowel?' he asked gently.

She didn't look up. 'If I had a trowel, I wouldn't be using a soup spoon, would I?'

'Fair point,' he said, and walked back into the kitchen. He opened a few drawers until he found what he was looking for and then went back into the garden and got down on his knees next to Ellie. She looked at the fish slice in his hand but kept on shovelling earth out of the hole.

Jack started to slice chunks out of the hole too. Every now and again he noticed Ellie stop and wipe her eyes with the back of her hand; she had a smear of earth down one cheek. He had no idea what she was doing or why she was doing it. But *how* she was doing it was definitely scary, like she was possessed. He fumbled for something to say, some little bridge to build between them.

'Ellie, this hole you're digging?'

'It's not actually for Edith, before you ask.'

There was that physical pain, as if she'd punched him in the chest.

'Ellie, for God's sake, do you really think I would say something so heartless? I liked Edith. She was ... she was a one-off, funny, sharp as a knife ... wicked. Why would I say that about her?'

'I don't know, Jack, but then I don't know anything any

more.' Jack winced at the bitterness in her tone as she continued to gouge great lumps of earth with her spoon. 'I mean, I wouldn't have thought two daughters would sit there pricing up their mother's possessions and agreeing what a laughing stock she was when she's probably not even completely cold yet. So, hey, what do I know?'

Again Ellie wiped her hand roughly over her eyes, leaving another smear of dirt behind and Jack wanted to reach over and wipe it away with his fingertips.

'Different people deal with grief in different ways, Ellie,' he said.

'Oh, what the hell would you know about it?' Ellie chucked a spoonful of loose earth on to the growing pile. Then he saw her stop and close her eyes. 'Sorry,' she said, opening them again. 'Of course you'd know.'

Another punch to his chest. He dragged in a couple of deep breaths and kept his head down. 'Forget it.' He hacked at the sides of the hole, dislodging great lumps of earth.

They worked together in silence. Jack was glad to be close to her, even under these circumstances. Every now and again their hands would meet in the hole and once or twice he timed it deliberately so that they would. All he could do was try to help her with whatever this manic task meant to her.

She threw down the spoon. 'That's deep enough.'

Jack watched as she felt behind her, brought out an old

biscuit tin and then took the lid off and tipped its contents into the hole. He reached out and picked up a photograph of a young, smiling man in an RAF uniform.

'An old boyfriend of Edith's?'

Ellie nodded. 'An affair, before and after she was married to George. He's Pandora's father. Pandora doesn't know. Nobody but me knows and that's the way it's going to stay.' She took the photograph out of his hand and placed it back on top of the other papers.

'He died?' Jack said, not really wanting to ask that question at all.

'No, went back to his wife. Edith never saw him again.' Ellie started to shovel the earth back into the hole and Jack helped her, trying not to think too deeply about Edith's lost love.

If he wasn't careful, he'd have another lost love of his own on his hands. Another one to add to Helen. He stopped shovelling so that he could gaze at her. Drink her in.

Here she was, still looking after Edith. He felt as if in that very instant, kneeling next to Ellie in the garden, he understood everything about her and loved her even more because of it. Such determination to do good.

Very soon the hole was filled and Jack took the spoon from Ellie and started to pat down the soil.

'You look like you're smashing the top on a boiled egg,' she said, and then stood up and turned away from him. He saw her shoulders juddering and her hand go up and pass across her eyes again and he desperately wanted to grab hold of her and kiss it all better.

Everything was completely still in the garden; around them the air was warm and perfumed with flowers and the lights were creating little glowing pools in the bushes and the trees. The perfect evening for romance if he hadn't so spectacularly, magnificently, shagged everything up. It was going to take tiny steps to get back to her, even if she would let him. He stood up very quickly, determined to take one of the steps now.

'Ellie, I know that tonight isn't the right time to talk about this—'

Suddenly the back door opened and a corridor of light flooded out into the garden. They both turned to see Frank striding towards them.

'Ah, there you are,' he said, and then stared at the fish slice and spoon in Jack's hands. His brow crinkled. 'What are you doing?'

'Planting bulbs,' said Ellie.

'This time of year?'

'Edith bought some and never had a chance to plant them. I thought it would be apt if I did it now.'

'Right,' Frank said, still looking at the spoon and fish slice. 'Right, well, good. Anyway, it's nearly time to turn in and the girls have sent me out to ask about sheets and things ... Could you show them where they are?' He noticed the biscuit tin and bent to pick it up and then

turned it over in his hands. 'Very nice, bit ropey condi-
tion, but it might be worth a bob or two.' He put it under
his arm, oblivious to the look he was getting from Ellie.
'Come on, then, time to stop all this spooning in the
moonlight.' Mightily pleased with his own joke, he started
to chuckle but stopped when he caught Jack's eye. He
looked quickly at Ellie. 'OK. Well. Let's go and find those
sheets, then.'

Ellie followed him into the house and Jack watched
them go, not sure what to do next. Nothing in life had
really prepared him for the correct way to end a day that
included a botched declaration of love, a death, burying
the evidence of somebody's parentage and standing in a
garden with a fish slice in your hand.

CHAPTER 43

Ellie rolled over and then sat up quickly and scrabbled out of bed. Ten thirty – she was going to miss the Creative Department meeting.

Then she became aware of two things: she was still wearing yesterday's clothes, and Edith was dead. That second thought made her sit back down on the bed with a bump. No more filthy Scrabble; no more huge neat gin; no more crazy clothes; no more of Edith's sheer exuberance at being alive.

All that love and companionship they'd built up over the years, gone in minutes.

Ellie sat there bringing up deep sobs until there seemed nothing left to mine. She reached out for a tissue and blew her nose. Her chest felt as though somebody was sitting on it.

Yesterday had been like that rollercoaster ride Lesley and she had tried out. The high of seeing Jack, the low of arguing with him and then the depths of Edith dying. No, not a rollercoaster ride: more like a vertical drop down a mine shaft. No wonder she'd flaked out last night. She remembered finding the bedding for Constance and Pandora and then going to sit up in her own room for a bit of peace.

Jack's shoes and socks were by the bed and Ellie wondered if he'd spent the night in the room with her. Perhaps he'd put her to bed.

Yesterday morning she would have been beside herself with joy at the thought of spending another night with Jack. Now she wasn't sure she cared any more. There was too much else careering round her brain. Thinking about a man who had dumped her and then reappeared talking regretful gibberish was too much. She kicked out at his shoes and then went to have a shower and find some paracetamol.

The house was silent as she phoned Lesley to tell her she wasn't coming in. That conversation was torturous. Lesley had left a message on the answerphone the night before asking how Edith was, but Ellie had not been able to face telling her the truth. Listening to the shock in Lesley's voice, followed by the sound of her crying, set Ellie off again. It was some time before she got down into the kitchen to find a note on the kitchen worktop: *Gone to sort out registrar and funeral details. Back late afternoon. Constance/Pandora.*

At least she had time to get herself pulled together.

Ellie's mind limped over the events of the evening before, but when she started to go over the bit about digging the hole for Edith's letters, she forced herself to stop. That would mean thinking about how kind Jack had been and she didn't have the emotional battery power for that right now.

Once the kettle had boiled, she made a cup of tea and headed for the garden. Someone had left the back door unlocked.

Outside, she took a step back at the brightness of the sun. The temperature was already high and it was going to get higher. Even in her thin kimono she felt hot and overdressed. She sipped at her tea and wandered over to where they had buried Edith's letters and photos, and saw that somebody had scattered a handful of small stones over the area, so that it was almost impossible to tell that the earth had been moved.

The person whom she supposed had done it was standing at the end of the garden looking up at the back of the house with his arms crossed. Barefoot and with stubble shadowing his cheeks and chin, Jack looked like something wild that had strayed into suburbia. He was heart-stoppingly sexy and he was still here, but what that meant she didn't know, and right now she was fed up with trying to second-guess what Jack was up to. She'd been trying to work that out since that first night in his flat.

She saw him glance her way.

'What are you looking at?' she asked, turning to peer up at the roof.

'The roof.'

She finished her tea and fumed. One- or two-word sentences from Jack weren't good enough right now. What she wanted were pages and pages of explanation for the way he had treated her.

'Any particular reason?' she said.

'Think there's a slate missing.'

Ellie felt all her remaining nerves snap one after the other. Reappearing unannounced back in her life and coolly discussing the roof right after Edith had died wasn't on. It wasn't even his roof.

'Tell you what, Jack,' she said slowly, 'why don't I get you a ladder and you can climb up and have a good look. With any luck you'll fall off it and break your bloody neck.' She walked off down the garden, but not before seeing Jack's face. She registered that he didn't look surprised or angry, just resigned.

Ellie pushed open the back door and went into the kitchen again, switching the kettle on as she walked past it. She needed more tea – what she did not need was a session of playing riddles with a taciturn Yorkshireman.

Jack appeared in the kitchen. 'Ellie—'

'Leave it, Jack. Go back to New York, work your way through all of the women in North America and leave me alone. I've had enough of trying to guess what you're up to, what you really feel. I don't need another of yesterday's half-hearted little speeches telling me how you didn't want to want me.'

Ellie wrenched the top off the jar holding the teabags, grabbed one, threw it in her cup and then sloshed water from the kettle on top of it. 'Do you remember how you were always trying to get me to raise my game? Well, you were right. I shouldn't settle for the callous way you treated me. I deserve better.'

She jabbed a spoon into the teabag in the cup and then fished it out and slung it in the sink, not caring that it left a trail of brown liquid across the worktop.

'Funnily enough, Jack, I'm a little bit upset this morning, and to be honest I'm surprised you're still here. Shouldn't you be off shagging someone else? It must be all of twenty-four hours since you've had sex. Unless of course you had a go at me while I was asleep.'

Jack hung his head as she pushed past him to get the milk from the fridge. 'Ellie,' he said, 'I know you have so much else on your mind. I know I cocked it up yesterday, but let me explain.'

'Don't kid yourself, Jack,' she said, pouring milk into her cup. 'You cocked it up way before yesterday.' She picked up her tea and walked past him back out into the garden. This time she stayed on the patio and settled herself into one of the chairs.

Jack came to sit in the chair opposite and gave her that intense, grey stare of his.

'Ellie, sit and listen to me for ten minutes.'

'No, Jack, don't try and tell me what to do. You're not my boss here in this garden. When I've finished this cup of tea, I'm going back to bed.'

Jack sighed. 'OK, OK. I know you're really angry with me.'

'Oh, you picked that up, did you?'

'Ellie ... please ...' It was the same tone he had used in the meeting room yesterday, the one that had almost made her turn back when she had been heading for the door. Even this morning it managed to take the sharpest edge off her anger. She made a vague 'go on' gesture, but deliberately didn't look at him. She wanted to hear what he had to say, not be distracted by the way he looked.

Jack leaned towards her. 'Yesterday I was rubbish. If it had been a pitch to a client, I would have blown it. I said all the wrong things, started in the wrong place. Completely the wrong place.'

Ellie took a sip of tea that was far too hot and felt it burn its way down her throat.

'I should have started by telling you that I love you, Ellie. That last night we spent together, well, I knew then that I was in trouble.'

'Trouble?' Ellie slammed her cup down on the table. There he went again, talking about her as if she was something to be avoided, something bad that had happened to him.

'Damn,' Jack said, and rubbed his hand over his chin. 'I used to be able to talk in a straight line without putting my foot in my mouth.' He picked up her cup of tea and held it out for her to take. 'I'm sorry, just ... just drink your tea and give me another go.'

His tone once again swayed her and she slowly reached out and took the cup from him, but the familiar flip of her stomach that had greeted the phrase 'I love you' had now fizzled away to nothing. If Jack loved her, and it was a big 'if', he had a funny way of showing it.

She saw Jack shift in his chair. 'I don't find this easy, talking about Helen, laying out all my emotions as if they were things at a car-boot sale for people to pick over.'

Ellie looked down the garden and focused on how the heat was making little mirages of water appear on the lawn. She wanted to tell Jack that she wasn't any old 'people', but it was his turn to talk, not hers.

Jack bent down, picked up a piece of loose stone from the patio and looked at it as though it had upset him in some way.

'Helen dying was incomprehensible,' he said sadly. 'I'd known her for nearly seven years, four of them we'd been married, and then it was all gone. A matter of months. I had everything I wanted and then I had nothing.'

'Afterwards ... being around everyone I'd grown up

with, I couldn't do it. So I took myself off to Manchester and just ate and slept and worked.' He gave a mirthless laugh. 'For the best part of two years I didn't even think about anyone else.'

Ellie didn't comment, just kept concentrating on the lawn and the shimmering heat haze.

'Then one night I went out to a bar and picked up the first woman I could. The sex was good. I woke up in a sweat in the morning half expecting to find Helen's hands round my throat, but there was nothing. So I kept on doing it.'

Ellie had a vision of Jack hanging around the bars in Manchester and felt intensely sad.

'Don't look at me like that, Ellie. I know it wasn't a good way to act.'

'I wasn't judging you, Jack.'

He looked unconvinced. 'Well, anyway, it wasn't always one-night stands. Sometimes it was two nights, a couple of weeks, a few months. Nothing heavy, though. It worked for me. Every time I had sex it was like putting two fingers up at fate. Like proving I was still alive.' Jack looked down at the stone and transferred it to his other hand.

'I told people in Manchester nothing. Let them think I was what they saw. Made it easier – I'd had a bellyful of "poor widowed Jack".' Ellie saw him scowl and the stone ended up on the patio.

'When I moved to London, it became even easier. More

women who only wanted to keep it cool. Of course, every now and again I'd get it wrong. Someone would start getting a bit keen. But I knew the signs. They'd cook a meal for me, or buy me a tie, or a book.' Jack shook his head. 'Books. What is it with women and books? My sisters were the same. They were always buying books for boys they fancied.'

Ellie bent down and picked up the stone and put it on the table. 'It's like sending a love letter without having to write it yourself,' she said softly.

Jack studied her for a while and then turned his face away. His voice when he spoke again sounded dry and tired. 'Well, I didn't want their books or ties or lovingly prepared meals. When that happened, I bailed out. I know it was horrible, that I was turning into the kind of heartless bastard I used to sneer at, but I didn't want to get emotionally involved again. I gave the impression that I did, but at the end of the day I couldn't have given a toss.'

He reached out and picked up the stone again. 'So how did I find myself a few months after meeting you, having a good time playing Scrabble with your great-aunt and getting genuinely upset that both your parents were dead?' He shrugged his shoulders. 'I guess at the start you came up on my blind side. I couldn't recognise you for what you were. I saw a scruffy, tricky, underachieving member of staff. I suppose I should have twigged when I found myself getting so irritated by you ...' Jack palmed the stone again and closed his fingers over it. 'Then when I did realise why you were irritating me, it was too late. All I could hope was that the sex was going to be rubbish, or once I'd had you, I'd lose interest.' He snorted. 'Well, those two ideas crashed and burned spectacularly.'

Despite her earlier resolution to keep looking at Jack to a minimum, Ellie had found herself watching his face as he talked, particularly his eyes. She couldn't believe how miserable he seemed. Like he was describing some kind of accident that he'd been in. He had her emotions zigzagging all over the place. Should she be pleased she had at least had some effect on him? That he had been shaken up by her even though the whole experience had obviously been so unpleasant for him?

Then, quite unexpectedly, Jack laughed. 'That first time in my flat, you were so . . . surprising. You weren't pretending to be cool or experienced. You weren't playing any little power games. You were so damned open. When you actually thanked me, in my kitchen, for making you less timid, I felt . . . God, I don't know . . . like I'd done something great for once. Almost something honourable.' He shook his head. 'Then the sex bit kept getting better and better and I started to like you more and more and . . .'

Ellie had that old familiar somersaulting-stomach feeling again.

'Every time I tried to end it, I couldn't. I knew I was

scrabbling to stay upright and remain in control. It bugged the hell out of me. I wanted to shake you and tell you to leave me alone.' He darted a glance at her. 'Going to New York seemed the best solution and even then . . . your visit . . . I . . .'

Jack pressed his lips together tightly and Ellie waited.

Everything in the garden seemed to be holding its breath along with her.

'No matter how hard I tried, I couldn't stop thinking about you,' he eventually said. 'What you were doing, what you were thinking. Even what you were eating for your bloody lunch.'

The intensity of Jack's stare ripped through Ellie's determination to be quiet. 'But you didn't want me to replace Helen. I was right, wasn't I? You can't let her go.'

Jack shook his head. 'No. Helen's been dead ten years. She's a huge part of who I am, but I've had to get on with life.' He put the stone very deliberately back on the table, and when he spoke next, it was so quietly that Ellie had to strain to hear him.

'It wasn't about Helen's death, it was about yours.'

For a second Ellie could not even make sense of the words.

'Mine?' she said incredulously.

Jack shot her a look of the blackest misery. 'Yeah, your death. I was afraid you might die too.'

'I don't—'

'When I began to care about you, it all started up again. That feeling of worrying about someone else and then ... well, then that bastard with the scythe came back. The one who came for Helen.' Jack's gaze shifted away from her as though he was too embarrassed to maintain eye contact. 'Every time we got together there he was grinning at me, telling me he could whisk everything away whenever he wanted. Who the hell was I to think I could be happy again? I couldn't bear it, Ellie. I couldn't go through it all again.'

She saw his hand go to his eyes and was unwilling to embarrass him by staring. She could hear him struggling to keep in control.

'It's not like in the movies ... someone lying there and drifting gently away. I mean, it might be for some people, Edith perhaps ... And for Helen at the end ... but there were times, Ellie, when I didn't think I could bear to keep watch any longer. I was so scared. And none of those things you normally tell people to comfort them were going to work, were they? "Don't worry"? "I'll look after you"?'

He took his hand away from his eyes and looked straight at her. 'When I realised that I really, really loved you, I had to run, try to get back to not caring about what happened to you.'

Ellie felt a tiny little flame of elation spring up as Jack said 'really, really loved you'. Everything she had believed she had seen in his eyes on their last night together *had* been there.

Then just as quickly the flame was extinguished by the realisation that there was absolutely no future for them. He had been unable to comfort Helen with the usual platitudes and now Ellie was going to fail to comfort him. How could she tell him nothing bad would ever happen to her? She was not immortal.

She got shakily to her feet, feeling as if her lungs were full of sand and she was barely managing to dredge up a breath. There was a man here who loved her desperately, but he couldn't push aside that grinning skull to get to her.

She had to move away from the table or she would suffocate.

'There's nothing to be done, then, Jack,' she managed to say, and took a step towards the house.

Jack's hand shot out and grabbed one of hers. 'No . . . don't go . . . I haven't finished,' he said, his voice panicky. She was aware of his face tilted up towards hers, but she didn't dare look at it.

'I got it wrong, Ellie, so wrong. Sitting in Central Park one lunchtime, I realised I'd killed you off myself. I'd done exactly what I'd been scared of. It hadn't taken an illness or an accident. If I was never going to see you again, you might as well have been dead.'

Involuntarily Ellie's gaze went to the patch of earth they had dug yesterday and Jack turned his head too.

'Yeah, that hit a nerve last night,' he said. 'Henry might as well have died – the end result for Edith was the same.' He turned back to look up at her. 'I thought about you still being out there in the world without me, making a life with someone else, lying beside him in bed, having his babies . . .'

Suddenly Jack was on his feet and he grabbed her other hand and held it tight as if he was afraid she was going to make a run for it. 'I wouldn't blame you if you told me to get lost, Ellie. The way I treated you . . . the things I said in that restaurant . . . the pain I caused. I'm not sure if you're going to be able to forgive me for that. I don't even know if I deserve it.'

She felt him squeeze both her hands. 'But whatever you decide, you have to know that for the first time since Helen died I'm not thinking about what might go wrong in the future. I'm thinking about what I could have right now with you.' She felt his thumb start to rub along her knuckles. 'I love you, Ellie. I want to take a chance again and bugger what might happen.'

He gave her hands one more squeeze and then let them go. It was a movement that said, 'It's up to you now,' as clearly as if he had spoken the words.

Ellie looked at him and thought how much it must have taken for him to admit his fears to himself, let alone to her. How hard it must have been for him to lay bare all those feelings he'd kept buttoned up.

All the love that she'd been trying to beat away over the past weeks came pouring back into her and she reached out and grabbed him firmly with both of her hands.

'Come here, you idiot,' she said, and wrapped herself around him.

Jack made a strange gasping noise and brought his head down on to her shoulder. His hair lay against her neck and she felt his chest convulse. She said nothing, just rubbed his back gently until whatever it was had passed.

When he finally lifted his head, the look in his eyes made Ellie raise one of her hands to his face and this time he didn't pull away. He took it and kissed the palm and then bent and kissed her on the mouth. It felt like an affirmation of everything she had believed: Jack Wolfe loved her.

She could feel his heart hammering in his chest as strongly as her own.

When they stopped for air, Jack said, 'I can't tell you that I won't nag you about getting taxis when it's late or force you to go for all your check-ups. I'd wrap you in cotton wool if I could. But I don't want to know what's ahead any more.' He cradled her face in his hands. 'The future seems too vague and distant a thing to ruin what I've got here.'

'And the man with the scythe,' Ellie said, 'he's not standing behind me?'

Jack rubbed his thumb over her cheek. 'Bugger him. I know where the fish slice is kept and I'm not afraid to use it.'

He leaned in to her and Ellie was aware of his stubble rough against her face and then his mouth was on hers and they kissed again for a very long time. The deep, searching kisses left both of them breathless in the heat.

'We'll get sunstroke if we stay out here much longer,' she said, reaching up and touching the top of his head. 'Your hair feels so hot.'

'It can burst into flame for all I care.' He pulled her into him. 'Ellie, I love you and I want to come home.' Ellie knew that if Jack had not been holding her at that point, she would have fallen on to the grass and melted in the heat.

He ran his hands down her body as if he were checking that everything was still there and it seemed right to grind her hips against him, feeling his lovely, familiar hardness. His mouth came down on to her neck and this time his kisses had more hunger behind them.

He stopped and took a step back from her. 'Oh hell, I'm sorry, Ellie. You don't need this today. Not so soon after . . .'

His eyes strayed to her shoulder, where the kimono had slipped a little. Ellie saw him swallow and she tried to pull the material back up. When it simply slipped again, he stood there looking at her shoulder and breathing hard.

'Perhaps I should go in and get dressed,' Ellie said. 'It's been an emotional twenty-four hours. I'll just . . .' She made a move to go, but after all the talk of death and sadness she wanted to feel exhilarated and alive again, and she wanted Jack to feel like that too. She shot out her hand and pulled him towards her. 'I need to feel your heartbeat,' she said, and wrenched his shirt out of his trousers.

In an instant Jack had her kimono down round her waist and Ellie felt the sun on her bare breasts, closely followed by Jack's fingers. Her hands burrowed under his shirt to find the warm skin of his back.

Jack was cupping her breasts, trailing his thumbs gently over them. 'Sorry,' he panted, 'I'll stop . . . I just needed to touch you again . . . We should take it—'

'Slowly,' Ellie said, and tore his shirt open.

Everything seemed to speed up after that and they were both naked and down on the grass. Ellie felt it hot against her back and the ground was hard and dry and all she could think about was getting Jack inside her. Jack was scrabbling through the pockets in his trousers until he managed to find what he was looking for, even though by then Ellie already had her hand wrapped round him, caressing him.

'Hell's teeth,' he hissed at her, and, after a few tortuous moments of waiting and one dark, dangerous look, he pushed himself into her in a way that suggested he was never, ever going to be persuaded to pull back out again.

'You little Southern tart,' he growled at her, and Ellie let out a cry that made Jack try even harder.

They thrust and clutched at each other, rediscovering how it felt, oblivious to the noise they were making. The sun poured down and everywhere their skin touched was soon wet and slippery. Ellie tried to pull Jack deeper into her and then she felt him get his hand between them and his thumb was moving across that very place, that very place that was already on fire. Ellie could not stand it any more. She tried to get away from him, but he held her close and finished her off, smiling down at her as she called out something incomprehensible. Then she heard his own cry and saw him fight to catch his breath.

'Good God,' a voice said, 'don't tell me you're planting seeds this time.'

As much as two post-orgasmic people could freeze, Ellie and Jack froze. And then Jack took a quick look round at the people standing transfixed on the patio and tried to grab his discarded trousers and shield Ellie's body with them. It was a limited success and Ellie screwed up her eyes tight to try to shut out the view of Pandora, Constance and Gerald standing there open-mouthed. Frank was holding on to one of the chairs and laughing.

Finally Constance said in a little strangled voice, 'We left some papers behind. We came back to collect them.'

Jack bit his lip. 'Right,' he said, half turning and then abruptly resuming his original position. 'Right. Well, if you go and get them, we'll see you later.'

The group shuffled back into the house, all of them silent except for Frank, who continued to make rude puns about gardening.

Ellie opened her eyes and tried not to laugh, but when she failed, it bubbled out, lovely and clear and uninhibited.

Jack felt Ellie's laugh ripple all around him, and could not remember ever hearing a better sound. He put his head down on her breast and started to laugh himself, a strong, rumbling laugh that he felt low in his belly. Then he rolled off her. They lay there, side by side, helpless with laughter and squinting up at the sun.

When they had calmed down and their breathing had softened, Jack saw Ellie turn towards him. 'I bought you a book, you know,' she said. 'Never had the chance to give it to you.'

Jack groaned, 'Oh, Ellie, and you cooked me a meal – that salmon, remember?'

'Hey, you cooked me a steak. And you bought me a dress. I never bought you a tie.'

She had a point. Jack turned his head to look at her properly, her curls around her shoulders and her body long and soft and naked in the grass. If she wasn't careful, some delicate, usually covered-up bits of her were going to get scorched. He placed his hand over one of them.

'What was the book?'

'*Dr Jekyll and Mr Hyde.*'

Jack gave a huge laugh and decided to protect her from burning with the whole of his body. He rolled back on top of her and brushed her hair gently away from her face before bending his head to kiss her on the lips. It was a gentle kiss, but he still felt her toes wiggle against his leg. 'Dr *Jekyll and Mr Hyde*, eh? Was I really that bad?'

Ellie rolled her eyes in answer and then raised her hand to dislodge a piece of grass that was stuck on his cheek. Her hand strayed to his hair and she smoothed it down gently.

'So, what book would you have bought me, Jack, if you were a romantic fool?'

Jack screwed up his eyes in thought. '*Little Red Riding Hood*,' he said at last.

Ellie laughed and pulled his hair, and then Jack watched the happiness go from her face.

'Thinking about Edith?' he said.

'Yes. I don't know if it's insensitive to be lying here laughing like this.' Her eyes were shimmering with tears.

'Do you seriously think Edith would mind? She'd be pleased you were rolling around naked in her back garden. She wouldn't see it as insensitive or disrespectful, she didn't think like that. She'd be laughing her glittery socks off.' He dropped a kiss on her hair. 'You made her happy when she was alive, that was the main thing. And you were there when she was dying, still holding her hand. You never forgot she was part of you.' He jerked his head towards the patio. 'Unlike the fearsome foursome.'

'I wish I'd taken more care of her.'

'Ellie, stop it. You couldn't have made Edith stay in every evening with a mug of cocoa, even if you'd wanted to. She didn't want to sit around and wait for death. She was thumbing her nose at it as long as she could.' He rubbed his own nose against hers. 'That night I played Scrabble with her, she didn't stop going on about how lovely you were. How you didn't tell her off like her daughters. She wouldn't shut up about you.'

'She wouldn't?'

'No. So stop beating yourself up. It's easy to run around wringing your hands when somebody's dead, doing the "sympathy and the flowers" bit. It's looking after them when they're still alive that's damned difficult.'

She held his gaze for a while and he knew she had understood exactly what he meant.

'I love you, Jack,' she said, and he felt her pull his mouth back on to hers.

When she had stopped kissing him, she said, 'I really wish Edith had known you were back. She said you had hidden depths, but she really liked you.'

'I liked her too, sweetheart.'

Jack thought about the way the word 'sweetheart' sounded in his mouth and let it roll around his brain for a while, along with thoughts of how Edith would have laughed to see them here on her lawn. Then he saw a little cloud drift across Ellie's thoughts again.

'Jack,' she began hesitantly, 'Edith was a perceptive woman – she said I didn't "do" half-hearted and I have to agree with her. So . . . if you were under the mistaken impression that I was one of those cool, sophisticated women who turn a blind eye to the men they love sleeping with other women as long as they don't flaunt it, then—'

Jack put his finger on her lips. 'Amazing as it may seem, Ellie, when I was married I didn't have a problem with the "forsaking all others" bit. It was the "till death us do part" coming so quickly that freaked me out.' Suddenly, making her believe that seemed the most important thing in his life.

He saw her nod slowly. 'I'm going to trust you on that, Jack. Really, really trust you. Besides, I haven't forgotten that Bryan North said you laughed about the women who were after you and went home to Helen.'

'Too bloody right.' Jack made a note to send Bryan a bottle of whisky along with his Christmas card this year. 'Besides, Ellie, it wasn't even working any more. All that sex. It wasn't making me feel alive. Quite the reverse. It was only a matter of time before I started wearing a medallion and fake tan.'

He was relieved to hear her laugh and they held each

other without speaking until she said, all in a rush, 'I can't promise not to die. I wish that I could take that fear away from you completely. All I can tell you is that I will try my very best to stay alive. I won't take any stupid risks. I won't even use the bus any more if that makes you feel happier. And . . . well, whatever happens, I won't go without a big fight.'

Jack felt his throat close up at that and put his head down for a while. When he lifted it back up, she was smiling mischievously at him.

'What?' he said.

'Well, you silly sod, how could I even think of going before you? Don't I always have to have the last word?'

It was the first time Jack could ever remember finding anything funny about death.

Perhaps that was what had reeled him in: Ellie's sense of humour. Bursting through the neat compartments he'd surrounded himself with. All that warmth wrapping around him and making him realise how cold he'd become.

After another bout of kissing Ellie said, 'But what about New York, Jack?'

'I'll delegate it.'

'A whole city?'

'Yup. Too far from you. Too far from Yorkshire.'

He ran his hand over Ellie's smooth skin and bent again to kiss each place he touched. Warm, yielding, his. Enough optimism in that one body to make him believe that history didn't have to repeat itself. That scythe man might be a niggling presence he'd have to learn to fit around his life, not allow to shape it entirely.

He felt Ellie tense under his hand.

'Good grief,' she said, her eyes wide. 'Poor Mrs White.'

'I don't know any Mrs White,' Jack said, sure he hadn't slept with any married woman on his travels.

'You do now.' Ellie nodded her head towards the next-door house. A lady with white hair was standing in an upstairs window with a similar expression on her face to the ones that Edith's relations had been wearing earlier.

Jack groped around for his trousers again. 'Any bright ideas about how we get out of this?'

'We could tell her we're pagans and we're worshipping the sun.'

'Or we could run for it.'

Covering as much of themselves as they could with one pair of trousers, they sprinted for the house.

CHAPTER 44

'Look, I am not telling you. It is meant to be a surprise, so stop trying to wheedle it out of me. And if you open your eyes once more, I'll have to blindfold you.' Jack's voice dropped to a whisper. 'You know how much I'd enjoy that.'

Ellie kept her eyes tightly shut. 'Oh, I know you would, Jack, but think how much you'd embarrass the taxi driver.'

'Bet he's seen worse. Now, shush – it's not far.'

Ellie felt the lurch of the taxi as it set off from the traffic lights and clutched at Jack. He put his arm round her and she could feel his hot breath on her cheek.

'Don't do that,' she whispered. 'It's getting me excited.'

'What, me breathing? You're saying that's all it takes? I'll not bother with the champagne, then.' He lowered his voice and thickened his accent. 'No good squandering good money, lass.'

'Ooh, stop doing that too. You know you make me think

of ruddy Heathcliff when you do that.' She clutched him tighter. 'And you have champagne?'

Ellie heard the rustle of a carrier bag and gasped as an ice-cold bottle was pressed against her leg. 'I have champagne, I have those little pancakey things, I have those fish-egg things, and I have that gloopy sour stuff.'

'Wow, you make it all sound so nice.'

The taxi slowed and came to a halt and Ellie's pulse speeded up. She loved surprises; in fact, she'd been planning to give Jack one of his own before he'd whisked her off in the taxi. It was fizzing up inside her even now and threatening to spill out. But there would be time later. Right now Jack's surprise was maddening her and she'd run out of ideas about where they were going. Jack had answered a simple 'no' to all her guesses.

'Right,' Jack said, 'eyes still closed.' Ellie heard the taxi door being opened and Jack paying the driver and then she felt Jack's hand on hers. 'OK, come on, and mind the step.'

She groped her way forward, feeling Jack push her head down gently so that she didn't brain herself on the door. Then he was leading her by both hands. 'That's it. OK, now you can open your eyes.'

Ellie did and found herself looking at a pair of intricate wrought-iron gates. She recognised them at once: they were the gates of the park round the corner from where Edith and she used to live.

'They're the park gates,' she said.

Jack nodded. 'They are.'

When she continued to stand, unsure of why she was there and what she was supposed to do next, Jack leaned into her.

'Brilliant concept, Ellie. They're on hinges and see' – he pushed on one of the gates and it opened – 'you can go from standing outside the park to standing inside it.' He gave her a little nudge through the gates and shut them behind her.

'Why am I here, Jack?' she said. 'I mean, I can see they've finished doing up the park. It looks great. But why am I here? Why are we here?'

Jack said nothing, just raised his eyebrows.

As long as Ellie could remember the 'park round the corner' had been degenerating. Its battered benches were home to intimidating little gangs of drunks, the grass was patchy and strewn with paper, and it had an unloved, unvisited, depressing atmosphere about it. The patch of water in the middle, laughingly called a pond, had been the final resting place of supermarket trolleys and used condoms, and any self-respecting waterfowl had long ago abandoned it.

Edith could remember the park in its prime, when people had actually wanted to visit it and sit under the trees, or sail little boats on the pond, but it was unlikely that many other people in the area could.

All that had changed when a local builder had bought a series of derelict buildings adjoining the park and as part of the deal with the council had been persuaded to contribute substantial funds to bringing the park back to life. Work had still been in progress when Edith had died.

Ellie had a good look around, taking in the neatly mown grass and blooming flowerbeds, the elegantly curving wooden seats and the gravel pathways. Off to their left, a woman was lying on a rug with two small children having a picnic. A man sat and read his paper.

'Walk a little?' Jack suggested, and she followed him, wondering where the Special Brew and cider drinkers now gathered and why nobody had vandalised the place. Part of the answer appeared in the shape of a community policeman who wandered past.

Ellie kept on walking, the part of her that wasn't confused now interested to see how the pond had been rejuvenated.

'Oh,' she said, as they came out from the trees and got their first clear view, 'it's gone.'

In its place was a large, circular paved area, much of it wet.

Ellie frowned. 'I didn't know it had rained earlier.'

'It didn't,' Jack said, 'and if I were you, I wouldn't stand right there.'

She was going to ask, 'Why?' when a jet of water emerged from the paving stone next to her feet and she leaped backwards. The whole paved area was alive with them, little fountains of sparkling water dancing for a minute or two and then stopping as abruptly as they started.

'Wow,' Ellie said. 'It's like at Somerset House. A lot smaller ... but still ... beautiful.'

'Fun too,' Jack said, watching a small boy creep up to one of the holes, stand there for as long as he dared and then run away squealing when the jet of water shot out again. 'Nearly got him.'

Jack was laughing, the carrier bag now up in his arms, but Ellie sensed he wasn't completely relaxed; he was still being driven by the need to show her something.

'So the champagne's to celebrate ... what?' she prompted.

'Just wait,' he said gently. 'Have a walk around.'

She gave him a puzzled look but set off round the edge of the paved circle, stopping now and again to laugh at the children darting in and out of the fountains and noticing that at the edge of the paving were little brass plaques.

Some of them bore the names of large national banks or businesses, but there were many more with less well-known names on them. 'Siddicoat's the Butchers', read one; 'Patmir's News' another.

'Local businesses,' Ellie said, reading them off as she went round. 'Ah, there's Mr Arundi's name. He runs the launderette, or did when I lived here. Oh, and here's the florist.'

'They all helped refurbish this part of the park,' Jack explained. 'Donated money towards it.'

Ellie had a vague recollection of having heard about the fundraising appeal, but it had drifted from her mind in the intervening eventful year since she had moved from the area to live with Jack.

She walked on a little further. 'Oh look,' she said, 'there are other names I recognise too. Those are the Hopgoods – they're the family who had the son with the motorbike – and the Elliots. She was always a bit stuck-up, but he was a sweetheart. Used to wave at me from his wheelchair.' She frowned. 'So individuals gave money too?'

Jack gave her a funny little smile and she kept on walking and reading, realising that on this particular run of plaques there were sometimes little messages or snatches of verse.

'They're memorials,' she said, and then she stopped.

'Edith,' the plaque next to her feet said, 'always sparkly, never still.'

As her vision blurred, she saw that the letters of 'Edith' had been written on brass Scrabble tiles.

'Oh God, Jack,' she said, 'this is our Edith, isn't it?' and then speech was beyond her.

She felt him come and stand beside her. He spoke to her softly. 'Last weekend they had a grand opening and I was thinking of showing you then. Only, it occurred to me that you might prefer to see it for the first time without other people gawping. And you weren't feeling that well, so I waited.'

She still couldn't do anything but swallow painfully.

His hand closed round hers. 'Did I get it wrong?' The doubt was obvious beneath his words. 'I thought about putting a plaque on a seat, but Edith didn't sit down for long. A fountain seemed more . . . more like her.' He stumbled on, 'Perhaps I should have asked you first, but I wanted it to be a surprise. I suppose if I had told you, Lesley could have done a proper design and you'd have thought of better words.'

Ellie turned and threw her arms round him.

'No,' she said into his chest. 'It's perfect. Absolutely perfect. Nobody could have done it better.'

Once again she was crying all over Jack.

'You've squashed those little pancakey things,' he said after a while, looking down at the carrier bag, which was wedged between them.

'I don't care,' Ellie replied. 'You're such a clever, clever man. What a perfect way to remember Edith – somewhere full of life and people having fun.'

She kissed him then for quite some time before pulling away and having another read of the plaque. Very soon she was waterlogged again.

Jack passed her a handkerchief this time.

'Where did you get this?' she said, sniffing.

'Bought a pack at lunchtime. I know how you like a

good blub and my shirt's not thick enough.' His tone was light, but Ellie felt his arm round her shoulders.

'Come and sit down and I'll rub your back,' he said, and she let him lead her away down one of the paths to an empty seat under the trees.

He waited for her to stop crying.

'I thought we could drink a toast to Edith and eat the squashed pancakes and fish stuff. Celebrate Edith's memory in a way she would have approved. And you know, anytime you want to come here you can. Paddle in the fountain, have a think about her.' He reached down into the carrier bag by his feet and extracted the champagne.

Ellie tried to blow her nose as delicately as she could in Jack's handkerchief and then said, 'I don't know what to say. I'm still a bit dazed and . . . overwhelmed. It's such a considerate thing to do.' She paused. 'You're so good at surprises . . . the driving lessons . . . that jewellery when we got married.'

'And all I got was five million lousy ties and a library's-worth of books,' he said, chuckling.

'And me. Don't forget you got me.'

'Yeah, I got you. That *was* good.' He leaned over and pinched her nose gently. 'Beautifully wrapped, even nicer unwrapped.'

'Smut, as usual,' Ellie said, and he grinned and started to tear the foil off the champagne and fiddle with the little wire cage over the cork. She watched him work and was not sure if she should leap in now and surprise him as much as he had surprised her. No. Let them toast Edith first. And in the meantime . . .

A mischievous thought sidled into her brain.

'I still wish I'd given you something else for a wedding present,' she said.

'Really?'

'Yes, something that would have told everyone how I felt about you.'

'I thought marrying me did that.'

'Ah, but not as much as a specially composed poem would have done. You know, like the one Lesley and Megan wrote for their wedding.'

She was delighted to see that her words had the desired effect. Jack went absolutely still and there was more than a trace of panic in his voice when he spoke.

'Please no, don't you dare,' he said. 'Don't you dare start reciting that poem again. I mean, it was a lovely thought. It was a great wedding; I will never forget the sight of Rachel with the whole back row of that rugby team, but no, not the poem. Even thinking about it makes my toes curl.'

'You're just jealous because they knew more words that rhymed with "vagina" than you did.'

Jack pointed a finger at her. 'That's it, Ellie. Stop it. Stop it now or you and I are paying a trip to the shrubbery.'

'You can't, not on a solemn occasion like this.'

'I think we established long ago that Edith wouldn't mind what we did as long as it was fun and we raised a glass to her now and again. So don't push your luck, Eleanor Wolfe.' Jack put the bottle down on the ground and gave her a challenging look. 'One line of that poem and you're in the rhododendrons.'

Ellie felt a shiver of anticipation run through her. 'Really?' she said, getting up and dancing a little away from him. You don't even want to hear that bit that went, "When your lady garden I first espied, I couldn't wait to get inside"?'

'No, no, absolutely no,' Jack cried, shooting to his feet and making a grab for her. She managed to dodge away from him.

'"And when I saw your soft, soft breasts, I knew our love would stand all tests. So place your hand— "'

She got no further before Jack caught her.

'You're a bad, bad girl,' he said, lowering his voice to a deep growl, 'and it is only because that policeman person is walking our way that you have escaped a severe horticultural-themed punishment.'

'Thank you, Mellors,' she said, giggling.

He led her back to the seat and they sat very primly as the policeman walked past. He slowed as he saw the bottle of champagne, but kept on walking.

'Seemed a bit scared of you,' Ellie said.

'Should think so too.' Jack resumed his efforts to open

the bottle. 'Shame you're not still scared of me. Might get a bit more respect.' He was having a job not to laugh.

'I wasn't ever scared of you, Jack. I was wary, that's different. That was when I thought you were granite all the way through.'

'I think I was. Then,' he said simply, and gave her a tender look.

Ellie drank it in and wondered how it was possible to keep on adding to the love you felt for someone. Day by day she had watched Jack step away from the past and relax into the present. Now he only scowled when she asked him to. Plate glass shattered long ago.

The cork shot from the bottle and champagne spurted out all down his suit and on to the grass.

'Ooh, mind your trousers, Jack, or you'll have to take them off when we get home,' she said with a straight face.

He shot her a glittering look and deliberately shook some more champagne down them.

'Naughty, naughty Jack,' she said, and he smiled. It was the smile from the photograph, the one Bryan North had shown her. Ellie had seen it many, many times since Jack had come back from New York. Especially on their wedding day. It hadn't even disappeared when Frank had sidled up to them during the reception and asked them how much it was all costing.

'To Edith,' Jack said, taking a drink from the bottle and passing it to her.

'To Edith,' she repeated, and took a little sip, letting the bubbles fizz around her mouth and remembering Edith in her prime, dressed like an explosion in a clothing factory and enthusiastically embracing any new experience she could lay her hands on.

'OK?' Jack asked.

'Never better,' she replied, and reluctantly handed the bottle back to him before taking a few seconds to decide how to phrase what she had to say next.

She had to be very, very careful how she broke any news to Jack. While he might have conquered his fear of death enough to be with her, it hadn't disappeared entirely. She'd found that out a couple of weeks after they were married and she'd had to admit to him that she had dented the car during her driving lesson. As she'd put on a serious face and said, 'Jack, I have something to tell you . . .' she'd seen his eyes widen in alarm, all the colour drain away from his face.

It was a mistake she hadn't repeated since.

'So,' she said brightly, 'you know how the two of us working together can sometimes be a bit tricky?'

'Not for me,' he said, picking up the carrier bag and plonking it on the seat next to him and then reaching in and bringing out a pot of sour cream.

'No, well, I don't mind either, but anyway, I think I might have solved it.'

'Oh?' Jack put his hand back in the bag and pulled out

the packet of blinis. He screwed his face up at how battered they were.

Ellie pursed her lips. 'Are you listening?'

'Yes, of course.'

'OK, well, put it another way, I think there's going to be a dip in sales in the San Pro market for a while. They won't be getting my custom.'

'Right,' Jack said, putting the blinis down and reaching into the bag for the pot of caviar.

'You're not really paying attention, are you?'

Jack stopped feeling around in the bag. 'Yes, 'course I am. What were you saying?'

'Cubs, Jack, what do you think about cubs?'

'Well, I enjoyed it for a few years, but the Scouts never really appealed to me. It all seemed a bit homoerotic.' Jack stopped and gave her a searching look. 'Hang on. Are we talking about cubs as in boys in uniforms or cubs as in cubs?'

'Patter of tiny little paws, Jack,' Ellie said, and grinned.

She thought that this was one of those moments in life that you could never get back. She watched her husband and saw the exact second when understanding hit him.

'Hell's teeth,' he said, and threw the bag on the ground. He was standing in front of her the next instant, pulling her to her feet.

There was that smile again.

'When?' he said in a voice that sounded a little wobbly.

'Well, it could have been anytime, but I think it might have been when we were down by the river and you dared me to take—'

'No, you daft wench, I mean when is the baby due?'

'Oh, March, late March. And less of the wench.'

Jack placed his hand gently on Ellie's stomach and gave her that intense, grey look of his that had stolen her heart all those months ago and made her yearn for him even now when he was standing in front of her.

'New life,' Ellie said softly.

Jack nodded. 'Damn right, Ellie. New life.'

Then he pulled her in close and wrapped his arms tightly round her.

And just this once, Ellie didn't say anything smart or funny. She didn't search for the perfect pun.

She stayed quiet and let Jack have absolutely, totally, the last word.